ANTIQUITAS LOST

THE LAST OF THE SHAMALANS

BY

ROBERT LOUIS SMITH

ILLUSTRATIONS BY GEOF ISHERWOOD

MedLock
PUBLISHING

MEDLOCK PUBLISHING
TULSA, OKLAHOMA

Antiquitas Lost
The Last of the Shamalans

Robert Louis Smith

Copyright © 2011 by Robert Louis Smith

All rights reserved. No part of this book may be reproduced or transmitted in any form or by any means, electronic or mechanical, including photocopying, recording or by any information storage and retrieval system without written permission from the publisher, except for the inclusion of quotations in a review.

 MedLock Publishing
Tulsa, Oklahoma
www.antiquitaslost.com

Illustrations by Geof Isherwood
Book layout: www.TheBookProducer.com
Editing by Michael J. Carr
Maps by Robin Kuprella: www.fantasy-cartography.com

The Girl From Ipanema (Garôta De Ipanema)
Music by Antonio Carlos Jobim
English Words by Norman Gimbel
Original Words by Vinicius de Moraes
Copyright © 1963 ANTONIO CARLOS JOBIM and VINICIUS DE MORAES, Brazil
Copyright Renewed 1991 and Assigned to SONGS OF UNIVERSAL, INC. and WORDS WEST LLC
English Words Renewed 1991 by NORMAN GIMBEL for the World and Assigned to WORDS WEST LLC
    (P.O. Box 15187, Beverly Hills, CA 90209 USA)
All Rights Reserved Used by Permission
Reprinted by permission of Hal Leonard Corporation

Printed in Palatino Linotype font by the Maple-Vail Book Manufacturing Group, York, Pennsylvania

First Edition

Library of Congress Control Number: 2011910604

ISBN: 978-0-615-46047-5

eISBN: 978-0-9838512-0-2 (kindle version)

eISBN: 978-0-9838512-1-9 (epub version)

Dedication

For Aimee, Sam, and Anna Kate.

Follow us on Twitter @AntiquitasLost
Like us on Facebook! Antiquitas Lost

Contents

ANTIQUITAS LOST

THE LAST OF THE SHAMALANS

Ambush at Ondor

A tendril of smoke from the campfire's last embers curled into the sky. Sarintha sat alone, mesmerized by the orange glow that brightened and dimmed with each passing breeze. She wept quietly, her thoughts drifting as the last coals died away and darkness enveloped the clearing. Heroic memories of her father flooded in, making her feel altogether too young and untested for the job ahead. Lost in her reverie, she barely noticed the sound of footsteps approaching and turned to find her old friend Marvus standing behind her. She hoped he hadn't noticed her tears.

"You should rest," he said softly, laying his small hand on her shoulder. "We are safe here."

She put her hand atop his and attempted a smile. "I am fine," she said. "It is you who should sleep. We have a full day tomorrow."

He studied her, and the corners of his mouth turned down. "You mustn't keep reliving it in your thoughts," he said gently. "A sleepless night accomplishes nothing. The time to address our plight will come, but first we must get home."

Her gaze moved beyond him, into the forest. "I just can't believe all that has happened," she said, choking back tears. "They cut us to pieces. It wasn't supposed to be like this."

He squeezed her shoulder. "But what's done is done, and we won't resolve the crisis tonight. We will have to take it up with the council when we get home tomorrow."

She jerked her head upward, startling him. "I do not trust the council!" she hissed. "How do we know that Waldemariam himself isn't to blame for what has happened?"

"Waldemariam is the chancellor," he said in a placating tone. "What cause has he to betray us?"

She stared into the forest, looking away from him, and her melancholy face wrenched into a scowl. "Under his rule, the empire has fallen to depths our fathers would not have dreamed possible. And after these past days, do not tell me to trust in the council."

Marvus sighed. "You need to reconsider your distrust of Waldemariam," he pleaded. "We have no choice but to rely on him. Without the support of the council, we have nothing."

She looked long at her friend. "This is no longer the kingdom of my father."

"But it will be again. He lives on in you." Marvus smiled ever so slightly and reached out for her hand. "You will know what to do when the time comes."

She grasped his hand and turned as footfalls came from just beyond the fire ring.

Like Marvus, the newcomer was a gimlet and quite short. "Why aren't you two asleep?" he said, rubbing his eyes.

"Dear Jingo," said Sarintha, "you should both go get some rest. With the loss of Grimaldi, you are the only ones left whom I can depend on." She spoke softly, with affection. "Let's talk no more of betrayal and ambush. Tomorrow we will complete our journey home. There we can discuss our options and mourn the loss of our soldiers. In time, we will avenge my father's death and turn the tide of this horrid war." She looked to the ground, searching for the confidence she wished to portray. "Let's go to sleep so we will be ready for the walk to Harwelden."

Marvus smiled. "A wise plan. I wish you sleep."

And with that, the gimlets left her alone.

But sleep was still far from Sarintha, and she sat by the fire, unable to drag her thoughts away from the awful events of the past few weeks.

The empire is dead. The words resonated in her thoughts. She didn't want to believe that the northern hordes, after all of these seasons of war, had finally extinguished the light of the failing empire. But in her heart, she feared that they had already struck the mortal blow. She shuddered at the thought of what Malus Lothar, emperor of the hordes, might have done if the troops from Iracema had not arrived when they did, rescuing her from his brutal assault. If all went well, they would reach the safety of the castle by sunset tomorrow.

By the dim light of the crescent moon, she surveyed the field of sleeping, exhausted warriors and thanked the elders for the sacrifice of her courageous gimlet army. A short time ago, the gimlets would not have known what to do with a weapon of war. But as with all the Carafayan folk, the protracted war had taught them how to wield blades and shoot arrows. Their loyalty to the empire—or, rather, to the motley band of warriors and politicians who sought to restore it—moved her.

Gazing out at the forest one last time before lying down, she heard a twig snap behind her. Thinking that Marvus had come back, she turned toward the sound—just in time to see the flash of a Vengan war ax.

She screamed and ducked the assassin's weapon, hitting her shoulder hard against the packed dirt. The ax continued its arc and embedded itself, just above her head, in the trunk of a huge moss-covered tree. Rolling toward her attacker, she unsheathed the dagger at her ankle and drove it through his calf as he wrenched at the ax to free it from the wood. Roaring in pain, he fell to the ground as she jumped to her feet.

Marvus and Jingo emerged from the darkness, their faces showing a mix of fear and anger. Jingo already had his dagger out.

"Run!" she yelled.

The two gimlets stood defiantly before her, staring at the would-be assassin writhing in pain on the ground.

"Leave now and send word to Harwelden," she commanded. "There will be more of them!" And pulling a shell horn from her belongings, she sounded the battle call.

In seconds, hundreds of gimlet troops were at the ready, loaded crossbows in hand, prepared for the fight that surely lay ahead.

She turned a steely gaze to Marvus and Jingo, and they hurried away as gimlet soldiers rallied around her.

With the troops alerted and her friends safe, Sarintha turned her attention to the assassin at her feet. Coolly, she picked up her sword from beneath the tree and stood over him.

"How many travel with you, serpan?" she hissed, holding her blade to his throat.

The serpan laughed gently, mocking her. "You're as pretty as they say, young one. I would've been honored to carry such a comely young head upon the spike of my halberd."

"How many?" She pressed her blade into his skin.

"You'll see soon enough."

The sword's tip penetrated his leathery skin, bringing forth a trickle of blood. "I don't intend to ask again."

"The malus will be pleased to see you again," he said, looking her up and down. An unsettling grin spread across his lips. "What they say of you is true. You are a beautiful creature."

He smiled, revealing a row of crooked teeth, and opened his mouth to speak again, when an arrow slammed into his chest, embedding itself so deeply that only half the shaft remained exposed. The gimlet commander who loosed the arrow moved to her side as the mortally wounded behemoth locked eyes with her. His grin remained even as he struggled to breathe.

"You will die like an animal," he gurgled. "They'll have their way with you and feed your gizzard to the simitars before the next bright moon." His voice trailed off, though the intensity of his gaze remained. "You will meet your death slowly, and beg for it many times before it comes." A rattle escaped his throat, and he closed his eyes, as if giving up the ghost. But they opened again, fixed on the princess. "Valderon is rising," he whispered. Then his eyes lost their luster, and his body slumped back on the forest floor.

For a moment, the night was quiet, but a chill rolled up Sarintha's spine. Steeling herself, she turned to the gimlet commander at her side and nodded.

"Gimlets, be on watch!" he yelled to his troops. "There'll be more where this scum came from. It seems we will draw our enemies' blood one last time before we see Harwelden."

The first salvo of arrows came from behind them. Sarintha, from her vantage point facing the troops, was the first to see them, flying so densely that, for a split second, they cast a shadow in the moonlight.

Then, with the gimlet troops still facing away from the threat, the arrows fell like lethal hail. Gimlet warriors collapsed in droves, arrows protruding from their backs in an eerie reenactment of the scene from Prytania just twenty days before.

The surviving warriors, about half the original regiment, raised their crossbows and turned north. Though the enemy remained hidden in the shadows, the gimlet commander ordered them into the inky blackness of the ancient woods. With swords and crossbows at the ready, the warriors rushed over the corpses of their fallen comrades and into the darkness. And almost in the shadow of the towering, proud spires of Harwelden itself, they threw themselves on the serpan legions that had infiltrated the forest.

Though the diminutive gimlets fought with all the fierceness that only recently characterized their race, they were badly outmatched. The serpan warriors bested them not in courage but in size, numbers, and cruelty, and they spilled rivers of gimlet blood. In no time, this latest ambush was over, the battle terribly lost, and Sarintha stood alone beside the great mossy tree with the Vengan war ax still embedded in its trunk.

A wall of heavily armed serpan warriors descended on her, their grotesque features distorted in the shadowed moonlight. Standing alone against them, she raised her sword just as a stone from an enemy sling struck her forehead.

A serpan warlord advanced and plucked her up from the mossy ground and hoisted her over his shoulder. "Her flesh is smooth," he said, rubbing the back of her thigh. "Malus Lothar will be pleased to have her back."

His men roared with delight, and the warlord set off into the forest with his captive. His troops followed, cackling as they wended their way among the trees and the corpses of massacred gimlets.

⚑ ⚑ ⚑

With the departure of the serpan horde, the night grew eerily still, and Marvus and Jingo emerged warily from beneath a tree uprooted in some long-ago storm. They wore simple tunics, unlike the armor of their brethren, and instead of swords, they carried on their belts only short daggers, better suited for cutting meat or rope than for warfare. They were the stewards of the princess, whom they now feared murdered. On her orders, they had hidden themselves before the first flight of serpan arrows came.

Now, dazed, with the smell of their comrades' blood still in their nostrils, they hurriedly set out toward Harwelden, to bring the awful news of the massacre and the loss of the princess to the Grayfarer Council.

Chapter 1

A New Home

Elliott sat at his mother's bedside, holding her hand and watching as she slept. He was frightened at how thin and gaunt she had become these past few months. He longed for her to wake up, but she needed her rest. Although he had never had many friends, he had been especially lonely since they came to New Orleans.

"Get well, Mom," he said, dabbing her forehead with a damp cloth. "I don't know what I'd do without you."

To his relief, he caught the faint rise and fall of her chest, then suddenly felt a little silly for wanting to hold a mirror under her nose to see if she was still breathing. He surveyed the bottles of pills on the bedside table and wondered if she had taken a sedative. If she had, she might sleep for the next several hours.

He heard footsteps in the hall and turned to find his grandfather standing in the doorway. The old man was unusually tall and had a certain unkemptness about him: the mop of white hair flying wildly in all directions, the bushy white beard that grew almost to his chest. Elliott often wondered how he kept from getting food in it when he ate. As usual, the old man had on the same threadbare gray suit that he wore every day. Elliott noted the usual hint of a smile on his face, as if he knew a secret that no one else was privy to. And for the umpteenth time, the boy couldn't help thinking that the old man looked strangely regal, especially now, as he stood in the door frame with the sun streaming in behind him.

"Feel like taking a walk?"

"Yeah, I guess," Elliott sighed, stealing another glance at his mother as he stood up. "We won't be gone long, Mom," he murmured, joining the old man in the doorway. Then, thinking better of it, he went back into the bedroom, to the old record player on the dresser. "Wait just a minute," he said. He picked up a worn record and placed in on the turntable. Then, flicking the switch, he lowered the needle to the vinyl, waiting for the music to begin before turning to rejoin his grandfather. His mother's favorite song, "The Girl from Ipanema," rolled and swayed out of the tinny speakers. "Get some rest, Mom," he said. "I love you."

His grandfather nodded, and together they walked down the hallway to the grand wooden staircase.

Although slight for his fifteen years, Elliott was accustomed to feeling particularly small in the presence of this lanky old man. He was pleased to see the sun shining through the windows—a welcome change from the tropical storm systems that had dominated the weather since his arrival.

After going down the stairs, they walked out the front door into the sunlight, and Elliott paused to look at his surroundings. "The gardens are beautiful," he said. "Thank goodness the rain finally quit. I haven't been outside in days."

The old man smiled.

"Maybe it won't be so bad here after all," Elliott mumbled, so softly that his grandfather didn't hear.

They went out the gate and onto the street. "So how are you liking New Orleans?" his grandfather asked. "Is your bedroom agreeable?"

"I'm getting used to it," he replied. He was still uncomfortable around this strange old man, whom he had just met when they arrived on his doorstep a few weeks ago. "I miss being home sometimes."

"Well, I think you'll find this place has a lot to offer," the old man said.

The two of them continued down the street in silence. The glorious old homes of New Orleans's Garden District were lovely in the sunlight.

"We sure didn't have any neighborhoods like this back home," Elliott said. "Mom says some of these houses are older than the United States."

"It's true; there's a great deal of history here." The old man looked at him as if gauging his interest. "Wealthy American settlers built the oldest of these houses in the seventeen hundreds." He made a sweeping gesture with his arm, indicating the row of homes on the block ahead. "Back in those days, the French Quarter was the only civilized part of town, but it was filled with Europeans, and they didn't much like the American settlers. So, to avoid persecution from the French and Spanish, the Americans built their homes out here, developing this part of town in the bargain."

Not in the mood for a history lesson, Elliott changed the subject. "So how old is your house?"

His grandfather chuckled. "Our house is one of the oldest ones in the district. It was built in 1796, not long after the American Revolution. At the time it was built, there weren't many homes in this part of town. By all accounts, it was the grandest one around."

"Wow," said Elliott, happy to be finally having a normal conversation with his grandfather. "So it's more than two hundred years old? I never would've guessed."

"And it has quite a colorful history," the old man added.

Elliott was unsure whether to take the bait, but he was happy for the exchange. "So tell me," he said.

The old man grinned. "As the story goes, our house was built by a very odd character—odd enough that people still talked about him years after he died. His name was Darius Orion—not that it matters, I suppose." He pronounced it *Dairy-us O'Ryan*. "Rumors about him have endured almost to this day."

Elliott looked up at him, urging him to continue.

The old man gave a slow nod. "As far as anyone can tell, Mr. Orion arrived in New Orleans in the early 1790s. When he first showed up, the locals thought he was a vagrant: only one set of clothes, unshaven and unwashed, no wagon or even a horse."

Elliott nodded.

"But he had sacks and sacks of gold," said his grandfather. There was a gleam in his eye, and Elliott could tell he was enjoying himself. "Mr. Orion wasn't a merchant, and as far as anyone knew, he didn't have any trade skills. He never worked a day in his life after moving here, yet he always had lots of money."

Elliott tried to form a mental image of Darius Orion.

"And he never made friends," his grandfather continued. "No matter how hard people tried, he never warmed up to anyone. He didn't have family, either, except for a son that arrived to claim the house when he was on his deathbed." A knowing smile crossed the old man's face. "In spite of his appearance, the locals eventually assumed he must be from an aristocratic family up north, because he was so rich and obviously not from the South. When his son showed up, it was a bit scandalous, as one of the few things known about him was that he never married. Those sorts of things were important back then."

"How do *you* know so much about him?" Elliott asked. "I mean, that was such a long time ago."

The old man pointed across the street. "There's a bookstore right over there that has books with the histories of these old homes. Because of Mr. Orion, the history of our house is well known."

"He does sound like an odd fellow," said Elliott.

"Indeed," said his grandfather, raising an eyebrow. "Though many thought Mr. Orion was from a wealthy Yankee family, others thought he might be a criminal—perhaps even a pirate from one of the old ships that sailed in and out of the port in those days. Some said he might have been in league with the most famous pirate of the times: Jean Lafitte."

Elliott soaked it all up eagerly. Although he had been in New Orleans only a few weeks, he had heard some of the local lore about the notorious pirate Lafitte. There were many things in town named after him. Elliott's young mind marveled at the idea that he might be living in a house bought with pirate loot.

"Also," his grandfather continued, "the location where he built the house was strange, though you wouldn't know it now. Back then the Americans in New Orleans lived up that way, along St. Charles Street." He pointed north. "That would have been the natural place for him to build a house. But he insisted on building it closer to the river, farther away from the community. It was controversial back then because there were agreements with some of the local Indians, and the place where he built his house was in the middle of an area that the Choctaws claimed as sacred ground. There were a lot of cultural nuances back then, you see, what with European settlers, American settlers and frontiersmen, African slaves, and the Indians. It wasn't easy keeping things harmonious between all the different groups, and the Americans, not wanting to stir up any animosity among the Indians, lobbied the governor to stop Mr. Orion from building where he did. But he was bound and determined to build on that spot and nowhere else." The old man grinned. "Obviously, he eventually won out. Some say he bribed the governor to get approval." He dropped his voice to a whisper. "A lot of that goes on around here, you know." He winked at Elliott.

"In any event, after building the house, he lived there for many years and later willed it to his son. Eventually other people built their houses around him. The Indian community grew smaller and smaller, and the outcry to stay off their land was eventually forgotten. Now the house is just one of many here in the district, but with one of the most colorful histories. It has passed from generation to generation within the same family, father to son, until it ended up with me."

Entranced in the tale, Elliott walked with his grandfather past the old Lafayette Cemetery's rusty iron gates, draped in bell-shaped white flowers. The air was so thick and humid and sweet with wet honeysuckle, he felt he could almost drink it. Looking up at the old man, he said, "So how did *you* get the house?"

"I inherited it from my father, the great-grandson of Darius Orion."

"You mean to tell me you're the great, great-grandson of the man who built the house?"

"That's right. And you're his great, great, great, great-grandson."

"Wow," said Elliott. "Then you must know even more about him than what's in the old books."

"Unfortunately, I don't," his grandfather replied. "Our family didn't pass down much lore from one generation to the next. But we still have many of his belongings in the house. Some of the things he left behind are . . . well, a mite unusual."

Elliott had a hundred questions zipping through his head. He opened his mouth to speak when suddenly a pack of boys whizzed past them on bicycles.

"Hey, look! There goes Stripes and his crazy old grandpa," one of the boys shouted. There was laughter from several of the boys, and one of them passed so close he almost knocked Elliott over. Seconds later, they were gone.

"Unbelievable," said Elliott. "I haven't been here two weeks, and already I'm an outcast." He looked down at the backs of his hands, seeing the familiar symmetrical birthmarks that ran from the webs between the fingers almost to the wrist. They looked like angry red welts, each forming a palpable cord just under the skin between the tendons. He had similar birthmarks between his toes as well. He hated them. His mother, who also had the strange marks, had urged him to ignore the taunts he had received all his life. But, of course, this was easier said than done.

"Don't let them bother you, son" said his grandfather, who had similar birthmarks between his fingers. His were a deep purple. "Kids can be mean, but you shouldn't listen to them. There are wonderful things in store for you if you're willing to work hard and do something with your life." And there was that gleam again in those gray eyes.

This seemed to Elliott the standard response adults offered to kids who got picked on. Having been the butt of cruel jokes for most of his fifteen years, he recovered quickly from the boys' insults and continued with their earlier conversation.

"So did you grow up here?" he asked. "And what about your parents—my great-grandparents?"

"Yes," replied the old man. "I was born in our house. So was your mother. My mother died in childbirth, and your grandmother died while giving birth to your mom. The women of our family haven't been blessed with longevity, I'm afraid." A frown darkened the corners of his mouth.

Elliott cringed, thinking about his own mother. "What do *you* think is the matter with Mom?" he said. "She's been losing a lot of weight. She hardly ever gets out of bed. I guess the main reason we moved down here was so you could help take care of her."

The old man stopped in the street and placed his hands on Elliott's shoulders, bending to look him in the eye. He held the boy's gaze for several seconds. "Your mother is very ill," he said, and paused, waiting for a reaction. When none came, he said, "She's been diagnosed with breast cancer and has been afraid to tell you. The doctors aren't sure, but they think it may have spread to other parts of her body." He spoke slowly, all the while gazing into Elliott's face. His smile was gone. "When they determine the extent of the disease—how far it has spread—she will begin treatment. In any case, her prognosis is very guarded. So there it is, son—we have been trying to figure the best way to tell you."

Elliott stared into his grandfather's face. Tears welled up in his eyes and rolled down his cheeks. *Cancer.* It was the last thing he was ready to hear, and for a moment he just stared at his grandfather, digesting the news.

"We have to do something," he said finally. "We should take her somewhere they can help . . . to a university or something."

Elliott's grandfather was silent for a long moment. Finally, he said, "We're doing all that can be done."

Elliott turned and ran back toward the house. His grandfather called after him, but he kept running, wanting to be alone—wanting to be anywhere but in New Orleans, living with a weird old man he hardly knew.

Rounding the corner onto his block, he slipped and skinned his knee on the asphalt. Slowly, trying to collect himself, he got to his feet, just as the pack of boys whizzed past on their bikes again. Seeing him, they turned around and rode toward him.

"What's the matter with little Stripes?" said the biggest one. "Did he fall and hurt his little knee? Aw, look at little Stripy, crying and running home to his mama." All the boys laughed as if this were the funniest thing they had ever heard.

Elliott turned to face them. Blood rushed to his face.

The fat one circled and rode up to him and got off his bike.

Elliott stared at him for a few seconds before casting his eyes to the ground. He knew what was coming next.

The fat one dropped his bicycle and methodically closed the space between them. The other boys followed suit, closing in around him, working up their nerve.

Feeling panicked, Elliott looked from one boy to the next. They had made a tight circle around him. "Come on," he said, still staring at the asphalt. "I don't want to fight. I didn't do anything to you."

The fat one poked him in the chest, pushing him backward.

"Just let me go home," Elliott said.

The fat one moved closer, standing nose to nose with him. "All right, then, he said, "get out of here." He pushed him.

Clenching his teeth, Elliott started to walk away. But as soon as he turned, the fat one punched him in the back of the head, knocking him to the ground. He hit the pavement face-first, and blood gushed from his nose onto the street.

The boys descended on him like a pack of dogs. He drew his arms around his face to protect at least that much of himself from the flurry of blows. He sobbed uncontrollably, pleading with them to leave him alone.

Just then, he heard his grandfather's voice. "Break it up!" he barked. "All of you." He rushed to Elliott's side and peeled the boys off him one by one, jerking the biggest one so hard that he fell backward onto the pavement. "Get!" he yelled at them. "Out of my sight, or you'll wish you had never laid eyes on me."

"Look at this," said the fat one, dusting himself off. "Crazy Grandpa comes to the rescue." But his voice lacked conviction. "Come on," he said to the others as he picked his bike up off the ground. "You haven't seen the last of us, Stripes," he said, glaring at Elliott as he turned to ride away. "You're gonna pay for this."

Elliott's grandfather cocked a fist, and the fat one flinched.

As the boys rode away, the fat one yelled over his shoulder, "Watch yourself, Stripes. When you least expect it, we'll be back."

The old man reached down to help Elliott up. "Are you all right?" he asked.

Elliott grasped his hand and pulled himself up. "Yeah, I'm all right." He wiped the blood from his face with the back of his sleeve, feeling ashamed for the beating he had just taken.

"Animals," said the old man. "What's the world coming to?" And for several seconds, he stood in the road and looked at Elliott with a strange expression, as if debating whether to say more. "Let's go home," he said at last.

Elliott nodded. Staring at his feet, he followed his grandfather down the street. As they walked the remaining distance back to the house, the old man looked at him with that same inscrutable expression. "You know, son, violence is not the solution to every problem."

Elliott looked up at him.

"But it *is* the solution to some problems." He put his arm around his grandson's shoulder, and they walked home in silence.

When they reached the house, the old man started to speak, but Elliott bounded up to his bedroom and slammed the door, threw himself on the bed, and buried his face in the pillow.

A loud crack of thunder boomed across the sky, signaling the return of the storms that had been a daily occurrence since his arrival in New Orleans. Eventually, he fell into a restless sleep. The day turned into evening while he slept, dreams of happier times filling his head.

Later that night, with rain still thumping against the ceramic rooftop, he awoke and ventured downstairs. Outside, darkness had fallen. He had been holed up in his room for the past several hours and was hungry, though the shame from the

Staring at his feet, Elliott followed his grandfather
down the street as they walked the remaining
distance back to the house.

beating earlier in the day loomed foremost in his mind. Also, he wanted to see his mother. He arrived at the dining room table to find his mom and his grandfather talking in whispers. His mom, bone thin and ghostly pale, was crying. Hearing him approach, the two ended their conversation, and his mother looked over at him and hurriedly collected herself. To Elliott, though he loved her so, she looked like death itself.

"Come here, Ell," she said, opening her arms wide. "Give your mama a hug." A weak smile formed on her lips as she reached out to him. Outside, the wind kicked up, and rain pelted the rooftop.

As he went to embrace her, he realized that she looked scared despite the smile on her face. He hugged her and breathed in the smell of scented soap from her skin.

"I heard you had a rough day," she said, caressing the back of his head as she held him.

To his own surprise, he began to cry. It embarrassed him, breaking down here in front of his granddad, and he struggled to regain his composure.

Perhaps sensing his discomfort, the old man stood. "I need a drink of water," he said softly, and went through the swinging door into the kitchen.

"It's all right, Elliott," she said gently. "One of these days, the bullies are going to leave you alone." She held him at arm's length, brushing the bangs from his face. "I'm so sorry all this has started up again. I had hoped that by coming here you'd be able to get a fresh start." Gently she wiped his tears away. "You're such a handsome boy," she said. "And strong—deep inside, where it counts."

"You always say that," he said quietly.

"Do you remember the Christmas after your daddy left?" she asked, her voice perking up. "You were so young then."

"Yeah," he said. "I remember."

"You waited until I'd gone to sleep, and then got out of bed," she said, smiling. "It was just you and me in the house."

"Yes," said Elliott. The hint of a smile formed on his lips. Strangely, the first Christmas after his father left remained a happy memory for him.

"While I was sleeping, you snuck into my room and opened my jewelry box. And you took my jewelry into the living room and wrapped all the pieces into Christmas packages." Now she was smiling, too. "When I woke up the next morning, I found you asleep under the tree, surrounded by all the packages you had made for me. "I opened them to find all of my own jewelry. You told me that Daddy always gave me jewelry to make me happy and that you wanted me to have a happy Christmas." She beamed at him.

"And you gave me the bicycle," he said. "And we spent all day on the couch, watching movies under the blanket and eating microwave popcorn." He laughed.

His mother laughed, too. "You're a good boy, Elliott," she said. "And you are blessed with compassion and a kind heart. Those things are harder to come by than the ability to push others around. Showing kindness is its own kind of strength, and it will bring you more success in life than any of those boys will ever know."

"If you say so," he said.

"I do say so," she replied. "When you grow up, you'll do marvelous things, because there are marvelous things inside you." She always had that knack for making him feel better. "Now, I hope you didn't do anything to provoke those boys."

He chuckled. "I didn't do anything to provoke them. They're just the same old bullies I've been dealing with my whole life."

"Well, whatever happens, I expect you to take the high road," she said. "Do you understand me?"

"Don't worry, Mom, I don't think I'm going to be mistaken for the school bully anytime soon."

He sat down at the end of the table and looked around him. The walls were burgundy and, like the rest of the house, decorated with glossy paintings in carved gilt frames. *No velvet Elvises around here,* he mused, feeling a little better than before as he recalled the kitschy decor above the sofa in his father's mobile home. He had been young when his father left, though not too young to remember the smell of cheap whiskey, the beatings and hateful words rained on his mother. He hadn't spoken to his father in years, and that suited him just fine. Elliott and his mother were a team. He looked out for her, and she for him.

Returning to the present, he looked at the chandelier hanging from the high ceiling, and the myriad rainbows shimmering onto the walls from its hundreds of cut-glass prisms. The room was wainscoted and crown-molded with carved cypress wood, and at its end, two windows with drapes of olive green and gold looked out at the twin magnolia trees swaying like drunks in the gale-force wind. Like most of the other rooms in the house, the dining room felt more like a museum than a cozy retreat. As he plopped down into the chair at the end of the table, he thought to himself, and not for the first time, that this place was a bona fide mansion.

"So, Mom," he said, "about your . . . um, sickness . . ." They needed to talk about it, though his guts twisted in knots at the thought. "I'm fifteen years old now. You don't have to be afraid to talk to me." His voice cracked a little, betraying the fear he was trying so hard to mask. "I'm going to be here for you. We'll get through this—together, like always."

This seemed to catch her off guard. "Oh, Elliott," she said, "let's not talk about that just now." She glared toward the kitchen, her eyes shooting daggers at her father through the carved cypress door.

Elliott gazed at his mom, recalling how she used to sing him to sleep those nights after his father left. He remembered how she tried to teach him to play baseball when he was in the fourth grade. She couldn't throw the ball straight to save her life, but she didn't want him to miss out on what the other boys were doing. An ungainly attempt, to be sure, but he loved her for it. He thought back to when he developed a terrible crush on Lisa Hastings, and how she tried to give him advice about girls. Later she tried to comfort him when Lisa laughed at him after he asked her to the ninth-grade dance. Seeing his mother so pale and thin, he felt he couldn't bear it if anything should happen to her—if she should die.

He rose from his chair and hugged her. For several minutes they just held each other, neither of them saying anything, the air thick with the awareness that very soon they might not have each other to hold ever again.

Eventually, Elliott's grandfather returned and the two of them helped her up the stairs and into her bed. They had tried to get her to eat some dinner, but she was nauseated and hadn't really tried to eat. After getting her tucked in, they returned to the dining room, and the old man went into the kitchen and came back a few minutes later with two roast beef sandwiches and two glasses of milk. Ravenous, Elliott tore into the sandwich as his grandfather began to speak. From upstairs, he thought he heard a single muffled sob.

"Well, *I'm* glad you finally know," his grandfather said. "We were concerned about how you'd take the news."

Again feeling a little uncomfortable in the old man's presence, Elliott continued eating his sandwich and said nothing.

"I'm really worried about her, son. She needs you right now."

"I know," Elliott said, taking another bite though his mouth was already full.

"What if there was something you could do to help her get better? You'd want to know about it, right?"

"What do you mean?" Elliott said, feeling both uneasy and a little put off by the cryptic question. "Of course I would."

"Well," said the old man, the familiar mysterious smile returning to his face, "I don't want to get your hopes up, but there may be something you can do." Again he looked toward the stairs. "Your mother made me promise on my life that I wouldn't bring it up, but I can't sit by without saying any-thing—too much is at stake."

Elliott began to wonder if the boys who beat him this af-ternoon might be onto something. Maybe his grandfather *was* crazy. "Tell me what you're talking about," he said, putting down the half-eaten sandwich.

His grandfather looked at him, as if wondering whether to continue. "Elliott, I'm pretty sure I know why Mary's got-ten sick, and if I'm right, there's more to it than you could possibly realize."

"What are you *talking* about!" Elliott demanded. The old man was starting to scare him.

"Don't be alarmed, son," his grandfather said. "I know it sounds crazy, but I think your mother's cancer has something to do with . . ." His voice trailed off.

"With *what*!" Elliott practically shouted. "Tell me what you're talking about!"

"Well, it has something to do with this house, with our family history, and with those birthmarks you have between your fingers and toes."

Elliott recalled his father telling him that his grandfa-ther was crazy—that he "had dangerous ideas," to be exact. Calmly, he said again, "You have to tell me what you're talk-ing about."

"I'm going to tell you everything, son. You're old enough, and you have the right to know the whole lot, whether your mom wants you to or not."

A flash lit up the two magnolias outside the dining room window, and the next instant, thunder cracked like a rifle shot in his ear. Now the rain fell with a vengeance.

The old man leaned forward, looking into his eyes. The cryptic smile was absent. His voice deepened. "Our family history is a rich one, son, full of power and secrets and places you can only dream of. You are the legacy to that history. And now, I fear, you have a terrible job you must fulfill."

The wind rattled the windows so loud, it sounded as if the glass might break. The old man stared at him. His white hair springing out in all directions added to the impression that he was a little unhinged. Elliott grew more afraid of him. Shadows danced across the room as the swaying magnolias outside moved back and forth in the light of a streetlamp, casting erratic shadows and then withdrawing them.

"I think the key to your mother's well-being"—the old man's voice softened—"and to many, many other things, lies directly in your hands."

Elliott gazed at his grandfather, wondering whether he had gone off the deep end.

"In the basement of this house is a small collection of, shall we say, *artifacts*, left by Darius Orion. Tonight, while your mother sleeps, I want you to go to the basement and spend some time looking through those things. After you've had a chance to explore the various things you'll find down there, you and I will talk again. I have much instruction to offer you in the coming weeks. You'll need to be well prepared if we are to succeed."

Elliott stared at his grandfather. He had no idea how to respond.

"When the timing is right," his grandfather continued, "we'll start with a test. You will have to demonstrate that you can perform a simple task—one that I myself, for reasons I don't understand, have been unable to complete." The old man's voice trailed off. He sighed, looking suddenly, inconsolably sad. "The key to all this is down in the basement. The reason Darius Orion chose this site for his house was because there's something special down there, something only he knew about—something that had to be protected from outsiders at all costs. I am speaking of a secret that can give you the power to control many things, Elliott, including your mother's illness—*if* you are the man I suspect you are."

Elliott was flummoxed. "Do you have any idea how crazy that sounds?"

With a broad smile, his grandfather replied, "The basement, Elliott. Go to the basement. Tomorrow, while your mother is at the doctor's office, we'll talk again. We have many things we must discuss before your journey can begin."

"I have school tomorrow," Elliott protested. "Mom's not going to let me stay home from school, especially when she hears about the crazy things you're telling me." Elliott was surprised by the tone of his own voice. He sounded angry.

The old man slammed his fist onto the table, startling him. A stern glare replaced his smile. "Your mother must not hear a word of this. If she learns that we are going to begin the cultivation, son, all will be lost. The consequences of inaction will be immeasurable . . . and your mother will die."

The cultivation. Elliott digested the words. Strange.

"Don't dare breathe a word of this to her. I can promise you, her very life depends on it. Tonight when we're asleep, just go to the basement. Look through the things you will find there; then we can discuss them in detail tomorrow. More is at stake than you can possibly imagine." The old man held Elliott's gaze for a few seconds, then abruptly rose and went upstairs.

For several minutes, Elliott sat at the dining-room table in stunned silence, listening to the storm howl outside. He hadn't even known this place *had* a basement. His mom would want to know about what his grandfather said, and he was going to have to tell her, first thing in the morning. After all, they were a team. He rose from the table and went up to his room.

As he lay in his bed, thoughts of his mother's illness consumed him. He hadn't been crazy about the idea of picking up and moving to New Orleans to live with a grandfather he didn't know, but once they were here—at first, anyway—he had felt that maybe things would be better. His grandfather clearly had resources that could help them while his mother was fighting her illness. But after the conversation tonight, he wasn't so sure. The old man was crazy as a bat. He wondered what his mother was going to say when he told her about the conversation. Probably she was going to be angry. She always seemed uncomfortable leaving the two of them alone. Either way, his decision was firm. The last thing she needed to be dealing with was this crazy old man trying to pull him out of school and "cultivate" him, whatever the hell *that* meant. With these thoughts running through his mind, he turned off the light, pulled the covers around him, and gradually fell into a fitful sleep.

⚜ ⚜ ⚜

Several hours later, he awoke with a start. The room was pitch black. He looked around in an effort to identify what had woken him, but all he saw was darkness. The wind howled, and water pelted the clay tile roof. This place was creepy in the dark. Feeling suddenly wide-awake, he tried to lull himself back to sleep by recalling the dream he was having moments ago. In it, he was at the school dance with Lisa Hastings.

Lisa was wearing a black miniskirt that accentuated her long, tanned legs, and he caught a hint of cleavage when he stole a glance at her chest. Her hair smelled like shampoo—strawberry Suave, maybe— and the scent of her perfume was ever so slightly detectable. He stared into her eyes and could see from her expression that she was in love with him. The two of them were in the center of a dance floor, swaying to his mother's favorite song, "The Girl from Ipanema." He knew the words by heart.

> Tall and tan and young and lovely,
> The girl from Ipanema goes walking,
> And when she passes, each one she passes goes, "Ah" . . .

Everything happened in the perfect slow motion of dreams. His hand rested on her waist, and he felt her body press against his. As they swayed back and forth to the sultry music, a crowd of admirers watched with envy. In the crowd were the boys who had harassed him earlier in the day. The fat one looked longingly at Lisa Hastings and remarked to his friends that he would never get a girl like that. To Elliott, the song had never sounded so perfect.

> Ooh, but I watch her so sadly.
> How can I tell her I love her?
> Yes, I would give my heart gladly,
> But each day when she walks to the sea,
> She looks straight ahead, not at me . . .

Lisa gazed into his eyes. Elliott felt the way he felt only in his best imaginings: confident, powerful, handsome. As they swayed back and forth, he looked over at the fat bully, all the while relishing the feel of Lisa's body and silently communicating to all that he, Elliott, had the girl and they did not.

As the two spun around, moving in perfect synchrony with the music, he saw his mom watching them from across the room. She wore a beautiful white evening gown, and her hair was pulled up in a movie star do. Her skin, dark like Lisa's, was glowing with the radiance of good health.

"You did it, Ell," he heard her say, tears welling in her eyes. The jewelry he had wrapped for her on that long-ago Christmas glistened in the light of a chandelier overhead. *God, she looked beautiful. You don't need to sing to me anymore, Mom, he thought. Everything's going to be fine. Tonight I'm dancing with Lisa Hastings. Lisa's face moved ever so slowly toward his.*

> *. . . And when she passes, I smile, but she doesn't see.*
> *She just doesn't see . . .*
> *She never sees me . . .*

Lisa tilted her head to the side as she moved in to kiss him. Consciously making an effort to imprint the moment forever in his brain, he focused on the melody as they moved together. He pulled her closer. As they circled in their embrace, he saw the fat bully mouth the words "no way" to the kid standing next to him. All the while, Lisa's mouth moved closer to his. Her wet lips glistened with ruby red lipstick.

As he anticipated the kiss, he glanced over Lisa's shoulder and saw his grandfather in the corner, towering above everyone around him, wearing his usual gray suit. His hands were folded in front of him, and the purple birthmarks between his fingers stood out like beacons. The ever-present faint, smirking smile lit the corners of his mouth.

Although the old man didn't speak, Elliott heard his voice in his head. You're the one, boy, it said. Lisa's nose brushed his. He closed his eyes. When their lips touched, he began to kiss. She kissed back. Lost in the moment, he knew he had just claimed the most beautiful girl in school as his own. He thought, this is what heaven must be like.

A thunderclap jolted him awake. His heart pounded in his chest. *Just when it was getting good!* He pulled the covers over his head and tried to recapture the moment in the dream. He knew he would never be the object of the affection of someone like Lisa Hastings. His lot in life was to be ridiculed, beaten up, and abandoned—first abandoned by his father and now, perhaps, by his mother, too. He lay there lamenting that he was neither lucky nor cool. For several minutes, he tossed and turned, but after some time, he realized he wasn't going to nod off again, so he decided to go downstairs for a glass of milk. By the clock on the nightstand, it was 3:15 a.m. He chided himself for having slept so long this afternoon.

Yes, no doubt about it: the house was creepy at night. Although his eyesight slowly adjusted to the darkness, he couldn't make out the top of the ceiling in the blackness of the hallway. Paintings loomed over him, the figures ever frozen in their tasks, some of them frighteningly lifelike in the nocturnal shadows. Rain pelted the rooftop. As he passed his mother's bedroom, he stopped and slowly opened the door, careful not to make any noise. He stood in the doorway, barely able to make out her sleeping figure in the bed across the room. Looking at her, he thought of how vibrant and alive she had appeared in his dream, and felt a pang of sadness deep inside. Shaking it off, he continued downstairs and into the kitchen.

He turned on the kitchen light and went toward the refrigerator, on the way passing the door to the pantry. Just beyond it, secluded in the corner, was a door he hadn't noticed before— a long, thin door that matched the wooden paneling so well, it was almost indistinguishable. When he saw the door, he instantly thought of the weird conversation with his grandfather. Curious, he walked over to it. Although its borders were now clearly visible, it didn't have a knob. He ran his hands along the edges of the wood, wondering how to open it, all the while hearing his grandfather's voice in his head. *Go to the basement.*

He pushed on the edges of the door, with no effect. Placing his hand in the center of the door, he gently applied pressure. There was a click, and it swung open. His breath caught in his throat as he looked down into a dark, narrow passageway leading underground.

Chapter 2

The Chamber

He stood at the head of the stairs, peering into the darkness. Gradually, he could make out the beginnings of a narrow, claustrophobic passageway leading downward. The steps before him were deep, carved from stone and recessed in the center, as if worn from many years of foot traffic. The height of the passage, he estimated at about five and a half feet. The walls were stone and mortar, rising in an arch only slightly higher than his head. He tried to imagine his grandfather, stooped over and walking through the passageway, and the image made him smile. The old man probably had to sit and scoot on his butt to get downstairs.

Summoning his courage, Elliott glanced back at the kitchen. Realizing that it would probably be pitch black after the first few steps, he opened the third drawer by the sink, where he just might find a flashlight. Not finding one, he settled for a lighter nestled in a pile of coupons and rubber bands. He pocketed it and returned to passageway.

Unable to see more than a few feet ahead, he stepped down on the first stair. His heart rate quickened, and he thought about going back. After all, this was silly . . . and a little scary. But something inside him said press on, and he took another tentative step, pressing against the cool stone wall to steady himself. When he reached the fifth step, a whooshing sound made him jump, and he was immersed in darkness. The door to the kitchen had closed. He took a deep breath, urging himself to stay calm. The dream of Lisa Hastings lingered in his mind, beckoning him to turn back, but a strangely insistent curiosity about Darius Orion countered the impulse. He fished the lighter out of his pocket. It was an old Zippo, with the steel striking wheel, and he realized he hadn't even checked to see if it worked. Thankfully, it lit on the first attempt, revealing the dim stone passage below.

Shadows played on the walls, and a musty odor filled his nostrils. He held the lighter in front of him, brandishing it against the darkness, and counted the stairs as he descended. At twenty-five, he wondered how far beneath the house this basement was. After all, the flight up to the second story had only twenty steps, and those were shorter than these. At this rate, either the basement had a very high ceiling or he was headed into an underground chamber several feet beneath the old house's foundations.

By the fiftieth step, he was scared. The air seemed thinner somehow, and his breathing became faster and shallower. In the Zippo's feeble light, he noticed a change in the composition of the walls. No longer stone, they were now of earthen brick. Sconces holding dust-covered torches jutted from the walls every dozen steps or so, reminding him of the stairwells in old castles he had seen on the history channel. This was like no basement he had ever seen. He wrestled one of the torches free and held the lighter to its wick. To his astonishment, it erupted in flame. Thankful for the light, he pocketed the Zippo and continued the claustrophobic trek downward.

He finally reached the bottom. He had counted seventy-seven steps in one long, unbroken flight. Holding the torch at arm's length, he surveyed the room before him, thinking it looked more like a burial chamber than a basement. Like the tunnel that led him down here, the chamber had a low ceiling, perhaps six and a half feet, and earth instead of stone. The walls were of the same earthen brick that lined the bottom half of the staircase, and the floor was dirt, packed so tight it felt like smooth concrete beneath his bare feet. The chamber itself was not much larger than a closet—certainly not what he would have expected for a basement seventy-seven steps beneath such a grand home.

A primitive wooden chair sat in the corner, flanked by a chest and a small table. Fine paintings hung from iron spikes hammered into the mortar. But who would have used these Spartan furnishings when such a grand mansion was available upstairs? Above the chair were two more torches. Using his torch, he lit them, filling the chamber with flickering amber light.

A thick layer of dust coated the chair as well as the chest and table beside it. A wide, thick, yellowed book sat on the table. After staring at the book for a moment, he gave the paintings a closer look. One by one, he inspected them. They were exquisitely detailed, though the scenes they depicted were otherworldly, like something out of a children's tale.

The first painting, set in a carved golden frame, showed a city in a desert wasteland of rolling dunes. The city, set in the middle distance, was built of something that looked like shimmering black glass. Wondering where in the world such a place might be found, Elliott stared at it. It was beautiful. At the corners, spindly glass watchtowers stretched skyward, and a wall of thick glass brick, interrupted periodically by massive wooden gates, surrounded the city. Many of the buildings within the wall were tall, giving the impression of a skyline, though they were narrow and oddly built—again, like nothing he had seen before. A soft apricot glow, emanating from the heart of the city, enveloped the structures in a serene wash of color. The painting, despite its strangeness, felt somehow pleasing.

Beside it hung another painting, depicting a forest of massive trees. The trunks were more massive than any Elliott had ever seen, some even wider than a fair-size house. A clearing with a circle of stone statues filled the center of the painting. The statues were tall and oblong and planted upright in the ground, evoking images of Stonehenge. But unlike the megaliths of southern England, these stones were carved into lifelike busts of royal figures. In the center of the ring of statues, a boy in a burgundy robe stood before a stone table, arms upraised. His eyes were closed and his mouth open, as if he were praying aloud.

Intrigued, Elliott walked around the chamber and looked at each of the other paintings. One showed a castle atop a sprawling green mountain, with purple mountains rising in tiers behind it. Towers of varying heights and widths rose from all sides of the castle, and a massive wall enclosed the entire mountaintop. Lining the roof of the castle, in fine detail, were rows of menacing statues carved in the likeness of winged monsters. Large and muscular, with doglike faces and with oversize wings folded behind them, they reminded him of the gargoyles decorating the university buildings back home. Overall, the scene was beautiful, and the castle's architecture reminded him of the Gothic European buildings he had seen in pictures from one of his mother's many books. The winged monsters made him uneasy, though, for they seemed to be staring out of the picture at him.

The last painting also depicted a castle. Like the first, it appeared to be a massive architectural undertaking, and it, too, sat atop a mountain. But the castle in this picture was black, and the mountain it rested on was a bare crag without vegetation. Winged monsters lined the roof of this castle as well, though they were larger, with red eyes and long, pointy tails. To Elliott, they looked like demons.

The door of the castle, made of riveted iron, was opened to receive a long column of men with metal collars around their necks, each chained to the next. Their faces showed anguish and torment, and some clawed at the bindings around their necks.

The last painting also depicted a castle.
Winged monsters lined the roof of this castle...
to Elliott, they looked like demons.

Then he noticed the captives' hands and felt an eerie chill. For each had birthmarks like his own. At the front of the line was a hairy brown creature with thick, muscular arms and legs. His head was bald, his ears too large. With vacant eyes and a toothy grin, he looked back upon his trail of prisoners and tugged at their chains. Farther in the background, rising from the spires of the castle, plumes of black smoke billowed skyward. Elliott looked into the eyes of the squat brown creature and shuddered.

Not quite sure what to make of the paintings, he turned his attention to the chair in the corner and was again thankful for the torchlight in the dank underground chamber. He brushed the fine dust from the seat, filling the air with it and making himself cough, and could not but wonder how long it had been since someone sat here. After the dust settled and he could breathe easily again, he sat down in the chair and reached for the book on the table.

The soft leather cover was decorated with strange markings. The glyphs were unfamiliar, though they rather reminded him of characters from the Cherokee alphabet, which he had learned about in school. Gingerly, careful lest he damage it, he opened the yellowed book. The pages, though brittle, were filled with beautifully handwritten text. With torches blazing above him, he began to read.

First Entry
Give me strength, Baruna. I know not what my fate will be. I have been in this hole now for three days—at least, that is my guess—and I cannot find my way back to the forest. It is a curious thing, how I got here. My comrades and I were convened in Ondor for the Festival of Opik. As during every celebration of the equinox, our numbers were uncountable, with virtually every shamalan from the empire in attendance. We amassed not only to

celebrate but also to scheme against the dark forces that have assembled against us for the last several revolutions of the Enstar. Our meeting was raucous and different from any I can remember. Many of the shamalans, for the first time in memory, feared for the empire's future. I, of course, presided over the assembly with what courage and wisdom I could muster. My brother, Galeren, was with me as always, but he acted quite strangely, leading me to wonder if perhaps he had played a role in the events that unfolded that day. We had just sat down to offer our thanks to the elders when it happened. With sudden force, the disturbance in the Shama overtook me like a war hammer smashing into bone. The next thing I knew, they were on us. Serpan warriors poured into our forest in uncountable numbers. The sky became so thick with arrows that, for a moment, the light of the two suns grew dim, and before my eyes, my brethren fell around me. Anguish fills my heart. It was through Lothar's betrayal that my people were slaughtered in the peaceful gathering of the equinox, and through his machinations that I have passed into this dreadful place. Surely he must think me dead, and perhaps I may as well be. I have begun to fear that I shall be stuck in this hole forever. Despite my keenest efforts, I am unable to overcome the hex that has banished me here. During my cultivation, I learned of the daughterlands, but never did I imagine I would someday find myself exiled to one. Because my fate is uncertain, I have decided to make this record. I will leave it here, deep underground and near this passageway, so that only those who know the strange and terrible secret of this place will see it. I am about to run out of what little food and wine I had with me at the time of the betrayal. Thank Baruna I was

wearing my knapsack at the time of my banishment!
Yesterday I found a tunnel that appears to lead out of
this cave. When I awaken tomorrow, I shall climb out to
find sustenance for my survival. Give me strength, great
Baruna, for I will need it.

A mixture of confusion and wonder overtook Elliott. Had
his grandfather planted the book down here? Was *this* what he
was supposed to find tonight? The torchlight cast eerie shadows
on the walls, adding dramatic effect as he digested the strange
account. He was beginning to feel the discomfort of a distended
bladder, but he wasn't about to set the book aside, not with so
many pages left. He turned the page.

Second Entry
I traveled out of the hole for the first time today. Above
me stands a forest much like Ondor, though the trees are
much younger. The smell of water is rich in the air, and I
think I must be near an ocean. I prayed to Mileva to send
food, and she blessed me with fresh meat. The creature I
slew was one I have not seen before, but it tasted much
like dammas. Thanks to Mileva, I will have fresh meat
for a few days while I explore the lands above this cave.
I have not yet found water, but I was able to slake my
thirst by chewing on some leaves from the trees. I do
not think it will be hard to find water—I can smell it
everywhere.

Enthralled, Elliott turned the page.

Third Entry
Today I climbed out and followed the scent of the water.
I discovered not an ocean but a river, one that is great

and wide, like Tantasar. Thank Baruna it is less than a half day's journey from the cave. I was so thirsty, I drank until I felt ill. I lay down on the banks of the river, holding my belly, and thanked Baruna for the bounty he has brought me in this isolation. There is only one sun in this place, but it burned hot and bright on my skin as I lay by the river. For a moment, I felt so good, I could almost imagine that I was back home and that none of this had happened. Thanks to the elders, I think I will be able to survive in this daughterland until I find my way home. I filled my wineskins with water before returning to the cave. I should have at least seven days' worth, and it is only a short trip to the river should I need more. I was tempted to explore the riverbed and see what sorts of creatures live in the water, but I shall save that task for another time. For now, I shall focus my efforts on the surface—and on returning to my home.

Fourth Entry
Mileva blessed me with more fresh meat today, and I broadened my travels through the lands above. Imagine my excitement to find a road cut through the middle of this wood! I pray that either gimlets or men built it, as it wasn't a road hewn by shamalan or susquat. The road was well kept and had many fresh footprints. Oh, how I wanted to join with the Shama today! But I did not, as it is not clear whether that would be safe. Tomorrow I will do what my ancestors did in the ages before the enlightenment: I will find myself a raven.

Fifth Entry
Although I have not sent up a prayer to Opik since my arrival, water fell from the sky today in torrents. I left

the cave only briefly, but I heard voices in the forest. I pray they were not serpan. I was unable to find a raven today. Until I do, I must be careful during my excursions through the forest and to the river. If the storms continue, I have enough fresh meat and water to sustain me for several days. Because of the storms and the voices in the forest, I spent much of the day down here, trying to find a way back home. I am looking at the passageway even as I write this. It seems that it should be so easy to return to my home. Why, therefore, do I fail? Baruna, please show me the way. I shudder to think of the turmoil that must be brewing in Pangrelor and on Mount Kalipharus. I am sure my old friends the grayfarers are doing all they can. I pray they will have the strength to repel the northern hordes and the cowardly soul who commands them. I have not written of the betrayal, but these events are perhaps the most important that I shall have to tell. I vow to record what happened while it is still fresh in my thoughts, but not tonight, for I am going to get a good night's sleep. Tomorrow I must find a raven.

Sixth Entry

I emerged today to find the ground soft and the lone sun shining brightly. I would never have imagined that a single sun could provide so much light and warmth. I spent much of the day calling for a raven, but alas, none came. Perhaps there are no ravens in this strange land. As the sun began to fall, I made a trip to the river to replenish my water. If the storms come again, I want to be prepared to stay in my hole without concern for such things. I also felt like making the walk, as most of my day was spent in meditation while I called to the ravens. When I approached the river, I heard voices. Fearful that serpans may be approaching, I hid behind a tree and waited. As the voices came closer, I realized that they were coming from the direction of the river. I saw a boat approaching. It was made from great wooden slabs and powered by wind. The seamen from Lon Carafay often use something similar when oarsmen are not readily available. The vessel was not as large as a warship and did not appear to have any weaponry. Although this heartened me, I kept hidden until it was well out of sight. To my great disappointment, I did not get a look at the crew of the vessel. From the sounds of their voices, though, I doubt they were serpan. I traveled back to the cave in the darkness. To my great fortune, a moon was shining brightly in the sky. It was frightening how close it appeared, but I thanked Cerus for its light and guidance. What an odd land this is, with only one sun and this strange moon!

Seventh Entry

I have not written for a few days, but I have much to tell. On the morning after my last entry, I contacted a raven! I had begun to doubt my ability to do so, as so many days passed without an answer from one. When I contacted him, though, he granted my request and allowed me to see through his eyes. How much I have learned in the last few days thanks to my wonderful and wise raven. Thanks to Mileva for sending him! The road I have written of leads to a large village to the east, less than a half day's journey from here. Men inhabit the village. They are smaller than the men back home but larger than gimlets. They do not appear to be particularly warlike or fierce. To my great interest, I have seen that there are many different breeds of men here. Most are pale, with color in their eyes and hair. Others have brown skin and eyes and short black hair, much like the gimlets of Obsidia. The pale ones seem to govern over the brown ones. I have also seen small, fair-skinned men with slanted eyes who seem to function in the same capacity as the brown ones, though there are very few of them. These men speak in so many different tongues, it is a wonder they can function as a village. Much to my delight, I have also seen a fourth group of men. These have smooth, olive skin and dark eyes, much like the men back home. However, they are not a part of the same culture that makes up the village. They live in clans in the forest and clothe themselves with the skins of beasts. Their hair is fine and black, and they wear jewelry of bone and wood. Through my raven, I have learned that they do not like the inhabitants of the village, whom they regard as trespassers. How homesick it made me to see this noble race of men! They look much like Pangrelorians. The village itself appears to be a center of commerce. There are many primitive wooden dwellings, which begin just outside the town center and radiate outward in an almost uniform fashion. In the center of town stands a structure that I believe to be either a temple or a palace, for it is larger and more ornate than its surrounding buildings. The town seems to be laid out around it, though it is quite crude by Pangrelorian standards. The temple faces the river, and a dock lies just in front of its gate. I have not seen battlements or warships. There are guard towers at the corners of the village, but this does not look like a land ravaged by war. If I can obtain proper dress, I think I can visit the village and learn more about this place. How nice it will be to break from this long isolation, though I am loath to leave the passageway unprotected with so many men milling about.

Eighth Entry

I named my raven Griogair, after the conquering shamalan emperor. With such a noble moniker, he is certain
to bring me good fortune. Today Griogair circled the
village so that I might get a feel for its layout. It is bordered on both sides by water. Behind it is an inlet of a
vast ocean. Large seafaring vessels were docked there.
Crude wooden roads lead from the docks, through a
forest, to the back of the village. Strangely, much of the
land behind the village is nearly underwater, making me
wonder why anyone would establish a village in such a
wet spot. Not even we shamalans, with our great affinity for water, would build in such an inauspicious place.
The front of the village faces the river and is built on
higher, sturdier ground. As with the rivers back home,
the highest ground seems to be near the riverbanks. At
my request, Griogair spent some time inspecting the
temple, for it was the focus of much activity. It is indeed
a crude building, constructed of timber, mud, and unfinished stone. It faces the river, and a communal square
lies between the temple and the riverfront. As Griogair
circled the square, brown men in chains were placed on
the auction block and bartered to the highest bidder for
goods and coins. They were sold side by side with pieces
of fruit, bits of cloth, and trinkets of jewelry. And in front
of the temple! Oh, Baruna, what barbarism is this? I shall
have to proceed cautiously if I am to enter this place, lest
I be captured and bartered for meat! In the middle of the
square, posts were planted, with men chained to them.
Children passed hand in hand with their keepers near
these posts and jeered at the prisoners. Primitive and
treacherous this place must be—more like Vengala than
my beloved Harwelden, I fear. I shall have to conduct

myself with caution when I enter this village, if I hope to return here and make it back home. On either side of the temple are buildings that house warriors. Perhaps some type of army reigns over this place, though I have seen no evidence of threat other than the men who would sell their brothers for coin in the square. A crude wooden palisade surrounds the village. I shall likely sneak into the village through the palisade, for it stands unguarded. I am not inclined to pass through the gates—there are many questions that I fear I would be unable to answer. I do not want to end up chained to a post in the square!

A flurry of questions tumbled through Elliott's mind. Was the journal Darius Orion's? Clearly, the "village" he referred to was old New Orleans, with Lake Pontchartrain behind it, and the Mississippi River in front. The temple he described must have been an early version of the St. Louis Cathedral, with Jackson Square lying between it and the river. His grandfather had said the house was built in 1796. Was that how New Orleans looked at the time?

And what about the chamber? It must have been the site of the "passage" the author referred to, though Elliott couldn't fathom why anyone would refer to this dank hole as a passage. Was the chamber the reason Darius Orion had insisted on building the house here—to protect the hole that lay beneath it? And did the Indians back then know about the chamber? Perhaps its presence was the reason they considered the place sacred and had tried to keep Darius from building his house here.

The author of the text had described the Indians and reported that they "look much like Pangrelorians." Also, he had repeatedly referred to his "home," apparently a place called Lon Carafay. Elliott ransacked his memory for any mention "Lon Carafay" or "Pangrelorians," but nothing came up. He rescanned the pages he had read, looking specifically this time for strange, alien-sounding words. He found references to ser-pans, grayfarers, susquats, gimlets, and shamalans. Unknown place names also cropped up: Vengala, Obsidia, Mount Kali-pharus, and Harwelden. And the author wrote of a place with two suns. It was like something out of a fairy tale. Elliott had to wonder: did Darius Orion have weird raspberry birthmarks between *his* fingers and toes?

By now, Elliott had to pee so badly, he had trouble concen-trating. Standing up to ease the pressure, he looked at the nearest of the paintings, with the city of black glass. In the upper right corner, a big orange sun shone brightly. And in the background, more distant, a second, more yellowish orb, about half the size of the first. A passing cloud partially obscured it, but there it was.

With growing excitement, he looked at the next painting, which showed the gray stone castle. Again he found a large or-ange sun and a smaller, yellow one, their rays glinting off the stony backs of the monsters that kept watch along the castle battlements. The two remaining paintings showed no suns or moons in the sky, even though one depicted the black castle near dusk. Elliott shivered when he looked again into the eyes of the hairy brown creature leading the line of prisoners into the castle. Shamalan, gimlet, grayfarer, susquat, serpan—the creepy little guy was probably one of these.

Despite the discomfort his bladder was causing him, he decided to look around just a little more before heading back up the many stairs. He could sit down and finish reading the journal when he came back. He went back to the corner, to the small chest beside the chair. It was crudely made of unpainted, unfinished wood, colored by age but sturdy looking. He lifted the creaking lid and found only a leather knapsack inside, coat-ed in a thick layer of dust. After making sure nothing else was in the chest, he grabbed the knapsack and pulled back the flap.

Inside, he found a heavy cloth sack, cinched at the top with a yellow drawstring. It jingled when he picked it up. Opening the sack, he gingerly stuck his hand inside to find it full of gold coins. He withdrew a coin and inspected it in the torchlight. It was stamped or cast with pictures, but they were irregular, as if made with crude technology. On one side was a soaring bird with a hooked beak, and beneath this, the word "Parados." On the opposite side was the picture of a bizarre striped monkey with unusually large eyes. Its ears lay back on its head, like those of a cat ready to pounce. Beneath it was the word "Wedjat." The sack was heavy with coins. Curious about their value and recalling his grandfather's tale about Darius Orion's endless wealth, Elliott set the sack aside and reached back into the knapsack.

This time he pulled out a bracelet of thick, hammered silver, set with nine polished stones. The gleaming cabochons were identical in shape and size but of different colors. He turned the bracelet over in his hand, feeling its weight, and the thought occurred to him that his mother might like it. He placed it on his wrist—a perfect fit—and snapped the latch closed.

The next thing he pulled from the knapsack was a stone. He turned it over in his hand—it was smooth and about the size of a baseball, though surprisingly light. Unlike the sack of gold coins and the bracelet, it didn't appear to be valuable in any way. He set it aside and stuck his hand back inside the knapsack, scraping the bottom with his fingertips. It appeared empty, but what was this? His pinky had brushed something smooth under a fold of leather. A moment later, he was looking at a small slingshot. It was of sturdy polished wood and only eight or nine inches long. Pulling it back, he was surprised to find the rubber still elastic, but otherwise it seemed quite ordinary—just a child's toy.

Gathering up the sack of coins, the rock, and the slingshot, he put them back in the knapsack. The silver bracelet

remained on his wrist. Now he could think only of going upstairs and relieving his bladder. He slung the knapsack over
one shoulder, grabbed a torch from one of the sconces, and
walked toward the stairs. He had much to discuss with his
grandfather tomorrow.

Approaching the stairs, he heard a sound that made him
start: a barely audible whisper, lasting only a second. Frightened, he swung around, brandishing the torch in front of him.
Seeing no one, he chided himself. It would have been quite
a trick for someone to sneak down here with him sitting and
facing the stairs the whole time. His imagination was playing
tricks on him. Best to get out of here.

But as soon as he turned toward the stairs, he heard the
whisper again. In a hushed feminine voice, it said, "*Pangrelor.*"

His heart pounded. His shadow wavered against the wall
in the flickering torchlight. No one else could be down here,
but where was the voice coming from? "Who's there?" he demanded, trying to sound in charge and hoping he could keep
from peeing in his pajamas.

No response.

He swung the torch around the room, illuminating the
corners. No one here. Confused, he reasoned that the whisper
must be coming from the staircase itself. Perhaps his grandfather had sneaked down behind him and waited a little way up
the stairs, just out of sight. Yes, that must be it. He moved toward the steps.

"*Paaaangreloooor . . .*" The soft whisper came from behind
him—louder this time, and definitely not from the staircase.

"Who is that!" he said. "Grandfather, is that you?" His
voice cracked.

"*Paaaangreloooor . . .*" The word sounded more drawn out
and softer, but in the same seductive voice. Elliott spun toward
the whisper, raising the torch high. To his right, he saw a gleam,

for just a split second, coming from the behind the painting of the gray castle.

"Who's there?" he demanded, trying to stay calm.

No response.

Summoning his courage, he approached the painting. Nothing here he hadn't seen before. Finally, about to wet himself, he turned to go back upstairs.

"Ellllioooooott . . ."

Gasping in fright, he whirled around just in time to see the glimmer again—a dull yellow light with about the duration of a flashbulb. It came from behind the painting of the gray castle.

Easing the torch back into its sconce over the chair, he turned and faced the painting, determined to discover the source of the glimmer and of the voice. Heart pounding, he grasped the painting and hoisted it off its hook.

"Ellllioooooott . . ." Although the whisper was barely audible, the voice was impassioned, insistent.

The wall behind the painting was marked with a myriad of strange symbols, and in their midst an outline of a hand, as if someone had held their hand up to the wall and outlined it with a piece of chalk. On the hand were lines—four, to be precise, originating in the webbed spaces between the fingers and extending almost to the wrist. Elliott stared at the picture, entranced. Again he heard the whisper, but could not make out what it was saying. This time it was not a single voice but a collection of many voices, speaking at once though not in unison. A cool breeze blew across his forehead—odd, for until now the chamber had been still as a tomb. He stared at the hand, watching as the lines, the birthmarks, seemed to pulse. The whisperer called with increased urgency. The picture itself seemed to beckon him. He knew what they wanted him to do. Tentatively, he raised his right hand to the wall and placed it within the drawing. It fit exactly.

Coldness.

He was surrounded by darkness and unbearable cold. He felt as if a bucket of water had been dumped over his head. He shivered violently and gasped, but there was no air to be had. A frigid wind buffeted his face. He tried to open his eyes but could only squint. Desperate to breathe, he kicked his feet but felt no ground beneath them. Through the slits of his eyes, he saw pinpricks of blue light.

Then, as quickly as it had begun, it was over. He gasped again, and his lungs filled with air. The wind was gone, and he felt the ground beneath his feet. Shaken, he opened his eyes. It was pitch black. He ran his hands over his body to reassure himself that he was in one piece. Then he reached out in front of him, feeling for the chamber wall, but felt nothing. There was a rank odor of decay in the air, as if some dead thing lay nearby.

Disoriented, he took a cautious step forward, and something crunched beneath his bare foot. It felt as if he had just stepped on the dried bones of a tiny rodent. As he strained to orient himself, two thoughts vied for primacy in his mind: *Where in the world am I?* And *I have to pee NOW.* Unable to hold on any longer, he pulled down the front of his pajamas and let loose.

As the sound of the stream hitting the ground grew louder, he heard a raucous cawing in the distance. His mind raced. *What just happened? Where am I?* When he finished peeing, he turned and stepped slowly, holding his hands in front of him. With each step forward, he felt the same unpleasant crunching beneath his feet. Near tears, he stopped in the midst of darkness, at a complete loss for what to do next. He was about to call out for help when he heard the shrill cawing again. This time it was much louder, as if the creature making the noise had come closer. It sounded like a large animal, but he was certain he had never heard this awful sound before. Off to his right, he heard the same crunching noise that his own footsteps had caused, though he hadn't moved an inch. Sensing that he was in danger, he tried to gather his thoughts. He had no idea what to do next. Again he heard the call of the strange animal, and the crunch of its footsteps as it moved toward him.

Chapter 3

Hooks

The beast stood still as a tree trunk, his chest barely moving as breathed the crisp spring air. From his hiding place near edge of the forest, he had a perfect view of the farm. Across the field, the farmer pushed his plow along a crop row despite the oppressive heat of the twin suns. Beyond him stood a humble wooden farmhouse. Other than the farmer, not a soul was in sight.

The beast's stomach growled. As quietly as he could, he took a deep breath and held it, then glided to the edge of the forest, between two trees that bordered the little farm. His movement was seamless and graceful, and despite the dry leaf litter covering the forest floor, he made no sound as he planted his massive feet at the edge of the field. He was within striking distance of his goal.

Before him, a corral of fat, squawking opilions pecked at the ground, plucking worms for their breakfast. In the distance, the farmer bent over his plow, his back to the corral.

Eyeing the opilions hungrily, the beast stood stock-still. He would have to do this carefully to remain unseen, for the opilions, if they should sense his presence, would raise a loud ruckus, alerting the farmer. Typically, he raided the opilion corrals at night, staging his thievery to look like the work of dire wolves or perhaps a simitar. Today, though, his grumbling belly made him bolder. It had been several days since he had a decent meal. Using piloerection, a skill peculiar to his race, he manipulated his fur to look like the bark of the trees he hid among. Most creatures could pass within a few steps and never detect his presence.

After a time, his patience paid off. A female opilion moved to the edge of the corral, within striking distance. She pecked absently at the ground and lifted her head to look out into the forest. Perhaps she detected his scent. Her long neck protruded above the top rail of the corral, beckoning him.

In a fluid motion, his paw darted outward, grabbing her neck and squeezing hard, obstructing her airway so she couldn't sound the alarm. And continuing the same movement, he lifted the massive wingless bird over the fence and sprinted away from the scene of the crime. The other opilions in the corral, oblivious, pecked away at the ground, and a final glance over his shoulder confirmed that the farmer hadn't seen a thing.

He zipped through the trees at a dead run, the opilion flopping lifelessly in his great, clawed hand. Only when he was deep in the forest, satisfied that no one followed, did he finally stop to catch his breath. Grinning, he held his prize before him, pleased at its weight. His mouth watered. He turned the creature over, exposing its soft white breast, and raised it to his mouth, closing his eyes in anticipation.

Just as his jaws closed on the succulent flesh, he heard a twig snap above him and looked up, but too late. A large net of thick cord fell from the treetops, covering him. His meal forgotten, he pulled and clawed at the net, cursing himself for lowering his guard, and scanning the forest to see who might be after him.

A dozen Harweldenite soldiers rushed in from behind the trees, pointing their crossbows at him.

Disgusted, he dropped the opilion. Though he smelled the soldiers' fear and saw it in their eyes, he was draped in a heavy rope net and surrounded—there was no escaping.

Just as his jaws closed on the succulent flesh,
he heard a twig snap above him and looked up,
but too late.

"We've caught him!" crowed one of the soldiers. "It's really him!"

A commander emerged from behind the line of soldiers and walked up to the netted beast, glaring at him, challenging him with his eyes.

The beast stared back, cocking his head to the side.

"Are you the beast Hooks, of the Valley of Susquatania?"

Surprised to be recognized, Hooks said nothing. He knew better than to talk to a soldier.

"Don't want to talk?" said the commander, motioning to one of his soldiers. "So be it."

An arrow whizzed past Hooks's head and thwacked into the tree behind him. Though momentarily startled, he steadied himself at once. This was no time to show fear.

"That was your warning shot," said the commander. "Now, drop to your knees."

Hooks was not used to being bullied or pushed about. He glared at the soldiers, taking particular note of their crossbows and weighing his chances should he decide to fight. He didn't want any trouble with the empire, though, and grudgingly he knelt, keeping his eyes on the commander.

The commander motioned to one of the soldiers, and for a split second Hooks thought he was going to be executed right there and then. He was relieved when the soldier dropped his crossbow to the side before approaching. After a momentary hesitation, the soldier reached up and brushed away the fur at Hooks's left cheek to reveal a long, jagged scar.

"It's him, all right," said the soldier, running his finger across the scar. "It's just as the chieftan described."

"Remove the net," barked the commander. "Don't be afraid of him—we'll protect you."

The soldier nodded and, after an uneasy look back at his fellow men-at-arms, stepped forward and lifted the edge of the heavy net. When it was off, he quickly stepped back, nearly falling in his haste.

Hooks glared at him.

"All right, then," said the commander. "Stand up, beast. And do it slowly."

Locking eyes with the commander, Hooks did as he was bidden.

"Now, turn and put your hands behind your back."

Hooks paused again to consider his options, then finally turned, hands behind his back. He looked at the opilion in the dirt at his feet, and his stomach growled.

The nervous soldier tending him unstrapped a thick cord from his belt and tied the big hands, being wary of the claws.

The commander smirked. "It is done," he said. "The council will be pleased to learn of his capture. It's going to be a good night for us, men."

The soldiers laughed and congratulated one another on their good fortune, though they kept their weapons trained on the captive. Nudging him onward at arrow point, they began the trek back to the castle.

Hooks was in a dark mood. In all his years of wandering, he had never before been captured. He cursed himself for ever setting foot in the Forest of Ondor.

After a time, the troops and their captive emerged from the forest and into the foothills of an expansive mountain range. At the top of the mountain nearest them, Hooks saw the castle. Though he had never been to Mount Kalipharus, he had heard of it since childhood—still, nothing could have prepared him for the sight. The ancient castle atop the mountain was as splendid a thing as he had ever seen. Whatever one said about the shamalans, in the castle of Harwelden they had wrought one of the wonders of the known world. Falling away behind Mount Kalipharus, a purple-hued mountain range extended as far as the eye could see. These, he knew, were the Azure Mountains, and under different circumstances, he might have found it a beautiful scene.

He gazed up at the soaring towers of gray cut stone and the balconies that allowed the inhabitants to stroll along and enjoy the majestic view from so high above the mountaintop. Craning his neck, he supposed that one could probably see the entire Carafayan continent from such a height. Though he had seen much in his travels, nothing rivaled the precise crafts-manship of the shamalan masters. The castle was every bit as magnificent as the stories boasted.

"Move, beast," said one of the soldiers, poking him in the back with his crossbow. "We're expected before nightfall."

Hooks looked back down at the trail and began the ardu-ous trek up the mountain.

"I suggest you enjoy the beauty of the sunset," said the soldier behind him. "It's the last you'll ever see."

Hooks gave the soldier a puzzled look. *Last sunset?* He ex-pected to get thirty days in the dungeon at most. His crimes consisted of pilfering coins from farmhouses, raiding fields and orchards for a bit to eat, and, of course, snatching the occasional unwary opilion. None of these crimes fetched a harsh punish-ment, and the Grayfarer Council at Harwelden was generally known to be fair. But the soldier's comment made him uneasy. Thinking about it, he surmised that the soldiers had been hunt-ing for him specifically, for they had known his name and had known of his scar. He searched his mind for some offense that might warrant hunting him down and meting out serious pun-ishment, but nothing came to mind. Although, if the Grayfarer Council had learned that a Susquatanian beast roamed their for-est, robbing local farmers, they might have sent an inquiry to his homeland. The leaders of his old clan would have no trouble concluding that it must be he, Hooks, causing mischief on the outskirts of Harwelden. Now that he thought of it, it wouldn't surprise him if they had sent Susquatanian warriors to assist in his capture, they reviled him so.

"Keep moving," said the soldier behind him, poking him hard with the crossbow. "Night approaches."

Hooks turned and gave a deep, low growl, the most menacing he could muster. The soldier gulped and left him alone.

As darkness fell, they reached the summit of Mount Kalipharus. Hooks stared in amazement at the wall surrounding the mountaintop. From the foot of the mountain, the wall had seemed merely an afterthought when compared with the castle it enclosed. But now, as the massive drawbridge lowered to receive him, he saw that the great crenellated wall, more than three times his own considerable height, stretched on either side as far as the eye could see. Even now, crossing over the drawbridge, he saw soldiers in the wall's towers, watching him.

By the time he entered the castle, night had fallen. Already, hundreds of torches blazed along the inside of the wall, and oil lamps lit the cobblestone walkways. Finely carved fountains and statues of long-dead nobles decorated the plaza ahead and the many courtyards that lay in the shadow of the great castle. Indeed, the whole city was aglow. Rows of dwellings, finely built from finished stone and timber, surrounded the castle complex, and gimlets and men bustled about, carrying baskets of fruit or pushing carts full of cloth or stone, while others strolled about the city streets just taking in the sights.

"Get going," said the soldier behind him, apparently emboldened now that they were safely within the city walls. "They'll be expecting us."

Hooks gave him a baleful glare but plodded on through the plaza and onto the town's central promenade.

As he marched through the town, people everywhere stopped and gaped. A small girl actually spat on him as he passed, and all around him, people pointed and stared, speaking to one another in whispers. Perhaps many had never seen a beast of the valley.

Still, the hostile reception baffled him. Traditionally, Susquatanians had enjoyed an agreeable enough relationship with shamalans, men, gimlets, and even the grayfarers, so it couldn't be his race that generated such ill will. Surely the theft of a few coins and opilions couldn't explain it.

As Hooks and his captors continued their march down the Boulevard of Kings, little knots of heckling men and gimlets, some brandishing torches, gathered on either side of the walkway. The attention of the entire city seemed focused on him. Even the soldiers began to look nervous as they watched the growing rabble. Hooks watched in disbelief. Fists were raised into the air, and torches waved. A blur of screaming faces surrounded him, and it began to look as if the mob might rush him.

Finally, they reached the courtyard at the castle entrance. For perhaps the first time in his adult life, Hooks was scared. He had seen blood in all those hostile eyes. With a sigh of relief, he passed through the front door of the castle, safe at last from the growing throng, who kept right on screaming even after the castle door swung shut.

The foyer of the castle was big and round, lined with arched entryways to various halls and rooms. Hooks, who had lived in caves and forest dwellings his whole life, was amazed at the extravagance. The ceiling was a golden dome that soared several levels above his head. Beautiful frescoes depicting ancient events in shamalan history adorned the inside of the golden dome and the high walls of the foyer. One showed a shamalan knight extending a hand of friendship to a fearsome grayfarer general. Another showed nine gimlets, each with a halo of light above his head, seated behind a long wooden table. A shamalan priest bowed in deference to the gimlets. Another

showed a shamalan king kneeling over a leering serpan warrior and holding a dagger against his throat. The archways were
ornamented with hammered gold, and between them hung tapestries with more scenes from shamalan lore.

The soldiers nudged Hooks forward and led him through
one of the golden archways into the castle's great hall. The room
was long and wide, with a pair of windows at one end offering a
sprawling view of the moon-shadowed Forest of Ondor. At the
opposite end of the hall, a long table of heavy timber stood on a
wooden dais. Torches lined the wall above the dais, dimly lighting
the far end of the room. Seven tall figures sat behind the table, each
wearing a dark tunic with the hood pulled forward. Although
Hooks had seen no one in the forest other than his captors, they
must have sent a runner to inform the council of his impending
arrival—again, unusual measures for a petty crime. The Grayfarer
Council was assembled and waiting for *him*. Hoots and catcalls
from the mob outside infiltrated the great hall. Despite the hour,
the castle was charged with excitement at his arrival.

"Bring the prisoner before us," boomed a voice from the dais.

With his hands still bound behind him, Hooks followed
his captors to the far end of the hall, where the council awaited.

"You may unbind him," said the figure seated at the center
of the table.

He could discern very little about the councilmen's appearance from where he stood, but no matter—all grayfarers
looked much the same. The soldier nearest him unsheathed a
dagger and sliced through the cords, and Hooks felt the welcome rush of blood to his hands and shoulders. Rubbing his
wrists, he looked up at the hooded figures.

"Are you the creature Hooks, of the Valley of Susquatania?" queried the councilman in the center.

"I am," said Hooks, deciding it was in his best interest to
cooperate, at least for the moment.

"I am Waldemariam, chancellor of the Grayfarer Council and acting governor of Harwelden and all her territories. We have been looking for you for quite some time now."

Hooks stared back at the chancellor, awaiting further remarks, but was met with stony silence, which made him uneasy. "Why are *you* the acting governor?" Hooks said with a note of scorn. "Where is King Gregorus? If I am to stand judgment before the eyes of Harwelden, I demand an audience before the king."

"You are in no position to demand anything, beast," said Waldemariam. "Tell us, please, of the circumstances surrounding your capture today."

Hooks paused for a moment. It seemed an odd question. "I was about to have my lunch when I was accosted by your soldiers, Chancellor," he said, standing tall, refusing to be cowed by pomp and pageantry. "With the stealth of a pack of rats, they ambushed me from the shadows of the forest where they hid."

A group of onlookers at the back of the room tittered.

Waldemariam slammed his fist on the table. "You will show this council proper respect, beast, or we will add immeasurably to your misfortune. Do I make myself clear?"

Hooks nodded, though the smirk on his face remained in place. "Yes, Chancellor," he said. "Please accept my most abject apologies."

The onlookers chuckled again at the sarcasm in his voice.

"You stole an opilion from one of the hardworking farmers of the valley," said Waldemariam. "The man is working his fields alone this season, as he recently lost both his sons to the dreadful war that is raging. He fears that his profits for the season will not be enough to cover his debt. He plans to use his opilions to make it through the coming winter."

Hooks said nothing, though the smirk left his face.

"But that is not the reason you are here," said Waldemariam.

Again the feeling of uneasiness came over Hooks. "If not that, then why am I here?"

"You are from the clan of beasts that reside in the Valley of Susquatania, are you not?" asked Waldemariam.

"Many seasons ago this was so," Hooks replied, "though I have been separated from them for quite some time."

"And why is that?" asked Waldemariam. It seemed a loaded question.

"I'll keep that to myself," said Hooks. "I don't see what relevance it has to anything here."

"I have recently met with leaders of the Susquatanian clan," Waldemariam continued. "I found them to be gracious and accommodating, as their reputation suggests. Chieftan Keats has shared with me the tale of your crimes and the reasons for your banishment from your people. They do not speak fondly of you." The words dripped with accusation. "Your chieftan spoke rather frankly about you."

"I am sure *Chieftan* Keats told you everything you wanted to hear," Hooks said. "He's a politician, like you. I'm sure he was interested in what you might give him for the information."

"*Hmph!*" Waldemariam picked up his gavel and rapped the table seven times, signaling the beginning of a more formal phase of the proceedings. "Hooks of Susquatania," he said, "you stand before the Grayfarer Council of Harwelden, accused of the high crime of kidnapping grayfarer fledglings and selling them to leaders of the serpan army, who slaughter them in a misguided attempt to weaken the army of Harwelden. For this, we find you guilty of murder."

"Now, hold on!" said Hooks, dumbfounded. He held up a massive hand in protest. "I've done no such thing!"

"Silence!" Waldemariam yelled. "You will show respect to this court. You will not speak again unless asked. Do you understand me, beast?"

Hooks glowered into the hoods of his accusers. The hairs of his thick pelt stood on end. "I have done no such thing," he repeated.

"Silence!" Waldemariam pounded his fist on the table. "Soldiers from our army have been seeking your capture for much of the past season. In your absence, a trial has been conducted in this very hall. Powerful and trusted witnesses have spoken against you. Your devilish crimes have not gone unseen, stealthy though you may be. What have you to say about this?"

"Lies!" Hooks growled through clenched teeth. "I demand an audience before the king! I will not stand and listen to this."

"For the crime of murder, you have been slated for death. In three days' time, you will be drawn and quartered in the public square. I suggest you seek absolution before that time, lest your spirit be sent to the eternal torments of Hulgaar. That is all." Waldemariam banged the gavel down, and the council stood before the condemned.

On this cue, soldiers on either side of Hooks moved to retake him. Hooks swung a massive arm, and three soldiers on his right flew across the hall and slammed into the wall. Hooks bellowed and turned to the soldiers on his left, his eyes darting about the room, searching for a point of escape. "Lies!" he yelled. "I thought this council was just! I have not done the things you accuse me of!"

Soldiers with trembling hands trained their crossbows on him as, with a frightful bellow that resounded throughout the hall, he advanced on them. But before he reached the soldiers, something hard struck him on the side of the head. Dazed, he looked back toward the entrance. More soldiers rushed in to contain him as their leader loaded a second stone into his sling. Hooks turned his back to the charging soldiers and faced the councilmen, who remained behind the table.

"I'll be out of here before daybreak," he growled. "You will never hold me." As he turned to face the soldiers at the entrance, a second stone struck him in the head, and he stumbled and went down.

$$\Phi \ \Phi \ \Phi$$

He awoke shackled hand and foot to the wall of a tiny, dank cell, no doubt somewhere in the bowels of the dungeon beneath Harwelden. His vision was blurred and his head throbbed. Somewhere far away, a bell chimed, signaling midday. In two days' time, as punishment for a crime he had not commited, he would be disemboweled and pulled to pieces in the public square of a city respected throughout the land for its civility and justice. He had been in plenty of scrapes, but this time he didn't have a clue how to get out.

Chapter 4

Pangrelor

Ca-caaaaaaw! With rhythmic uniformity, the crunching foot steps grew louder, nearer. Elliott could hear his own heart thumping and feared the sound would draw the creature, whatever it was, to him. He stretched out his hands, trying to locate something solid in the darkness. Cautiously, he sidestepped left, shifting his weight as gently as possible, but he couldn't quiet the crunching beneath his feet. Finally, the coarse texture of a stone wall met his outstretched palm. The stone here, unlike the smooth walls of his grandfather's basement, was rough and creviced. Running a hand along the rough surface, he moved forward, grimacing at the noise he made with each step.

Ca-caaaaaaaaaw! Although the call sounded birdlike, it was from no creature he knew. He thought of how he might defend himself if the thing attacked, but he had no weapons and no ideas. Frantic, he pulled the Zippo lighter from his pocket and flicked the striker wheel.

The flame cast a pool of light around him. The walls were indeed of rough stone, veined with glistening quartz. The roof, high above his head and only barely visible, was festooned with thick stalactites that hung like stone daggers. He looked down at his feet. Beneath them was a carpet of fat purple insects. Stifling a scream, he scanned the floor of the cave and saw thousands of them. Crunchy bits of insect carcass poked at his bare soles. The bugs were the size of mice, with eyes protruding on stalks from either side of the carapace. He hoped they weren't poisonous.

The crunching footfalls sounded closer, though he still could not see his pursuer in the Zippo's weak light.

Scared to take another step, he held out the lighter and looked down at the carpet of bugs. Though terrified that they might come swarming up his legs, he squatted for a closer look. Nothing moved—not so much as a flicker of an antenna. He willed himself to pick up one of the creatures, grasping it warily between thumb and forefinger and turning it over to inspect it by the lighter's flame. To his relief, it was dead. Purple and a good three inches long, it had a pair of wiry antennae in front of its stalked eyes. He had never seen anything like it. Holding the flame closer, he found that he could see right through the violet carapace to his thumb. He pinched the exoskeleton, and it crumbled to dust. As he suspected, it was the abandoned shell of some molting insect—something like the shells of cicadas back home.

Another cry from his mysterious stalker made him jump. It was right behind him, though he was too terrified to turn and look at it. No longer concerned about the noise of his footsteps crushing the molted bug shells, he broke into a dead run.

The flame of the Zippo flickered precariously as the air rushed past him, but up ahead, he could see a tiny spot of light. Again the throaty cry echoed off the stone walls as he snapped the lighter shut and pocketed it without breaking stride. The footsteps behind him grew nearer as the animal gave chase.

CA-CAAAAAAAAW! He began to fear for his life as the animal gained ground, grunting and panting behind him, rhythmically crushing the hulls of alien arthropods with each footfall. Only a few more yards to the opening to the cave.

Just as he broke out of the syrupy darkness into dazzling sunlight, the creature lunged, knocking him over. He screamed. It was on top of him now, and he rolled, reflexively holding his arms out in defense.

The first thing he saw was a massive beak of bloodstained bone, with sawlike rows of teeth and a lolling red tongue that licked at the air. It looked like some sort prehistoric killer ostrich. Scarlet feathers encircled its awful face, and its breast and neck were draped with bright crimson plumes, and long yellow clusters flopped behind its head.

Elliott shrieked as the creature thrust a great, scaly leg onto his chest, pinning him. He felt the talons pierce his skin as its weight forced the air from his lungs. It lowered its head and licked at him, as if to taste its next meal. Then it lifted its head and gave a long, triumphant bellow, and in that moment it occurred to Elliott that this was surely the last sound he would ever hear. He struggled to breathe under the terrible weight. Consciousness faded.

The creature reared its head back to strike, then paused, as if having second thoughts, and looked upward. A confused *caw* escaped its beak, and it swayed. It was then that Elliott saw the dagger, buried hilt deep in the neck feathers. He heard a meaty *thunk,* and now a second dagger hilt jutted from the plumed neck, inches below the first. With a last sway, the predator staggered and fell, looking bewildered at this sudden reversal of its fortunes.

Elliott awoke a short time later to find two small men standing over him, eyeing him curiously. He breathed deeply, thankful to be free of the predator's weight.

Elliott squinted, unwilling to believe his eyes. The two men were very short, the taller being perhaps three feet tall. They wore leather trousers and jerkins, with empty scabbards at their waist. And they were hairy. Not hairy like apes, exactly, but hairy like some men at the neighborhood swimming pool back home—the ones his mom used to say shouldn't take their shirts off in public. They had large ears that stood straight out, and roundish little bellies that somehow gave the impression they were friendly.

They stared openmouthed at him, their eyes darting back and forth between the birthmarks on his hands and the stone-encrusted silver bracelet on his wrist.

Elliott pushed up onto his elbows and felt the back of his neck, where the creature had snapped at him, knocking him down. "Thanks," he said feebly, looking at the smear of blood on his hand.

Not wanting his saviors to think him rude, he tried not to stare. They didn't say a word.

"Where am I?" he asked tentatively.

They remained silent, looking almost as if they were in shock.

"Hey," he said. "Where am I?" When they didn't respond, he rose to his feet and dusted himself off. *Of course,* he realized. They didn't speak English. Cautiously, he turned his attention to the carcass of the predatory bird. "Wow," he mumbled, reaching out to stroke its soft feathers. "What is this thing?"

"It's a magby," said the smaller of the two men without taking his eyes off Elliott's birthmarks.

Elliott smiled. "Thanks for that," he said, nodding at the bird as he extended his hand in friendship. "My name's Elliott." The silver bracelet gleamed in the sunlight. The two men stared at it, but neither took the proffered hand. Embarrassed, he retracted his hand and looked up at the sky. The sun looked unusually big and orange. Then he saw, behind it, a smaller, pale yellow sun. "Where am I?" he asked again.

Finally, the taller of the two spoke. "Why, you're in the Forest of Ondor, of course."

Of course.

"I'm Marvus, said the taller one. "And where are you from, Sir Elliott?"

"Uh," he said, pausing for a moment. "I came from a long way away."

"All right, then," Marvus said, inspecting his pajamas. "Please excuse our behavior. We do not mean to be rude. It's just that we haven't seen a shamalan in the forest in quite some time. Have you come to meet with the council?"

Elliott stared at him, trying to decide how to proceed. He was thinking about asking them if they had ever heard of Darius Orion when the shorter one intervened.

"I thought all the shamalans were dead," he blurted. "Except for the princess, I mean."

Marvus gave him a stern look.

After an uncomfortable pause, a look of recognition crept across the short one's face. He stared at Elliott with renewed interest. His mouth hung open. After several seconds, a grin spread across his lips. "Oh, my," he whispered.

"Excuse my young friend, Marvus said," stepping in front of him. "His name is Jingo. We are stewards of the princess. Please consider us at your service." He bowed.

Elliott nodded and smiled.

"What may we do to accommodate you, Sir Elliott?" Marvus said, still staring at the pajamas despite the politeness of his tone.

"I really don't know. . . ." Elliott looked back at the mouth of the cave. "I have traveled here from very far away. This is a strange land to me." He felt like an actor in a bad movie. Still, he couldn't think of anything better to say.

"Are you from Gaya?" Jingo asked, staring at the birthmarks on his hands.

Marvus glared at him disapprovingly.

As Elliott pondered how to answer, Marvus, thankfully, intervened.

"We require no explanation from you, Sir Elliott. Please allow us the pleasure of escorting you to Harwelden, where you can obtain good food and a safe night's rest. You will be a most welcome guest of the council, to be sure."

"All right," said Elliott, deciding he should say as little as possible. "Thanks again, though, for saving me from the, uh . . . magby."

Marvus knelt over the huge carcass and removed the daggers from its neck, then carefully wiped the blades clean on the bird's thick plumage. He sheathed one of the daggers and handed the other to his companion.

"We'll have to do something about your garments, of course," he said, looking at the pajamas. "Those will never hold up."

Marvus, being the taller of the two, took off his knapsack, which was remarkably similar to the one Elliott wore, and pulled out a pair of leather trousers and a leather shirt.

"Try these," he said, handing the suit to Elliott. "You may step into the cave for privacy, if you like."

Elliott accepted the suit and, glancing back at the cave, walked behind one of the huge trees surrounding them. Changing out of his pajamas, he stuffed them into his knapsack. The leather clothes were a poor fit—baggy around the middle and too short in the arms and legs—but they would have to do. He tied the waistband and stepped back onto the path, feeling a little ridiculous.

"Hmmmm," Marvus said, inspecting him.

Jingo giggled.

"Just a few more touches, I think," said Marvus, burrowing in his knapsack and coming up with a pair of moccasins and some strips of white cloth. He tossed the moccasins to Elliott. "Perhaps you'll be more comfortable wearing these."

Elliott sat down and pulled the moccasins over his feet. They were at least two sizes too big. Jingo giggled and reached into his own knapsack.

"Try these," he said. "It's a long walk to Harwelden."

Elliott put on the smaller moccasins. They were still too big but much better. "Thanks," he said.

Changing out of his pajamas, he stuffed them
into his knapsack. The leather clothes were a poor fit...
but they would have to do.

"Just one more thing," Marvus said, approaching Elliott with the strips of white cloth in hand. "Hold out your hands."

Elliott obliged. "What's this for?"

Ignoring the question, Marvus crinkled his brow, then walked over to the dead magby and smeared the strips of cloth in the blood. Then, while Elliott watched, he wrapped his hands, making it appear as if they had been wounded.

"Gross," Elliott murmured.

"Gross," Jingo parroted, wrinkling his nose. He seemed to be having fun.

"Perfect." Marvus grasped Elliott's shoulder. "Time to go."

Elliott looked to the mouth of the cave one last time before turning to follow them down the trail.

After a few steps, Jingo stopped and held up his hand, directing Elliott to stop.

Confused, Elliott complied.

Nodding, Jingo unclamped the bracelet from Elliott's wrist and handed it to him. "You should put this in your knapsack."

Marvus nodded. "He's right—I didn't think of it."

"Okay," said Elliott. "Whatever you say." He buried the bracelet deep in his knapsack, hiding it beneath the pajamas.

"Right this way, then," Marvus said."

Elliott followed them down the footpath, bordered on either side by the magnificent trees of the Forest of Ondor. "By the way," he said, nodding at the daggers on their waists, you guys are pretty good with those. Another second, and . . ." His voice trailed off.

"No need to keep thanking us," Marvus replied, smiling. "Though I must confess, it's Jingo that can throw a blade, not I."

"Well, then, thanks to you, Jingo. I think I owe you my life."

Jingo giggled, looking at Elliott with something like adulation.

Elliott smiled, though he did find the little one a bit peculiar. Soon he was lost in the strange beauty of the forest. The trees were like none he had seen before. Their trunks were massive, like those in the painting in his grandfather's basement. Even the lowest branches towered high above his head, and moss hung from them in wispy streams, adding to their otherworldly beauty. Vibrantly colored red and blue birds peeked down from the treetops, chirping their alien calls, and occasionally he heard the sounds of larger beasts off in the distance: sometimes a roar like that of a great cat, and other times the forlorn howling of a wolf. But since his escorts seemed unafraid of these sounds, he didn't worry. At one point, Marvus and Jingo stopped. In a clearing, a tiny, furry brown elephant, perhaps the size of a collie, dug in the dirt with its pointed ivory tusks, as if rooting for tubers or grubs. Grinning, Jingo reached for his dagger, but Marvus slapped his hand away. Sensing the commotion, the tiny elephant looked up and trotted into the forest. When it was gone, Marvus tugged at Jingo's arm, beckoning him onward. Elliott followed, his amazement growing at every turn.

As the afternoon wore on, they moved more quickly through the forest. It seemed Marvus and Jingo had walked this route a thousand times, and though they were much smaller, Elliott struggled to keep up. After a few hours, the trees grew less dense, and he could see that they were nearing the edge of the forest. At last, they emerged into a clearing.

Stretched out before him was a beautiful vista, and there in the center, the green mountain from his grandfather's painting. Far above, at the top of the mountain, sat the gray castle, its towers shining against the blue summer sky. Elliott scanned the panorama, taking in the range of purple mountains that fell away behind the castle. It was the very scene depicted in the painting, and from almost the exact vantage point, but orders of magnitude more beautiful. *Like something out of a fairy tale.*

After a brief rest, his companions led him through the clearing to a narrow trail heading up the mountain.

"We'll be at the gate soon," said Marvus. "The council will be so pleased to see you."

Elliott nodded and smiled. It seemed the right thing to do, though he wondered what to expect from this council. He tried to keep the pace, but he kept gazing up at the castle, thinking it the most wonderful thing he had ever seen. He looked up so much that several times he tripped over rocks or roots and almost fell.

When they were halfway up the mountain, Jingo stopped and pointed toward the roof of the castle. Elliott had already noticed the statues of winged monsters along the rooftop. For a moment, he stared at them, thinking they were what Jingo wanted him to see. But as he watched, he saw movement. With the suns glaring in his eyes, he could just make out the silhouettes of two adults escorting a child between the statues along the battlements. It gave him vertigo just looking at them. Jingo grinned, and Marvus, too, smiled as he looked to the roof. Elliott opened his mouth to speak, but Jingo said, "*Shhhhhhhsh!*" Making a visor of his hand, he turned to watch the people on the ledge.

The two adults paced back and forth opposite each other, like caged dogs preparing to fight. The child stood deathly still between them. A chorus of cheering voices arose from the courtyard beneath the scene, though the massive stone enclosure kept him from seeing the crowd. Suddenly, the two adults, flanking the child, hoisted it into the air, swinging it back and forth as if they intended to throw it to the ground below. Elliott looked in alarm to Marvus and Jingo, wanting them to do something, but they just stood there, watching calmly as the two adults prepared to fling the child from the roof.

In ever-lengthening arcs, they swung the child back and forth over the precipice. The chorus of voices chanted in time with the swinging. As the swinging intensified, Elliott looked on, horrified to think that he was watching a sacrifice.

Then the adults let go, launching the child into the air, and the crowd fell silent as the little one tumbled toward the ground.

Panicked, Elliott looked to Marvus and Jingo, wanting them to do something. Their smiles had evaporated.

The child fell like a stone. Because of the slant of the mountain and the height of the wall, Elliott could see only five stories of the castle from where he stood.

The child tumbled past the uppermost level . . . then the next . . . As it fell past the next story, it screamed.

Just as it was about to fall past the wall and out of sight, a pair of wings, which Elliott hadn't noticed before, sprouted from its back. His jaw dropped.

The wings captured a gust of wind, slowing its downward spiral, but it continued to fall.

A collective gasp came from the crowd. Elliott imagined them scattering, making a clearing for the winged child to smash into the flagstones.

Finally, it flapped its wings. The fall reversed itself as the fledgling regained a few feet of the height it had lost. The wings flapped again.

Elliott had the impression that the winged child was really struggling to make these small gains, for its movements were awkward and out of rhythm. It made flying look hard. Then, with great effort, it regained the rooftop, where the adults waited with arms outstretched.

The child tried to land on the roof, but a gust of wind caught it, tossing it back. After a short while fighting the wind, it seemed to grow tired, and the flapping of its wings grew clumsier as it began to lose altitude.

When it became clear that the child would not regain the rooftop, a pair of wings erupted from the back of one of the adults, and with the speed and grace of an eagle, it swooped down and grabbed the child by the shoulders, lifting it back into the air as it slumped, exhausted, in its parent's embrace. While the crowd cheered, the parent soared effortlessly in circles high above the castle roof.

The row of winged monsters lining the rooftop stood and cheered.

Elliott nearly fell over. Just as he thought the display was nearing its end, the parent dived toward the crowd, pulling up at the last second, then flew in a loop overhead, holding the child out for all to see.

The crowd went wild.

Finally, the parent flew back up to the rooftop, holding the child in a tight embrace, to join its waiting mate. The crowd screamed and cheered as the winged monsters huddled around the family, congratulating them. The parents hugged the child, and as the family walked across the rooftop and disappeared from sight, the winged monsters resumed their positions squatting along the rooftop.

Jingo pointed to the rooftop. "Those are grayfarers," he said.

"Congratulations, Sir Elliott," Marvus said. "You have just witnessed a first-flight ceremony."

Elliott nodded and smiled. *Gargoyles,* he thought as they wended their way up a boulder-strewn slope. *Grayfarers are gargoyles.* Exhilarated by the display he had just witnessed, he hardly felt the long, arduous climb. In fact, he felt oddly energized.

They reached a large wooden drawbridge that opened into the mountaintop, and as Marvus and Jingo spoke in low voices with a pair of guards, Elliott looked up at the stone enclosure, some thirty feet high, that wrapped around the mountain. It must have taken a hundred years to build such a wall.

The drawbridge's chains groaned, and as it began its descent, Marvus and Jingo completed their negotiations. It was time to see this Harwelden firsthand. With a growing sense of wonder, Elliott followed his two diminutive guides through the entrance.

Inside the wall was a bustling city, with the towering stone castle looming at its center. Elliott's eyes darted this way and that, trying to see all the strange sights at once. Throngs of people moved about the cobbled boulevards. Some looked rather normal, but many were short and hairy, like Marvus and Jingo.

Walking through a parklike plaza toward the main thoroughfare, Elliott paused to look at a giant statue, surrounded by fountains. The handsome bearded figure held a three-pronged spear, reminding Elliott of the Greek god Poseidon. An inscription at the base of the statue read, *King Griogair, founder of Harwelden.*

Beyond the plaza was a boulevard, lined with shops and magnificent statues, each depicting a heroic figure. Some of the figures also held the trident weapon he had seen on the statue of Griogair, and all of them bore birthmarks like Elliott's. The statue nearest him was still under construction, with artisans chiseling away as he walked past.

Everyone in town seemed eager to greet Marvus and Jingo, sometimes practically falling over one another to get at them, while sparing Elliott no more than a curious glance. To his surprise, Marvus and Jingo ignored the townspeople and proceeded down the boulevard in silence. They were being treated like rock stars, and he couldn't fathom why they should behave so rudely. He started to put his hands in his pockets but couldn't because of the bulky, blood-soaked bandages. He looked up in time to see Jingo furtively checking on him, glancing nervously at his hands. As they made eye contact, Jingo averted his gaze, offering the impression that he didn't want to draw the crowd's attention to him.

Happy with the anonymity, which gave him more freedom to gawk at his surroundings, Elliott gazed up at the castle, fascinated by it. When he was a child, his mother had often held him on her lap, sharing pictures of Notre Dame Cathedral, the Louvre, and Vatican City. *Someday you'll visit these places, Ell,* she had told him as they looked at the pictures. *And until you do, you can dream about them. The best journeys begin in the heart of the traveler.* Looking ahead at Marvus and Jingo and thinking of the grayfarers, he wondered who had made this wondrous city.

Before he knew it, their march was over. The castle Harwelden loomed before them.

Marvus and Jingo conferred with the guards, and the doors quickly opened, allowing them passage, then closed before the clamoring mass of people behind them.

Jingo grabbed Elliott and pulled him into the castle, and they stood in the foyer as Marvus spoke in whispers to the liveried majordomo who greeted them. It seemed that Marvus knew everyone.

The foyer's golden ceiling soared seven stories above them. Contrasting with the gold dome, countless frescoes portrayed men, grayfarers, and the short, potbellied race of Marvus and Jingo. The figures battled, prayed, dined, and rejoiced, forever frozen in various attitudes of glory and tribulation. Elliott looked at his two new friends. *Shamalans, serpans, susquats, gimlets*—he recalled the terms from the journal in his granddad's basement. Which were the little ones?

The frescoes weren't just on the ceilings, but extended down the walls to the second story, ending at the shimmering archways of hammered gold. Elliott had never seen anything to rival it. There must be thirty or forty such archways encircling the foyer, and between them hung tapestries, each depicting some important event.

"If I may beg your pardon, sir Elliott," Marvus said, "our presence is required in the great hall."

"All right," Elliott said, wondering why his presence should be required anywhere. Marvus looked at him strangely, then led him out of the foyer and through an archway.

The room they entered, in dramatic contrast to the ornate foyer, was bare but for a stone dais at the far end of the room, and some torches and flags that periodically broke the austere expanse of stone and mortar. At a long table atop the dais sat seven imposing figures in hooded robes that obscured their faces, which seemed unusually large.

Heralds on either side of the hall trumpeted a brief fanfare—some type of formality, no doubt—then scurried away through unseen exits.

"Why don't you sit, for a moment, Sir Elliott, and enjoy the glorious view?" Marvus whispered, motioning to a pew beneath a large window that opened onto a spectacular view of the forest.

Wanting to improve on his communication, Elliott replied, "Why, thank you, Marvus, I believe I will. That sounds most pleasant." Kicking himself for adding the last sentence, he took a seat.

"The council will call for you momentarily, sir," Marvus said, and left him at the window.

Elliott watched as the hooded figures stooped over the table, straining to hear Marvus, who spoke only in whispers. But the acoustics of the long stone room were strange, and the place was deathly silent except for the conversation at the dais. Elliott found that if he listened intently, he could eavesdrop on their conversation.

". . . That's right," said Marvus. "They smacked her in the head with a stone and carried her off toward the desert. For all we know, they've killed her." He spoke in hushed tones, and Elliott couldn't tell if he was sad or afraid.

"*Hmmmph!*" said the hooded figure at the center of the table. "That is the worst news you could have brought." He paused for a moment, digesting the report. "I shouldn't have let her go to Prytania. It was a fool's errand from the outset." He stared at Marvus from under his cowl. "Was Malus Lothar with them when they captured her?"

"No, Chancellor," Marvus replied. "We didn't see the malus in the forest, but he was there when they ambushed us at Prytania. He must have known we were there all along."

"You are lucky to have escaped with your lives," said the chancellor. "He isn't usually so careless."

Marvus continued his account. "The army you sent to help take Prytania arrived just in time to rescue us, but we lost many soldiers. We retreated as fast as we could, but they pursued us like wolves. When we reached the Forest of Ondor, we thought we were finally safe, but they attacked while we slept. We weren't a stone's throw from the tombs of the elders when it happened. The entire gimlet army was slaughtered." His voice caught, and he had to pause a moment.

"Calm down," said the chancellor. "Where is General Grimaldi?"

"Captured at Prytania. I don't know if he is alive or dead."

The chancellor stared at Marvus for a moment. "I should never have listened to her," he said. "*Now* look at the mess we find ourselves in!"

Marvus looked at his feet.

"Leave us," said the chancellor, placing his head in his hands. "The council has much to discuss."

"But wait," said Marvus, looking back at Elliott. "There is something else."

The chancellor stared at him, waiting for him to say more.

Cautiously taking the cue, Marvus said, "After they took the princess, as we hurried to bring you the news, we found a strange boy in the forest."

Elliott's palms began to sweat. The chancellor looked up at him.

"I fail to see the relevance of this," said the chancellor.

Marvus shifted his weight nervously.

Elliott didn't like being the topic of conversation, and the dour hooded chancellor did nothing to ease his self-consciousness.

"Well," Marvus stammered, "the boy has the markings of a shamalan."

The seven hooded figures began talking excitedly, speaking over one another. They stared at Elliott, who suddenly wished he were anywhere else.

"Go on."

"The boy speaks strangely, sir, and I don't feel that he's been truthful with us."

For the first time, Jingo spoke up. "I think he's from Gaya."

This brought another eruption from the councilmen. Marvus glared at Jingo.

"Preposterous!" the chancellor barked.

"If I may," said Marvus, "we all know that my young friend sometimes speaks out of turn. But frankly, the boy *is* quite strange."

Elliott watched the exchange with growing fascination. He looked at the bloody bandages on his hands.

"There is something else you should know," Marvus said.

"Proceed," said the chancellor. "What else do you have to say that requires our attention?"

Marvus winced. There was a long pause.

Elliott scooted to the edge of the pew, straining to hear every word.

"He has the bracelet of the nine clans," Jingo blurted.

"Impossible!" cried chancellor, jumping up from his seat.

"The prophecy of the ancients unveils itself," Jingo finished.

The chancellor snarled, "If you open your mouth one more time, gimlet, you'll find yourself shackled in the dungeons, sharing your gruel with the rats. Do you understand me?"

"Yes, Chancellor," said Jingo, bowing his head.

In a singular motion, Marvus, Jingo, and the seven hooded councilmen turned to Elliott. He suddenly felt hot.

"Boy," said the chancellor, his voice booming off the walls, "rise and approach the council."

All eyes were on Elliott as he stood and began the long march across the room.

Chapter 5

Across the Burning Sands

Sarintha woke with a start. Already the serpan encampment was abuzz with activity. The scrub trees surrounding her, and the vast desert landscape ahead, told her where she was. Her captors had carried her to the edge of Ondor, and today they prepared to begin the journey north across the burning sands of Toltuga and on to the Vengalan continent. The serpans, restless to leave the forbidding confines of the shamalan forest, packed their supplies and loaded their horses hastily. Warriors mounted their horses as, off in the distance, the heated air had already begun to rise from the sweltering sands, causing wavy distortions in the landscape.

She looked around the encampment, searching for familiar faces, but found none. She tried to stand, but her legs were dead weight beneath her. Her head ached, and she wished her hands were unbound so she could hold them against her throbbing temple.

A serpan warrior, low ranking by the look of his dress, approached and poked her in the ribs with a stick. "Rise, shamalan," he said. "You've slept late this morning, and we have a long journey ahead."

Staring fire at him, Sarintha struggled unsteadily to her feet. "Poke me again, and you will pay the price."

The serpan laughed and poked her, knocking her down. "You are a prisoner—act like one. In time, you will learn your place among my people. It is not a good place."

Careful not to fall, she stood to face her tormentor.

He grinned and stepped toward her, raising his hand as if to strike her, and she flinched. This brought gleeful laughter as other serpans rode over and surrounded them, watching the exchange.

She spat on him, and he slapped her, knocking her to the ground. Her nose began to bleed, and though she didn't intend to, she cried out.

The mounted serpan warriors laughed, nodding their approval, and tightened their circle around her, enjoying this bit of entertainment before the long ride ahead.

Her tormentor dropped his stick and unsheathed a dagger. His grin was gone as he wiped the spittle from his face and knelt over her. She had humiliated him—stupid, she knew, especially with so many watching. With one hand, he rolled her onto her stomach. Then he raised the knife and slashed downward.

The result was a welcome one as the bindings fell away from her wrists, then her ankles. Her hands and feet tingled as feeling returned. Cautiously, she rolled onto her back and pushed up onto her elbows.

He glared at her, caressing the knife, still seething from the insult of being spat on.

She struggled to stand, defying him with her eyes.

"Today," he sneered, "you walk."

A mounted serpan tossed him a rope with a noose at the end. Catching it, he sheathed his dagger and cinched the noose around her waist, then began to tie the other end of the rope to a saddle.

Sarintha spat again in his direction, and with a snarl of rage, he tried to backhand her. But she ducked the blow, grabbing the dagger from the sheath at his waist as the swing brought him around to face her, whereupon she plunged the blade into his chest.

Sarintha plunged the blade into his chest.

His eyes looked in wonder at the knife, then to the faces of the warriors around him, then back to her. He fell to his knees.

"I said you'd pay the price, scum!" she hissed.

At once, a half-dozen serpans jumped down from their horses and took her to the ground. She screamed out under the flurry of blows, and her surroundings grew dim.

She woke a few seconds later with one eye swollen shut and the taste of blood in her mouth. The noose tightened around her midsection as the horse she was tied to began the trek into the desert. All around her, the other serpans joined the march as the suns rose higher and the sands began to bake.

𝇉 𝇉 𝇉

By midday, Sarintha was spent. In the killing heat, her legs felt wooden, and she began to stumble. Her swollen tongue stuck to the inside of her mouth, and though she tried to stay focused, her thoughts grew jumbled. She stumbled and fell, staggered to her feet, and fell again and did not rise. The noose tightened around her waist, cutting into her as the horse dragged her over the dune, filling her mouth with hot sand. She clawed at the rope, and fearing that the end was at hand, she prayed. Her death would not be a noble one, and all she could do was ask for forgiveness.

Suddenly, the line of horses stopped. Fading in and out of consciousness, she imagined that she had just come out of the sea, cool and refreshed and no longer parched.

The line of serpans gazed into the sky, shielding their eyes against the suns' glare. Following their lead, Sarintha looked upward, searching, wondering what had caused them to stop. And in the sky above, she saw them: four great, soaring birds approaching from the north. She thought of her father and the stories he had told when she was a child. In the stories, the parados, the great birds of life, came forth from Antilia in times of great need. Sometimes they came to escort one to the glory of the afterlife. She smiled. They were beautiful. She closed her eyes.

She woke to a splash of water on her face. She was not in Antilia but still in the burning Toltugan sands. A serpan knelt over her, rousing her from her torpor. He slapped her face, grinning. She struggled to focus, and the idea that she had just arisen from the sea would not leave her thoughts, though in time she returned to the present, understanding at last the grim reality of her circumstances. Thankfully, the heat had released her from its grip, and she no longer noticed the thickness of her tongue, or the sand caked in her mouth. Thinking of the parados, her eyes returned to the sky. They soared above her like angels.

Water splashed against her face once more, and the serpan kneeling over her pointed to the sky, directing her attention again to shadowy creatures overhead.

But there were no parados in the skies above the desert. Instead, four scaly golgomites—fire-breathing lizards from the bowels of the Deccan Traps—descended on them. Beneath the four lizards, shaded by their wings and hanging from chains they held in their talons, hung the sky chariot of their master, Malus Lothar. She had seen the sky chariot once before, as it descended on the bloody scene at Prytania.

The golgomites, drooling fire, began their descent. As they approached the dunes, they flared their leathery wings and set the chariot down gently, careful not to jar its lone rider. The serpans stepped back, clearing a line for their lord, whose steel mask glistened in the sunlight as he walked toward his captive.

Chapter 6

The Dungeon

Two days had passed since the Grayfarer Council pronounced Hooks's sentence. He was slated for execution at midday tomorrow. He pulled vainly at his chains, then slumped back against the wall. The cell was not made to hold susquats, but his captors had risen to the challenge and found a way to hold the first susquat that had ever found its way to the dungeons beneath Harwelden.

The cell contained two sets of shackles: one on each opposing wall. Each set, designed for man, gimlet, or serpan, had manacles fastened near the top of the wall, and leg shackles near the bottom. But because of Hooks's great size, his jailers had used both sets. His wrists were manacled above his head to one wall, and his legs, splayed in front of him, shackled at the ankles to the bottom of the opposing wall—an unconventional arrangement, but it did the job.

No matter how he squirmed and fidgeted, Hooks could not find a comfortable position. He could not bend his knees or elbows, nor could he straighten at the waist. The manacles holding his limbs were too small, and his wrists and ankles were chafed and throbbing. Chained in this position for two days now, he had never been more miserable.

More worrisome, however, was the fact that he would be released from the cell tomorrow morning. For a few glorious moments, the manacles would come off, and he would flex his joints. Then, after a brief march to the square, he surmised, the manacles would be replaced. The new set, however, would be attached not to chains along the walls of a cell, but to the saddles of four mountain horses. At the chiming of the midday bell, his belly would be slashed open and his innards spooled out on a device that resembled a dough roller, and perhaps even burned before his eyes. After that, the horses would be slapped on the hindquarters, and each would gallop off toward an opposite corner of the square. When this happened, of course, he would be ripped into four pieces.

He wondered whether his head and torso would depart attached to an arm or to a leg, or if it would remain in the middle of the square, limbless, after he was pulled apart. He supposed that he might remain conscious for a few moments after the dismemberment, and wondered if his last view would be of the twin suns, shining down upon the public square, or if his face would go skittering along the ground behind the arse of a mountain horse as it galloped down the mountainside. Though he struggled to divert his thoughts to something cheerier, the grisly images refused to leave him.

He gave another futile tug at his chains. How had it come to this? Though innocent of the crimes for which he was to be executed, he would die in disgrace, shaming his clan one last time before departing this mortal world. His thoughts turned to the family he had not seen since his youth, and to the idyllic seasons back home in the valley, before the death of his parents and before his exile from his beloved birthplace. For just a moment, he smiled. But then his thoughts turned again to the falsehoods spoken against him, and the terrible fate that drew inexorably closer with each passing second.

He had been convicted of kidnapping grayfarer fledglings and selling them to the serpans. Incredibly, that was what the chancellor had said. He snorted in disgust. Though he had no love for the self-righteous grayfarer protectors of Harwelden, he would never lower himself to kidnapping their young. Even a thief had his limits. And anyway, indirectly, the grayfarers were his allies against the serpans, even if no one seemed to realize it. For who hated the warring hordes more than he? The serpans, he reasoned, were the cause of his exile, the source of every loss he ever suffered, and now he was to be executed for joining their side. If only he could get a second hearing before the council, perhaps he could make them see.

During the past season of war, the serpans had grown bolder. Throughout the continents of Vengala and Lon Carafay, the claims were repeated: *Valderon has returned. Valderon is rising. The empire is dead.* With each claim of Valderon's rise, the serpans' audacity grew, and with each defeat of the imperial forces, their bloodlust increased. On several occasions, he had caught scent of serpans in the very Forest of Ondor, the once sacred place where they dare not enter until a few seasons ago. Could it be that they themselves were taking the fledglings? It seemed unlikely. Serpans were easily identified by both appearance and scent—if they came near Harwelden, they would be captured. They had to have an ally within the castle walls. A traitor with access to the fledglings was somehow behind these dastardly acts, and Hooks was the scapegoat. And in one day's time, the scheme of the real culprit, whoever it was, would be complete.

Half lying and half sitting on the floor of his cell, he tried in vain to come up with some way to escape. He was a consummate survivor, and his resourcefulness always came through. But never had he found himself in such dire circumstances, with no glimmer of hope for a way out. In desperation, he wept.

Down the hall from his cell, he heard the groaning of an iron door. Footsteps approached.

Unable to wipe away the tears, he looked into the face of the approaching guard, wondering what he wanted.

Unable to wipe away the tears, Hooks
looked into the face of the approaching guard,
wondering what he wanted.

"In spite of your crimes, beast," said the guard, "the council would like to offer you a final supper. Anything you request will be made available to you."

Hooks stared at the guard and felt his contempt. "Opilion," he mumbled.

"Cooked or raw?"

"Raw."

In time, the guard returned with a fat opilion, freshly strangled. He opened the door of the tiny cell and released one wrist from the manacles. With his free hand, Hooks received the bird, and the door clanged shut. As the footsteps of the exiting guard echoed through the halls of the dungeon, Hooks clumsily turned the fowl over to expose its soft breast. Though he typically would have devoured the bird in great, greedy mouthfuls, his bites were tentative, and eventually he discarded the thing, half eaten, onto the floor of his cell.

He felt as though he might vomit. In his mind's eye, he saw himself drawn and quartered. He thought of his parents and of his childhood home, the Valley of the Beasts. He thought of the handsome female, so sweet and innocent, whom he had loved so many seasons ago, before love had left him forever, and who would have been his bride had he not been exiled. He had lost so much, and now his life would end in shame.

The guard reappeared, removed the half-eaten opilion from the floor of his cell, and replaced his wrist in the manacle.

Chapter 7

A Shamalan's Test

Marvus and Jingo watched with obvious trepidation as Elliott approached the Grayfarer Council. This was not the reception they had led him to believe he would get. As he looked into the black ovals of the hoods, he knew he was in danger. At least he should be allowed to see their faces. He wanted to go home.

"I am Waldemariam, chancellor of the Grayfarer Council, and acting governor of Harwelden and all her territories," boomed the voice of the figure seated in the middle. "And what is your name, boy?"

"Elliott," he said meekly, trying to suppress the quiver in his voice.

"And where do you come from, *Elliott*?" The voice seemed to be mocking him.

Again unsure how to respond, Elliott repeated the flimsy-sounding line he had told the two gimlets in the forest. "I come from a long way away."

Several of the councilmen chuckled. "And where, exactly, is 'a long way away'?" Waldemariam asked, sounding amused.

Elliott had no idea what to tell them. Jingo shifted uncomfortably beside him.

"I asked you a question, boy!" the voice boomed. "It is not in your interest, I assure you, to withhold secrets from this council."

Elliott shuddered. What was he to tell them? That he was from Earth? The United States? New Orleans? Gaya?

The silence weighed on him as they awaited his response.

"I come from a city beneath the sea," he said. Although he had no idea where it had come from, he was pleased with the answer. New Orleans, his granddad had told him, was one of only two cities in the world that sat below sea level.

For the umpteenth time since he entered the great hall, Elliott heard a collective gasp from the hooded figures on the dais. Marvus, standing next to him, stared openmouthed at him. Jingo grinned. Whatever Elliott's answer implied, it carried some unknown weight.

Slowly, Waldemariam stood. Even cloaked, he looked fearsome. Elliott was suddenly not so sure he wanted to see his face. The guy must be seven, maybe even eight feet tall. Standing before him, the chancellor looked like the Grim Reaper, come to take him to the afterlife. Waldemariam raised his hands to the cowl and pulled it back from his face. As he did so, the six remaining councilmen, three on either side of him, did the same.

Elliott winced. He couldn't believe what he saw. Their appearance was somewhere between canine and human, with pointy ears and long, toothy snouts. He found them striking. Their color was somewhere between pale gray and olive. Wrinkles lined their faces, and some of them were going gray. Their eyes were inquisitive, and bright with intelligence.

Waldemariam, who seemed younger than most of his colleagues, had a thick shock of black hair that descended to a widow's peak just above his brow ridge, which somehow added to his wolfish appearance. A golden amulet hung at his throat. Elliott could not help finding him, in a strange way, handsome.

"The council shows itself to you, boy. Now show yourself to the council. Remove the rags from your hands."

Elliott looked to Marvus and Jingo, who nodded.

Slowly he removed the bloody bandages and dropped them to the floor. Unsure what to do when he finished, he held

Standing before him, the chancellor looked like the Grim Reaper.

Waldemariam raised his hands to the cowl and pulled it back.

his hands out before him. In the light of the great hall, the birthmarks stood out. The grayfarers gawked openly.

"It is true," said one.

"He bears the markings of a shamalan," said another.

Waldemariam stared at the birthmarks, then looked left and right, receiving nods from each of his colleagues. "Very well, then," he said. "The boy shall be tested."

Confused, Elliott looked to Marvus, who looked worried, and Jingo, who was grinning outright. But before he could ask them what this meant, the chancellor continued. "I understand you hold an object of importance to this council. May we see it, please?" Though his words were polite, his tone was combative.

It took Elliott a moment to realize that Waldemariam referred to the bracelet hidden in his knapsack. Unslinging the pack, he dug out the bracelet and held it out so they might get a good look at it.

"Bring it to me," Waldemariam said.

Elliott took the bracelet to him, and the chancellor held it, feeling its weight and turning it so that he could carefully inspect each of the polished stones embedded in it. Like an appraising jeweler, he examined the bracelet for several seconds before finally passing it to the councilman beside him. In this fashion, it passed to each of them, until all had inspected it. When the last councilman finished with the bracelet, he passed it back to Waldemariam, who placed it on the table.

"Tell us how this item came to be in your possession."

Elliott searched his mind for the right thing to say.

"Do not trifle with me, boy," Waldemariam snapped after waiting perhaps two seconds.

"It belongs to my grandfather," Elliott said meekly.

"And who is your *grand father*?" Waldemariam made two words of it, as if the term were unfamiliar to him.

Elliott had no idea what to say. "He is a man from the city beneath the sea."

The councilmen gave no reaction but merely stared, waiting for him to say more. But he didn't know what else to say.

"And does this man beneath the sea bear the markings of a shamalan?" Waldemariam asked.

"Yes."

"May we meet this grand father?"

"No," said Elliott. "He remains in his home beneath the sea."

They stared at Elliott for several seconds. "You shall be tested," Waldemariam said at last. "Bring his knapsack to me, Jingo."

Jingo walked over to Elliott and retrieved the knapsack from the floor in front of him, looking up at him apologetically. Without a word, he brought it to the chancellor.

"When shall the test begin, Chancellor?" the councilmen to his left asked.

"Now."

Marvus gasped.

Waldemariam pulled the cowl forward again, cloaking his features, and the other councilmen did likewise. Then he said, "Take him to the testing room."

A pair of burly guards came forward and stood at Elliott's sides. "This way," said one.

Realizing that he had no say in the matter, Elliott looked to Marvus for guidance. Marvus frowned and looked at the ground. Elliott then looked to Jingo, who, though not as sullen as Marvus, looked plainly worried. He nodded to Elliott, indicating that he needed to comply.

Elliott walked with the guards, out of the great hall and into the castle foyer. For the first time since his flight from the cave, he was on his own.

The guards, one in front and one behind, led him through an archway opposite the one leading to the great hall, along a series of hallways and down a short flight of stairs to more hallways, twisting and turning their way through the depths of the castle.

Finally, they entered a small room, bare except for a wooden hatch in the center of the floor. While one of the guards waited in the doorway, the other went to the hatch and slid two thick iron bolts free, then lifted the heavy door open.

"Right over here, sir," said the guard, his tone curt but polite, motioning to the small, dim chamber beneath the hatch.

"What are you doing with me?" asked Elliott.

"Please strip out of your garments and get in the testing chamber," said the guard.

Elliott balked. He didn't know precisely what this "testing chamber" was, but it didn't look inviting from here.

"Please don't make this difficult," said the guard holding the trapdoor, maintaining a degree of politeness. "The council has decreed that you shall be tested, and we shall enforce the will of the council. Now, strip out of your clothes and move to the testing chamber."

Grudgingly, Elliott stripped. He felt self-conscious standing there in his boxer shorts.

"Into the chamber," said the guard, straining to hold the heavy door open while the guard in the doorway looked on, with both hands on his crossbow.

Realizing that he had no choice, Elliott sat on the smooth stone floor at the hatch's edge. He could make out the floor some eight feet below. Carefully he lowered himself until he hung by his arms from the hatchway, then let go and dropped the last couple of feet to the bottom. He looked up in time to catch a glimpse of the guard's face before the trapdoor slammed shut, immersing him in darkness. Above him, he heard the iron bolts slide into place, then silence.

He felt his way to a corner and sat in the musty pitch blackness. And as his head filled with dire imaginings of what this test might be, a rhythmic creaking sound came from somewhere overhead, followed by the sound of running water. An instant later, his bottom felt wet and cold. He jumped up. The chamber was filling with water.

As the creaking continued, frigid water rushed into the chamber. Frantic, he yelled, "What's going on!"

But no one answered. The water rose past his ankles, then to his knees. Soon it was waist deep, and he was shivering. He began to scream as the water rose to his chest, his neck. The creaking sound above came faster, more insistently, and his mouth filled with water. Though he had no idea how to swim, he sensed that it wouldn't matter—the water would rise till the chamber was full. He folded his knees, then kicked against the bottom, propelling himself to the surface just long enough to take a breath before sinking again.

Driving up from the floor again, he sucked in another breath. This he did again and again, until soon his head knocked against the hatch door with each upward push. Exhausted, he pushed up and found no more air below the hatch. The chamber was completely filled.

Above the hatch, the creaking stopped. All he could do was float in the icy darkness, holding his breath until his lungs screamed. And at last, he could no longer override the urge to breathe, and against his will, his body inhaled. The cold water stung his nostrils as it rushed through his airway and into his lungs. The last thoughts that entered his mind were of his mother: that he would die in this strange place and leave her alone. She would face her own death without him, wondering why he had left her and where he had gone. With these thoughts in mind, he convulsed, then succumbed to the blackness. Gradually, his body ceased its writhing and sank to the floor.

Chapter 8

A Gimlet's Curiosity

Marvus and Jingo stood alone in the great hall, horrified. Outside, the suns were setting on the long and eventful day.

"We should never have brought him here," Marvus said, shaking his head as he walked to the window. "It was a grave error. Waldemariam's reaction was not what I expected."

"It's going to be all right," Jingo replied, walking behind. "The boy is shamalan."

Marvus stared out over the moonlit forest. Outside, the early evening was shaping up to be quite pleasant, though clouds loomed on the horizon. "I don't share your conviction. Only one shamalan remains in all Pangrelor, and in our hearts, we both know this." His voice fell. "I hoped that finding the boy might mean something, but we've made a grave mistake. He will be killed."

Jingo looked out over the forest. "The boy is shamalan," he said, placing a hand on Marvus's shoulder. "And from Gaya."

Marvus smiled. "Sometimes you're truly impossible," he said, tousling his protégé's hair. "I wish I had your faith, Jingo, I really do. But times are changing." His voice grew melancholy. "The time of the shamalans is ending." He cast his eyes downward, ashamed of his own words. "The princess, if she still lives, will be taken to Sitticus. And our spies say that the malus is planning a siege of this place." He looked out across the great hall, grateful to be secure within the castle but also wondering how long even these stout walls would stand. "I'm afraid for the future of the empire."

"Have faith," Jingo said as they left the room. "We are not defeated yet."

Later that night, after Jingo had bathed and put on fresh garments, he returned to the great hall. He was starving. Despite everything that had happened, it was good to be home. Rows of rough-hewn wooden tables now filled the hall, and servants bustled to and fro with platters of roasted meats and pitchers of ale. The room had been transformed from tribunal to dining hall, and all Jingo's friends who worked in the castle were here, enjoying the evening meal. At the end of the room, a band played merry tunes on their harps and horns.

After looking around the room, Jingo spotted an empty chair. As he sat down, a fellow gimlet named Zeppo scooted over to make room. They had grown up as neighbors on the outskirts of town and had obtained employment at the castle during the same season long ago. Zeppo now served as a tailor on the second level of the castle. He was also a tireless gossip, and Jingo resolved to choose his words carefully.

"I can't believe what happened yesterday," Zeppo said, not even waiting for Jingo to fill his plate. "They captured the susquat." He looked at Jingo, awaiting a response.

"What are you talking about?" Jingo asked, relieved that the topic had nothing to do with the princess's capture or the discovery of the boy in the forest.

"The beast from Susquatania. The one that's been stealing the grayfarer fledglings for bounty." Zeppo lowered his voice, apparently not wanting the sensitive subject to fall on grayfarer ears.

Jingo knew little of the situation regarding the captured susquat, only that the army had been seeking the beast. Of course, he also knew of the disappearance of several grayfarer fledglings during the past few seasons. Like the rest of the town, he had mourned their loss alongside the grieving parents. Responsibility for the crimes was long ago assigned to a wayward beast, and capturing him had become a top priority for the council.

"At midday tomorrow, the susquat will be drawn and quartered in the public square," Zeppo said. "He went before the council yesterday."

The council has been busy, Jingo mused as a servant set a mug of ale by his plate.

"A good batch," Zeppo said of the ale. "It's been cooling in the river all day."

Across the room, a grizzled grayfarer jumped up noisily onto a table, laughing and pouring a mug of ale down his throat. Jingo recognized him as a crusty old soldier of the grayfarer army. He stretched his wings, straining to make them as long as he could, while two half-sloshed gimlets got up and stumbled to opposite ends of the table, eyeing his wingtips to see if they reached past the ends of the table. Everyone watching cheered. After some discussion, the gimlets decided that the wingspan was indeed longer than the table, and each gave a thumbs-up, making the onlookers howl in delight.

"Arbusto wins!" said one of the gimlets.

A roasted opilion haunch flew across the room, and the drunken grayfarer snatched it from the air, laughing. He tore a bite from it and waved the rest over his head as the hall erupted in cheers, and the band played louder.

"So where did they capture the beast?" Jingo asked, returning to the conversation. "I've never actually seen one before."

"I hadn't, either, until they marched him down the Boulevard of Kings bringing him into the city. He's huge! They captured him in the forest, just a half day's journey from here. He had just raided an opilion corral when they got him."

"Hmmm," Jingo said, his curiosity piqued.

Zeppo slurped his ale and gave a satisfied belch. "Will you go to the execution tomorrow? The whole village is buzzing about it."

"I've no taste for those things," Jingo said, taking a long drink of ale. "I haven't been to an execution in many seasons. I feel ill every time."

"Well, you can bet *I'll* be there," Zeppo said, digging into his meat pie. "So how is the princess tonight? She must be pleased to be back home."

Jingo cringed, wishing he had chosen another table. News of the princess's capture had not yet gone further than the Council, though many had noticed her absence when Jingo and Marvus entered the city. No doubt, her whereabouts were the topic of whispers at many tables.

"The princess is well," he replied. "But we'll not talk politics tonight." His tone was cordial but firm.

"Sorry," Zeppo said sheepishly, and poked at his food.

They finished the meal with small talk. Jingo praised the ale, and Zeppo promised to make him a new suit of clothes. Throughout the dinner, though, Jingo's thoughts kept returning to the beast in the dungeon. He had always wanted to see a susquat, but he had no stomach for executions. Later tonight, he decided, he would go to the dungeon and see the beast firsthand. He had heard they were taller than three gimlets standing on each other's shoulders, and weighed as much as a mountain horse.

After finishing his meal, Jingo bade farewell to Zeppo and the others at his table. He could see that Marvus had already left—his mentor was not one for parties and merrymaking. And though the party was just beginning, he, too, was tired and ready for some time alone.

Jingo's room was small and spare, but it had a sweeping view of the Azure Mountains. He scooted a chair to the window and propped his feet on the ledge, relishing the beauty of the mountain-scape, and the relative quiet of his bedchamber. He passed some time gazing contentedly out at the mountains, thinking about the boy from the forest and the susquat in the castle dungeon.

"Well, you can bet I'll be there," Zeppo said,
digging into his meat pie. "So how is the princess tonight?
She must be pleased to be back home."

The moon shone brightly, and the night was quite peaceful, even with all the noise coming from the great hall. And despite all the turmoil of recent days, he couldn't help but feel a twinge of happiness to be back finally, safe and comfy in his bedchamber. If only Sarintha and the others could have made it home, too.

As he sat at his open window waiting for the noise to die down, a pair of drunken young grayfarers appeared in the sky over his perch, gamboling and wrestling and hooting with laughter. Eventually, their reveling took them to the skies on the other side of the castle, and the night grew calm again. Pulling his pipe from his shirt pocket, Jingo filled it and thought of the strange boy from the forest as he sat smoking. He was shamalan—had to be.

Eventually, the noise in the great hall died down, signifying that the revelers were at last wandering off to bed. This was what Jingo was waiting for. His heart quickened at the thought of seeing the fearsome exotic beast.

It took several minutes to descend through the castle's labyrinthine passageways to the dungeon. But once there, it was a simple matter to talk his way past the guard, for Jingo had free run of the castle ever since coming into the princess's employ. Slowly, he walked through the dungeon corridors, peering into each cell in search of the susquat. Not a single cell was empty, and one pair of forlorn eyes after another watched through the iron bars as he passed. He had to wonder what so many citizens had done to come to such a sorry pass.

Halfway down the corridor, he spotted the beast. The thing was huge, nearly filling a cell designed to hold two men. It appeared to be sleeping, but as Jingo watched, it opened its eyes.

"What do you want, gimlet?" it asked. "Why don't you leave me in peace?"

Jingo was taken aback. He hadn't expected it to speak to him. "Shut up, beast" he said, staring at him through the bars. The creature was larger than he expected, and he was instantly fascinated.

The susquat stared back in contempt.

"Why did you do it?" asked Jingo. If the beast wanted to talk, then he would talk.

"Why did I do what?"

"Kidnap fledglings for bounty, of course."

"I've never laid hands on a stinking grayfarer fledgling in my life," said the beast.

"Ironic, then, that you find yourself about to be executed for your part in their disappearance," Jingo said, rather enjoying himself—though he was glad for the sturdy iron bars between them.

"I hope your shamalan boy drowns like a dog," the creature said.

Jingo gaped, surprised that anyone, let alone a condemned prisoner, should know of Elliott's presence.

"The guards have long tongues," said the beast, sensing his bewilderment. When Jingo did not reply, he cocked one furry eyebrow. "Another shamalan lives, you know."

"We'll not talk politics, beast," said Jingo.

"I'm not talking about the princess, little fool. Another shamalan hides in the wilderness, far from this place. He has fed and sheltered me many times."

"Explain yourself," said Jingo. "And while you're at it, explain why I should believe a criminal who will very soon be dead."

"Why don't you go over to the guard and fetch a key to the manacles," the susquat replied. "Release my limbs so I can stretch them on this, my last night, and I'll tell you more."

"I'll do no such thing," Jingo said, chuckling at the very audacity of such a suggestion.

"Look, gimlet, you can reach through the bars and un-shackle the wrist nearest you. When my hand is free, you can give me the key and I'll release the rest of my limbs. The bars will remain between us, and I'll remain safely locked in the cage. What harm can come of it? If you do this one thing, I'll tell you of a shamalan who hides in the wilderness. I'll even tell you how you can find him. You'd want to have this information before I'm executed, I assume."

Jingo stared, contemplating the proposition.

"In the morning," the susquat continued, "the guards will release me from my cell and march me to the square. The crowds will cheer when they see me torn asunder. If you release me from the manacles, that won't change, and no one will be the wiser."

A part of Jingo couldn't believe he was even considering it.

"And a nice price you'll have for your troubles. Imagine the council's reaction when they learn that, unbeknownst to them or anyone else, another shamalan lives."

"Why didn't you mention this to the council?"

"I wish I had," Hooks muttered. "I was so surprised by their accusation that I didn't think of it."

What the beast suggested was ludicrous. After the Great Betrayal, when most of the shamalans were murdered, the sur-vivors had collected at Harwelden. Like precious flowers or rare birds, they had been numbered and counted. In the many sea-sons since the Betrayal, the shamalans had slowly succumbed to the ravages of age, sickness, war, and assassination until only the princess remained. It was inconceivable that one had sur-vived in the wild, unbeknownst to Harwelden. This beast was trying to hoodwink him.

"His name is Crosslyn."

Jingo searched his brain. Where had he heard that name before? After a moment, it came to him. Crosslyn was a priest during the reign of King Dagnar. And like all of Dagnar's court, he had been slaughtered in the Great Betrayal. Every gimlet schoolchild knew the story. But how would a beast from Susquatania know the shamalan lore? And how would he know the name Crosslyn?

"He's very old," said the beast, with a hint of eagerness in his voice.

He would have to be quite old, thought Jingo, doing the calculations in his head, taking into account the long life spans of the shamalans.

"And he waits for the prophecy to unfold."

As quickly as that, Jingo was hooked. There was simply no way a susquat could know of the prophecy. Clearly, this one knew *something*.

"All right, I'll hear you," Jingo said softly.

He walked to the end of the hall to find the guard with his chair tilted against the wall, dozing in the corner. After a quick search of the desk at the guard's station, he returned to the cell and reached through the bars to unlock the manacle nearest him. The beast's wrist almost exploded from the cuff as it popped open. Then Jingo tossed the key to the floor, and Hooks tried clumsily to pick it up. After flexing his fingers for a few seconds, he managed to pick it up, and before long he was rubbing his wrists and ankles and groaning with relief.

"Now, tell me the tale of the shamalan living in the wild," Jingo said.

Hooks continued rubbing his wrists, then flexed each elbow, then his knees.

"If you are honorable, you will tell me of the shamalan in the wild," Jingo persisted. "I have kept my end of the bargain."

Hooks continued to rub his wrists and looked absently at the floor.

"Fine, then." Jingo turned and started to walk away. I will

bring word to your clan that you lied to the very end. You bring shame on your family, beast, even in your final hours."

"Wait," Hooks said, looking up.

Jingo stopped. The beast looked as if he might say something, but when he didn't, Jingo walked briskly toward the exit.

"Crosslyn has foreseen the events that now come about. Two seasons ago, he foresaw my arrest. He warned that I would be held for a capital offense against Harwelden."

Jingo stopped again, trying to decide whether to believe him.

"He predicted the finding of a strange shamalan boy in the forest. And he foresaw that a young gimlet, with my assistance, would prove invaluable in turning the tide of the war."

Jingo's mind was spinning. Shamalan priests did have the gift of foresight. "Go on, then, beast. Honor your words. Tell me where I might find this Crosslyn."

"Get me out of here, and I'll take you to him. We can be at his doorstep before the turn of the seasons."

Jingo chuckled. "That is not going to happen."

"Then locate him you shall not," said Hooks.

"I could have the shackles back on you in a matter of minutes," said Jingo. "One trip to the guard station, and you'll spend your remaining hours bound and cramped. Give me the information, and you will at least pass your final night in relative comfort."

"Then I shall wear the manacles, gimlet." The beast looked hopefully at him. "And Crosslyn's whereabouts will remain unknown. Oh, and by the way, the empire will crash down around your ears—all because you were too weak and shortsighted to fulfill your role in the ancient prophecy that tries to manifest." The beast stared deep into his eyes. "And an innocent life—mine, as it happens—will be taken in the bargain." He cast his eyes downward and held his arms above his head, indicating that he was ready to go back in the shackles.

At a loss for words, Jingo turned and left the dungeon, leaving the beast in his martyr's pose. He walked past the guard station without a word and ascended the many stairs to his room in the tower.

Sitting again at the window, he lit his pipe and gazed out into the shadowed wilderness. A cool breeze blew through the window, stirring the air around him. It would be easy enough to secure the beast's escape. But in doing so, he would mark himself an enemy of Harwelden. The army would hunt him relentlessly for the treason, and if they found him, *he* would be the one disemboweled and then ripped apart by horses in the city square. His family would be shamed. And what if the beast should simply melt into the night once they reached the forest? How could a mere gimlet ever hold such a huge, powerful half-wild creature to his bargain? Perhaps the beast *was* guilty of the kidnappings, after all. The stakes were high.

But then, what if it spoke the truth? What if this Crosslyn had, in fact, hidden himself in the wild all these seasons, patiently awaiting the fulfillment of the prophecy. It did seem possible. The beast had gotten his information from *somewhere.* Certainly, no beast from the valley would be schooled in the teachings of the Shama or know of the writings in the scrolls. If he was lying, then how had he known of the prophecy?

And what about the boy? And the bracelet of the nine clans? If Elliott survived the test, then the prophecy *must* be true. What else could explain the appearance of a strange shamalan boy in the forest—especially one who wore the lost bracelet of the nine clans? No shamalan had been birthed in Lon Carafay since the princess herself; this was common knowledge. Where, then, had the young boy appeared from, if not from Gaya? If Elliott was the one heralded in the prophecy, then Jingo was duty bound to assist him, even at the risk of his own life. A surviving shamalan priest, unknown until the very day of the boy's appearance, seemed too convenient for chance. If this Crosslyn really existed, he could bring Elliott through the cultivation. This had to be considered. So many questions, and each of enormous consequence.

For a moment, he considered approaching the council with his dilemma, but quickly discarded the idea. The grayfarers were warriors. Their predilection was toward battle, not faith. Just earlier today, had he himself not been threatened with imprisonment for merely *mentioning* the prophecy? No, he couldn't go before the council with the susquat's tale. The grays would consider no other fate for the beast but execution. Jingo longed to speak with the princess, but in her absence, he would have to settle for the next best thing: he would speak to Marvus.

With the castle asleep, he left his quarters and went quietly down the darkened hall to his mentor's room. Gingerly, he knocked on the door. After a time, Marvus appeared, smelling slightly of ale and clearly unhappy to be awakened at such a late hour. Jingo tried to think of a good way to begin, and Marvus, sensing his agitation, brought him inside.

With the room lit only by the moonlight streaming in through the windows, Jingo sat in a wooden chair overlooking the mountains. He said, "Have you heard about the beast that was captured in the forest?"

"Why have you woken me?" Marvus growled. "Have you any idea how late it is?"

"I went down to the dungeon to see the beast."

"Sometimes I swear you've taken leave of your senses!" Marvus said. "Why can't we talk about this in the morning?"

"He claims a shamalan named Crosslyn has been hiding in the wilderness since the time of the Great Betrayal. He wants to take us to him."

The sleepy expression left Marvus's face. He stared at Jingo. "All right," he said finally. "You have my complete attention. Start from the beginning and tell me the whole thing."

Marvus paced back and forth in the moonlit room, barely looking at Jingo as he listened to the strange account of the night's events. Jingo, for his part, made quite an argument for freeing the beast. The presence of a shamalan priest, if true, certainly changed everything. If Elliott had passed his test, would it not be worth the risk of trying to find this Crosslyn? Did the possibilities of the prophecy's fulfillment not *demand* it of them? Marvus, apparently unmoved, stared silently out into the wilderness as Jingo finished making his case. The young gimlet was prepared to rescue the criminal and steal away into the night. He looked to his mentor, unable to read his expression in the darkened room.

In a voice barely above a whisper, Marvus said, "I have lived the whole of my life in this castle. Many, many seasons ago, I was birthed in this very tower. All my days, I have served at the pleasure of the nobles. All my days, I have served Harwelden." A frown darkened the corners of his mouth, and his words came slowly, with great deliberation. "For countless seasons of war, we have watched as the enemy's hand strengthened. I stood with King Gregorus and Princess Sarintha when they learned of the fall of Prytania." He grew sadder. "I was with the princess at the moment she learned of her father's slaying by the darfoyle Ecsar."

As he spoke, anger encroached on his melancholy, and the tempo of his voice quickened. "We stood in the fields outside Prytania when the princess was ambushed, and we watched from the shadows as Malus Lothar held her in his arms." An errant cloud passed from in front of the moon, and silvery light streamed through the windows, so that his small face fairly glowed. "And we watched from a crevice beneath a tree as she was taken again in the Forest of Ondor, in the shadow of this once mighty place."

Jingo watched his mentor with fascination. He had never seen him like this.

"Now we sit in our castle and pretend that doom is not upon us. Though a traitor sits among us, we drink and feast and ignore the slaughter that comes to claim us. With the fall of each city, our resolve weakens. With the loss of each shamalan, we grow nearer the end days."

A cloud again obscured the moon. "So what shall we do?" Marvus said as he lit an oil lamp. "Shall we await oblivion and the executioner that marches toward us? Or shall we act? If we flee into the wilderness with the beast at our side, we will be hunted like animals by daybreak. Our loved ones will forget they ever cherished us, and will themselves sharpen their knives and join the hunt for us. To our beloved Harwelden, which we have served with honor all our days, we will become viler than the serpans that come to conquer us. It is a grave proposal you make."

Jingo had no idea whether Marvus was embracing the plan. "What will we do?"

"We will check on the boy," said Marvus, returning his gaze to the mountains. "If he is alive, then we shall hatch a plan to rescue the beast and will do as you propose."

Thunder flashed across the sky, and a flurry of rain pattered against the window. Beneath the two uneasy gimlets, the castle slept, oblivious of the brewing storm.

Chapter 9

A Shamalan Lives

In the darkness of the water-filled chamber, Elliott opened his eyes. At first, he had no recollection of where he was or how he got here. He inhaled, filling his lungs with water, but unlike before, it didn't sting his nostrils as it passed into his lungs. Remarkably, it was satisfying. He exhaled, expelling the water, and drew in another lungful, without coughing or sputtering or flailing or clawing at the door. He just floated, surrounded by the darkness, and the liquid medium soothed him. For a moment, it did not register that he was breathing water, that his body was extracting oxygen from it just as it had from the air he had breathed all his life. With each liquid breath, his head grew clearer.

Incredulous, he reached out for the walls, feeling his way to the rough wood of the hatch above him. A prickly sensation tickled the webbing between his fingers and toes. The birthmarks were tingling. He moved a hand in front of his face, trying to inspect the familiar welts, but all was pitch black.

Gradually, though, his eyes adjusted to the darkness, and he was able to make out the shape of his hand. It looked strange. The spaces between his fingers were gone, replaced by thin membranes extending all the way to the nails. And the fingers themselves were splayed more widely than usual, with his pinky extending almost perpendicularly outward. It looked not like a hand but like a wide, amphibious paddle. He inspected his other hand, then his feet—paddles all.

He was able to make out the shape of his hand. ... It looked
not like a hand but like a wide, amphibious paddle.

To see the strange membranes more clearly, he blinked his eyes against the water and reopened them. This made his vision sharper. Gone was the murky distortion that should be there. In yellow hues, he saw the stone and mortar of the walls surrounding him, and the webbing that stretched taut between his fingers and toes. *The markings of a shamalan.* Somehow, inhaling the water had contributed to the transformation.

As the bizarre realization dawned, the creak of hinges overhead jarred him from his thoughts, and he looked up into the relative brightness to see Marvus and Jingo, straining to lift the trapdoor. Only one thought entered his mind: that this had been an exceedingly strange day.

Eventually, the two gimlets got the trapdoor open. And while Jingo strained to balance it at ninety degrees to the floor, Marvus extended a hand to help Elliott out of the water.

Though he felt an unlikely dismay at the idea of leaving the water, he accepted the hand and kicked and was astonished to find himself launching out of the water and into the air, to land on his feet beside Marvus. Speechless, the gimlets hugged him.

He returned the embrace.

"You've done it!" Marvus crowed. "Praise Baruna, you have passed the test!"

"I knew it," Jingo exclaimed, staring at the webbing between Elliott's fingers. "You *are* a shamalan!"

They worked together to lower the trapdoor, and Marvus replaced the iron bolts into the latch. When they finished, they looked at Elliott, unable to stop grinning.

I passed the test, Elliott thought. Though he wanted to thank them for coming to his aid, a panic suddenly overtook him. Standing in the open air of the testing room, he realized he couldn't breathe. He opened his mouth and vomited buckets of water, purging it from his lungs. Some of it was still cold. In desperation, he looked to the hatch door. It was bolted shut, and he hadn't enough time to try to wrestle it back open. Frantically he searched the room for some relief to his suffocation, but except for Marvus and Jingo, the room was empty. His body shook as he coughed up more mouthfuls of water. He was drowning in the open air.

Falling to his knees, he could stand it no longer, and inhaled, filling his lungs with the musty air of the testing room. Like the water before, the air stung as it passed through his nostrils and entered his airway. His lungs and throat were on fire, and he thought surely he was dying.

After filling his lungs with the burning air, he coughed, expelling the air in a rush, and inhaled again. This time it was less painful. He exhaled. After a few cycles of this, his breathing eased and finally returned to normal. Knowing what to expect, he held his hands out before him. The membranes linking his digits had vanished. The birthmarks were back, though redder and more inflamed than before. Simultaneously with the retraction of the webbing, something happened to his eyes, too, and the yellow hues that had shaded his vision underwater were gone. *I am a shamalan*, he thought, gaping at the markings on his hands.

"Well done!" said Marvus, beaming. "It's been so long since I witnessed a transformation, I forgot to warn you about breathing air again. But don't worry, you'll get better with practice."

Still grinning, Jingo took some clothes from his knapsack and tossed them to Elliott, who dressed quickly, relieved to be clothed again. These clothes were a much better fit than those Marvus had given him in the forest.

When he was dressed, he looked at the gimlets in utter bewilderment. "I have so many questions, I don't know where to begin," he said.

"With all due respect, Sir Elliott, we've no time to dawdle here," said Marvus. "All your questions will be answered in time." He scanned the room nervously. "We have to get out of here before anyone sees us."

"All right," said Elliott. Marvus's change in behavior was making him nervous. He looked at his hands one last time and followed the gimlets out of the testing room, into the foyer and up the spiral staircase. Thankfully, they met no one.

When they got to Marvus's room, he hustled them inside, scanned the hall again, and shut and bolted the door. "Sit down, Sir Elliott," he said, motioning to a chair by the window. "We have a lot to discuss, and I'm afraid we don't have much time."

"All right," said Elliott, sitting in a chair by the window. He gazed into the mountains. Despite the rainstorm outside, the view was breathtaking.

"If all goes well," said Marvus, "we will be leaving the castle before daybreak."

Baffled by the comment, though a little relieved at the thought of getting far away from the grayfarers, Elliott just nodded.

"Since you left us earlier today," Marvus continued, "it has come to our attention that there will be a public execution tomorrow."

Elliott tensed, fearing that perhaps he was to be the star attraction.

"In a fit of curiosity," Marvus continued, "my pupil went to the dungeons and spoke with the condemned prisoner." He looked sideways at Jingo. "The prisoner told of a lost shamalan who survives in the wilderness, far from Harwelden."

Though relieved to learn that the condemned prisoner was someone other than himself, Elliott failed to grasp any deeper significance to what Marvus was saying.

"The presence of the shamalan in the wilderness, if true, would be of great value to your own purposes here, Elliott, whatever they may prove to be," said Marvus.

"I don't understand," Elliott said.

Marvus sighed, as if unsure how to continue. "The history of the shamalans is complex, and we cannot review all of it now. But before this evening, we believed that only one of your kind survived in all Pangrelor. When we found you in the forest, bearing the markings of a shamalan, we thought it inconceivable that we had stumbled across a second member of the dying race. But tonight you have proved yourself."

Elliott looked at his hands.

"You can understand, I'm sure, the significance of finding a second member of a dying race—especially when that race is shamalan." Marvus looked at him, gauging his understanding. "The prisoner claims he can lead us to the shamalan who hides himself from Harwelden. If the prisoner is telling the truth, the number of your race in all Pangrelor will have tripled in half a day."

"So there's one in hiding, and there's me," Elliott said. "Where's the other?"

The gimlets tensed.

"Oh, I get it," he said. "Sorry. You don't have to tell me."

"It's all right," Marvus said. "The other is Princess Sarintha, rightful heir to the throne of Harwelden and all her territories. She is the daughter of the slain king Gregorus."

"Oh." Elliott had no idea who King Gregorus was, but he sounded important. "Where is she?" he said, careful to sound respectful, and aware that something about the topic made them uncomfortable.

Marvus looked at Elliott the way he might look at a child. "Our princess has been captured by our enemies to the north. We have been at war with them for generations, and, I'm sorry to say, we grow closer to defeat with each passing day." Marvus looked sad. "She was taken from us just a short while before we found you in the forest."

The thought of his first meeting with them, and the magby attack, gave him a chill.

"Even setting aside Jingo's conversation with the prisoner," Marvus said, "today has been a day of great importance. The princess was captured, and then we found you."

Jingo opened his mouth to speak, but Marvus shushed him. "We have decided to rescue the condemned prisoner and flee Harwelden to search for the shamalan." His voice grew sad as he finished. "By morning, we will be hunted as traitors."

"Wait a minute," said Elliott, raising his hands. "You guys can do whatever you want, but I don't want to make any enemies—especially with those grayfarer guys. In fact, if you'll just take me back down to the cave where you found me, I promise I'll go back home and not be any more trouble for you."

"That won't be possible, I'm afraid," said Jingo.

"Why not?" Elliott surprised himself with the anger in his voice. "None of this has anything to do with me. I don't want to anger the council or be hunted as a traitor. I just want to get out of here." He crossed his arms.

"Even if we took you back to the cave, you wouldn't be able to go back home," Jingo said.

"How do you know that?"

"Because it says in the—"

Marvus cut him off. "You'll have to trust us. Your best chance of returning to your home lies in our plan. We must find the shamalan in the wilderness. Without a doubt, that will be the best thing for you . . ." He seemed unsure how to finish the sentence. "And for the rest of us as well."

Elliott felt uneasy.

"Freeing the susquat should be easy," Jingo said.

What in the heck was a susquat? Elliott wondered.

"But before we can leave, we have to find the bracelet," Jingo said. "That will be hard. And we have to act fast."

"You're right, of course," Marvus said. "And I know just the thing to help us find it."

"I don't want anything to do with this," Elliott said. He didn't know what to do, but he was pretty sure he didn't want to go with them.

"I'm sorry, Elliott," Marvus replied. "But this is the only way. Now, come on, we must hurry." Marvus collected a few things from his room, stuffed them in a knapsack, and turned for the door.

"There really isn't any choice for you," Jingo said. "You're safer with us than with anyone here."

Elliott uncrossed his arms and sighed. "If we get caught, you have to tell them this wasn't my idea."

"Agreed," Jingo said.

They made their way back toward Jingo's room but stopped at a door along the way. Marvus took a key from a chain in his pocket and unlocked the door, careful not to make any noise. Searching the halls to make sure no one watched from the shadows, they entered the room, and Marvus bolted the door behind them.

Like Marvus's quarters, the room overlooked the Azure Mountains, though it was much nicer. Thick, rich rugs covered the floors, and fine paintings crowded the walls. Like the frescoes in the foyer, the paintings depicted scenes from shamalan history, including several portraits of long-dead nobles. In the center of the room, amid an array of fine furniture, was a bed covered in silky linens. A portrait of a beautiful young woman hung above the headboard. The woman looked out over the room with a tranquil expression, as if the artist had captured her essence during a particularly pleasant thought. Elliott found her quite striking and had a hard time taking his eyes off her. "Wow," he said, staring at the painting. "Who *is* that?"

Marvus chuckled, appreciating the look on Elliott's face. "That's Princess Sarintha. I hope one day you two can meet."

"Me, too," Elliott mumbled.

Marvus went to a nightstand between the bed and the wall, and slowly, so as not to make any noise, he opened a drawer and removed a small stone, holding it out in front of him.

Jingo grinned at the sight of the stone.

Elliott wrenched his eyes from the painting and watched as Marvus turned the stone in his hand. It reminded him of the one he had found in his grandfather's basement.

"It's Princess Sarintha's seer stone," Jingo explained.

"I think I can make it work," Marvus said. "I am no expert with crystalomancy, but she let me use it once before." He went to a chair next to the window and sat. Elliott and Jingo gathered around him, and he closed his eyes, concentrating as he held the stone in the palm of his outstretched hand. Jingo, too, closed his eyes.

After a false start, the stone levitated a few centimeters above Marvus's hand. Elliott couldn't believe it! They must be playing a trick on him. He looked at the stone carefully, trying to discern how Marvus made the thing float, but he could find no strings or other mechanism to explain it.

Marvus squeezed his eyes shut tighter, and a greenish glow radiated outward from the stone, illuminating the three huddled faces. The stone rose a little higher.

The wheels in Elliott's mind spun, trying to make sense of what he was seeing, but there appeared to be no trickery involved. In disbelief, he stared at Marvus, whose face contorted with the effort.

Quietly, reverently, Marvus whispered, "Show me the boy's knapsack."

The green glow intensified and kindled into a bright wash of light. From within the stone, a scene appeared. It showed the entrance to the castle Harwelden.

Sensing the change in the intensity of the light, the gimlets opened their eyes and gazed into the stone. In the picture, two guards chuckled as they shared a joke. The view moved slowly past them and through the castle's closed door, then into the foyer and up the spiral staircase to the top level of the castle. Moving faster, the view went to the hall leading to the western tower, then up a second flight of stairs.

"It's going to the councilmen's chambers," Jingo whispered.

The picture in the stone ascended to the top of the western tower and passed several doors. At the fifth door, it stopped.

"That's Waldemariam's chamber," Jingo said.

Marvus glared at him, telling him with his eyes to be quiet.

The stone took them through the door. In the middle of an unusually large bed, the chancellor lay snoring, with his scaly wings folded on either side of him. After showing them the chancellor for a moment, the stone took them to the opposite end of the room, finally hovering over a wooden desk across from the bed. Sitting on top of the desk were Elliott's things: the knapsack, the bracelet, the coin sack, the shamalan stone, and the slingshot. The chancellor had obviously been inspecting the things before going to bed.

The light from the stone dulled, and the stone dropped back into Marvus's hand.

"This is going to be tricky," Jingo said.

"How did you do that?" Elliott asked. "With the stone . . ."

"Later," said Marvus. "Right now we have to hurry. The suns will be on the horizon soon, and we still have to worry about rescuing the beast."

"What beast?" Elliott said. "I didn't hear anything about a beast."

"The prisoner," said Jingo. "He's a susquat."

Though Elliott still had no idea what a susquat was, he decided this wasn't the time to ask. "How do we get the stuff from Waldemariam's room?"

"We steal it," said Marvus.

The matter-of-factness of this response surprised Elliott. Marvus just hadn't seemed the type to steal anything.

The gimlets worked out a plan while Elliott peered at the painting of the girl above the bed. She was a beauty—prettier even than Lisa Hastings. When they were ready, Jingo motioned to Elliott while Marvus pocketed Sarintha's shamalan stone and grabbed an oil lamp. On the way out, Elliott stole a final glance at the painting, willing himself to remember the lines and angles of her face.

Minutes later, they stood before the chancellor's door. The hall of the western tower was deathly quiet, and not even the patter of the rain outside penetrated the silence. With uncanny stealth, Marvus slipped a key from his chain into the lock, and with a slight click, the lock released and the door opened. Marvus pushed, and the hinges made a low creaking sound, prompting him to cover the lamp with his hand and peer nervously down the hall.

Jingo, unable to see the sleeping form through the cracked door, put his ear to the gap, then turned and nodded to his companions—the chancellor was still snoring away.

Breathing a sigh of relief, Jingo entered the room and tiptoed toward the desk, only a few feet from the sleeping chancellor. The knapsack and its contents were in plain view. With Elliott and Marvus watching from the archway, Jingo stole over to the desk and began quietly stowing the items back in the knapsack.

With his crime nearly complete, he reached for the last item: the silver bracelet. With bated breath, Elliott and Marvus watched from the cracked door.

At the exact moment that Jingo closed his hand around the bracelet, there was a bright flash, and an eyeblink later, a horrendous thunderclap tore across the skies outside.

Waldemariam rolled and sat bolt upright in his bed. He looked directly at Jingo, who stood frozen, clutching the silver bracelet.

Elliott gasped, then clapped a hand over his own mouth.

Jingo didn't move an inch. Caught red-handed, he stared at the chancellor, who, apparently still sleeping, flopped down onto his back and resumed his snoring.

With utmost care, Jingo stashed the bracelet in the knapsack and quickly tiptoed out of the room.

Marvus pulled the door shut and locked it, and with a collective sigh of relief, they hurried down the hall and back to the central tower. Marvus and Jingo were moving faster than before, and Elliott had to struggle to keep pace with them.

Jingo quickly gathered a few things from his room and put them in a knapsack. Then, with barely a word, they rushed from the tower and down to the foyer. Elliott felt a little sorry for the two gimlets as they paused in the foyer for a final, wistful look at their home. And after that brief pause, they hurried down to the dungeon.

The guard at the entrance was wide awake, and his eyes narrowed as they approached. Standing there and blocking the entrance, he had the look of someone prepared to meet them with force but at the same time calculating whether that would be smart or necessary. "What are *you* doing here?" he asked, fixing his gaze on Jingo. "It's too late for visitors." He spread his feet wide, standing square in front of the entrance.

"Hello again," said Jingo. His eyes flashed with the excitement of a young child. "I wanted to take my friends to see the susquat before he is executed." He grinned unabashedly, and his whole presence exuded innocence.

"What is in the knapsacks?" asked the guard, glaring back at them.

Jingo giggled. "Oh, nothing really," he said. "We've been out collecting souvenirs with our friend." He motioned to Elliott. "He is a visitor to Harwelden, and we've spent the evening in the central tower with some of the artisans. They've gifted him with some of their tools, which are different from anything he is used to." Jingo took a deep breath, as if excited by the thought. "I'm afraid we've had a bit too much ale, and we were so excited to see the beast, we forgot to drop them in our chambers."

The guard stared.

"Here, check if you like," said Jingo, holding out his knapsack, grinning all the while.

Elliott stiffened. The boldness of Jingo's gamble made a knot in the pit of his stomach.

The guard ignored the gesture and looked at Elliott, taking particular notice of his hands. "Who are you?" he asked.

Elliott froze, at a loss how to continue the charade.

Marvus intervened. "If I may be so rude," he said, stepping between Elliott and the guard, "the boy is a guest of the princess, and his presence here is not yet well known, so I must ask for your discretion. He is a shamalan of the highest birthright. Jingo and I have been instructed to entertain him, and he wants to see the prisoner. Surely you won't stand in our way?"

The guard stood his ground. His eyes moved uncertainly over the three visitors. "All right," he said finally. "But don't take long. I'll be listening for you." He narrowed his eyes and stepped aside, studying them as they walked into the dungeon.

Elliott heard Marvus exhale in a rush as soon as they were past the guard, and he noticed that Jingo's hands were shaking. They walked as casually as they could manage, past rows of questioning eyes to the cell where the beast was imprisoned.

When they finally stood before the beast, Elliott stared in amazement. Though he had never seen a susquat before, he knew immediately what it was. For he was gazing directly into the eyes of an imprisoned Bigfoot.

"What's his problem?" said Hooks.

Elliott nearly fell over. The thing could talk.

Ignoring the beast, Jingo turned to Elliott and whispered, "That," he said, "is a susquat."

With great haste, Marvus produced yet another key from his chain and opened the door to the cell. "Hurry!" he said to Hooks. "No time for chitchat. Jingo told us of your earlier conversation, and we are going to follow through on your offer. You had better not betray us, beast, or you will feel the full wrath of the princess."

Hooks chuckled as he got to his feet. "Can't get much worse than this, can it?"

Jingo scanned the halls, then waved Hooks out of the cell. He towered over them. Bending low, he grasped Jingo and lifted him off the ground, hugging him so tightly that he squeezed the air out of him.

He grinned. "I won't let you down. We'll find the shamalan."

The prisoner in the adjacent cell stirred. "What's going on out there?" he grumbled.

Elliott watched Marvus look at Jingo. The look on his face was sad and scared and exhilarated and deep with friendship all at once. It seemed almost as if he was saying good-bye.

"It's now or never," whispered Marvus.

Jingo nodded and turned in the opposite direction, heading for the exit. "I'll meet you at the base of the mountain. Good luck."

Marvus nodded and watched as Jingo walked off toward the guard's post. After a moment, he turned and led Elliott and Hooks down the opposite hall, deeper into the cell block.

The prisoner in the cell next to Hooks's, apparently unhappy at his neighbor's good fortune, began to scream for the guard. And in no time, all the prisoners in the cell block were awake and yelling.

With Hooks and Elliott following, Marvus began to run deeper into the cell block. Everywhere they went, a cacophony of prisoners' voices erupted in their wake. Elliott was fairly sure they hadn't counted on this.

When they reached the far end of the dungeon, at the end of a long hall lined with cells, they stopped. A sheer stone wall stood before them, and the prisoners in the cells lining both sides of the corridor screamed for the guard, beckoning him to their location.

With his heart thumping faster than he thought it could, Elliott turned in time to see the guard rounding the corner at the far end of the corridor. They were boxed in.

Marvus, somehow managing to keep calm, reached into his pocket and produced another key—a single one, not from his chain. Larger and more weathered than the others, it had a head as big as Marvus's hand, inscribed with an unusual character. Elliott realized that he had seen just such a glyph among the strange markings on the book in his grandfather's basement. Marvus crouched and felt along the border of a stone in the lower right corner of the wall. His hand was shaking.

The guard was halfway down the corridor toward them. "Stop what you're doing right now and surrender the susquat!" he shouted, clearly out of breath. "I don't care who you are—I'll shoot you where you stand!" He raised his crossbow, clumsily trying to aim as he lumbered toward them.

Marvus was working the big key into a narrow, barely noticeable crevice in the mortar. He turned it. Nothing happened. With a look of dismay, he turned and shook his head.

Elliott looked back. The guard was closing fast and had his

crossbow aimed in their direction. He fired on the run, and the quarrel struck the wall above their heads and broke.

"Some escape this is," said Hooks, turning to face the guard, who was fitting another quarrel to his crossbow. "This is what I get for counting on a gimlet."

Another guard rounded the corner. "You there—halt!" he screamed as the closer one drew the cocking lever back on his crossbow.

Frantic, Marvus jammed the key in the slit again, as deep as it would go, and turned it, This time a great screeching noise filled the hall as the entire section of wall began to move. When the door was exactly perpendicular to the wall from which it had sprung, Marvus shouted, "Go!" and pulled Elliott and then Hooks into the darkened passage. Without stopping, the door continued pivoting on its center until it completed a half turn, its stone edges meshing precisely once again into the wall.

In the dark, they could hear quarrels clattering off the opposite side of the wall, and the muffled profanities of the screaming guards. Elliott could hear Marvus and the susquat breathing heavily beside him. The chamber smelled of moisture and old dust. He was wondering what had become of Jingo when he heard a rustling of cloth beside him, then Marvus's voice.

"Light."

The princess's shamalan stone appeared in Marvus's open palm, glimmering with the greenish glow of a firefly, then quickly lighting up the chamber for several feet around them.

"Sorry I doubted you back there," said Hooks. "Looks like you got us out after all."

"Shut up," said Marvus.

Before them, illuminated by the light of the stone, the passageway branched in three directions. As if he knew precisely where he was going, Marvus struck out toward one, leading them down a stone staircase. Elliott, frightened by Marvus's tone with Hooks, didn't say anything as they walked. The others, too, kept silent as they weaved through the tunnels, with Marvus choosing the direction at every branching point. After a while, the crude stairs leveled off and they set off on a dirt trail. Except for the green glow of the stone, they were surrounded by blackness.

"We've reached the bottom," said Marvus.

They hurried along the underground trail for a while before coming to another stone wall. Marvus took out the weathered key and again felt along the bottom of the wall. Finding the crack, he wiggled the key into it, and the wall began to move.

As the gap in the wall widened, he said to Elliott, "Not many know of the mines beneath Mount Kalipharus. They're older than the castle itself."

When the door gap was wide enough, they went through to find themselves outside the mountain and looking out into the valley that lay between Mount Kalipharus and the Azure Mountains. Though dawn was near, the moon still shone feebly overhead, casting shadows across the mountains and into the wooded valley stretched before them. Rain pattered gently on the giant fern fronds above their heads.

Elliott heard a thunderous stomping of hooves, and turned to see the silhouettes of horsemen headed right at them. He turned to Marvus, wondering if they should duck back into the secret passage, or how else they might get away as, from the mountaintop, trumpets blasted the alarm.

Marvus looked up at the approaching horses and grinned. It was Jingo, thundering toward them on horseback and leading three more horses down the craggy mountain trail. Reaching the three fugitives, he pulled up and sat grinning before them.

"You did it!" Marvus said

"Yes. So did you."

Elliott goggled in amazement. "Where did you get them?

"Tied near the public square. These are the very horses that were to be used in the quartering of our troubled new friend." Jingo grinned at Hooks. "Now, hurry up, all of you," he said. "The whole castle is awake and coming after us."

Far above them, Elliott could see light in every window of the castle. He and Marvus each grabbed the reins of a horse and slid up onto its back, then waited for Hooks to do the same.

"I can't ride one of those things," Hooks said. "I'll break its back before we're halfway through the valley."

Marvus and Jingo looked perplexed.

"Just go," Hooks said. "I'll run alongside." And before they could protest, he loped off into the valley.

Luckily, riding was one of the few things Elliott's father had taught him, and bareback wasn't so different from saddled—he just had to sit low and move with his mount. Without a word, they kicked their horses and cantered after Hooks. Eventually, they caught up to him, and the four of them galloped up the valley in the shadow of Mount Kalipharus as the trumpets from the castle blared behind them.

Chapter 10

Viscount Ecsar

A dozen leagues north of Mount Kalipharus, Viscount Ecsar sat high on a hill outside Scopulus, watching from a distance as the remote enclave came to life in the early morning suns. The darfoyle, though similar in form to his grayfarer cousins, was much larger, and his great, scaly wings rose far above his head even when folded. Thus, he sat himself behind a great tree to conceal his dreaded silhouette from the gimlets of the town below. His thick talons scratched absently at the soil as he watched the unsuspecting gimlets go about their morning routines.

Behind the hill, hidden from the villagers, a horde of serpan warriors readied for attack, sharpening their blades and checking their saddles. The gimlet village lay less than three days' journey from Harwelden, and its conquest would provide another in the long line of stepping-stones that the serpans had captured on their march toward Mount Kalipharus. Soon enough, the castle itself would fall, and generations of war would come, at long last, to a glorious finish.

From behind Ecsar, a serpan warlord approached the hilltop. Ecsar eyed him suspiciously, flexing his wings as he stood to face him.

"What do you want?"

"It is almost time, my lord," said the warlord, casting his eyes toward the ground.

Ecsar stared at him. "Almost."

"My men will fight well for you, Viscount. We are pleased to have you as our new commander." His head remained bowed. "I want you to know that I won't stand in the way of your leadership."

Ecsar narrowed his eyes, and subtly extended his wings further. "I know you won't."

The warlord looked up at him. "The taking of the town promises to be a simple affair, my lord. We have been watching it in anticipation of your arrival. The grayfarers have had to withdraw their soldiers to Harwelden; the new strategy is working."

"Of course it is," Ecsar said. "The malus is no fool."

"And neither are you, my lord," said the warlord. "The killing of the shamalans has changed everything. Without their leadership, the enemy grows clumsy and complacent. We are grateful for your service and your vision. I look forward to serving under you."

The darfoyle viscount stared at him for a moment, then nodded.

The warlord looked him in the eye, and the tempo of his voice quickened. "May I ask about the status of the hunt for the Antiquitas Trident?"

Ecsar scowled. "I don't concern myself with such things," he said loftily, looking past the warlord as if he weren't there. "We have more pressing things to consider."

Ignoring the slight, the warlord said, "Before your arrival, I received a report that the trident's whereabouts remain unknown. They say the malus is bent on finding it at any cost. He believes it is the key to everything."

Ecsar grunted. "Malus Lothar has breathed life into the mongrel rabble of Vengala in ways I haven't seen before. His instincts for warfare against the empire are unassailable, but I don't share his belief in the promises of the old magic." He narrowed his eyes. "You should worry less about fables of the dark arts and more about the realities of war."

"Yes, my lord," said the warlord, raising an eyebrow. "But I will offer you some advice as well: be watchful of your comments. The malus holds close his allegiance to the old magic."

Their eyes met for a moment; then the warlord turned and walked back down the hill.

Ecsar adjusted his armor, tightening the breastplate, then loosening both pauldrons a little. Caressing his war hammer, he felt his heartbeat quicken, as it always did before battle.

Quietly, he left his hiding place behind the great tree and walked down the back of the hill. Though he was well known throughout Vengala for his individual victories against the shamalans, this was the first battle he would lead troops in, and he had yet to earn their loyalty and esteem. It was time to establish his leadership and prepare them for battle.

The legion of troops turned to face their new commander as he spread his wings behind him. The suns cast shadows, one dark and one faint, of his fearsome form onto the hillside behind him, precisely as he had planned.

"Today, brave serpans," he began, "we come to conquer Scopulus."

With one mighty voice, the troops, astride their warhorses, shouted their approval, raising their lances, blades, and war hammers above their heads. When their cheers died down, the viscount continued.

"On this glorious day, give praise to Valderon, for he holds your brave souls in the palm of his hand as you enter the battlefield." He looked over the troops, who seemed appropriately struck by his presence. "For generations, your peoples have starved while the enemy grew fat. On this day, your mothers and fathers continue their toil, farming weeds from the stone, while the enemy's grain molds in his storehouses. The empire takes everything from you, and they do it in the name of virtue as they follow their pagan gods."

The troops erupted in raucous cheers.

Ecsar's voice rose in intensity. "When they murder your children, they give thanks to their elders. When they burn down your homelands, they kneel to the forest in gratitude. But no more! This day we shall stand and fight. We shall take what is meant to be ours!"

With each pause in his speech, the troops shouted in unison.

"Mighty Valderon has foreseen our victory against the pagans who steal the food from our mouths," he said. He flapped his wings, rising a few feet above them, and hovered there, causing them to look up at him. "He leads us off the rock to which they have banished us, and out into the fertile world. He gives us victory in battle, and very soon we shall prevail. One day, the bounty of the Carafayan forests will fill your tables, and you will lick your fingers with gratitude as you fill your bellies with meat. Your children will thrive on the richness of these lands, and they will give praise to mighty Valderon for the sacrifice you make on this day."

Looking up at him, the troops cheered.

"The unnatural devils that rose from the seas in the olden times have been slaughtered. Soon the last of them shall be exiled forever to Hulgaar, and Valderon smiles on us for our efforts. Soon we will watch from within the walls of Harwelden as mighty Valderon reclaims his place among the living gods that once ruled this world. When our plan is fulfilled, the gimlets and men who have stolen food from your tables will carry your water, and the grayfarer dogs shall turn down your beds. The malus has decreed that it be so."

The serpan troops cheered again, shaking their weapons and holding them high.

Ecsar's voice rose in intensity. "This day we shall stand
and fight. We shall take what is meant to be ours!"

"So march into Scopulus on this glorious day. With each pagan cleansed, Valderon grows stronger. Those of you who fall today shall go to your maker with a smile on your lips. Antilia awaits you with arms open wide. If you are taken, you shall stand at the sides of your fathers in the afterlife, and they shall grant you dominion over worlds unseen. For your sacrifice, Valderon will make you gods in death. The Malus has decreed that it be so. Valderon himself has decreed it."

Even the horses grew restless as he spoke. Satisfied with his oratory's effect, he descended to the ground, flaring his wings and touching down at the base of the hill, and walked into the crowd. Wherever he trod, the troops scrambled to make room for him, looking at him with awe.

At the back of the line of troops, a squat young serpan sat his horse, watching his new commander with adoration. Because he was smaller than the other soldiers, Ecsar noticed him, and walked toward him.

"What is your name?"

The short serpan gasped, and his horse took a step backward. "I am Slipher, my lord." The soldiers beside him moved back to make room.

Ecsar stepped closer and looked him over, eyes pausing on his clubfoot. "Have you ever been in battle?"

Slipher's cheeks turned red, and he looked at the ground. "No. But I am ready to die for the malus." His eyes shone with zeal.

"Hmmm." Ecsar looked at him another moment, then turned and walked back to the front of the line as the soldiers nearest Slipher whispered and snickered.

When Ecsar reached the base of the hill, he lifted his war hammer from his belt and ascended into the skies. Raising the weapon above his head, he barked the command: "Forward! To Scopulus!"

The troops raised their weapons and kicked at their horses, following him down toward the town.

As Ecsar gained altitude, a small gimlet child in the town square turned and pointed up at him. Soon after, other gimlets in the square screamed and shouted. They scooped up their children and ran, though the child who had spotted him stood rooted, pointing up at him.

Grinning, Ecsar pointed back at him with his war hammer. And with his army screaming forward beneath him, he flew toward the defenseless town.

Chapter 11

Flight of the Susquat

Hooks howled with delight as they galloped across the sweeping plain of the valley. He hadn't run so fast or so far since he was a youth, and he was overjoyed to be free of the confines of his cell. Beside him rode Elliott and the two gimlets, hair flying in the cool morning breeze. The moment was triumphant. Without breaking stride, Hooks looked over his shoulder, toward Mount Kalipharus. To his dismay, a swarm of flapping grayfarers already darkened the sky above the castle, and it seemed the entire army of Harwelden was pouring down the mountain to give chase, spilling onto every trail like lava streaming from an unseen caldera. In the skies, the flocking grayfarers looked like a plague of insects at harvest, and he could hardly see the light of the rising suns through the mass of flapping wings. How could they have mobilized so quickly? He lowered his head, willing his legs to run faster. Ahead, the valley seemed an endless expanse, with the cover of the Azure Mountains still far in the distance.

As they raced through the valley, Jingo kicked at his mount, beckoning it to the front of the pack. "Follow me," he shouted, turning sharply to the right, leading the spare horse by its reins. He was now taking them due west, parallel to the base of Mount Kalipharus, into open valley terrain rather than toward the cover of the Azure Mountains. "What are you doing!" cried Hooks. "We need to head for the mountains! This is madness!"

The flocking grayfarers looked like a plague of insects. ...
Ahead, the valley seemed an endless expanse, with
the cover of the Azure Mountains still far in the distance.

"Trust me!" Jingo yelled back.

Though the mounted soldiers would take some time to descend the craggy mountain trails, the grayfarers, heading in a beeline for them, were gaining fast. Hooks strained to see if they held crossbows, and wondered whether they would really fire on Elliott and the gimlets. As if in reply, the first quarrel zipped into the ground barely three paces ahead of them. He turned to see the nearest of the grayfarers almost directly overhead and descending, probably to take better aim with their crossbows. Already, a stitch in his side made it painful to breathe, though the fear of recapture spurred him onward.

A second quarrel whizzed past Jingo's cheek and *thwip*ped into the ground. Hooks turned toward Jingo, wondering again why he wasn't heading toward the mountain terrain, where the trees and boulders would give them a fighting chance against the grayfarers. Perhaps he should split from the group and try to make his own way to freedom.

"This way!" Jingo yelled back at them. "Just a little farther."

Hooks looked to his left, scanning the perimeter of the Azure Mountains. He wasn't going back to the dungeons— he would rather die fighting. As more arrows sailed past them, closer and with increasing frequency, he decided to make a break for the mountains. Then suddenly, a deep, narrow ravine appeared on his left. He pulled to the right, stumbling, and nearly fell headlong into it. The tall grasses covering the valley plain had concealed it until they were nearly on top of it.

With the skill of a master horseman, Jingo moved his horses to the very edge of the ravine. Riding alongside it, he turned and nodded to the others before leaning back on his horse and giving it the reins, letting it pick its way down the steep slope. To Hooks, it looked as if the ground had just opened and swallowed them up.

Recognizing the hint of a plan, Hooks watched as Marvus and Elliott, too, directed their mounts to the edge of the ravine and vanished from sight. He looked to the foothills of the Azure Mountains, again weighing his chances alone. The grayfarers above were gaining with alarming speed. Already the swaying grasses hid his friends from sight, and to the north, the first wave of mounted soldiers had reached the valley and were thundering toward him. Deciding at last that he was safer following his companions, he stepped back to his left, looking for the path they had taken. But he had veered a few steps away, and for a moment he feared he had lost it. Then, almost beneath his feet, the ravine materialized again. He jumped down and ran westward, striving to catch up with the others. Above his head, the tall grasses blew lazily back and forth in the morning breeze, barely allowing the light of the suns into the hidden passage. Gasping for breath and pressing one hand to the stitch in his side, he lowered his head and ran.

⚑ ⚑ ⚑

By the time the fugitives reached the mountains, it was midday. They had been galloping along the narrow ravine for hours, perfectly hidden from sight. After many miles, the high walls fell away, and they stood on a stony beach by a pristine lake, in the shadows of the majestic mountain range. The skies above them were blue and empty, and the land behind them quiet.

"That was a close one," Jingo said, leading his horses to drink.

Marvus looked nervously eastward. "How did you know of the ravine?" he asked. "I've lived at the castle all my life and spent countless days in the valley beneath it, and I never saw that passage until you jumped headlong into it."

Jingo grinned. "I stumbled across it when I was a child, and I have followed it to this quiet lake many times. I suspected no one would know of it."

Still panting and holding his side, Hooks walked to the edge of the lake and dropped to his knees to drink. When he had drunk his fill, he lay on the beach until his breath slowed again.

"We still have a lot of daylight left, and they will be coming for us," Marvus said, scanning the skies for grayfarers. "They will figure out how we escaped."

"Quite right," Jingo said, looking east. It was eerily quiet.

Lying on the pebble beach, Hooks groaned. His legs hurt, and his side felt as if someone had left a dagger in it.

"So let's get going," Jingo said.

Chapter 12

Confusion at Harwelden

In the great hall of Harwelden Castle, the Grayfarer Council convened. Waldemariam could not recall a more troublesome day in his tenure as chancellor. Not even the fall of Prytania had shocked him so. He sat in silence at the table, forming in his mind the words he would use to address the council.

In a single ill-starred day, disasters had multiplied that would shape the future of the war. Scopulus had fallen. Marvus and Jingo, trusted stewards of the princess, had brazenly broken into his bedchamber, stolen the strange boy's possessions and the newly recovered bracelet of the nine clans, and freed the condemned beast from the dungeon. The serpans had captured Princess Sarintha at last. And now the boy himself was missing! It was not known whether he had survived the test or his corpse had been spirited away. A fourth had escaped Harwelden with the gimlets and the beast, but no one knew for certain whether it was truly the boy from the forest. Waldemariam stood. "A day of unparalleled importance this has been," he said.

The other six councilmen moaned in agreement.

"We should have foreseen the attack on Scopulus," he lamented. "Its fall drastically worsens our prospects. We should have had soldiers protecting the city." He walked to the window looking out over the benighted forest.

"We had no soldiers to send to Scopulus," said Councilman Baucus. "With due respect to the chancellor, why should we condemn ourselves for not having an army at Scopulus when we haven't enough soldiers to protect Harwelden?"

"It is true," said Councilman Landrew. "Even if we had been alerted to the planned attack, whom could we have sent? We have only two armies remaining. The gimlet army at Iracema cannot leave its post. If we had dispatched them southward, leaving Iracema unprotected, the serpans would have gained an even greater prize."

"And what of the army at Harwelden?" said Councilman Woolf. "I shudder to think what the serpans might have done had we ordered the forces of Harwelden northward to Scopulus. For the past four seasons, the serpans have anticipated our every move." He scanned his colleagues suspiciously, his gaze lingering on Councilmen Fanta and Oskar. "Sending our troops away from the castle would have been suicide. As soon as our soldiers leave the shadow of Harwelden, the enemy will be on us, and the castle will fall. I've no doubt they are privy to our every plan."

Waldemariam snorted. "And that really is the issue, isn't it? We can't even pursue an escaped prisoner to the base of the Azure Mountains without risking attack from the enemy. What has become of the glorious days of empire?" He paced before the window. "Scopulus is lost. We must focus our efforts on Iracema and Harwelden. It is only by holding this castle and the forest city that we shall remain viable."

"And what of the boy, Chancellor?" asked Councilman Alasdar.

"Yes," said Waldemariam, "what of the boy?" He cast his eyes to the floor. "I have personally questioned the dungeon guards about last night's events. They report that Marvus and Jingo entered the dungeon just before dawn. Another was with them, and one of the guards reports he had the markings of a shamalan."

"It must have been he," said Councilman Landrew. "And what would that mean? If the boy passed the test, then he is shamalan."

"And if the boy is shamalan," said Alasdar, interrupting Landrew, "we must think of the implications that arise from that fact, whatever his origins."

"We won't discuss any of that nonsense tonight," Waldemariam snapped, anxious to regain control of the discussion. "It's just as likely that the boy's corpse was fished from the testing chamber and hidden away, or that he was rescued before he succumbed to the drowning. I should have instructed the guards to stand watch over the chamber. It was careless of me . . ." He scanned the eyes of his colleagues. "Why shouldn't we conclude that a boy from the village traveled with the gimlets and the beast and that this whole event was staged to make us believe something that cannot be true? Your faith makes you vulnerable, Councilmen. Your belief in this shamalan gibberish makes you weak on the battlefield and plays to the enemy's strengths. The willingness to believe in this . . . this *prophecy* shall break us apart if we don't remain steadfastly allied to one another." He looked in particular at Woolf and Alasdar. "Tomorrow, I shall order a census of the village. We will take keen note of the young boys who live under our rule, and we shall locate the one who is missing. Aside from the princess, no shamalan inhabits these lands, and I won't be convinced otherwise until I see the child undergo the transformation with my own eyes." Waldemariam caressed the gold amulet that hung from a chain on his neck. "We will speak of this no more."

"But we *must* discuss it!" said Councilman Woolf. "Our shamalan nobles have spoken of the prophecy since before we were birthed. How do you so easily discard their teachings? And why would Marvus and Jingo stage the discovery of a shamalan in the forest? With all due respect, Chancellor, your words make no sense."

"I *said* we won't discuss it further tonight," Waldemariam growled. "We shall not rely on the fables of the shamalans or allow them to dampen our senses any longer. We are engaged in a mortal struggle against a formidable enemy." He slammed his fist on the windowsill. "We must face the possibility that Marvus and Jingo are the traitorous link that, as each of us knows, has been present within these castle walls for many seasons. Through their connection with the princess, they have been privy to every secret that has passed from our lips in the war room above, and with their actions tonight, they reveal themselves. They are enemies of Harwelden and shall be captured and punished for their treason."

"I, for one, do not believe that Marvus and Jingo are the traitors sending information to Mount Sitticus," said Alasdar. "In all their years, they have shown nothing but loyalty and service to Harwelden. What have they to gain from reporting our plans to the enemy?"

Councilmen Baucus, Landrew, and Woolf nodded in agreement.

"We will learn the answer to that question when they are captured," said Waldemariam. "The question for us to decide is how we will go about capturing them. The forces of the castle now rest safely within its walls, prepared to defend it from attack if necessary." He raised his eyebrows. "And who's to say the gimlets weren't *trying*, by their flight, to lead the armies of Harwelden away from the castle, leaving it unprotected from the enemy's advances? Why else would they free the condemned beast, who has little to do with the greater war? If this is their plot, we have wisely avoided its perils. With the castle's forces now back at their posts, we are safe for the moment. But we must make provisions for the capture of the gimlets, the susquat, and the boy, whoever he may be. With our armies unavailable for the search, it falls to this council to capture the criminals. The question is which of us it shall be." He looked at the six grayfarers sitting before him. "I am curious to hear from Councilmen Fanta and Oskar, who have remained silent so far." He looked to the only two members of the council whom he himself had appointed during his tenure as chancellor.

Fanta spoke first. "Though some of my colleagues may disagree with your theories, Chancellor, your words are prescient. I can think of no other reason why Marvus and Jingo would have broken into your room, stolen the bracelet of the nine clans, freed the susquat, and faked the boy's survival. If they are indeed the traitors who have been working against us, then an attempt to divert the forces of the castle, leaving it defenseless from attack, would be well explained."

Woolf tried to interrupt, but Fanta hushed him.

"Marvus and Jingo must want us to believe in the prophecy, to make it seem plausible. In doing this, they attempt to further weaken our defenses against the enemy. For if we believed that the prophecy reveals itself through this boy, would we not alter our strategy for warfare and defense? And if the boy is not shamalan, would that change in strategy not hasten our demise?"

"Ridiculous!" said Woolf. "Belief in the fulfillment of the prophecy will *strengthen* our army, not weaken it. You are foolish to believe otherwise."

Alasdar nodded, while Baucus and Landrew, both seated near the center of the table, seemed unsure what to think.

Waldemariam and Oskar scowled at Woolf. "Do not interrupt Councilman Fanta

again," said Waldemariam. "You shall extend him the same courtesy that he granted you."

"And finally," said Fanta, ignoring Woolf's scoffing, "the susquat's rescue also becomes reasonable when we think of Marvus and Jingo as the traitors. Only by freeing the susquat could they inflame the castle's forces against them, luring the armies of Harwelden away from their posts. It is fortunate that Chancellor Waldemariam had the wisdom to recall the armies rather than allow them to pursue the criminals hither and yon, for they might have led us into a disastrous ambush. Alternatively, an attack force might have been hiding in the forest, prepared to attack the castle while our forces were out pursuing the traitorous gimlets. We must remain steadfast in our protection of Harwelden, especially now that Scopulus has fallen, and we must take action against Marvus and Jingo, who would sabotage us at every turn. I, for one, would be honored to lead the hunt to capture them."

Waldemariam beamed. "And what have you to say, Councilman Oskar?"

"Of course," said Oskar, "I agree with everything Councilman Fanta has said."

"Very well, then," said Waldemariam, "it is settled. Fanta and Oskar shall leave Harwelden in the morning to search for the criminals." He turned and smiled at them. "We shall hold you in our thoughts as you go to protect the mighty name of Harwelden."

"No," said Woolf, standing. "I don't believe for a moment that Marvus and Jingo are traitors to Harwelden. And I think we must consider the possibility that the boy from the forest may be what he appears. If the princess were here, this discussion would not even be taking place."

Alasdar nodded in Woolf's support.

"But the princess is not here," barked Waldemariam. "And it is quite likely that she won't be returning. The whole of Harwelden now follows my lead, and you would do well to remember that, Councilman."

Though seething with anger, Woolf spoke in measured tones. "If you want a member of this council to go and find Marvus and Jingo, then I shall go and find them."

"Fine," said Waldemariam, looking at Woolf with a degree of contempt. "It will be Woolf *and* Fanta who shall go after the gimlets. In the morning, the two of you will take leave of Harwelden and set out for the Azure Mountains to search for the traitors. I suggest that each of you get a good night's rest—the days ahead will be difficult."

⚜ ⚜ ⚜

Later that night, inside his chamber, Councilman Woolf readied his belongings for the journey, then took flight from his window. Circling the valley behind Mount Kalipharus, he scoured the ground with his eyes. Suddenly, he swooped downward and caught a large rat in his talons. Careful not to injure the little beast, which squealed in protest at its capture, he climbed again into the night sky and checked his surroundings. Satisfied that no one had seen him, he flew back to his bedchamber, where, still holding the protesting rat gently in his claws, he went to his dresser and retrieved a small bag of fine white powder from his drawer. Gingerly he retrieved a pinch of powder from the bag and sprinkled it over the chattering rat.

The rat sneezed.

Holding it by the nape of its neck, Woolf stared at it.

The rat continued to chatter, and as Woolf looked on, the pitch of the chattering began to change. At first it sounded entirely alien. Then, thanks to the dab of kaphis powder that Woolf had kept hidden away for a score of seasons, the alien chatter slowly turned into recognizable speech. Woolf could understand everything the beast was saying.

"Put me down at once," it said. "This is an outrage. I demand to be returned to my nest this instant."

Woolf grinned.

"My brothers and I will visit a plague on this whole city if you don't return me to my nest at once," it said. "You've no idea of the damage a plague of rats can bring. Consult your scrolls if you doubt my veracity. The rats are a mighty enemy and not to be trifled with." It bared its four yellowish teeth.

Still grinning as he held the outraged rat by the nape, Woolf asked, "what is your name, friend?"

"I will divulge no information to the enemy!" said the rat. "You are in direct violation of the treaty of Rasmussen. Repatriate me or suffer mightily."

"Oh?" Woolf said, still grinning. "I was aware of no such treaty."

"Well, then, you'd better consult your castle's bylaws, knave! You have no right to harass me like this. This is kidnapping."

"Let us begin again, friend," said Woolf. "I am Woolf, a sitting member of the Grayfarer Council, and I mean you no harm. What is your name?"

For the first time since its capture, the rat fell silent. Then, hesitantly, it said, "A member of the Grayfarer Council, are you? Can this be true?"

"It is," said Woolf, smiling.

"Please accept my apologies for calling you a knave," said the rat. "I beg for your mercy. I have a family. My mate has just birthed a litter of pups. Please grant me your leniency."

"I mean you no harm, friend. Now, what is your name?"

"I am Taldar, elder of the vermin clan of the field."

"You hold a position of importance among your kind, then?" Woolf queried.

"I am a watchman, first line of defense against birds of prey."

Woolf chuckled. "Then I consider myself lucky to have caught you."

"Please accept my apologies for calling you a knave," said the rat. "I beg for your mercy. I have a family. My mate has just birthed a litter of pups. Please grant me your leniency."

Taldar blushed.

"I have brought you here because I must ask for your help," said Woolf. I request your participation in a secret operation that may play a role in the salvation of the empire."

Taldar's ears perked up. "I'm listening, grayfarer."

"If you are wondering how you have suddenly developed the ability to communicate with a grayfarer, it is because I have dusted you with an enchanted powder. King Gregorus himself gave me the powder several seasons before his demise.

Taldar blushed again. Apparently, it had not occurred to him that he should not be able to speak to a grayfarer, and he was embarrassed not to have noticed it. "My clan and I enjoyed good relations with the king," said Taldar. "Before his death, that is. His daughter, Sarintha, has yet to make contact with us."

"Is that so?" said Woolf, raising an eyebrow. "Perhaps we can talk more about that in the future."

"I suppose," said the rat. "I believe I am authorized to speak to a member of the council."

"In any event," Woolf continued, masking his surprise, "what I propose is this: I want to ask you to be my eyes in the castle as I begin a search of the wilderness to the south."

"I'm still listening," said Taldar.

"I will place around your neck a pendant with an enchanted stone. Around my own neck, I will wear a matching stone. This will allow you to know my whereabouts at all times."

"Yes, I am familiar with such magic," said Taldar.

Again Woolf raised an eyebrow, though he did not mention his surprise. "We will embark on a journey at sunrise. I will fly, naturally, and you will follow me as best you can on the ground below. It will be hard for you to keep up with me, but I want you to make contact from time to time. When I have not heard from you in a while, I will remain camped in one spot, when possible, so that you might reach me and we can exchange counsel."

"And I suppose you want me to keep tabs on Harwelden through a chain of communications with my kindred on the ground?"

"I must confess my surprise at your detailed knowledge of my plan," said Woolf. "I was not aware that such a strategy had been used in the past."

"So what do I get in return?" Taldar asked. "As I said, I have a new litter of pups to worry about."

"If our plan is successful, I will find a nice place in the castle for you and your family to build a nest. A place near the kitchen would be nice, I suppose, and I will ensure the safety of you and yours within the castle at all times."

"That would be a dream come true," replied Taldar. "No more worrying about freezing to death in the winter, or getting eaten by serpents or birds of prey."

"Yes," Woolf said, "I can promise a nice life for you and your family—that is, if we succeed."

"But it will be dangerous," said Taldar. "You are asking me, a new father, to leave the safety of my nest and leave my family unprotected. I will be exposed to the elements and the beasts of the wild. I may well lose my life."

"That is so," said Woolf. "Is this a risk you are willing to take? I must be able to rely on you. I prefer that you tell me now if you are not up to the task."

"Can you ensure daily feedings upon my installment in the castle? I expect that a rat who has gone to such great risk and sacrifice would not be expected to scavenge."

"I will guarantee daily feedings on one condition," said Woolf.

"What's that?"

"I will also ask that you seek information on the group I am hunting. They consist of a condemned susquat, two gimlets of Harwelden, and a shamalan boy."

"So it is true," Taldar gasped. "The shamalan boy is real."

"You are an amazing little creature, Taldar. Do we have an agreement?"

"We do. I am at the service of Harwelden. I will risk my life for the cause of the empire."

Woolf smiled. Setting Taldar on the top of his dresser, he pulled from a drawer a cloth sack, and from this he withdrew two bejeweled pendants. He placed the first of these around his own neck and, after adjusting the thong holding the second, he fitted it around Taldar's neck.

"Can you take me back down to the field now?" Taldar asked. "I have many preparations to make. This is rather short notice you've given me."

"I would be happy to oblige," said Woolf. "I think this is the beginning of a very productive relationship."

"I'm going to hold you to your word," said Taldar. "Installation in the castle with daily feedings for my family and me, and protection against cats and exterminators . . . and cooks. Now, I have to get back to my nest."

"You have my word, Taldar," said Woolf. And gently picking up his unlikely little ally, he flew him back to the field and released him, bidding him farewell for the time being, and returned to his room. After checking his kit and weaponry one last time, he blew out the candles and took to his bed. As he drifted off to sleep, he marveled at the revelations of Taldar the rat. Who could have supposed that a rodent from the field below would have such a keen knowledge of goings-on at Harwelden?

Early the next morning, Woolf met with his traveling companion, Councilman Fanta, and the two shared a light breakfast of steak and mead before flying from the roof of the western tower. Few words passed between them as they soared toward the chain of mountains. Woolf bided his time, waiting for the proper moment to take his leave of Fanta so that he might be first to reach the four fugitives.

Chapter 13

Slipher

Slain gimlets lay sprawled across the cobbled walkways lining the central market of Scopulus. Slipher limped through the litter of corpses, favoring his clubfoot and periodically leaning over a body to rifle the pockets for valuables. All around him, fellow serpan warriors did the same. With the battle won, it was time to reap the spoils. Though Malus Lothar frowned on the plunder of corpses—he thought the practice reflected a lack of discipline in his troops—the viscounts and warlords largely ignored the behavior. Such looting of the dead was a throwback to the days when the warlords ruled the hordes, and indeed, it served as a powerful motivator to the conquering serpan troops, who used the plunder to supplement their salaries and help support their families back home.

The battle for Scopulus was Slipher's first real test, for he was new to the battlefield. Because of his youth and inexperience, as well as his deformity, he had been relegated to the back of the pack as the fight got under way. It began and ended quickly, and by the time he reached the heart of the city, there was little for him to do, for the warriors of the front lines had done their job well. Distraught, he had rifled the pockets of one corpse after another, only to find that others had already stripped them of their valuables. Not only had he failed to kill a gimlet, he feared that he would come away empty-handed and return to Vengala not only in shame but broke, too. As he stood in the central square pondering his options, a group of elder warriors walked past him, their pockets jingling with gold coins. Slipher's hand went to his own pockets, which remained empty.

"What have we here?" said one, tousling Slipher's thick mane of hair. "The cripple looks about to cry."

The warriors laughed. "Don't you know that you must actually *slay* a gimlet to take a share of the spoils?" said another. "You can't expect to just march in here and empty the pockets of an enemy felled by someone else. You must *earn* your bounty, runt." One of them poked him hard in the shoulder.

"How did you get into the army anyway?" asked another, staring at his deformed foot. "Have the warlords become so desperate that they accept cripples on the battlefield? Why, you're scarcely bigger than a gimlet!" This met with more laughter. As they walked past him toward the gate, one of them turned for a final insult. "Go back home to your mama. There is no place for a runt on the serpan battlefield. Leave the fighting to those who can swing a war hammer, and go back to your farm."

Slipher felt the blood rush to his face. He had joined the army with great expectations. For months, he had imagined what he might achieve during his first chance at battle. He so wanted to make a name for himself and prove himself as a fighter despite his small stature, but things were not going as planned. As always, his dreams of becoming important kept bumping into reality. He knew he had to do something or face the continued torment of his countrymen.

Nursing his hurt feelings, he decided to poke around inside some of the buildings that had not burned. He couldn't return home without finding *something*, for among his people this indicated a lack of prowess. It was also the sign of a coward.

Sticking his hands in his empty pockets, he headed toward a building across the square just as Viscount Ecsar, his new commander, flapped his great wings and hovered above the central square.

Like the others, Slipher turned to behold the magnificent darfoyle commander, hanging in the air by his great scaled wings, the glare of the midday suns streaming from behind him. Ecsar's shadow fell over the young serpan, and he stood transfixed.

The darfoyle looked out over the soldiers and grinned a toothy grin. "Be proud, brave troops," he said, "for today you have exiled the vermin of this foul enclave forever to Hulgaar, where they will pay for their greed with suffering beyond measure." His eyes gleamed scarlet.

Forgetting his troubles for the moment, Slipher stared slack-jawed at the viscount. He thought the darfoyles a magnificent race.

"Because of your efforts on the battlefield today, the weakest among us in Vengala will soon reap the bounty of the forests, and the influence of the shamalans will be forever expunged from these lands. Your children will sing songs in praise of the noble works you achieved this day."

Slipher cheered, and the fire of zeal lit his eyes as he stood shoulder to shoulder with his comrades, in the shadow of their commander.

"And it is only the beginning for us," Ecsar continued. His voice softened. "For I have received word from Malus Lothar of our next assignment. We shall move farther south, toward the Forest of Ondor and Mount Kalipharus itself."

Slipher gasped, giddy at the thought that they were actually going to Ondor.

"We will build a base camp at the northern tip of the forest, within two days' journey of Harwelden. As the season draws near its end, we will be joined by legions of fellow warriors in preparation for our final assault. Before the next season begins, Harwelden will be within our grasp, and the armies housed within it will lie dead at the end of our blades. Soon this ancient war will fade to memory as our farmers work these rich lands and our children play in the shade of the great trees of Ondor. All this has been foreseen by the malus and by his lord, Valderon, who rises from the shadows to guide us to victory."

Slipher's face glowed with ecstasy.

"So hold your heads high on this glorious day," Ecsar said. "For your sacrifice, Valderon smiles upon you." He lowered himself to the ground as a roar of approval rose up from the soldiers and rang over the destroyed town.

Slipher gasped at the thought. The prospect of establishing a base camp at the outskirts of Ondor was both exciting and historic. Never before had such a bold endeavor been considered. Now, under the guidance of Viscount Ecsar, a direct extension of Malus Lothar himself, he was to play a key role in what would become the most consequential military campaign in the history of Pangrelor.

The troops, still wading through the carnage of the day's slaughter, laughed and slapped each other on the back as if they had just prevailed in a sporting match. Basking in the presence of his new commander, Slipher was overcome with emotion as he mulled the idea of helping build a base camp in the enemy's front yard. He felt renewed. He would become a great warrior. Perhaps one day they would sing songs about him in the fields of Vengala.

With renewed purpose, he headed for the building at the end of the square, on the hunt for booty. He entered through the front door of what appeared to be a temple.

Though the temple contained fine rugs and carved benches and altars, it was already picked clean of anything easily carried. A large coffer at the front of the room was overturned and emptied, and candles lay scattered on shelves and floors, stripped of their silver and gold holders.

Frustrated, Slipher turned to leave. But as he moved toward the door, he spotted something: a tuft of blond hair sticking out from behind the altar. Someone else was in the room, and it was not a fellow serpan.

Slipher brandished his sword in front of him. "Who's in here?"

No answer.

"Show yourself, and I shall end your life mercifully," he said, his voice quivering.

Still no answer, and the tuft of hair didn't move.

Steeling himself, he stepped cautiously toward the altar, blade at the ready. "I said show yourself."

Stopping after only a few steps, he picked up a candle from the floor and threw it, hitting the edge of the altar with a loud *thunk*.

With growing confidence, he came closer. As he neared the front of the huge, elaborately carved altar, he sidestepped in a broad, arcing path, giving it a wide berth.

"I'll cut you open like a dog," he said, his voice growing stronger as the lifeless form behind the altar came into view.

Behind the edifice lay a dead gimlet. A broken arrow shaft protruded from his chest, and his glazed eyes stared lifelessly at the frieze below the ceiling. He wore a flowing white tunic, now spattered with blood, indicating his station as some sort of holy man or priest.

Slipher let out a long sigh of relief and lowered his blade. Did priests carry coin? After cautiously kicking the corpse, he laid his sword on the altar and knelt beside the slain priest. To his chagrin, the pockets on either side of the tunic held no coins, so he patted down the body in an effort to glean something— anything—from his find. Outside, the setting suns sent their last rays blazing through the stained-glass windows.

Just as Slipher was about to give up, he noticed a slight bulge underneath the slain gimlet's tunic. Through the fabric, it felt like a small box. Perhaps the gimlet had tried to hide it in the moments before his death. Pulling the tunic roughly aside, Slipher discovered a small, oblong package wrapped in gold foil and tied with a silken ribbon. A gift, perhaps.

Inside the box, he found a small silver mirror and a smoking pipe carved from pale green stone. Next to the pipe was a bag of tobacco. A handwritten note read, *For my dear boy, Pongo. May all your days be filled with enchantment and wonder. Happy birthday, my beloved son.*

Slipher turned the note over and discarded it. Undoubtedly, Pongo had not survived the morning and had not had a very happy birthday at all. That the attack had happened on the boy's birthday struck Slipher as funny, and he chuckled, imagining the brat's horror when he saw a screaming horde of serpans coming for him. He wished he could have seen it—it would help make up for the fact that a rather unremarkable-looking mirror and a pipe were his only mementos of the Battle for Scopulus. Shoving them into his pocket, he poked around some more but found nothing of any value that he could carry away with him.

He reached for the temple door, then paused. Through the stained-glass window, he saw the familiar silhouette of Viscount Ecsar, standing on the flagstones outside the door and talking to the serpan warlord.

Slipher backed away from the door and slid to the floor. He would wait until they left before going outside. It was hot in the temple, and sweat trickled down his belly, so he took off his leather vest and set it beside him on the altar. Then, gingerly so as not to alert the viscount to his presence, he set his blade on top of the vest.

He hadn't *intended* to eavesdrop exactly, but the viscount's conversation just happened to reach him clearly where he sat.

"Indeed, it went well today," said the warlord. "The malus will be pleased when he hears of our swift victory. Scopulus will make a nice prize."

Inside the box, Slipher found a small silver mirror
and a smoking pipe carved from pale green stone.

"Yes," Ecsar agreed. "And he shall hear of it soon. After midday, when the battle had clearly fallen in our favor, I met with Viscount Erebus, who came from Obsidia to check on our progress. As we speak, Erebus flies to Vengala to inform the malus of our triumph."

Listening from inside the temple, Slipher grinned. He wished he could have seen the notorious Viscount Erebus. Somehow, being on the same side as the darfoyles gave him a feeling of strength and worth.

"Erebus has been in contact with our ally from Harwelden and has told me of a strange occurrence this morning at the enemy's castle."

"I did not know we had an ally at Harwelden," said the warlord.

Ecsar ignored the comment. "It seems a boy has surfaced who bears the markings of a shamalan. He was tested in the usual fashion, and he has passed. Our ally could not explain whence the boy came, but knew for certain that he was not of the royal bloodline."

"Oh, my," said the warlord.

"Exactly," Ecsar replied. "We know only that the boy's whereabouts are unknown to the authorities at Harwelden. I am not aware of the details, but the Grayfarer Council has declared him an enemy of the realm. Waldemariam has dispatched two of his own council members to capture the boy and return him to Harwelden."

"An unknown shamalan appears at Harwelden and they declare him an enemy of the empire? Curious," said the warlord.

"Though Malus Lothar will want the boy dealt with, I will stay with the army for now," Ecsar said. "We will wait to hear how the grayfarers deal with him."

"We would be sad to see you go."

"Walk with me to the supply shed on the outskirts of town. We need to see what is held there, and make arrangements for our departure." Ecsar's voice trailed off as he walked away from the temple.

After the two had moved a few paces toward the town center, Slipher could no longer eavesdrop, so he left the temple and recrossed the square.

Night was falling, and most of the warriors had left the town—with pockets full of treasure, no doubt—for their camp on the outskirts of town. Dejectedly Slipher made his way to the camp, where the smells of cooking meat replaced the stench of congealed blood that had been in his nostrils since morning. Drawing near the encampment, he heard the drunken laughter of his victorious comrades as they regaled one another with stories of the day's slaughter. Off in the distance, he could see some of his fellow warriors sitting around their fires with bags of plunder in front of them, showing off handfuls of gold coins or fine metal trinkets. As shame prevailed over hunger, he detoured around the edge of the camp, deciding to stay away until his colleagues were asleep. Eventually, he reached the hill where they had hidden this morning before the attack. He gathered some wood, struck a spark from his tinderbox, and, with a warm blaze going, leaned back against the hillside and looked into the starry night. In the distance, the warriors' raucous voices grew louder. It would be a long while before he could return to the encampment without fear of ridicule.

With his stomach growling, he reflected on the day's events. While every warrior in the squadron was participating in the merriment back at camp, he had managed to end the day in embarrassment. Typical. Gazing into the stars, he began to sob. His dreams of returning home as a wealthy conquering hero were shattered.

Patting his vest pocket in case a bit of jerky had gone unnoticed, he felt the unfamiliar lump of the little pipe and mirror. He filled the pipe with tobacco from the pouch and lit it with a stick from the fire. As he puffed, his thoughts slowly turned to the viscount and the conversation regarding the unknown shamalan who had surfaced at Harwelden.

It was common knowledge in Vengala that a few darfoyles had annihilated nearly all the shamalans who had survived the Great Betrayal, murdering legions of them, including King Gregorus himself. It was also widely known that Princess Sarintha was the only remaining shamalan in all Pangrelor. So where had this new shamalan come from? And what did his presence mean for the war? Slipher puffed on the pipe, pondering the implications. And as he puffed, the tobacco seemed to sooth him, and a feeling of serenity came over him.

Like all in Vengala, he knew of the prophecies. The Scrolls of Ondor had foreseen the annihilation of the shamalans and the ensuing slide into chaos. In vague terms, the scrolls told of the rise of a great and powerful enemy who would rise up against the shamalan motherland, raining destruction on the ancient race and ushering in a new age. Indeed, back in Vengala Slipher had often listened in awe as the conquering Malus Lothar regaled the people with passages from the shamalan scrolls about the promising future that awaited the Northern Hordes under his command.

But Slipher knew that the scrolls of Ondor also contained passages not referenced by the malus. In the dark corners of taverns and in the privacy of bedchambers back in Vengala, some were bold enough to whisper that the scrolls also mentioned a shamalan hero—a champion who would rise to avenge his slain race and restore order to a lost empire, casting out the serpans once again from the bountiful lands of the shamalan kingdom and restoring peace to the empire by reuniting the Antiquitas Trident. Before this happened, however, the greatest of all wars would unfold, and all races would suffer terribly. Finally, the enemies that had risen against the shamalans would be slain, exiled to eternal torment in Hulgaar. If the prophecies were true, then this unknown shamalan boy was a threat to the serpans' cause, and a threat to Malus Lothar as well.

Slipher felt himself growing calmer with each puff of his newly acquired pipe. Down in the camp, his comrades' boisterous singing and cheering grew louder yet, but Slipher sank deeper into his own thoughts and no longer cared about his failed quest for booty or the respect of his peers. His thoughts were on the shamalan boy. Somehow, his vision grew sharper, and the air smelled a little sweeter. Though a chill filled the air, he felt warm. Over and over he pondered the shamalan prophecy and its implications for the remainder of the war.

Then suddenly, it hit him: He must find the shamalan boy and kill him. Ecstasy gripped him as he thought of hunting the boy. In his mind's eye, he stood over him, plunging a blade into him over and over while the boy begged for mercy. He pictured himself standing between Malus Lothar and Viscount Ecsar in Vengala while crowds of admirers hailed him as the savior of his people. Images of grandeur flashed through his mind like pictures in a storybook. All around him, the air seemed thicker and more fragrant, and the stars shined more brightly.

Again he inhaled from the pipe. In a copse of trees a few paces away, the leaves vibrated and danced before his eyes. *That's the energy of life,* he thought. *The trees know what I'm thinking.* The bark of the trees also changed, dripping slowly toward the ground like wax dripping down a candle. It occurred to Slipher that the trees were trying to tell him something. He breathed in the fragrant air, tasting it in his lungs and thinking that he had never felt so good in all his life.

Just then he thought of the mirror in his pocket. He took it out and gazed into it. The face he saw there was his own, but somehow better, more handsome . . . and stronger.

"*Kill the shamalan boy,*" said his reflection.

Slipher winced and dropped the mirror.

The handsome reflection laughed. *"Do not be afraid, Slipher,"* it said. *"For I am you. Or, rather, I am who you shall become.*

Slipher stared at the reflection, nonplussed. "You can't be talking to me," he said. "You are only a reflection."

"Ahhh," said the reflection. *"True enough. But I am a reflection of what lies inside you."*

"Impossible," said Slipher, puffing again on the pipe.

"Listen to me!" said the reflection. *"It is time to shed your insecurities and take matters into your own hands."*

"What do you mean?" asked Slipher.

"While you sit and lament that you were unable to scavenge a few coins from the dead today, your chance at greatness lay beneath your very nose. And there it still is!" The reflection laughed at him. *"Go and hunt the boy. Seek your fortune, and you shall find it. You are smarter than your colleagues down in the camp, and your abilities are far greater. Do not be afraid to think of great things, Slipher. Great deeds are what you are destined for."* The reflection grinned at him.

Slipher dropped the mirror to his side. He no longer heard the drunken jeers coming from the encampment. Again he filled his lungs with smoke and looked toward the little stand of trees. Their leaves vibrated faster, more urgently. He looked into the mirror again.

"Save the malus from destruction," said the reflection. *"Deliver your kindred from harm. Make your place in the world, Slipher."*

He slumped. "I will do as you say," he said to his reflection. "I will find and kill the shamalan boy. But how will I find him?"

"You hold the answer in your hand, young one," said the reflection. *"Finish your pipe, and it will reveal the path you must follow."* In the copse of trees ahead, the leaves suddenly grew still. The bark was firm.

Looking out into the darkness, Slipher saw the lines of the landscape with more clarity than he would have thought

possible. Following the mirror's instructions, he pulled deeply from the pipe and exhaled a large puff of smoke. *What now?* he thought, holding the pipe between his teeth.

As if in answer to his question, the puff of smoke began to take form, organizing itself into a moving picture, which showed a Susquatanian beast leading two mounted gimlets and a boy through a mountain passage. The figures were rendered in astonishingly fine detail from billows of gray smoke. As Slipher watched, the figures began to decrease in size, becoming tiny in scale with the wilderness surrounding them, which also shrank. The smoke showed him the whole of the mountain they were crossing, with the fugitives represented as tiny figures moving along a mountainside trail. Then, as the picture continued to shrink, the single mountain grew smaller, so that he could see the entire chain of mountains. Finally, the scene depicted an entire mountain range, bordered on its northern tip by a grand mountain, atop which sat a magnificent stone castle—Harwelden, atop Mount Kalipharus. Above the mountains, immediately south of Mount Kalipharus, far away from the shamalan boy and his friends, two tiny winged creatures flew wide circles in the sky, peering down into the mountains. The puff of smoke then evaporated into nothingness.

He's in the Azure Mountains, thought Slipher. He sucked at the pipe again, exhaling another large cloud of smoke. The scene replayed in identical fashion, except that this time the susquat was speaking to one of the gimlets and pointing southward. Slipher held the pipe up to the firelight, marveling at what it had revealed. *I have been chosen,* he thought. *With these tools, I will locate the shamalan boy, and I will destroy him.*

Feeling suddenly tired, he stuffed the pipe and mirror back in his pocket and curled up by the fire to doze, smiling as he pictured himself standing over the corpse of the slain shamalan boy.

He awoke late the next morning with a headache. He was confused, for he was completely alone and the suns were high in the sky, signaling midday. As if remembering a dream, he recalled last night's events, including his communication with his reflection and the smoky pictures of the boy in the mountains. With panic twisting his gut, he walked around the base of the hill and stared at the bare piece of land where his squadron had camped. Everyone was gone. By strict serpan definition, he was now a deserter.

Feeling as if he might vomit, he considered his options. In the light of the new day, the revelations of last night seemed much less profound. Far more immediate was the reality that deserting one's unit was punishable by torture and death. And his was not just any squadron. Viscount Ecsar was his commander.

Rubbing his temples with both hands, Slipher tried to organize his murky thoughts into a plan. He could try to locate the company and sneak back into their ranks, but this was a risky proposal, for he was likely to be caught, and Viscount Ecsar was not known for his tolerance or clemency. Even if he explained that he had fallen asleep on the outskirts of the base camp and accidentally missed the departure of his colleagues, he would still be in mortal peril. He had heard tell of warriors being executed for just such a lapse. In fact, the warlord may already have been informed when he failed to return to camp last night. Unwittingly, he had committed the gravest of crimes.

Feeling the lump in his pocket, he cursed the trinkets and began to sob. He had thrown away his future and forever shamed his family. Broken, he sat on the ground and sobbed unabashedly, rocking back and forth. Over and over, through heaving sobs, he repeated to no one, "I didn't mean to do it."

Over time, his sobbing lessened, his rocking ceased, and again he noticed the lump in his pocket. After much time had passed, he settled on the only plan available to him. He would travel to the Azure Mountains to find the boy.

Feeling low, he walked into Scopulus to look for supplies. Most importantly, he needed to find a horse.

After a half day's search through the dead city, he found very little in the way of supplies. A raid of the town's supply hut yielded only a few bits of dried fruit, and in a field near the edge of town he found a lone donkey, wandering aimlessly near a cabin that housed a slain family of gimlet farmers. In the whole of the city there wasn't a single horse.

After much coaxing, he managed to befriend the donkey by feeding him bits of the dried fruit. "I will call you Pongo," he said, rubbing it gently on the neck. "You and I are going on a great journey."

In the farmhouse, he found a saddle and halter. After carefully saddling his new companion, he decided that his last remaining task before leaving the city was to find a weapon and armor. Though he remembered having his blade and vest with him in the temple yesterday, he had not been able to locate them all morning. Remembering his fruitless search of the town square yesterday, he decided immediately that he was not going to search the city for a blade. After a time, he located the hasty graves of the only three serpan warriors killed in the battle for Scopulus. With his hands, he dug up the grave nearest him and stripped the corpse of its leather armor, shield, and sword. Though the sword was too heavy and the armor too large, he put it on and mounted his donkey. Now, he reflected as he tightened the stinking leather vest around his chest, he could add grave robbing and desecration of the dead to his crimes. Though he would have looked comical to anyone who chanced to see him, no one could question the resolve on his face. His only salvation lay in ridding the malus of the threat posed by the shamalan boy.

Mounting the donkey and gently spurring him onto the trail, he held his back straight in an effort to look regal as he left the deserted town. *Beware, young shamalan,* he thought, *for I know how to find you.* And off he rode for the Azure Mountains.

Chapter 14

Through the Azure Mountains

Elliott stood on a craggy shelf, well beneath the summit but just high enough to see the snow-dusted peaks rising in tier after tier behind him. He gazed across the vast range, trying to orient himself, and finally saw Mount Kalipharus, now a mere speck on the horizon. In the three weeks since escaping Harwelden, they had traveled far, and the mountain terrain seemed to grow wilder with every league of distance. With his breath forming plumes of fog before him, Elliott hugged himself for warmth, examining the endless expanse and wondering how much longer he would have to endure the cold, thin mountain air. Marvus and Jingo, standing beside him, rubbed their hands together, trying to ward off the icy breeze that whistled down the mountainside.

Peering down at the trail, Elliott said, "How long has he been gone? If we don't get going soon, we won't make it down to the valley before nightfall—we'll freeze to death up here."

"Right you are," Marvus said. "That loathsome susquat is going to be the death of us. I have really begun to question our judgment in traveling with him."

"He just went to look for food," Jingo insisted. "He's coming back."

Marvus scowled. "Every time he takes his leave, I fear we've seen the last of him. I do not trust that stinking beast."

From behind them, Elliott heard the horses snorting and stamping against the stony terrace. He wondered what had gotten into them, and hoped he had tied them well. But just as he got up to check on them, Hooks appeared on the trail, a strangled opilion over his shoulder.

"There he is," Jingo said, giving Marvus a reproachful glare. "I'll gather some kindling."

Hooks walked up, grinning, and dropped the opilion at their feet. "I don't know about you three," he said, "but I'm starving." He looked to Marvus, perhaps for a word of thanks, when a low growl came from the trail behind him.

Elliott tensed and jerked his head to the sound. "What was that! Did you guys hear that?"

"What was *what*?" said Marvus, looking hungrily at the opilion. "Jingo, strike a fire."

The horses, picketed in the clump of grass beside the trail, began to whinny and pull at their tethers. Elliott noticed that their ears were lying back, and an uneasy feeling settled over him.

Ignoring the horses, Jingo dropped his hastily collected armload of kindling at Marvus's feet and knelt, eyeing the fat opilion. "This is going to make a feast!" he said. "My mouth is watering already."

Hooks looked down the trail, cocking his head to the side and listening.

The growl came again—deep, gravelly, and ill-boding. Elliott scooted closer to Hooks. "What *was* that?" he whispered.

Hooks sniffed at the air. Staring ahead, he pushed Elliott behind him.

This time the gimlets had heard it, too. The opilion forgotten, they huddled around Hooks.

On the trailhead in front of them, an immense, snarling black wolf slunk into sight. Pulling back its lips, it gave a low, guttural snarl and laid back its ears, holding its head low to the ground, watching them.

Elliott's breath caught in his throat. The wolf was the size of a full-grown jaguar—certainly too monstrous for any of them to tangle with.

"Don't move," Hooks whispered.

The wolf's eyes glowed with malice. It licked at its snout and raised its head.

Elliott had never felt more afraid. His mouth was as dry as cotton, and he began to breathe fast, as he often did when afraid. With his mind spinning, he stared ahead, scared to move a muscle, hoping somehow that the predator might lose interest and leave them alone.

Movement in the rocks and brush below the trail materialized into six more wolves, slinking up to join their leader.

Elliott glanced sideways and saw that his companions, like him, were frozen, though he rather wished someone looked as if he knew what to do next. Behind him, the horses whinnied frantically, and he heard the snap of a branch and more stamping of hooves. The horses were in such a furor that for a moment Elliott thought they might draw the wolves' attention.

Then, in a flash of dark fur and glistening fangs, the wolves came at them.

Jingo leaped into action. In the space of two heartbeats, he had unsheathed his dagger, spun to pluck Marvus's dagger from its sheath, and flung both, one in each hand. The blades hurtled end over end, and two of the wolves fell.

The others, unfazed, closed the remaining gap and leaped.

As Elliott stood paralyzed, the wolves slammed into his friends, knocking them to the ground. Dirt, grass, and spatters of blood flew, and his mind processed the vicious attack in successive images of dark fur, bright teeth, and snarls intermixed with the terrified shrieks of the gimlets and the horses' frenzied stamping and snorting. Three of the wolves had Hooks pinned, and Marvus and Jingo were locked in a death struggle with the other two. In the lee of the mountainside, the largest of the horses—a big chestnut gelding—reared up, finally snapping the branch he was tied to, and the other two yanked loose their picket stakes, and all three bolted in different directions.

Elliott stood amid the melee in stunned disbelief. He was breathing fast and felt dizzy, and his mind screamed at him to be anywhere but here. Deciding there was nothing he could do for his friends, he turned and ran.

Heart pounding in his temples, he fought a wave of nausea as he pelted down the steep, difficult trail. His instincts commanded him in simple terms, telling him only that things had gone horribly wrong and he needed to get away fast.

Something rustled in the vegetation behind him, and he looked over his shoulder, praying it was one of the horses, only to see a dark shape slinking toward him. He couldn't outrun the wolf, but he would not just wait for it, either. He sprinted away, with the growling, panting beast behind him.

Stepping on a tilted flat rock, his foot rolled over some bits of loose gravel to send him tumbling headlong into thick brush. Crashing through the thicket slowed him, and he skidded to a stop. He had wrenched his ankle, but somehow there seemed to be no time for pain. He looked back to find the hulking beast nearly on him, fangs bared and eyes glinting. Uphill, he heard a bloodcurdling scream from one of the gimlets.

He scrambled up and tried to run, but the ankle buckled beneath him. Falling again, he slid downhill once more, fetching up just before a gap between two massive stone outcroppings that jutted like plates from the mountainside. Frantic, he pulled himself between the huge stone flakes. If he could just slip deep enough into the narrow crevice . . . He was afraid to look back, though the beast's rhythmic panting seemed to drown out all other sounds.

He scrabbled at the rock, knowing he had only seconds, and worked his way into the gap. The growl came again, right behind him this time, and he knew the chase was over. The beast had his leather pant leg and was pulling and shaking its head, as if trying to rip meat from bone. Dropping its hindquarters to the ground, it yanked him backward, away from the sheltering crevice. Reaching for the edge of the rock, he kicked with all his might while the frenzied wolf pulled and ripped at his pants. It seemed to be gaining the upper hand.

In the space of an instant, myriad scenes flashed through Elliott's mind: the poor gimlets and Hooks being viciously mauled on the mountaintop, his mother in her bed, the boys in the streets of New Orleans, lovely Lisa Hastings, his father. His churning mind played out the scenes in rapid succession until darkness enveloped him.

⚓ ⚓ ⚓

He was cold. In the dim fog of semiconsciousness, he lay still, breathing in and out, with one portion of his mind willing him to wake up, and another willing him to sleep. His mind told him nothing except that he was cold. He drifted back off, and dreamed of his childhood home—the old one, before his parents split.

He was a little boy, standing in the driveway of the old clapboard house, waiting for his for his dad to arrive. Just a few minutes earlier, he had overheard his parents fighting on the phone, and his mother had insisted that his dad get back home now. Though he hated their constant fighting, he couldn't wait to see his dad and tell him about the surprise he'd made for him at school. He felt at the back pocket of his Toughskins to make sure it was still there.

It was a sweltering summer afternoon, and the driveway exuded the smell of hot oil. On either side of the drive, tufts of grass and dandelions encroached from the neglected lawn onto the cracked concrete. Looking across the street at the contrasting row of tidy houses with their clipped hedges and lawns, he felt embarrassed by the eyesore that was his home. But his dad would be coming soon, and the eagerness over this mostly crowded out the bad thoughts. Then, in the distance, he heard it. The low rumble of an approaching motorcycle grew louder, and his heart quickened. Excited, he ran to the edge of the drive.

With the roar of the vintage Harley resonating through him, Elliott craned his neck as his dad leaned around the corner. His dad's curly black hair blew behind him, and below the aviator shades, the corners of his mouth were turned down in a scowl. Elliott could see instantly that his dad was drunk and not happy to have been ordered home. Elliott's mood sank a little, though he hoped the present he had made—a construction paperframed photo of the two of them holding a string of fish in front of a lake—would turn his dad's mood. Waving excitedly, Elliott stepped to the side of the drive, making room as his dad pulled up beside him. Unable to control himself, he presented the picture, beaming.

His dad sneered and didn't look at the picture. He twisted the grip of the right handlebar hard, and the Harley vibrated and roared. Still Elliott held the picture out. His dad glanced at it briefly but held on to the handlebars, twisting the throttle again. Elliott hated that sound. He called out to his dad, straining to be heard over the Harley's oppressive racket, though his dad just stared fire at him. Elliott couldn't fathom why, but he thought he saw hatred in that hard, handsome face.

Determined to bridge the divide between them, Elliott pushed the picture toward his dad again, trying to smile. But in the strange workings of the dream, the picture was gone. Instead, in his outstretched palm sat a child's small hand, severed and bloody at the wrist. Reddish-pink shamalan birthmarks pulsated in vivid relief against the gray, dead flesh. Shrieking, Elliott dropped the hand just as it erupted in flames. He looked up, and to his astonishment, his father and the motorcycle were gone, and in their place stood a tall shadowed figure whose face he could not make out. The tall figure, cloaked and hooded in black, stood quietly about five feet away.

Elliott took a step back, wondering whether, somehow, this strange new presence might still be his daddy. Gooseflesh stippled his arms. From somewhere far away, he could hear distant, mocking laughter. Thick black clouds roiled in the skies overhead, blotting out the sun. Elliott turned toward his house, hoping to see his mom on the porch, but the house—and the neighborhood with it—had also vanished. He now stood on a flat, endless gray plain, alone facing the shadowy figure. The black, smoking lump of the burnt flesh and bone lay on the ground between them.

Overcome with fright, Elliott tried to run, but his feet were stuck as if in concrete. Straightening his back, he faced the shadowy menace and asked, "Who are you?"

The shadow man stared balefully back at him and reached into his flowing robe, retrieving a long three-pronged spear that glowed bright against the bleak gray plain. Its shaft was covered with fine jewels, and the whole thing arced and crackled with blue light, as if electrified. Elliott heard a mechanical thrumming from the spear, vibrating rhythmically as if some great unseen machine had just been switched on. The ground beneath Elliott's feet vibrated gently with the thrumming, and the nugget of fear that had been with him since his father first rode up blossomed into terror. The thrumming continued, pulsing like the determined beating of a sick heart. Whatever the glowing spear was, he felt its power.

"Here lies your path," laughed the shadow man, though the voice was unmistakably his father's. "The Trident awaits you." The shadow man squared his shoulders toward him. "One way or another, the Trident will claim you."

The ground began to shake so violently, Elliott feared he would lose his balance. Steadying himself, he watched as the hooded figure drew back the trident, aiming it at him. A shadow passed overhead, darkening the already gray sky, and lunatic laughter from somewhere above almost drowned out the thrumming sound.

Elliott screamed as he heard the shadow man's voice in his head: "This is how your journey ends." With that, the cloaked figure hurled the trident at him.

The force of the blow knocked Elliott to the ground, and he felt the prongs rip into his chest, and heard the crunch of his own bones. It didn't hurt at first, even though Elliott looked down to find all three prongs buried hilt-deep in his chest. Bewildered, he grasped the shaft with both hands, but it was fixed to him as if welded in place. He breathed in and felt a searing stab of pain, then looked down again to see scarlet rivers of blood bubbling from the holes in his chest and darkening the fabric of his Toughskin jeans. The thrumming grew louder in his ears, offering the impression that the thing was just beginning to power up, and the shaft glowed the brightest blue he had ever seen. As he stared slack-jawed at the glowing spear rising from his chest, it hitched inside him, as if alive, and turned a quarter inch. The pain was more than he could bear.

Screaming, Elliott grabbed the shaft and it hitched again, then began to twist and spin, ripping flesh and bone. Like an alligator dismantling its prey, the spear rotated, picking up speed, boring a gaping hole in his chest as the mechanical thrumming rose to fever pitch.

Elliott fell onto his back, the massive wound in his chest burning like fire. Having ripped apart the flesh surrounding it, the spear no longer had purchase, and fell to the ground. Gobbets of meat and splinters of glistening bone remained fixed to the wicked barbs at the ends of its steely yet somehow delicate prongs. As Elliott's consciousness began to fade, he saw the shadow figure approach and reclaim the spear. For a moment, the cloaked man stood over him, then tossed him the very picture he had given to his father. In his final moments, Elliott snatched up the picture and stared at it, remembering the day *he and his father had caught all those fish, and wishing they had had more moments like that.*

"You don't belong here," the shadow man said. "Go back to your home."

And as if from far away, Elliott again heard the vibrating roar of his dad's motorcycle and smelled the hot oil from his driveway, and he grew cold as he felt his life leave him.

Elliott jerked awake, hitting his forehead against something hard, and opened his eyes to find himself in a dimly lit space, on his back, with a rough stone surface only inches from his nose. For a moment, he was relieved to be free from the dream, but the feeling quickly passed as he tried to raise his arms. He couldn't maneuver them more than a few inches above his waist before they met cool, rough stone. Shaking the cobwebs from his mind, he found that his feet were similarly caught. When he breathed deeply, his chest met the stone ceiling, and the rumbling, guttural growl from the dream remained in his ears. Fully back in the present, and realizing that he was sandwiched in the deep, narrow crack, he turned his head toward the sound, relieved that he could at least do that much in the tightly confined space.

Outside the crevice, the wolf paced back and forth, periodically trying to work its massive head inside or clawing at him with a forepaw. The incessant, foreboding growl resounded in the narrow chamber. He listened to the thumping of his heart, which seemed almost as loud as the low snarling and growling. Already, the burden of claustrophobia gripped him.

On the floor of the stone crevice, between him and the opening, his pants, one shoe, and his knapsack lay just out of reach. Partly to distract himself from the growing panic, he tried for the knapsack but couldn't reach it. Frustrated, he willed himself to be calm. He closed his eyes and breathed deeply,

Outside the crevice, the wolf paced back and forth,
periodically trying to work its massive head inside
or clawing at him with a forepaw.

imagining himself in a wide-open field with endless blue skies above. This helped, and the hysteria building within him abated. But the moment he opened his eyes, the wall of stone above his face taunted him, and his heart rate ramped up again. Without wanting to, he imagined the weight of an entire mountain on top of him. He told himself to stop, but his thoughts had their own agenda. He was pinned in the crevice, with the wolf waiting him out. No one was coming to rescue him. He wondered how long he might survive without food and water if the wolf kept him prisoner, and how long his mind could endure being trapped in the stone tomb without being driven to madness.

The wolf clawed at him with renewed effort just a few feet away. With its huge head poking into the gap, it bared its fangs and snapped its slavering jaws.

Elliott tried to calm himself, but his fear and his thumping heart refused to listen to reason. He wondered which would be worse: to be mauled by the wolf or to remain entombed in the rock. The kernel of dread blossomed into full, irrational panic, and the weight of the mountain seemed to press in on him. He had to get out. With no plan in mind, he inched toward the opening—only to find himself stuck.

As if sensing his dilemma, the wolf renewed its efforts.

Elliott screamed with all of his might, kicking his legs and flailing his arms as far as he could, but his knees banged painfully against the stone. When the initial burst of panic subsided to mere dread, he found that he had inadvertently maneuvered himself deeper into the tomb and could no longer straighten his neck. Struggling to regain control of his thoughts, he closed his eyes and visualized the sky. Carefully, systematically, he wiggled his arms and legs, trying to discover exactly where he was stuck. Though tightly confined, all his extremities could move except for his left foot, which was caught in the deepest corner of the crevice.

He worked the foot, trying to inch it free. Back and forth he moved it, working against the pain of the twisted ankle. His breath quickened with the effort, and his chest met the stone ceiling halfway through each breath, so that he couldn't fill his lungs. With his head turned to the side, both ears abutted the stone, and another fit of unchecked panic welled just beneath the surface. Closing his eyes, he imagined the sky and worked his foot.

Finally, thankfully, it wrenched free. Euphoric, he scooted both legs outward, almost afraid to believe it. The wolf, following his progress, clawed at him from the opening.

His right leg was asleep, and his movements were awkward. He had trouble working his head free, and the stone ceiling continued to squelch his breathing. Finally, he edged a few inches toward the opening, gaining more inches of space above him. It felt like a huge victory. He reached for the knapsack and pulled it toward him. Though he could not turn his body to the side, he could get his hand inside the bag. The first thing his hand met was the polished handle of the slingshot.

Buoyed by his success, he pulled the slingshot to him. It was no bigger than a child's toy, but somehow it felt good in his hand all the same. Without any particular plan, he felt around for a pebble. Finding one, he gripped it in his left hand and scooted a little closer to the opening, just enough so that he could wedge himself almost sideways and draw back the slingshot.

Inexplicably, the wolf had retreated to a few feet away from the opening, giving Elliott his shot. He loaded the stone and pulled back the sling. Aiming as best as he could, he released the stone.

It flew from the sling with less force than he had expected, and his heart sank as it veered feebly off course. But then, as he watched, it stopped in midair, hovering in the opening in much the way the shamalan stone had hovered above Marvus's hand in Sarintha's room. And inexplicably, the launched stone corrected its course. After hovering a second longer, it rocketed toward the wolf like a pistol shot and made a perfect, bloodless hole in its forehead. The wolf fell, and Elliott looked at the sling-shot in astonishment.

After staying in the crevice a few minutes longer and watching to make sure the wolf was dead, he scooted out of the tomb and back into the light of day. While keeping an eye on the inert body, he collected the knapsack and its scattered contents from the cubbyhole in the rock and hastily pulled on his ripped pants and shoes, then limped back up the mountain trail, dread-ing what may have become of Hooks and the gimlets.

Dark was falling by the time he neared the shelf on the mountainside. He limped up the final steps of the trail, bracing himself for what he might find and wondering whether, if his friends were gone, he could make it back to Harwelden alone, afoot—and what fate awaited him there.

Cresting the final rise, he beheld the aftermath of the battle. Immediately in front of him lay the corpses of the two wolves that Jingo had killed at the outset of the attack. Another lay just beyond them, its head crushed under a large boulder, and a fourth lay at the base of a tree, its spine kinked sharply just behind the shoulders. The last two wolves lay almost touch-ing, each with a dagger protruding from its neck.

Hooks and Jingo sat on a rock with their backs to him, their shoulders hunched forward.

He cried out to them, and they turned, the shock of the battle on their blood-smeared faces. Slowly, as if arising from a trance, they awoke to his presence and stood up, then limped to embrace him. The shared emotion of their survival connected them in a new bond, and the three of them stood holding one another, cocooned in Hooks's long, furry arms.

"Where's Marvus?" Elliott asked, fearing the worst.

Jingo's face fell, and he pointed to where they had been sitting.

Marvus lay still on the summit.

"They got him in the throat," said Jingo, lowering his eyes. "It looks bad."

⊕ ⊕ ⊕

Late that night, after a long and painful walk down the mountain pass, with Hooks carrying Marvus over his shoulder, they reached the valley and built a campfire. Hooks's left thigh looked like chewed raw meat, and Jingo's throwing arm had a frightful gash. Elliott couldn't fathom how they could still walk. Though the night was chilly, the valley was much balmier than high on the mountain, and the fire made things almost cozy.

From his knapsack, Jingo pulled out his spare trousers and cut the leather into bandages. When they had finished helping each other bind the worst of their wounds, Jingo miraculously brought out most of the opilion breast, which he had carved from Hooks's kill before beginning the painful walk down the mountain. Soon he had the meat spitted on green sticks and roasting over the fire.

Marvus, unconscious, lay nearest the campfire, his neck a swollen, bloody mess. His shallow breaths made an unsettling whistling sound.

Jingo passed around the meat, and they devoured it in silence, huddled around the fire.

After gulping down his share, Hooks bent over Marvus. His long expression betrayed his concern that the gimlet would not likely recover from his devastating wounds. "Will he . . . be all right?"

Jingo laid a hand on Marvus's forehead. "If he is to have a chance, we must get him to a healer. How far are we from this shamalan priest?"

"If we continue through the mountains, ten days," Hooks replied. "Longer if you take our injuries into account."

"He'll never last that long," said Jingo, shaking his head. "We have to think of another way."

Before Hooks could reply, Marvus groaned.

"He's waking up!" Elliott gasped, scooting to his side. "Marvus, can you hear us?"

Jingo caressed his old friend's forehead. "Don't try to speak," he said. "You've been badly wounded, but the three of us are caring for you. You're going to be all right." He looked to Elliott as if he had been caught in a lie.

Again Marvus tried to speak, more urgently than before.

Elliott held up his hand. "He's trying to tell us something."

Marvus's lips moved, and his companions drew closer.

"He's watching us," croaked Marvus.

"*Who's* watching us?" Jingo asked. "What are you trying to tell us?"

"He's watching us," Marvus repeated. "Through the eyes of the wolves . . ."

Jingo stiffened. With his hand still on Marvus's forehead, he looked at the others, his eyes wide with fear.

"What's he talking about?" Elliott asked.

"Lothar," Marvus croaked.

In the brush, something stirred.

Turning toward the rustling leaves, Jingo reached for his dagger and murmured, "I should have known it."

At the edge of the campsite, the rustling intensified. Something large was out there. Jingo raised the dagger in his good arm, looking more frightened than Elliott had yet seen him. A bulky shape moved toward them, and Jingo was about to let the dagger fly when the big chestnut gelding emerged from the darkness, the dun mare on his flank.

Jingo exhaled heavily, lowering the dagger. Neither horse

looked injured. Slowly, so as not to spook them, Jingo went to them, muttering softly and holding out his hands. Though their ears flattened a little at first, they seemed to trust him, and eventually allowed him to take them by their halters. As soon as they were tied, Jingo seemed to tense again, and he returned to the fire ring. "We have to get out of here now," he said, scanning the valley. "Hooks, can you fashion a litter for Marvus? We can drag him behind the gelding. You'll have to work fast."

Hooks nodded and went off into the dark to find a couple of strong saplings for the litter.

"I don't understand any of this," Elliott said. "How could someone be watching us through the eyes of a wolf?" As soon as the words left his lips, he thought of the journal in his grandfather's basement. There had been several passages about seeing through the eyes of a raven.

Jingo scanned the ground and then the skies. "Lothar knows where we are. He'll send more wolves . . . or worse."

"So this Lothar," said Elliott. "He's able to watch us through the eyes of the animals, even this far away?"

"If he has some idea where we are, he can send any willing beast to spy on us or hunt us," Jingo said. "Marvus must have seen something today that led him to believe that the wolves were agents of Malus Lothar. If that is truly the case, we are in mortal danger."

At that moment, a raven landed on a branch overhead and sat staring at them.

Speaking barely above a whisper, Jingo leaned toward Elliott and said, "Ravens don't fly at night. Where is the slingshot you used against the wolf today?"

"In my knapsack," Elliott whispered.

"Get it," said Jingo. "And don't let the bird see what you're doing."

Elliott nodded. "Wow," he said loudly, "I'm still hungry. I'll see if we have any food left in my knapsack."

Getting up, he limped the few paces to where the horses were tied. After returning to the fireside with his knapsack, he opened it and began rooting through it, casually tossing things out of the way in his feigned search for food. "I don't see much in here," he said. "Maybe if I look all the way in the bottom . . ." Digging down, he grabbed the slingshot and tossed it to Jingo while still appearing to rummage inside the bag.

Jingo scooted toward Elliott, grabbing the slingshot in one hand and a small pebble in the other. "There's got to be something in there," he said. Hiding the slingshot from the raven with his body, Jingo plunged both hands into the knapsack and loaded the stone. The raven stared at them from its perch in the tree.

In a single movement, Jingo pulled his hands out of the knapsack and launched the pebble at the raven. With an alarmed caw, it flapped its wings and started to rise from the branch, but the pebble found its mark, and the bird fell dead to the ground.

"Amazing," Hooks said, watching from the edge of the campsite.

"It's an ancient shamalan weapon," said Jingo. "It hits whatever you target, regardless of the shooter's skill. Now, we've got to get out of here. I don't know how Lothar has located us, or how he even knows of our presence, but he aims to be rid of us without launching a single arrow. These lands are filled with wild beasts: simitars, mountain bears, dire wolves, and the like. If we don't get out of here, we'll come across more trouble."

"How can we hide from him if he can see us through the eyes of any animal?" Elliott asked.

"If he loses our trail, he won't know where to search, and he won't know which animals to send for us. He can't connect with more than a few creatures at a time."

"Well, he certainly knows where we are right now," said Hooks, cinching the litter with a piece of vine. "How can we escape from him if any creature in the wilderness can put him on our path?"

"How far are we from the Forest of Golroc?" Jingo asked. "If we can make it to there, the enchantments of the black forest will protect us from the eyes of Malus Lothar."

"We're not far from Golroc," said Hooks, "but I'd sooner be eaten by a simitar than enter that fell place."

"What's Golroc?" Elliott asked.

Jingo pointed to the east. "An ancient forest that Lothar cannot penetrate. In the Forest of Golroc, we can lose him. It's our only chance." He looked pointedly at Hooks.

"And we can lose a lot more than one gimlet," said Hooks. "The place is full of unnatural beasts. I won't go, and you won't persuade me otherwise. If you decide to enter that accursed forest, you can find the shamalan priest on your own."

"We have no choice," Jingo said, nodding at the litter that Hooks held by one end. "Now, help me load Marvus on that thing. Let's get out of here before we're spotted again."

Elliott and Jingo gently hoisted Marvus onto the litter and tied him on while Hooks fashioned a harness from a horse tether and strands of vine. Elliott marveled watching him, for the beast was a wizard at anything involving limbs and vines. When the rig was complete, they rode into the night, with Elliott and Jingo on the horses and Hooks limping behind.

They rode through the valley without incident. Occasionally, they encountered an owl or small rabbit in the path, and each time, Jingo killed the potential spy with the slingshot and retrieved the carcass to be cooked and eaten later. As they traveled through the winding valley, the towering mountains surrounding them became gradually less majestic, and by dawn, after ten hours in the saddle, they reached the easternmost edge of the mountain range.

"Good riddance to the Azure Mountains," Elliott said as they crossed a final valley between the mountains and an expansive swath of forest. The vast forest ran the length of the mountain range, north and south as far as the eye could see.

"Good riddance," Jingo echoed, checking on his gravely wounded friend in the litter behind him.

In full dawn, they rode to the edge of the forest and, at Jingo's prompting, dismounted and made a fire. It was Elliott's worst day in Pangrelor yet. Though the jostling ride was agony on his ankle, the others had to be suffering much worse, and Marvus had made barely a whimper since they left the valley.

They passed the next day and night camped on the edge of the forest, nursing their wounds, with the great, moss-covered trees of Golroc near enough to reach out and touch. According to Jingo, their proximity to the forest was already providing them some of the needed protection from Malus Lothar's enchantments, though to fully escape his watchful eye, they must enter the forest as soon as they could manage.

Throughout the day, Elliott and Hooks made several short trips to water the horses and fill the water skins at a mist-covered lake that bisected the valley between the mountains and the forest. With each trip, Hooks stripped his bandages and waded into the water to cleanse his wounds. Elliott was amazed that he could walk at all, but he merely said that susquats were fast healers. The trips to the lake were arduous, and both Elliott and Hooks had tried to convince Jingo to camp closer to it, but Jingo was adamant: they would stay at the edge of the forest, and that was that. During each foray away from the shadow of the trees, Elliott carried the slingshot, though the landscape was unsettlingly quiet and he saw no creatures. The wound on Marvus's neck, despite their best efforts to tend to it, had become inflamed, and the flesh surrounding the bite was an angry red, but at least the awful whistling sound was gone from his breathing. Marvus spent the day in a feverish sweat, with heat coming off him in waves, rarely speaking or opening his eyes.

As dusk approached, they sat around the campfire and discussed their sorry plight. Marvus's condition was worsening, and when he spoke, his words were confused. Jingo's arm pained him terribly and was useless for carrying or knife throwing. On the bright side, they had two rabbits, a nightjar, and Jingo's raven roasting over the fire.

"I can't keep going like this," Elliott said, wincing as he dabbed the dirt from his scraped calf with a wet cloth. "I want to go home."

"You're going to be fine, Elliott," said Jingo, who had encouraged him and urged him forward countless times since leaving Harwelden. "You're getting stronger. You look fitter with each passing day."

Elliott looked down at himself. He, too, had noticed the retreating baby fat. "Thanks," he said. "But your compliments don't make me want to stay. I have to get back home. I have things I need to take care of."

Jingo smiled. "What sort of things?"

Stonefaced, Elliott said, "Personal things."

"Very well, then." Jingo poked at the campfire with a stick, careful not to jar his bandaged forearm. "I do not mean to pry."

Elliott said nothing, though he was pretty sure the gimlet *did* mean to pry.

"Ever since you passed your test back at the castle," Jingo said, "I have wondered what type of shamalan you would become."

Elliott felt annoyed that Jingo was trying to change the subject. He stared at the fire and said nothing.

"There are many different paths a shamalan can take."

"I'm not a shamalan," Elliott snapped, cutting him off. He held his hands out before him, inspecting the birthmarks. "I'm a teenager," he said. "And I don't belong here. I'm not brave and I'm not strong," He thought of the recent abuse he had suffered at the hands of the pack of boys in New Orleans. "And even if I am a shamalan," he continued, still looking at his hands, "I want no part of your problems here—I have enough of my own back home. This is your war, not mine."

"As I was saying, there are many different paths a shamalan can take." Jingo looked into Elliott's eyes. "Some shamalans become masters, demonstrating a talent for architecture and artistry. The wondrous sculptures, frescoes, and towers of Harwelden were all created by shamalan masters."

As he rearranged the green wands of roasting meat, he said, "Others demonstrate an unusual ability to join with the Shama, the energy that infuses us with life and consciousness. These shamalans have an affinity for sorcery and for mastery of the elements. They are the shamalan priests." He finished turning the rabbits and looked at Elliott. The night was dark and deathly quiet—not even a cydonia bug chirped. Hooks sat nearby, listening quietly. "Then, of course," Jingo continued, "there are the shamalan nobles, born of royal blood. The skill of the nobles is for leadership. They search what is inside us and inspire us to achieve our potential. As you have heard, only one shamalan from the royal bloodline lives. I speak of Princess Sarintha. She has been captured by Malus Lothar, and we don't know what her fate will be."

Shifting in his seat, Elliott listened. His frown softened, and he looked down at the birthmarks on his hands.

"And finally," said Jingo, "there are the shamalan warriors. Before becoming a warrior, a shamalan must demonstrate fearlessness and ability for warfare. But the warrior's skills are not just for battle. Shamalan warriors cultivate skills of leadership, sorcery, connection with the Shama, art . . . They are the embodiment of everything it is to be shamalan, and they are the proudest of the race, save for the nobility, which can only be attained by birthright. It was the shamalan warriors who built and maintained the mighty empire that now crashes around us. They were a force for good in the world like no others before them. As I look upon you now, Elliott, your muscles grow firm and your body grows lean. Though you are a stranger to these lands, you show bravery and strength. Because of what I have seen in you during these past days, I have begun to suspect that you are fated to be a warrior." With a gleam in his eye, he added, "And you must show strength in these difficult times. There is more turmoil ahead. We need you, Elliott. Marvus needs you. Pangrelor needs you."

Elliott sat quietly, looking at Jingo. A nice thought, but he disagreed entirely with the assessment. In his heart, he knew that he was no warrior. The whole time on the trail, he had been considering his options for returning to the Forest of Ondor, to try to make it back to the cave and then back home. Fighting back tears, he thought of his mother, a world away, slowly dying of cancer. He also understood that Jingo was willing to put logic aside because he so badly needed something to believe in, even if it was only a pipe dream. In response to Jingo's words of praise, he said simply, "I'm not a warrior." He looked at the ground.

"No offense, Elliott, said Hooks, speaking for the first time, "but you sure smell like one."

Jingo smiled.

"So what is our plan?" Elliott asked.

"I'm afraid we don't have much of a plan," Jingo said. "We shall care for Marvus as best we can, but until we reach the shamalan priest Crosslyn, Marvus will have to survive on his own strength if he is to survive at all." Jingo's voice broke slightly. "At sunrise, we enter the Forest of Golroc. When we have traveled some distance through it, we shall emerge at its southern edge and resume our trek through the mountain passages until we reach the swamps where Crosslyn lives. It is my strong desire that our friend Hooks accompany us during this journey. We wouldn't have made it this far without him." Jingo looked to Hooks for a response.

Hooks poked at the ground with a stick and growled. "I wouldn't set one foot in that forest for all the opilions in Pangrelor."

"Why are you so afraid of the forest?" Elliott asked.

Hooks winced. "The Forest of Golroc is well known to my race. It is a foul place, where the creatures that roamed Pangrelor in the olden times still lurk in the shadows, counting their days until darkness reigns again. Before the shamalans, the clan that now resides in Susquatania was part of a much larger family. Susquats thrived across the Carafayan continent and inhabited woodlands from the southern islands to Vengala. The Forest of Golroc is the most expansive on the continent, larger even than Ondor or Susquatania, and susquat lore tells of many tribes that tried to take up residence there in ages past. But always the tribes that entered Golroc were lost. Our history tells of unnatural creatures that drink the blood of their victims like wine. They eat the flesh of their prisoners without even bothering to kill them. Among the susquats, it is said that these horrible creatures dwell in the deepest, darkest confines of Golroc. They torture for pleasure, and death at their hands comes slowly. It is said that the sort of death suffered in the Forest of Golroc is the worst a creature can have. The monsters of Golroc are more powerful than shamalan priests and show far less mercy than the worst of the enemies to the north. My elders taught me since birth to give the borders of Golroc a wide berth. I'll not enter it under any circumstances, and I'd advise you to do the same. Lothar is a frightful enemy, but he is a knowable one. The enemies that lie within the confines of Golroc will lead you to a fate a thousand times worse than any he could design."

Jingo sighed. "I, too, have heard of the superstitions surrounding Golroc," he said. "But that is all they are, Hooks. The
legends of the salax are for children's tales around the campfire.
They—"

"Don't say their name!" bellowed Hooks. "NEVER say
their name." His head jerked left and right, as if Jingo's words
might summon the nightmarish denizens of Golroc to them now.

They stared at him, bewildered by his reaction.

"All right, then," Jingo said. "Do what you will. In the
morning, Elliott and I will take Marvus into the forest. If you
are determined to go your own way, then I'll say nothing to
stop you."

"I will go my own way," Hooks said.

"We will need you to provide us with a detailed map of
how to reach Crosslyn."

Sheepishly, Hooks used his stick to draw a sketch in the
dirt. Jingo and Elliott scooted nearer him so they could inspect
the crude map by firelight. The map depicted the whole of the
Azure Mountain range, with Mount Kalipharus at the northernmost tip, providing a reference point. To the east of the Azure
Mountains, he outlined a broad swath of territory representing
the Forest of Golroc. The northernmost tip of the forest began
several leagues south of Mount Kalipharus, on the eastern edge
of the Azure Mountains, and ran parallel to the mountains all the
way to their southernmost point, sometimes encroaching well
into the mountain range. Just south of Golroc, Hooks depicted
a flat plain that culminated in a vast swampland stretching to
the sea. In the heart of the swampland, he drew an X. There the
shamalan priest was to be found.

"So if I understand this map correctly," said Jingo, we can
reach Crosslyn by traveling due south through the forest."

"That's right," said Hooks. "The Vitaean swamps are
his keep."

Jingo stared at the map. "Correct me if I'm wrong, but it looks as if traveling straight through to the southern tip of Golroc might shave some time off our journey."

Hooks gave a mirthless chuckle. "By that route, you won't survive long enough to reach the southern tip of the forest."

"You said it would take ten days or more to reach Crosslyn if we traveled through the mountains and entered the swamps from the west," said Jingo. "How many if we enter the forest and travel due south until we reach the end?"

"If you travel directly through the forest without interruption, you could reach the Vitaean swamps in three days—two and a half if you traveled swiftly."

"Then we could save Marvus," said Elliott. "That's wonderful news!"

"Maybe," said Jingo. "But three days on the trail will still be quite difficult for him."

Hooks looked at Jingo. "I wish you would listen to me," he said quietly. "If you enter Golroc, you won't live to spend your first night there. It is a fool's errand you consider."

Jingo returned his gaze. "Tomorrow we enter Golroc. We will travel to the center of the forest and then turn due south. By doing so, we protect ourselves against the enchantments of Malus Lothar and make a shortcut to the priest's home. It is the best plan because there is no alternative. In three days, we will be at the doorstep of the lost shamalan, and we will implore him to save our friend—and perhaps even speed the healing of our own wounds. After that, he will offer us guidance on how best to proceed against Malus Lothar and the serpans." He paused. "Hooks, we have known each other only a short time, but already our fates are intertwined." He looked at him pleadingly. "Please reconsider and come with us."

"Yeah," Elliott said. "We're going to be lost without you. Who's going to protect us if you don't come along?"

Hooks sighed. "I owe each of you a great deal for saving me. Even him," he said, motioning to Marvus. "But it is the height of foolishness to enter that wretched forest, and my decision will not change. In the morning, I'll return to the mountains and make my way to the western lands. After everything that has happened so far this season, I want to get as far away from here as I can."

"Elliott, Marvus, and I will enter the forest at first light," Jingo said.

"Then I guess that's it," said Hooks.

"I suppose so," Jingo sighed.

Without further discussion, they began to settle in for their last night together around the campfire. With the fire slowly dying, they stretched out and waited for sleep to take them. Despite all that had happened, all Elliott could think about was his mother, lying sick back in New Orleans. He longed to return to the mansion on Pleasant Street, to sit at her bedside, to walk once more through the Garden District with his grandfather. With visions of the grand old house filling his head, he drifted off to sleep. In the morning, after the good-byes, Hooks would leave for the western lands, and he would enter the Forest of Golroc with the gimlets.

Chapter 15

Sitticus

From the highest tower of the stony black castle atop Mount Sitticus, Princess Sarintha stared into the milky darkness of the Vengan mountainscape. She had little memory of her recent flight to Vengala in Malus Lothar's sky chariot, and that suited her just fine. Although Lothar's journey to pluck her from the torrid sands of Toltuga probably spared her life, the death that she had courted on the floor of the desert was surely preferable to whatever lay ahead. Despite her will to remain courageous, Malus Lothar terrified and repulsed her.

But it was not her recent trek over the sands of Toltuga that occupied her thoughts as she stared across the moonlit Sepulchre Mountains, a continent away from her homeland. Nor did she try to remember her flight with the Malus to the towering home of her enemy, here atop Mount Sitticus. Rather, as she sat in the tiny cell overlooking the spindly mountaintops, her mind's eye returned to her singular previous encounter with the Malus, and his treatment of her in the scrub forest outside Prytania last season. She replayed in her mind's eye the night she first beheld the notorious leader of the serpan hordes—the evening that their intertwining fates brought them inevitably together.

As often happened with matters of providence, a long series of events led up to her first encounter with the malus. Seasons earlier, the serpans captured the key shamalan stronghold of Prytania. The glorious and ancient gimlet city stood at the mouth of the western passage to Vengala and had provided a crucial staging ground for assaults on the northern homeland of the serpans—that is, until its capture. The loss of Prytania was a grave blow to the shamalan war effort and proved to be the turning point in the conflict. In the seasons since Prytania's fall, the shamalans had aimed virtually all their military efforts at retaking the magnificent lost city. And all those efforts had failed, precipitating the downward spiral of suffering that the once mighty kingdom now came to expect. A short time ago, Sarintha's beloved father, King Gregorus, was killed during an attempt to recapture the invaluable gimlet city.

Her own attempt to recapture Prytania came on the heels of her father's death, even before her own coronation, which was yet to occur. In the days before the doomed offensive, Waldemariam and most of the Grayfarer Council had argued fervently against her plan to lead a new charge into Prytania, though she had refused to be dissuaded. Prytania held great significance to their cause, Sarintha had countered, and its re-taking would turn the tide of war back in their favor. For the sake of military strategy, spiritual significance, and sheer momentum, she argued, Prytania *must* be retaken, and she was willing to stake everything on this conviction. General Grimaldi, commander of the Grayfarer armies, generally echoed her sentiments, and Waldemariam finally acquiesced. Following her wishes, the plans for the offensive to retake Prytania were painstakingly laid down in secret. No detail was left to chance.

Soon thereafter, she and General Grimaldi, leading a large army of gimlets and men, had embarked on the long journey to the outskirts of the captured gimlet city. After many days of arduous travel, the force made its way to the southern edge of the city, where it hid behind a stony outcropping that jutted from the ground at the northern edge of Toltuga. But late in the evening before the surprise attack was to occur, Sarintha and Grimaldi were themselves surprised by a moonlight attack, led by Malus Lothar. In the onslaught of flying arrows and smashing hammers, her troops were slaughtered before they could organize a defense, and the attackers, like flames through dry grass, engulfed their encampment. All the while, Malus Lothar strolled casually through the battlefield, as if oblivious of the chaos surrounding him. His singular purpose on that night was to capture Princess Sarintha. And early in the fight, he had found her, helpless and alone.

Sarintha trembled as the event played out in her mind. A cold breeze rolled through the window connecting her cell to the outside world, making her shiver all the more, as memories of her first meeting with the malus streamed forth unbidden. She had never felt so hopeless.

Her troops never had a chance at Prytania. Though her army was large, the serpan army was larger, and her troops could not find momentum against the crushing swarm unleashed against them. Moments after the midnight attack began, the malus held her in his repulsive embrace. Heedless of the battle raging on all sides of them, he had caressed her as if she were a long-lost courtesan. *"The world is changing,"* he had said. *"The end of the shamalans is near."*

She shuddered at the memory.

"Tell me the whereabouts of the Antiquitas Trident, and Valderon will spare your life. Keep your secret, and your doom is sealed."

Even now, as she sat in her cell, she could almost smell Malus Lothar's foul breath, as she had on that evening, when she stared into the black eyeholes of his steel mask. Tears spilled down her face as she gazed out into the Vengalan night. For the second time in a single season, she was at the mercy of Malus Lothar, and her heart sank with despair.

Footsteps outside her door jarred her from her thoughts. Solidly back in the present, she looked about for some sort of weapon to defend herself with. Someone was coming up the stairs.

She searched frantically but found nothing of use in the small, round, bare cell.

Outside the door, the footsteps stopped. The visitor had reached the top of the staircase and stood on the landing, just a few feet away. She heard the snick of a key in the lock, and a long creaking sound as the bolt slid from its bed. Slowly, the door swung open.

At first, all she could make out was a hulking black figure, laughing softly.

She sat on the floor, unmoving. Her breath caught in her throat as she peered at the figure in front of her, and her instincts told her she was in mortal peril. The moon peeked over the castle battlements, illuminating the figure in the doorway. Short and thick, he wore a flowing black tunic and exuded a fetid smell.

"Rise shamalan," he said. "Your presence is required in the master's chamber downstairs."

She remained motionless, eyes on her jailer's shadowed face.

"I said RISE!" he bellowed.

Though his voice frightened her, she did not get up.

"So be it," he said, and turned his back to her as if to leave, though remaining in the doorway.

As she watched, praying he would leave, a faint reddish glow appeared in the doorway, eerily illuminating the darkened cell. Though the captor before her stood between her and the light source, she could see his outline better. His thickness frightened her. If forced to defend herself, she would be no match. As she looked on, the red glow brightened, pulsating as the creature muttered incantations. He remained with his back to her, though his mumblings grew louder and louder.

"*Conquiesco quievi*," he whispered over and over, each time with more force than the last, until the glow filled the cell. With each rhythmic chant, his voice gained strength, and the glow he was shielding grew brighter. Then, with a final utterance, he turned to face her. Suspended before him was a small, horrible, pulsating red ball of light, rotating on its axis above his outstretched hands. In its glow, she fully saw his face. Rows of broken teeth gleamed in the pulsating light as he stood grinning, mocking her with his eyes. Then, suddenly, he hoisted the ball over his head and hurled it at her.

The heat of a thousand fires surged through her, and she screamed with all her being, though barely a whimper escaped her lips as she slumped to the floor. Her mind tried to discern what sort of hex had befallen her, but her knowledge of the new magic was limited. She tried to sit up but found herself paralyzed, unable to twitch even a finger. Slowly, she realized that she could not even fill her lungs with air.

The creature lumbered toward her from the doorway, laughing softly. He knelt beside her, caressing her with his leathery hand.

"It is useless to resist," he said. "From this day forward, your place is with us. You would do well to realize that."

Her hunger for air overwhelmed her. Tears streamed from the corners of her eyes, but they were no longer the tears of anguish that she had cried a few moments ago—they were her body's attempt to counteract her inability to blink.

He watched with amusement as the seconds passed, and laughed, seeming to relish her horror.

Sarintha struggled to collect her thoughts and prayed for safe passage to the afterlife. Though her eyes remained wide, her consciousness began to fade.

The grinning serpan raised his hand to her mouth. "*Aether,*" he said, and a thin strand of silvery light arose from his fingertips, dancing in the air for a moment before entering her mouth.

Instantly her hunger for air ceased. Perhaps they didn't mean to kill her. But then again, there were worse fates.

Kneeling beside her, the serpan put his hand to her face and closed her eyes. Then, without a word, he hoisted her onto his shoulder and carried her down the winding staircase, humming an unfamiliar tune.

Still unable to open her eyes, she couldn't see where he was taking her, but after several turns and a few short flights of stairs, he stopped. The beating of drums filled her ears, and she heard chanting, as if some sort of ceremony was under way. Through her immobile eyelids, she sensed the presence of light. For a few moments, her captor stood still as the chanting and drumbeats continued. Then, all at once, a hush fell over the room. She had the unnerving sense that all attention was on her. Finally, she heard the unmistakable voice of Malus Lothar, who seemed to be standing just a few paces away.

"This night, my friends, marks the attainment of a long-awaited milestone," said the malus. The timbre of his voice was smooth and assured. "Before us, the honorable sorcerer Golthel holds the last remaining shamalan."

The soft, rhythmic drumbeats began again, and serpan voices whispered excitedly.

"And with her death, the unnatural race of shamalans will be forever extinguished from the world."

A chorus of approving hisses arose from all sides. The force and tempo of the drumbeats increased as the malus continued, and suddenly she realized that all this pomp and ritual implied one thing only.

"Let us take a moment to give thanks to Valderon," said the malus, "and let us reflect on how far our cause has progressed. In less than fifteen revolutions of the Enstar, we have traded slavery for freedom. We have stood against the mighty shamalan empire and have lashed out against its evils. And, through Valderon's guidance, we have slaughtered the oppressors that rose from the blackness of the sea to dominate our lands. Through faith and the providence of Valderon, we have declared with our weapons that we will suffer no longer. And our enemy has heard us."

The serpan voices muttered their approval.

"It is on this night, forever distinguished from all others, that we shall see with our own eyes the death throes of the empire."

Her heart quickened.

"Faithful servant Golthel, place the prisoner on the altar and open her eyes."

Though unable to move, Sarintha could see a great deal once the sorcerer opened her eyes. She lay on a stone altar in the center of a chamber filled with hooded serpans.

From somewhere out of sight, the soft beating of drums continued.

The sorcerer and the malus loomed above her. Slowly Golthel raised his hands and turned her head to the left so that she might better see the chamber.

Torches lined the wall. Robed serpans stood shoulder to shoulder.

An open sarcophagus stood in the corner, and by the light of the flames, she saw that a painting decorated its outer surface. It was a painting of the princess—the serpans had made the thing with her in mind. Inside the sarcophagus, metal spikes jutted from the floor and lid. Sarintha knew that the stakes would be positioned so as not to penetrate a vital organ, thus prolonging her suffering before merciful death took her.

Her heart raced faster.

Several paces away from the sarcophagus sat a rectangular wooden rack fitted with metal shackles. On the side of the rack hung a large wooden wheel attached to a pulley. Lengths of chain connected the pulley to the shackles so that, by turning the wheel, the tormentor could stretch the victim until the joints were gradually pulled apart. The flat surface of the rack bore another painting of Sarintha.

Golthel slowly turned her head to the opposite side of the chamber, where the torchlight illuminated a wooden chair. Its long, narrow back was fitted with two metal bands. Yet another likeness of the princess decorated the wooden surface of the chair, showing how she would be positioned. The uppermost metal band was to go around her forehead, holding her head in place against the narrow back of the chair. The lower of the two bands would fit around her throat, like a garrote. A large metal screw protruded from the back of the chair, at mid neck level.

Golthel walked over to the chair. As he turned the metal screw, the garrote tightened, and the sharp metal screw protruded farther from the back of the chair with each turn. According to the portrait, the screw would pierce the back of her neck as the garrote tightened around it, slowly piercing her spine as the garrote cut off her air. After the demonstration, Golthel returned to the side of the altar.

The soft, rhythmic drumbeats continued.

"As you can see, Princess, a great deal of effort has preceded your visit," said Malus Lothar.

Either purposefully or through inattention, Golthel allowed Sarintha's gaze to remain locked on the executioner's chair. The helplessness she felt from her paralysis only heightened her terror. Her unblinking eyes watered, and she hated that this would be interpreted as tears of fear or despair.

"It is a long journey that we are about to embark on," said the malus, "though one that will take place in the confines of this chamber."

The serpans chattered quietly among themselves, apparently pleased at the entertainment to come.

"But before we begin, I want to introduce another of our guests," the malus said, nodding to Golthel.

"*Partos exos quievi,*" said the sorcerer, swinging his hand in an arc over Sarintha's head.

Immediately, she regained control of the muscles of her head and neck. Instinctively, she squeezed her eyes shut. After several seconds, she opened them and found that she could turn her head. She opened her mouth to speak, but no words came; except for her head, she remained paralyzed.

As the drumbeats continued, the sorcerer left the room. Shortly thereafter, Sarintha heard clanking chains and frantic, muffled yelling arising from somewhere outside the chamber. The clamor grew steadily louder, and Golthel returned to the room with a prisoner. As Sarintha watched in horror, he escorted a hooded captive to the center of the chamber. The onlooking serpans hissed in delight.

The unfortunate soul was much larger than Golthel. He wore a long hooded robe, which blinded him and hid his face from view. Beneath the confines of the robe, chains clanked as Golthel paraded him around the room before stopping at the rack. There Golthel commanded him to stop and face the altar.

The prisoner obeyed, though not in silence. It was clear from his voice that he wore some type of gag underneath the hood, and except for the prisoner's loud protesting, the room grew deathly silent as even the drumbeats stopped.

From the altar, Sarintha watched in revulsion. Her heart raced in fear for the prisoner. Noting his size—roughly twice that of his tormentor—she was certain she knew who he was.

Golthel walked to the corner of the chamber and took a bulky wooden club from a selection of weapons on the wall. Returning to the prisoner, he whacked his knees with the club.

The prisoner grunted and fell to the floor, but Golthel was not finished with him. He raised his club and slammed it into his back, arching him backward in pain

"Well done," said Lothar. "Now, fix him to the rack so that we may get started."

The sorcerer motioned to two nearby serpans to help him place the prisoner on the rack. As they approached, Golthel took a dagger from his belt and cut away the hood hiding the prisoner's face, and then the cloth gag.

Sure enough, it was Sarintha's dear friend General Grimaldi, commander of the grayfarer army. He had been captured during her failed attempt to retake Prytania. Until this moment, she hadn't known whether he was alive or dead.

Captivity had not treated Grimaldi well. He had lost much weight since Prytania, and his eyes looked huge in his gaunt skull. He was barely conscious.

Once Gothel's attendants had Grimaldi shackled, his massive wings, previously hidden by the robe, were plainly visible, lashed behind him on the rack. Golthel began turning the wheel, stretching the grayfarer general's inert body to its full extent. Golthel turned to face the malus.

"Wake him from his stupor," said the malus.

Golthel nodded. "*Expergo*," he said, holding his hands in front of him.

A red glow appeared in the space above his hands and, rotating slowly, coalesced into a sphere the size of a plum. This Golthel hurled at Grimaldi, hitting him in the chest.

Grimaldi awoke, and the screams began anew, although lower in volume than before.

"Silence him," said Malus Lothar. "There is nothing more abhorrent than the screams of a coward."

"*Confuto*," said Golthel, releasing a strand of silvery light from his fingertips. The bright filament entered Grimaldi's mouth, and the screams stopped. The chamber was deathly quiet.

Grimaldi's eyes widened and darted from side to side, and his mouth opened and closed soundlessly. He thrashed

From the altar, Sarintha watched in revulsion....
Captivity had not treated Grimaldi well.

about on the rack, and as his head whipped about, he caught sight of the princess, and in that moment, his body went limp. He locked eyes with her, and the two exchanged a wordless communication: they were both going to die tonight, together, in this room.

Golthel tightened the wheel, and Grimaldi's thrashing began again in earnest. Blood flowed from his wrists and ankles as the steel shackles cut into his skin, and Sarintha could only imagine the blazing agony as the tendons and ligaments of his shoulder and hip joints stretched to the breaking point.

Malus Lothar leaned to the side of the altar where Sarintha lay paralyzed, watching the horrible spectacle. "Dear Princess," he whispered, "through my grace you shall have a choice." He stood and began to pace the length of the altar. "This war of ours has been a dreadful affair. There is not a soul in this room who hasn't lost someone dear." He looked out over the room. "On this night, before all to witness, I offer you a choice. I offer you the chance to end this long war—and to live."

The serpans hissed their loud disapproval.

"Silence!" said the malus, raising a hand. "I offer you the choice to save your race. You may even one day reproduce," he said slyly, "preserving some semblance of the shamalan bloodline."

Sarintha looked into his steel mask with horror as Grimaldi continued to thrash about on the rack.

"More than this, I offer you the chance to preserve the life of your friend, General Grimaldi. And all I ask in return is one simple thing."

Sarintha stared into his steel mask, longing to speak.

"Tell me the location of the Antiquitas Trident."

She glared at him and shook her head.

"I should inform you," said the malus, "that if you agree to my terms, your friend Grimaldi will be released at once and allowed to return to Harwelden unharmed. Tell me the location of the Trident, and he may live in peace to the end of his days. But if you defy me, I will have no choice but to snuff out his life—that is, after my sorcerer has interrogated him thoroughly."

Sarintha looked at Grimaldi, stretched and bleeding on the rack. She had known him nearly all her seasons and counted him among her closest allies.

Grimaldi returned her gaze and shook his head. They both knew that Sarintha did not know the whereabouts of the ancient shamalan weapon. With heavy heart, she turned back to the malus and spat on the shiny steel mask covering his face.

"So be it," said the malus, wiping the mask with his sleeve. He motioned to Golthel, who took a hammer from the cabinet, and four sharpened metal stakes from a box on the floor, and set them by the rack where Grimaldi lay.

"When one hammers the spikes through bone and fixes the extremities to the rack, the level of pain inflicted during stretching far surpasses that achieved by the rack alone," said the malus. "Golthel has expended a great deal of effort perfecting this technique."

Golthel appeared pleased with the compliment.

"Because I am patient," the malus continued, "I offer you a final chance to change your mind. Divulge the location of the Antiquitas Trident, or your general forfeits his life. Decide carefully, princess. If you agree to my terms, an immeasurable number of lives will be spared, including your friend Grimaldi's as well as your own. If you refuse, I will give the order to stake the grayfarer to the rack and continue this grim exercise. I should point out that I have rather specific plans for you as well." He looked meaningfully at the executioner's chair.

Silently, Sarintha prayed for deliverance from this place, though she knew it would not come.

"Though you may lack the good sense to agree with my plan, we possess the means to make you change your mind." Malus Lothar paced the length of the altar. "It would be a great shame if you should allow this loyal friend to perish, only to change your mind after a little more persuasion."

Getting only a hate-filled stare, he said, "Stake the grayfarer."

The beating of the drums began anew as the serpan onlookers began to chant.

Nodding to the malus, Golthel positioned a stake over Grimaldi's left wrist. He raised the hammer over the head of the stake and brought it down slowly, squaring his shot, then raised the hammer again and swung, smashing the stake through the bone of Grimaldi's wrist and into the wood beneath.

No-o-o-o-o-o! Sarintha mouthed the silent scream.

Grimaldi's face twisted, and his back arched so violently that one leg of the rack rocked up off the floor. His eyes widened, and he looked at Sarintha, perhaps pleading for her to do something, though Golthel's spell kept him mute.

She watched, powerless, as Golthel raised the hammer for a second blow. Again and again the hammer struck with great precision, until he had staked all four extremities.

Grimaldi stopped thrashing, perhaps having resigned himself to defeat, and looked into Sarintha's eyes. *Be strong,* she thought, willing the message to enter his mind. *Soon, we will stand together in Antilia, and we shall be whole.*

"Well done," said Lothar. "Now, return to the altar." He turned his attention to Sarintha. "We have more work to do."

Chapter 16

The Forest of Golroc

Elliott was back in New Orleans, in his grandfather's den, with Lisa Hastings. Rain tapped against the clay roof tiles of the old house as a storm raged outside. Lisa stood before him. Her clothing was strange. She wore a flowing white tunic that reached to the floor, covering her feet. She was breathtakingly beautiful.

In the corner of the room, the door from the kitchen opened, and the fat kid from his grandfather's neighborhood stormed into the room, slamming the door behind him. Standing in the corner, the kid glared at him. Lisa didn't seem to notice the kid, and she smiled at Elliott.

His mother appeared on the landing upstairs. Her face was pale, and her eyes were sunk deep into her head. She was very thin. "Help me, Ell," she said. "You're my only hope."

He looked at his mother, wondering how much longer she would live, knowing it couldn't be long.

Then he heard a snarl in the corner and turned to the direction of the sound. It sounded exactly like the snarl of the wolf on the mountaintop. But it hadn't come from a wolf; it came from the fat kid in the corner. As Elliott watched, the fat kid's forehead grew thick, and his face grew wide and flat. A wide, bony ridge grew outward from his brow, causing his forehead to flatten. Broad, broken teeth jutted from his mouth, and coarse black hair grew out, covering his skin except for his face. His limbs grew thick and muscular, and his arms grew too long for his body. The monster, still wearing the kid's jean shorts and striped shirt, said to Lisa Hastings, "Your master awaits you." Its voice was unnaturally deep.

Lisa turned to face the monster, but somehow she was no longer Lisa. An unfamiliar though equally beautiful girl had replaced her. Birthmarks covered the skin between her fingers. The new girl looked thoughtfully at Elliott, staring at him with sad eyes. After several seconds, she turned away and walked to the monster in the corner and took its arm, glancing over her shoulder at Elliott before leaving with the monster.

Feeling an intense though familiar pain of rejection, Elliott stood motionless. After the pair had left, he looked up on the landing and saw his mother lying dead on the floor. The sight jarred him, and he felt as if he might vomit.

At that moment, his grandfather emerged on the landing and stood over the corpse of his daughter. He looked furious. "This is all your fault, boy," he said. "You could have ended it."

Elliott stared at his grandfather, bewildered. Then a door on the landing opened, and someone—or, rather, something—that looked like a rotting corpse walked out onto the landing and stood next to his grandfather. The animated corpse was much shorter than his grandfather and wore a leather shirt and pants tied in the front. It was Marvus. As Elliott and his grandfather looked on, Marvus opened his mouth to speak, but instead of words, thick, black serpents writhed out of his mouth, falling to the floor and squirming about the landing and over his mother's corpse. Just then Marvus's corpse, with a hint of surprise on its face, went limp and fell lifeless onto the corpse of Elliott's mother.

His grandfather pointed a long, bony finger at him as his face twisted with rage. "You, boy—this is your fault."

Elliott looked sadly toward his grandfather, but in the strange world of his dream, the old man was gone and Elliott was no longer standing in the house in New Orleans. He was alone, standing on a spindly mountaintop in a desolate, gray place with dark skies. It was sweltering hot. In the distance, he saw the lone silhouette of a cratered mountain. Lava spewed from the crater, rolling down the side of the *distant volcano and spilling into a sea of molten lava that extended as far as he could see. He looked to his feet. Far beneath him, lava licked at the base of the spindly mountain, and he realized that he stood atop a lone island in some strange, hellish world. He heard a whooshing sound above him and turned to see a shadow in the sky. Before he realized what was happening, the shadow crashed into him, knocking him from the craggy stone spire. He screamed. The air swished in his ears as he plummeted toward the sea of lava. Closing his eyes and wondering if it would hurt, he plunged into it, screaming.*

He awoke with a start, bathed in sweat. His muscles had never felt so stiff. For a moment, his surroundings confused him. He was in the middle of a forest, flanked on all sides by gigantic trees. Sunlight streamed through the mossy treetops and onto his face. It felt good. Slowly, he caught up to where he was. This was the Forest of Golroc.

A few feet away, Jingo slept, holding the slingshot tightly against his chest. Marvus lay next to him, his chest rising and falling slowly with each labored breath. Blood-soaked bandages draped his neck. He had hardly spoken since the attack of the wolves, and he looked even worse than last night.

Dread filled Elliott's mind as the past three days' events returned in a flood. As realization continued to dawn, the sense of doom that remained from the unnerving dream gave way to the more imposing doom of the present.

With Marvus asleep next to him, he heard leaves crunching behind him. Recalling Hooks's many warnings about the malicious inhabitants of the forest, he turned toward the sound just in time to see a blur of orange as someone or something dashed out of sight behind a tree. Jingo slept on, clutching the slingshot. Marvus, of course, was no help in his current state, and Hooks had taken leave of them yesterday morning, when they entered Golroc. Already, he missed him. He looked at the tree that hid the interloper, but couldn't say what lurked behind it. He considered calling out to Jingo but discarded the idea, not wanting to make any noise and attract the unwanted attention of who knew what sort of horrid creatures.

Just then a strange frantic, high-pitched chattering erupted from behind the tree. Leaves and dirt flew up in all directions, though the intruder remained hidden.

Elliott's mouth felt dry, and his heart pounded. A glance to his side confirmed that Jingo, amazingly, still slept. To his surprise, the two horses, picketed at the far edge of the campsite, continued grazing, unconcerned with the intruder.

Behind the tree, leaves and dirt flew up in a fury. And as Elliott watched in astonishment, a creature the size of a small monkey emerged from behind the massive tree trunk, making a high-pitched howl that finally jolted Jingo awake. Indeed, it appeared to *be* a monkey, though its coloring was strange: orange with black stripes, rather like the markings of a tiger. It had an expressive, humanlike face. Howling and baring its teeth, it threw up leaves and dirt in an aggressive display. The creature frightened him.

Jingo, now sitting bolt upright, had the slingshot aimed at the monkey. But his expression changed from belligerence to wonderment as the thing howled and threw up more leaves.

Jingo dropped the slingshot and stared, for the little creature's eyes glowed. It howled and danced about, beating the ground with sticks, seeming to accuse them of intruding into its space. Without a word, Jingo closed his eyes and turned his face toward the sky. He placed his hands over his chest and mouthed a prayer. Elliott recognized the rapt expression on Jingo's face. He had seen it before and had come to find it annoying.

Slowly, the ruckus abated until the tiger-monkey stood quietly before them, craning its head back and forth between them.

After several seconds, Jingo opened his eyes and stared at Elliott. "You have summoned a wedjat," he said in tone almost of reverence.

"No, I didn't," Elliott whispered. "I didn't do anything. I was just sleeping."

Jingo smiled. "You have summoned a wedjat, and that is cause for rejoicing."

The tiger-monkey paced back and forth at the base of the tree, watching them all the while. After a moment, it scuttled up the tree and sat high above them, staring down at their campsite.

With the creature settled on its perch high in the treetops and looking somewhat aloof, Elliott turned to Jingo. "What *is* it?" he whispered.

"It is an omen," said Jingo, "and a good one at that."

Elliott waited to hear more, but Jingo just stood up and said, "Ready your pack. It's time to get going." He couldn't stop smiling.

"But wait a second," said Elliott. "I want to know—"

"Ready your pack," Jingo snapped. "We must proceed through the forest with caution. We must limit our conversation and keep alert."

Annoyed, Elliott packed his blanket into the knapsack, brushed himself off, and stretched, already dreading another day sitting a horse bareback. From the way Jingo was acting, there would be no breakfast this morning. Elliott looked to the treetops and saw the strange tiger-monkey high above, watching with detached interest as they loaded Marvus onto the litter, mounted their horses, and started deeper into the forest.

Elliott winced in pain with each movement as they headed down the overgrown trail, with the wedjat following in the canopy high above.

The forest was unlike anything Elliott had seen—grander even than the Forest of Ondor, where he had first entered this strange land. As in Ondor, the trees were massive, their broad trunks wider than African baobabs, their tops soaring far overhead, trailing aerial roots and streamers of moss that wafted in the cool breeze. The ground was stony and covered with brightly colored leaves. Occasionally, they passed great formations of glistening white rock honeycombed with caves. And unlike the silent outskirts, the deeper forest was filled with animals. At one point, while searching the treetops for the wedjat, Elliott glimpsed an enormous multihued bird soaring overhead, but before he could ask Jingo about it, it vanished in the canopy.

He was growing accustomed to the strangeness of the place. Several times he saw giant furry beasts with long limbs hanging from the treetops, apparently sleeping the day away as they hung suspended from the high branches. Jingo, in a talkative moment, informed him that they were larilars and, despite their size and bizarre appearance, harmless. He also saw several large beasts on the ground, and several times Jingo stopped in the trail, raising a hand for silence, while strange animals crossed the trail in front of them.

⚑ ⚑ ⚑

Late in the day, Elliott was dozing off on his horse when it suddenly jerked sideways so violently it nearly threw him. Confused, he yanked at the reins, but the mare ignored him. Behind him, Jingo's gelding had also turned and had started to whicker. Elliott squeezed his knees against the mare's ribs and stroked its neck with his palm, whispering to it until, finally, he managed to calm it, though by now it had loped perhaps a hundred yards back down the trail.

When Elliott finally looked up, he saw that Jingo had regained control of the gelding, but he also saw at once the reason the horses had spooked in the first place: Up ahead, a large cat sat in the trail, licking its paw. The creature was brown with white stripes, and a pair of long, curved fangs jutted down from its upper jaw. As they watched, it took notice of them, and stared for perhaps a minute before roaring and slinking back into the trees. The fearsome cat spooked Jingo. He whispered that it was a simitar and would have eaten them whole had they not been cloaked in the wedjat's protection. Elliott tried to question Jingo further about the saber-toothed cat, but Jingo insisted on silence, raising a finger to his lips each time Elliott tried to ask a question. In time, the horses calmed enough that they could resume their trek, but as the day progressed, Elliott couldn't get the cat out of his mind.

Later they paused to watch a giant, bucktoothed beaver shepherding her kittens across the trail. At one point, she stopped to wait on a straggler. Patiently, she waited until the kitten caught up to her; then, ever so gently, she scooped it up with her mouth and placed it on her huge paddlelike tail.

And so it went, with morning turning into afternoon, then dusk. Everywhere around them, Elliott saw creatures big and small, all content to let the little party carry on unmolested, so that he wondered if perhaps Hooks hadn't been wrong after all. So far, despite the appearance of the saber-toothed cat, the forest was far more pleasant than the cold and perilous Azure Mountains.

In marked contrast with Elliott's growing optimism, Jingo remained wary and hardly said a word. Periodically he stopped to check on Marvus, each time appearing more concerned, sometimes dabbing at his friend's forehead with a cloth or rearranging his bandages, other times adjusting him in the litter to make him as comfortable as possible.

As daylight faded, they entered the heart of the forest. The trees were denser here, and the thick triple canopy kept out most of the waning sunlight, giving the place a dark and gloomy feel.

Out of nowhere, a deep sense of foreboding arose within Elliott. Though he couldn't put his finger on it, he had the sense that something terrible was about to happen, and he felt overcome with the desire to spur his horse to a dead run until they were out of this dreadful place. His horse, too, seemed spooked and was getting harder to control.

With darkness falling rapidly, they emerged into a clearing. At its edge stood a crumbling stone building, and Elliott had to wonder what sort of place it was and what sort of being would build it in such a place. It looked ancient.

The growing unease at the corners of his mind elbowed its way inward, blossoming into low-grade panic as they approached the building. He had a very bad feeling about the place, and his anxiety threatened to swell into outright terror as they rode closer.

The building was an ancient stone fort, surrounded by crumbling walls in various states of disrepair.

Get out of here, said a voice inside him. *You are in danger.*

Jingo, up ahead, craned his neck, giving Elliott the sense that he, too, was uncomfortable. Neither of them spoke. As they drew near, the horses whickered and sidestepped and seemed ready to bolt. And eventually, with the crumbling fort standing just before them, The gelding whinnied and kicked up its hind legs, nearly toppling Marvus's litter.

Something brooded inside the fort. Elliott felt it. "We have to get out of here," he whispered.

Jingo turned to him and nodded. His face was ghostly white. Without a word, he pulled his horse to the left and trotted away, looking behind to make sure the litter was secure.

With night falling quickly, Elliott followed. In the distance, he heard a roar like that of the simitar earlier in the day, and began to realize how vulnerable they were. And the anxious mare seemed ready to charge off at the slightest provocation.

In time they had traveled far enough from the clearing that the feeling of panic abated, though Jingo led them well past the outskirts of the fort. At last, he slowed the gelding to a walk and began looking for a place to camp.

This had been an unsettling start to the night, and Elliott had no idea how they were going to get any sleep. Over and over he heard Hooks's warnings in his mind. Like never before, he wished the big susquat were still with them.

"We'll make camp here," Jingo whispered, dismounting.

"What *was* that place?" Elliott whispered back.

Jingo turned his face to the treetops, searching for the wedjat. His demeanor was strange. "I don't know," he said, unslinging the pack from his horse. "Help me unload Marvus, and then take the horses to the stream and water them. I have a bit of dried cheese we can eat for supper, and I must redo my bandages, but after that, we must try to get some sleep. We'll have to take turns sitting watch."

"What are you afraid of?"

"Just do as I tell you," the gimlet snapped.

Elliott nodded and helped get Marvus off the litter. After checking the neck wound and covering him with a blanket, they took down the litter, and Elliott led the horses the few paces to the stream, filling the waterskins while the horses drank. Although the gimlets were only a short distance away, he felt uneasy and alone and hastily led the horses back when they had drunk. After picketing them in some long grasses, he returned and rolled out his blanket on the ground, feeling jealous that the horses could fill their bellies with grass while he would have only a rind of dry cheese.

"No campfire tonight," Jingo said, laying a damp cloth on Marvus's forehead. He handed Elliott the cheese. "Perhaps it was a bad idea to come here. Eat quickly and try to get some sleep."

"Thanks," Elliott said gruffly, tearing a bite from the wedge. "Wake me when it's my turn."

"I will. And try to think cheerful thoughts as you go to sleep."

Jingo was scaring him. "Why?"

"Because the forest makes you dream."

With thoughts that were anything but cheerful, Elliott finished his Spartan meal and lay down. Again he heard the roar of a simitar in the distance. The darkness pressed in on him, and he pulled his thin blanket to his chin against the cold.

Jingo got his water skin and sat at Marvus's side, wetting his fingers and placing them on his mentor's feverish lips. He sat between Marvus and Elliott, pulling his knees to his chest against the evening chill.

⚜ ⚜ ⚜

Elliott awoke with a start. He had no idea how long he had been asleep. Leaves rustled behind him. Something was in the campsite. From the corner of his eye, he saw a flash of motion.

Jingo and Marvus were gone. A furtive glance to his left confirmed that the horses, too, were missing.

He scanned the campsite, remaining motionless so as to appear asleep. He was terrified and could see little in the darkness. From the corner of his eye, he saw another flash of movement. He nearly screamed. To his right, he heard a footstep. He turned his eyes toward the sound but saw nothing. Terror gripped him. There was another flash of movement to his left, but from a different place than before. All around him, shadows darted back and forth behind the trees. Ready to run, he sat up.

Without warning, a lithe, hairless creature leaped from its hiding place and landed quietly beside him. The thing was all muscle, with long, spindly humanlike arms and legs, and oily skin that glistened in the scant moonlight. Like a demon from the darkest recesses of his psyche, it sat on its haunches and licked its lips, cocking its shiny bald head sideways and looking at him.

He screamed at the top of his lungs.

More of the bizarre creatures dropped into the campsite, landing all around him like gangly paratroopers. With great, froglike leaps, they moved into position around him. Though their eyes seemed to lack intelligence, they moved fast, closing in a coordinated attack. They appeared to be all arms and legs, with sinewy forelimbs that ended in claws rather than hands. Their black eyes were large and alien. They reached for him.

He screamed and pushed away.

The creature nearest him smiled, revealing a mouthful of small, perfect teeth. It reached out and grabbed him, and he screamed again as, with seemingly little effort, it hoisted him under one arm and leaped out of the campsite.

Elliott screamed until he was hoarse while his captor moved quickly through the forest, covering several meters with each soaring leap. In the darkness, he couldn't see anything, though he sensed the motion of the other creatures hurtling along beside them in the darkness. He tried to fight the creature, but he was no match. As the forest grew denser, his flailing body began to bump against the tree trunks, and his captor jumped into the treetops. High off the ground, it moved just as fast, leaping from branch to branch, moving higher and higher into the canopy.

After some time, a break in the foliage allowed a ray of moonlight into the forest, and for an instant, his vision returned enough to give him a glimpse of his captor. Its thin chest heaved with effort, and its gray skin was covered with a sheen of sweat. Its muscles glistened in the moonlight. For a split second, he could see that they were high in the treetops. If the creature dropped him, it would be a long, undoubtedly fatal fall to the

Like a demon from the darkest recesses of his psyche,
the creature sat on its haunches and licked its lips...
Elliott screamed at the top of his lungs.

ground. Elliott's head swam, and he felt woozy, as though he might pass out.

The next thing he knew, he was standing against a tree in the middle of a strange encampment. A large bonfire blazed in front of him. Jingo and Marvus were nearby, though the horses were nowhere in sight. Elliott was bound to the trunk of a tree so tightly that he couldn't move a finger. Marvus and Jingo were similarly bound, though Marvus remained unconscious. Jingo looked as terrified as Elliott felt.

A dozen of the grotesque creatures milled about the clearing. In the light of the bonfire, he could see them well for the first time, and they were frightful indeed: lean and muscular with long, sinewy arms and legs and squat, unnatural bodies. Some of them were feeding. Horrified, he watched them fight over a giant, furry drumstick torn from an unseen carcass. In the firelight, the drumstick looked like a meaty susquat leg, though the fur covering it was black rather than the brown of the only susquat he had ever met. One after another, they grabbed for the meat, each tearing away gobbets of flesh or licking at it with a long red tongue before another snatched the leg away. Row after row of sharp teeth ripped flesh from bone until, within a minute or two, it shimmered glistening white. When the bone was licked clean, one of the creatures tossed it onto a pile at the edge of the campsite. Then an awful ripping sound preceded the appearance of another leg, and the sequence repeated.

Though it might have been Elliott's imagination, he thought he heard a whimper coming from the feeding circle, and shuddered to think that the legless victim might still be alive. One of the creatures spat out a black clump of fur before wading back into the melee for its next bite.

Trying to keep the panic at bay, Elliott took stock of his surroundings. The blazing bonfire was in the center of a clearing surrounded by a circle of giant trees. All manner of creatures were bound to the trees surrounding the campfire, each suspended above the ground and held against the tree by some sort of silvery webbing. Elliott and the gimlets were bound with the same material.

Furry black susquats were bound to some of the trees. A few struggled against their bindings while others hung their heads in despair. A pair of huge wingless birds, similar to the magby that had attacked him in Ondor, were also bound. Directly across from Elliott, the giant beaver they had seen in the trail struggled against its bonds, its great tail slapping at the ground. Next to it, its imprisoned kittens mewled frantically.

As the frenzied demons finished the carcass they were eating, one of them broke from the group and leaped toward the beavers. With a single slash of its claw, it released the mother and slung it under an arm, returning with it back to the circle. It tossed the giant beaver on the blood-soaked ground, and they descended on it. Desperately the tail slapped at the ground, and it bellowed an awful sound. It occurred to Elliott that it must be something like the sound a cow made when being slaughtered. Then the terror of his own circumstances gripped him, and he began to sob.

The creatures finished with the beaver in short order. Amazingly, they still appeared hungry, and one of them scanned the perimeter of trees, deciding on the next victim. Its eyes settled on Elliott. Terrified, he looked to Jingo.

"No," Jingo sobbed. "This cannot be."

The creature leaped over to Elliott.

"No!" Jingo shouted. "Take me, you filthy devil. Leave him alone!"

It slashed at the webbing and hoisted Elliott under its arm.

"This cannot be!" screamed Jingo. "Take me. Take me!"

With Elliott in its grasp, the creature lowered its head and squatted. But before leaping back into the circle with him, it paused. Cocking its head to one side, it held him out in front of it and looked at his birthmarks. Finally, it leaped toward the feeding site.

Elliott and Jingo screamed in unison as the creatures surrounded Elliott, bobbing eagerly up and down, blood dripping from their chins.

Elliott closed his eyes. Then, inexplicably, the creature holding him leaped away from the circle and into the forest. Elliott's last vision was of the blood-spattered creatures in the circle, staring dumbfounded after him as he was carried deeper into the dark forest.

Chapter 17

Slipher's Quest

S lipher rubbed his donkey's nose and fed it a piece of fruit. "That's a good boy," he said. "Fill your belly—we have a long way to go."

Pongo licked at the fruit, then devoured it in a single gulp.

Slipher laughed and fed it another piece. "We have made much progress," he said, rubbing its muzzle. "You're doing a fine job. That's why Slipher gives you so much fruit."

The donkey brayed contentedly, licking at the second piece before swallowing it whole.

"Let's get some water. You're thirsty after our long day on the trail, no?"

The donkey stared at him, licking its lips, and he led it to the pristine lake just a few paces from their camp. "Have a good drink," he said. "We've got to keep our strength up." Slipher knelt to drink and chanced to see his reflection in the smooth water. He was much thinner than he remembered, and the stolen armor hung comically from him, giving him the appearance of a child wearing its father's clothes. He turned his head to the side, trying to gauge how his profile looked, and the helmet slipped down over his eyes. He adjusted it and tried again, this time scowling into the water to appear fearsome. "I am Slipher," he said to his reflection. "I bring greetings from Malus Lothar." He snatched at his sword, struggling to free it from its scabbard, and plunged its tip into the water, breaking his reflection into concentric rings.

"Take that, shamalan!" he said, his helmet slipping over his eyes again. "The malus gives no quarter to pagans."

Reclining against an embankment, Slipher reached for his pipe. "We're getting closer, Pongo," he said. "Imagine how pleased the malus will be when he hears that we've killed the shamalan boy from the prophecies!"

"Who knows what he'll do," Slipher continued while the donkey swatted flies with its tail. "Perhaps he'll reward me with a chest full of riches." He imagined himself standing before an adoring crowd, receiving such a chest from the malus. "Or perhaps he'll make me a general. Who knows how important I'll become! He may even give me a room at the castle, Pongo—far cry from a mud hut on the outskirts of town, eh?"

The donkey lowered his head and sniffed at the ground, perhaps scouting for another piece of fruit.

"And there will be a reward for you, too, Pongo, once the malus hears how you helped me slaughter the pagan."

The donkey sniffed at the air and urinated a noisy stream.

Slipher laughed. "I see that you, too, have disdain for the shamalan. You are a good friend." He finished packing his pipe. Then, realizing that he had no way to light it, he gathered some dry moss from the ground and fashioned it into a nest. After getting out the bow and socket from his pack, he found a straight stick and twisted it in the thong until it was taut. After working the bow back and forth, he soon had a tendril of smoke, and with a bit of blowing, he had a flame. Soon enough, a roaring campfire blazed before him. Grabbing a stick from the fire, he lit the pipe and took a deep puff. With the first pull, he felt his body relax.

"Let's see what they're up to," he said, exhaling a puff of smoke.

The smoke organized itself into a picture, and he watched, mesmerized, as it showed him and Pongo at the edge of their campfire. The picture expanded, giving a bird's-eye view of the Azure Mountains to his east, and the vast plain of the western lands, where he and Pongo were camping. As the picture zoomed out, the landmarks grew smaller as more of the landscape was revealed. Finally, he saw the whole of the Azure Mountains, with a large swath of forest on their eastern edge, before the picture zoomed in on the forest. And there it hovered, revealing nothing more. The puff of smoke disintegrated.

"I don't understand, Pongo," Slipher said. "Where is the boy?"

Pongo sniffed at the puddle of his urine.

Slipher took another drag on the pipe and tried again, with the same result. "I don't understand," he said. "Perhaps if we look for the grayfarers, we'll see something." He closed his eyes and concentrated on the two grayfarer councilmen who were also hunting for the boy. He had seen them several times while tracking the shamalan in the smoke. Holding an image of them in his mind, he puffed on the pipe, and again the smoke became a picture. It showed one grayfarer flying over the valley between the Azure Mountains and the swath of forest Slipher had seen in the earlier apparition. As usual, the picture zoomed outward, this time revealing the entire length of the forest before zooming back in on its southern tip. At the southern end of the forest, a second grayfarer scanned the perimeter between the edge of the trees and a large patch of swampland. A great distance separated the two grayfarers. And still the shamalan boy and his companions were nowhere to be seen.

"Ahhh," said Slipher. "The grayfarers have separated since last we looked upon them. I wonder if they know something. Still, it is strange that we cannot see the shamalan boy. What could this mean?" He stared into the distance. "Tomorrow we will travel through the last of the western lands and cut across the southern base of the Azure Mountains. We will go to the forest where the second grayfarer searches for the boy. We will wait for them at the edge of the forest." Pleased with the plan, he said, "Wouldn't it be glorious if we coordinated killing the boy with Viscount Ecsar's siege of Harwelden?"

Pongo's eyes were closed. He had fallen asleep.

Slipher took a deep puff on the pipe while holding the viscount in his mind's eye, then exhaled. The smoke became a bird's-eye view of Harwelden before zooming out to show the valley to the north, then the entire length of the Forest of Ondor. At the northern edge of the forest, the picture zoomed in on a large encampment, where scores of troops labored to build shelters that spread out over many acres. As Slipher watched, legions of troops arrived from the north. Viscount Ecsar sat at a wooden table with a cadre of warlords. The puff of smoke evaporated. "Oh, my!" said Slipher. "I have never seen so many warriors gathered in a single place. The army of pagans at Harwelden surely cannot sustain an assault from such a large force. These are historic times, Pongo. And we must make haste. It appears that the siege of Harwelden is imminent."

He dragged at the pipe again. "I will cut the boy into ribbons, and anyone who tries to stop me will understand his folly too late." The smoke drifted into the twilit sky, revealing no more, though he continued to puff contentedly.

As night fell, he took out the mirror and, pushing back his helmet, stared at his reflection.

He was pleased with what he saw. The handsome reflection looking back at him was nothing like the one he had seen in the water. As before, it was stronger, handsomer, and more confident. Turning his face to the side, he looked sideways at his profile. He found it striking.

"*Yes, quite striking,*" said the reflection.

Viscount Ecsar sat at a wooden table
with a cadre of warlords.

Though he had known what to expect, the comment unnerved him nonetheless. He dropped the mirror and scooted away from it.

"Overcome your trepidation," it said. *"I am a reflection of you—there is nothing fearsome in that."*

Slipher looked around the campsite. Except for the sleeping donkey, he was alone. He scooted toward the mirror and picked it up.

"Don't be such a coward," his reflection scoffed. *"You embarrass yourself."*

"I'm not a coward!" he insisted, though the hand holding the mirror trembled.

"How do you expect to complete your journey when you act such a fool? It is time you behaved like a warrior."

"Do not speak to me in such a tone," Slipher growled, "or I'll smash you against the rocks!"

The reflection laughed. *"To hurt me is to hurt yourself. I am the better part of you, and you'd do well to listen to what I have to tell you."*

He stared into it, turning his head to see if his reflection mirrored his actions.

It did.

"What, then, tell me," he snapped.

"The malus needs you. You must kill the boy."

"I know that," he sneered. "That is no help to me."

"It is help, indeed," said the reflection. *"You are weak. If you hope to kill the boy, you must do what I tell you."*

"It is *you* who must do what *I* tell you."

"Don't act the fool. Focus your thoughts. Find the boy and kill him."

"I'll teach you," Slipher muttered, putting the mirror back in its box and covering it with the cloth. "I'll not take that from you or anyone." He stared at the box. "I knew that would shut you up. Nobody calls me a fool." He took another puff on his pipe and leaned back against the embankment.

He woke late the next morning, with the suns high in the sky. The donkey stood grazing at the edge of the lake.

"We must ready ourselves for our journey, Pongo," Slipher said. "We've no time to spare. Soon we will find the boy and claim our rightful place in history. Have no doubt, one day they will sing our praises in the fields of Vengala."

He adjusted his armor and looked at his reflection in the lake. Striking various poses, he practiced his lines: "I am Slipher, and I bring greetings from Malus Lothar." he swung his sword in a flat arc. "Prepare for the tearful journey to Hulgaar." He thrust his sword into the water, breaking up his reflection.

After filling the water skin, he plucked several fist-size purple fruits from a nearby tree and stowed them in his pack.

"Soon, I will eat nothing but meat!" he said. And mounting the donkey, he kicked its flanks and pointed it east, toward the southern edge of the Azure Mountains, bordering Golroc. As they rode off, he held his back rigid in what he fancied a warrior's pose, and pushed his helmet back, tying it snug so it wouldn't slip forward again.

Chapter 18

Grimaldi

Across the room from where Sarintha lay paralyzed, Grimaldi hung on the rack, nailed there with Golthel's four stakes. A lone rat licked at a half-congealed puddle of blood beneath him. The serpan audience had been dismissed, and only Lothar and Golthel remained with the prisoners.

Sarintha lay with her eyes open, hoping they would think her unconscious.

Malus Lothar knelt over her, then looked up at Golthel, who was busy caging a pair of bloated Deccan cave spiders, each the size of a person's head. "It is enough," he said. "For now."

Golthel nodded, smiling at the fanged spiders as if they were pets. "It is a good beginning, master."

"But we must be careful," said Lothar. "As long as the Trident remains hidden, she is of use."

"Agreed," said Golthel. I will carry her to her cell and await your orders."

Lothar nodded. "Perhaps she will be more agreeable the next time we question her," he said, looking meaningfully at the box that held the spiders.

"Perhaps," said Golthel.

"Next time, we will learn what she knows of the boy."

"You know how I feel about that, master," Golthel replied. "I think the boy is of little importance."

"Viscounts Ecsar and Erebus agree with you, but we must

Grimaldi hung on the rack,
nailed there with Golthel's four stakes.

leave nothing to chance. His presence can inflame old superstitions and sow doubt among the troops. We must remove him from the picture."

"I agree that he must be killed," said Golthel. "A shamalan's blood is cheap."

"Yes," said Lothar. "I nearly had him in the Azure Mountains, but he has escaped to the Forest of Golroc. If he survives the journey through Golroc, I will send another beast for him. He won't elude me again."

Lothar walked to the window, turning his back to Golthel. "It is passion that motivates our warriors," he said. "Above fear, greed, and all else, it is their passion that ignites them."

"Yes," said Golthel, joining him at the window. "Their passion for warfare."

"Not that. It is their faith in Valderon that gives rise to their passion. Our warriors must find purpose in their acts if we are to succeed. The shamalans have always understood this. It is belief in the rise of Valderon that best motivates our troops, and we must fan the flames of that belief. Passion leads to victory, Golthel, and passion comes from faith."

"Aye, my lord," said Golthel. "And killing the boy will hearten them further."

Still gazing out at the courtyard, Lothar inspected the row of massive timber crosses he'd had planted around the edge, just beyond the central fountain. The crucified remains of disloyal serpans, in various states of decay, stared back from their perches. "Our people know of the shamalan prophecies," he said. "And the boy's presence may give rise to questions. We mustn't allow that to happen. I know not if our spies report the truth—if the boy has survived the test of a shamalan. Indeed, I've no idea of his purpose or whence he came, but we will not let him foil our preparations. We are too close to victory to let that happen."

"How, then, to dispatch the boy?" said Golthel.

"I've many different ways," Lothar replied. "It is only a matter of time before I shall nail his severed hand to my shield and present his corpse to the troops as they gather at Ondor."

Golthel grinned at the prospect.

"Imagine their delight to hear of the capture of an unknown shamalan in these final days of empire! Imagine their zeal when they see the shamalans' prophecy shattered!" The malus's eyes burned. "Valderon *will* rise, and Harwelden will crumble beneath the weight of the serpans' zeal, and we will know victory at last."

"If I may ask," said Golthel, "how go the plans for the siege of Harwelden?"

Lothar gave his sorcerer a baleful look.

"I . . . I do not mean to be forward, my lord," said Golthel, peering out at the line of unfortunates who had provoked his masters vengeance. "I apologize for my brazenness—your military strategies are best left to the viscounts. Please forgive me." He bowed and stepped backward.

"Remember whom you address," Lothar snarled. "I am not in the habit of discussing military strategy with my sorcerer."

"Yes, master. I will do well to remember." Golthel hunched before him, looking at the floor.

Lothar stared for a moment, then said at last, "Our plans for the siege of Harwelden are progressing."

Golthel exhaled a sigh of relief and looked up at him.

"Viscount Ecsar is amassing an army on the outskirts of Ondor," said Lothar. "An army the likes of which no one has ever seen. As we speak, troops march from Prytania and Obsidia to join Ecsar's forces. By the end of the season, all of Vengala's forces will join the viscount at the edge of the shamalan forest. We will strike Harwelden at the equinox, during their Festival of Opik."

"Splendid," Golthel murmured. "You've an eye for the symbolic, my lord."

Lothar seemed pleased.

"I am honored to serve you," Golthel said, "and to bear witness to the fall of the shamalan empire. When Harwelden is taken, my ancestors shall rejoice in the afterlife."

"And we'll have *another* surprise for the vermin at Harwelden," Lothar continued. "For Viscount Erebus has departed for Corythalia, where he will summon the armies of the Haviru to join us."

Golthel gasped.

"The Haviru owe us much," said Lothar. "Viscount Erebus will do whatever is necessary to secure their aid. With the added might of the Haviru, we will quickly rout the remnants of the shamalan army. Soon I shall sit atop the shamalan throne, and your people will migrate off this barren rock at last. Remain true, and you shall sit by my side in the great hall of Harwelden."

"I am humbled, my lord," Golthel replied. He looked up. "Shall I return the princess to her cell, then?"

Lothar nodded.

"And what of the grayfarer?"

"Do with him as you please. He knows nothing the princess cannot tell us, and his demise may encourage her cooperation." Lothar turned and left the room.

Golthel knelt over the princess and leered, then hoisted her over his shoulder and left the chamber.

⚜ ⚜ ⚜

Sarintha lay on the floor of her tower cell, shivering in the dark. She struggled to sit up, and though her body shrieked in pain, she was pleased to find that she could move again—though she fell on her first attempt, bumping her head against the stone floor. Again she struggled, and managed to sit up.

When the dizziness subsided, she tried to examine her wounds, but she could see little in the dark. Running her hand over her belly, she found dozens of swollen punctures and wondered if the spiders had injected her with venom. The bites stung with a vengeance, just as the malus had promised they would. Even this much motion exhausted her, and she lay back on the floor.

I am sorry, Father, she thought. *I am sorry, Baruna, but I can endure no more.* She thought of dear Grimaldi. *I could have saved him. And now his death will be for naught, because I can endure no more.*

Her thoughts turned to the chamber, and she imagined being placed in the sarcophagus. She pictured herself on the rack and cringed as she remembered Grimaldi's silent scream when his limbs were staked to the platform. And she pictured herself, finally, placed in the executioner's chair, the garotte tightening around her neck, the screw boring into her spine. Lothar was right. She had let Grimaldi die, and it was all for naught. She hadn't the strength of her fathers. She was not suitable to be queen. *Deliver me from this place, Baruna. I want no more of it.*

Steeling herself against the pain in her belly, she stood and walked the few steps to the window. A cold wind blew against her face as she stood overlooking the Sepulchre Mountains.

Looking down to the rocks far below, it occurred to her that she could fit through the narrow window. It was a coward's end, but she could do it. As she stood contemplating this final, terrible act, a strange voice entered her head.

You are right, Princess—it is a coward's end you consider.

Sarintha stiffened. *Who speaks to me?*

A friend, whispered the voice in her head.

This is some sort of trick, she thought, not intending her thoughts to be heard.

It is no trick, said the voice. *I am a friend of the empire, and I offer you my service.*

Who are you? Sarintha asked. *Show yourself.*

She heard laughter in her thoughts. *I am Grinjar,* said the voice. *Close your eyes and I will reveal myself.*

Again Sarintha peered out her window onto the rocks far below. She closed her eyes. *Show yourself, then.*

Light flashed behind her eyelids. In an instant, she was back in the torture chamber, peering across the room. Her vantage point was the floor beneath a corner of the rack where Grimaldi's body lay stretched out in agony.

Ah, yes, whispered the voice. *You can see through my eyes—good. Now, we must hurry, for we have little time.*

Her eyes remained closed as she stood in her cell. Something was letting her see through its eyes. She watched as the creature scuttled across the floor, through a puddle of blood, and up onto the rack where Grimaldi lay.

In the distance, she heard humming—Golthel, humming the same tune as when he carried her down to the chamber hours ago. She had to concentrate to realize that she heard Golthel not through her own ears but through the ears of this Grinjar. Golthel was close to the torture chamber.

What is your plan? she demanded. *I can hear the sorcerer.*

Yes, said the voice. *We must hurry. He will return soon.*

What are you? she thought, watching as the creature positioned itself near the pin locking the rack's wheel in place.

I am Grinjar, the voice repeated. *I was sent to keep watch on the malus, though no one has contacted me for some time. It was your father, King Gregorus, who asked me to come here.*

So her father had had a spy at Mount Sitticus. *What are you?* she repeated.

A rat, said Grinjar, *and I have seen what the malus has done to you and Grimaldi. The rats are no friends of Malus Lothar. But come—there is no time for talk.*

Grinjar moved directly in front of the pin holding the wheel in place. As she watched, he bit and pulled at it, trying to release it, but the pin didn't budge.

In the background, Golthel's humming grew louder.

From her cell far above, Sarintha watched breathlessly as the rat tugged at the pin with his teeth. Still it didn't move.

Suddenly, Grinjar leaped off of the rack and scuttled across the floor. She watched through his eyes as he crossed the room and ran into a hole in the corner. *What are you doing?* she asked.

I must get help, Grinjar replied.

He ran through a series of catacombs, twisting and turning until he reached a nest where several large rats lay sleeping. Grinjar squeaked in rapid fire, waking them. Noses twitching with excitement, they jumped up and followed him back to the chamber. Soon a cluster of rats stood staring at the pin on Grimaldi's rack.

Golthel's humming grew louder, as if he were in the next room.

Whatever you have in mind, thought Sarintha, *you'd better hurry. The sorcerer is close.*

With Grinjar squeaking directions, three rats bit the pin and tugged in concert, while two others pushed with their tiny pink paws from the other side.

To Sarintha's astonishment, the pin moved infinitesimally.

The rats gave another collective heave, and it popped free. Immediately, the wheel turned, releasing the tension on Grimaldi's tortured limbs.

And with every fiber of his being, Grimaldi screamed. But Golthel's spell held, and though his face contorted in agony, he made not a sound.

He's alive! thought Sarintha. *Praise Baruna, he lives!*

Though Grimaldi's cries were silent, the turning wheel made considerable noise. Simultaneously, Grinjar and Sarintha realized that Golthel's humming had ceased. In breathless anticipation, they listened, hoping to hear it resume. Instead, they heard footsteps. Golthel was approaching the chamber.

Grimaldi, now fully conscious, remained staked to the platform. Every cell in his body ached from the ordeal, and long holes were torn in flesh and bone where his limbs had pulled against the stakes. With the release of the tension, he found that he could lift his mutilated limbs over the narrow heads of the stakes, and slowly, agonizingly, he freed himself from the platform.

As he pulled himself free, the rats went to work on the ropes binding his wings.

Sarintha felt overjoyed. *Hurry, Grimaldi!* she thought. *Golthel is almost there!* Although she knew well that grayfarers were not given to that form of communication.

As the rats chewed feverishly at the ropes, Grimaldi struggled to free himself. He retched from the pain as he dragged himself from the platform and struggled to stand.

Hurry! Sarintha urged, watching the scene through Grinjar's eyes.

Golthel's footsteps drew closer. It sounded as if he would enter the chamber any second.

With his limbs free at last from the platform, Grimaldi struggled to stand, but something held him. Though he had managed to free himself from the stakes, he remained shackled to the rack.

As he struggled in vain, the clank of chains echoed throughout the chamber.

Grinjar squeaked instructions to the rats, and off they ran to the corners of the rack, where they began pulling at the pins holding the shackles in place. One by one, the pins pulled loose, and the shackles popped open.

Sarintha's breath caught in her throat as, through Grinjar's eyes, she watched Golthel enter the room and walk toward the rack.

"It cannot be!" Golthel shrieked, seeing the empty chains before him. Frantic, he scanned the room, inspected the chains again, then turned and ran from the room. "Sound the alarm!" he shouted. The grayfarer has escaped!"

Grinjar and his friends emerged from the shadows in the corner of the chamber, and all except for Grinjar scuttled back to their hole. Grinjar looked up to the rafters at Grimaldi, perched overhead. And after stretching first one wing and then the other, Grimaldi flapped, rose into the air, and gracefully left the room through a separate door in the corner.

Listen carefully, said Grinjar to the overjoyed princess. *We haven't a moment to spare.*

I'm listening, she replied.

The malus plans to strike Harwelden during the Festival of Opik. A great army assembles near the Forest of Ondor.

If I get out of here, thought Sarintha, *I will tell them.*

The malus hunts for a shamalan boy near the Forest of Golroc, the rat continued.

She gasped. *A shamalan boy? It is not possible!*

He hunts for the boy, Grinjar said, *and he means to kill him.*

I don't understand, Sarintha replied. *Explain yourself further.*

Dozens of serpan guards rushed into the chamber.

I can do nothing more, said Grinjar. *May the fates be with you.* And unnoticed by the guards, he skirted along the wall and retreated to his hole.

Many thanks to you, Grinjar. Sarintha opened her eyes. For the second time that evening, she peered out her window, this time looking not to the rocks below but to the skies. Outside her door, hurried footsteps drew nearer.

"Secure the princess!" someone shouted from the foot of the stairs below. "The grayfarer has escaped!" Footsteps bounded up the staircase, and she heard a key rattling in the lock.

Outside her window, Grimaldi appeared and perched on the sill. He was still unable to speak.

Sarintha climbed out and onto his back, placing herself between his wings as she clutched at his neck. She cried tears of joy. "I've never been so happy to see you, dear friend!" she said.

He gave her a weary smile.

The cell door opened, and a serpan guard rushed into the room—just in time to see Grimaldi fly away into the night, with the princess on his back.

Chapter 19

The Salax King

Jingo, held fast by the silvery webbing, stared after the gangly monster as it leaped out of the encampment with Elliott under one arm. Another of the creatures lifted its head and scanned the circle of bound prisoners, finally settling its gaze on Jingo. A single leap brought it eye to eye with him, whereupon it leaned into him, sniffing him up and down.

Jingo squeezed his eyes shut, steeling himself for the awful end that would soon come. Then, inexplicably, the creature jumped sideways to Marvus, as if having deemed Jingo somehow unfit. After sniffing at Marvus, it raised a claw and slashed through the webbing that held him. Oblivious, Marvus fell forward into its grasp. It tucked him under its arm and leaped back to the feeding circle.

Jingo watched as the salax spirited Marvus over to the feeding circle. No longer merely terrified, he felt defeated and, at bottom, sad that their lives should end this way.

The salax tossed Marvus into the middle of the circle, and the grotesque things moved more slowly, as if bloated by the all flesh they had already consumed. Nonetheless, they surrounded Marvus and squatted before him, just as they had done with all the ill-fated beings preceding him.

Desperate, Jingo looked to the treetops, searching for the wedjat, hoping against hope that something might happen to unseal their desperate fate. But there was no wedjat. Broken, he looked to the ground, unable to watch.

From somewhere in the distance, an ear-shattering screech filled the night.

Jolted, he looked up, searching for the source of the alien cry.

The demons in the feeding circle froze, staring into the forest, with the unconscious Marvus at their feet. A moment later, they left him unattended as they hopped to the edge of the forest, cocking their heads sideways and peering into the trees. One of them screeched, returning the call that had floated from the darkness.

In response, another high-pitched screech echoed in the distance.

The salax grew increasingly agitated. With abbreviated leaps, they scurried about the encampment, intermittently squatting and slapping at the ground, and staring into the forest.

Jingo watched with a mix of dread and curiosity, wondering what new horror was about to come calling.

Again the unearthly screeching pierced the silence. It was deafening now, as though whatever made the sound had come much closer.

The creatures scuttled and hopped randomly through the campsite, staring into the forest and growing more agitated.

From just beyond Jingo's line of sight, footsteps approached.

With the sound growing louder, the demons at last fell still, sitting on their haunches and facing the sound.

A second, larger group of salax shambled into the campsite. Elaborate patterns of gold and red paint decorated their faces and chests, and they wore crude bone jewelry. Their black eyes stared ahead, and they scarcely acknowledged the smaller members of their race squatting before them. Rather than leaping as the others did to get about, they walked upright, their long, muscular legs eerily out of proportion to their squat torsos. They walked in a formation of sorts, holding a wooden platform above their heads. Atop the wooden platform, another of the creatures sat hunched. It differed from its kindred in many ways. Its skin was not gray but blood red, and it was twice the size of the others. It wore a crown of bones on its head and carried a smooth wooden staff, decorated at the top with brightly colored feathers of many hues. Like those who carried it, it had painted its face and arms, although, unlike its naked brethren, it wore a shirt of fine golden threads that shimmered in the firelight. When his bearers brought him into the encampment, the red salax gave another ear-shattering screech. By the light of the bonfire, Jingo saw that the creature wore Elliott's bracelet—the lost bracelet of the nine clans.

The smaller gray salax, looking suddenly less fearsome, bowed to their king.

When the painted newcomers reached the center of the encampment, they stopped, and the red salax looked over the camp. He scanned the ring of trees and the prisoners bound there, paying special attention to Jingo.

Then he screeched again, and a third group of salax entered the encampment. These were also painted, and they carried a second platform, with a large stone cauldron on top. Straining under its weight, they marched into position beside their leader and lowered the cauldron to the ground. Water splashed over its rim as they worked it next to the bonfire.

With the cauldron in place, the red king leaped from his platform to the ground and lumbered over to inspect the cauldron. Apparently satisfied with what he saw, he turned to the forest and screeched.

In a single bound, one of the smaller, gray salax hopped from the cover of the trees into the center of the camp. It was the same creature that had carried Elliott away in the night. Nestled under its arm, Elliott flopped, dead to the world, as the creature carried him over to the cauldron.

By the light of the bonfire, Jingo saw
that the creature wore Elliott's bracelet—
the lost bracelet of the nine clans.

Jingo watched in silence, terrified to think that may have killed him already.

The salax tossed Elliott into the caudron, and he slid beneath the surface.

The salax, both gray and painted, surrounded the cauldron, jostling and nudging one another and bobbing up and down in their excitement, alternately peering over the rim of the cauldron and looking up to their king.

The king peered into the cauldron. After several minutes had passed, he reached into the water and lifted one of Elliott's limp arms above the surface, eyeing the birthmarks.

He seemed to find what he was looking for. Elliott's birthmarks widened and separated, and the hand grew wide, like a paddle, and thin sheets of webbing unfolded between the fingers. Underneath the surface of the water, he had transformed.

He's alive, Jingo thought, relieved.

The king threw back his head and screeched.

The other salaxes rejoiced, jumping up and down and slapping at the ground, and one of the larger, painted creatures from the king's retinue leaped over to the bone pile and banged two bones together.

All the while, the king sat holding Elliott's hand above the water. Spittle dripped from the corners of his mouth, and he screeched gently, prompting his subjects to quiet. He looked at the salax that had placed Elliott in the pot, and screeched at it in several different pitches.

Nodding, the smaller one leaped over to the feeding circle and picked up Marvus, placing him underneath one arm.

Jingo stiffened.

Then the salax leaped across the encampment and sat Marvus back up against his tree. Holding him there with one claw, it opened its mouth and spat a glob of sticky saliva onto Marvus's chest. The glob quickly solidified into the weird silvery webbing. The creature spat again and again, contorting its stomach and neck with each effort, as if working the material up from deep within. With each spit, another swatch of silvery glue matted Marvus to the tree. When finished, the creature lumbered back to the cauldron.

The king mewled rhythmically, and the smaller salax closed in around him, bobbing up and down as if entranced by his mewling tones.

Jingo understood what was going on. Gimlet lore held that shamalans were a particular delicacy to the salax, who believed that tasting the flesh of a shamalan would bring them long life and curry favor with their gods. To a salax, this was surely a once-in-a-lifetime event.

The salax king hoisted Elliott's limp body up out of the water, holding him by the arm.

Please, no, thought Jingo.

He lifted Elliott fully out of the water and, still holding him by only one arm, tossed him up in the air. The motion was as casual as that of a simitar toying with a rodent. The king caught Elliott easily and held his body lengthwise, over his head.

Even though Jingo had seen Elliott transformed once before, he was nonetheless amazed by the change in his appearance. His shimmering wet body was sinewy and muscled and differed greatly from his soft appearance in the castle less than a half season ago. The paddles that had replaced his hands and feet swung lazily beneath him, seeming disproportionately large. They looked to Jingo as big as the massive paws of a simitar.

The king adjusted Elliott's body over his head so that his grip was more comfortable. The king's blood red skin shimmered in the moonlight, accentuated by the golden glimmer of his shirt and the bright yellow and green paint covering his arms and face. Even the bony crown atop his head glistened in the firelight.

As the smaller salax and their many hapless prisoners looked on, the king turned his head upward and snapped playfully at Elliott's fingers with his razor-edged teeth.

Jingo was mortified. The salax king was preparing to take a bite of Elliott's hand. The smaller salax eagerly inched closer.

Then, with the speed of a serpent, the king's head darted forward and struck at Elliott's swaying hand. When the head withdrew, it had the end joint of Elliott's right index finger protruding from its mouth.

Elliott's scream filled the night.

The smaller salaxes mewled, swaying back and forth, and closed in, apparently aroused by the blood squirting from the stump of Elliott's severed finger.

Elliott struggled to free himself, but his strength was far outmatched. And while Jingo watched in horror, the king repositioned Elliott's body above him. Again he tilted his head upward, preparing to strike. He screeched, and his head struck forward and his arms dropped to his side so that, for a moment, Elliott was suspended in midair. The king then caught Elliott in his jaws, sinking his teeth into his side.

Jingo heard a cracking of ribs as the powerful jaws clamped down. Like a dog with a bone, he held Elliott in his mouth.

The smaller salaxes, still surrounding their king, bobbed up and down, their gleaming black eyes on Elliott as they edged closer to their master.

Elliott screamed, and Jingo fainted dead away.

Chapter 20

Slipher Prepares
to Attack

"Oh, Pongo," said Slipher, "we have to take a bath—we're beginning to stink." He laughed. "Can you believe we have traveled so far? Valderon has great plans for us."

Pongo just lumbered along the trail. To their left, the Azure Mountains stretched northward, seemingly to infinity.

"I could never have imagined seeing the Azure Mountains from this end of the range," Slipher said. "And look, I can see the beginnings of the forest depicted in the smoke. If we keep up this pace, we can be there in a less than a day's time. We'll be there waiting for the boy and his friends when they leave the forest."

The donkey paused to sniff the ground, then continued along the animal trail skirting the base of the mountains.

"I've been thinking about what we might do," said Slipher. "When I meet the child, I will rush him and run my sword right through him. He'll never know what got him. With Valderon guiding us, he won't stand a chance." He caressed the sword hilt at his waist, causing his oversize helmet to slip forward yet again. "Curse this thing!" he muttered, adjusting it and pulling at the chin strap.

"Or maybe I'll ambush him. When he passes by, I'll jump on his back and slit his throat. Then you and I will carry his head to Vengala and present it to the malus." He grinned. "Or maybe we'll force that stinking susquat to carry it for us. In fact, that thing is big enough to carry the whole carcass."

Pongo lumbered stoically on.

"And wait until I get my hands on those gimlets." Slipher stared blankly ahead, lost in thought. "We're making a good plan. With Valderon on our side, we cannot fail. Someday, young serpans will study the lore scrolls and read about us. They'll read about what we're doing right now. They'll probably read about this very conversation." He patted the donkey's neck.

"And don't worry, I'm not going to take all the credit. I'll be sure everyone knows you helped me. Slipher and Pongo!" He grinned.

As they plodded along, the sun sank low, and they stopped to make camp. After dining on rotten fruit—he had to pull bugs from the soggy flesh of the putrid fare before dividing it—he prepared a campfire and stretched out before the dancing flames.

He gazed out at the rising moon. *I wonder what Mother is doing right now,* he thought. *Probably preparing Oort for bed.* Slipher's younger brother, like him, was small for his age, and suffered the added insult of having been born deaf. When the defective child was born, Slipher's father and brothers were all for abandoning him at the base of Mount Scar, a forlorn wasteland at the outskirts of their village, where the white simitars came to scavenge at night. Though this was a common practice, Slipher's mother would not hear of it. Slipher, too, had argued against abandoning Oort, though the rest of the males in his family knew that he did so because he understood how close he himself had come to being left to the simitars. In Vengala, runts brought shame on their fathers. As the night grew cooler, he stoked the fire and added some sticks to the embers.

I wonder what they have heard about me back home, he thought, wincing at the shameful separation from his regiment.

Perhaps they've heard that I'm dead. The past two nights, he had considered calling up an image of his mother in the smoke, though he always found an excuse not to. He didn't admit it to himself outright, but he was afraid of what he might see back home. In Vengala, being the mother of a deserter was a difficult burden to bear.

Again he jabbed at the fire with a stick, causing the flames to brighten once again.

But soon I will redeem myself, he reflected. *All I must do is kill the boy.* The thought brought him some comfort, and he smiled and packed his pipe.

The chirping of cydonia bugs filled the air. It was a peaceful night, and in what had become his evening ritual, he took a stick from the fire and lit the pipe. He had learned many days ago that the tobacco pouch was literally bottomless. No matter how much he smoked, it was always full the next time he packed his pipe.

He pulled deeply, inhaling the coarse smoke, and as always, his body relaxed with the first inhalation. While he held his breath and let the smoke take its effect, he pictured the boy in his thoughts. Slowly, he exhaled, and the smoke whirled and took shape before him. First, he saw a smoky version of himself and Pongo in their camp. Then the scene pulled back, as usual, reducing his camp to a speck while revealing the whole Forest of Golroc. Then the focus moved to the southern half of Golroc. Here the image froze high above the forest. For the past two days, the pictures had consistently stopped over the Forest of Golroc, always failing to show him the boy.

"What's the matter with this thing?" he muttered, shaking the pipe. To test it, he decided to focus on another scene—the one he had been loath to call up. Steeling his nerves, he pictured his mother and his little brother, Oort. Then he drew on the pipe and exhaled. The smoke showed him the entire length of the Carafayan continent, with the Azure Mountains forming a rocky spine along the eastern portion. It then panned, depicting the neighboring Vengalan and Carafayan continents, connected by the narrow land bridge known as the Deccan Traps. Then the scene narrowed on Slipher's village in the foothills of the Sepulchre Mountains, and finally on his mother.

It was daytime in the village. She knelt on the ground outside a crude gate fashioned of wooden palings that were sharpened at the tip and angled outward. Her headscarf whipped behind her in the wind.

Slipher winced. His mother was outside the gates—a sure sign that she had been cast out from the village.

She was thin and wore threadbare clothing, and she was shivering. Beside her lay the frozen corpse of a young male. She held the stiff little body in her arms, caressing its cheeks and rocking back and forth. The picture disintegrated.

Slipher stared at the space where image had been, then slumped against the log. Tears formed in the corners of his eyes.

After a time, he wiped his eyes and relit the pipe. He thought of his father, whom he hadn't laid eyes on in many seasons, and inhaled the smoke. When he exhaled, the smoke showed him a battlefield on the outskirts of Obsidia, the city of black glass in the center of the Toltugan desert. The battlefield was covered with bones. Above this battlefield, the smoke lingered briefly, then disintegrated.

His father was long dead; nothing remained of him but bones in a field. At least three revolutions of the Enstar had passed since the battle for Obsidia.

Slipher drew again on the pipe, this time thinking of his eldest brother, the one who had treated him the most cruelly, but whom he most wanted to emulate. The smoke showed him a picture of a battlefield outside the forest city of Iracema. The battlefield was lined with rotting, flyblown corpses. After lingering above the Iraceman battlefield for a few moments, the smoke disintegrated.

Shaken by the images, Slipher inhaled again, thinking now of his only remaining brother. Again the smoke showed him a battlefield, this time at the edge of Prytania, where Viscount Ecsar had slaughtered King Gregorus last season. The smoke hovered briefly above a litter of gimlet and serpan bones before disintegrating into nothingness.

Slipher could take no more. He threw the pipe into the dancing flames of the campfire and sobbed.

He felt warmth on his breast. *"Stop blubbering, fool,"* said a voice.

He reached for his pocket and removed the mirror. It was hot. The handsome reflection stared back at him. It looked angry. "What do you want from me?" he asked, his voice barely rising above a whisper.

"Collect yourself," it said. *"I am ashamed for you."*

"But," Slipher whispered, "my family . . ." He stared at his reflection.

"Release the bonds you once held dear," said the reflection. *"They make you weak."*

He threw the mirror against a rock, hoping to shatter it, though it remained whole.

"Shut up!" Slipher screamed. "You will not talk to me like that!"

The reflection laughed at him. *"Your mother does not cherish you. Your family did not love you. Even little Oort was ashamed of you. Is it really possible that you never realized this?"*

"Shut up!" he shrieked. And grabbing a stone from the ground, he hurled it at the mirror.

"Every night before she went to bed, your poor mother bemoaned that she never abandoned you when she had the chance. Now look at what you've done to her."

"It's not true," Slipher whimpered, slumping to the ground.

"*Oh, it's true,*" the mirror replied. "*You owe them nothing. Renew your allegiance to yourself. Stand strong and hunt for the boy. Carry his head to the malus, and you will gain the respect you deserve. Sit blubbering in the wilderness, and you will die like the dog your family thought you were.*"

"Stop!" Slipher placed both hands over his ears.

"*Kill the boy! Free yourself from the bonds of sentiment and accomplish the act you are destined to perform. Now, stop blubbering--it sickens me.*"

In a fit of rage, Slipher got up and unsheathed his sword and drove its point into the mirror. But the mirror did not break. His reflection laughed at him.

Frustrated, he threw his blanket over the mirror. For the moment, it was quiet. Satisfied, he sat back down by the fire.

From beneath the blanket, he could hear his reflection laughing at him.

Whether from exhaustion or the effects of the smoke, he finally fell asleep. But even in his dreams, the muffled tones of the laughing mirror continued to haunt him.

♦ ♦ ♦

When Slipher woke, it was late in the morning. Pongo stood hobbled several paces away, grazing on thistles. After rolling up his blankets, Slipher dressed himself in the ill-fitting armor. After some inner debate, he put the mirror in his breast pocket. Thankfully, it was silent. Before mounting the donkey, he walked over to the coals of last night's fire and stirred them with a stick. There amid the ashes lay the pipe, unharmed. He stared at it for a moment, then pocketed it, too. And mounting the donkey, he rode off down the trail.

They walked all day, making good time and stopping only to drink from the creeks they crossed near the edge of the approaching forest. By nightfall, the scrub trees at the outskirts of the Forest of Golroc surrounded them. The massive, moss-covered trees of the forest were now close enough to throw a stone at.

"We'll make camp here," Slipher said. His helmet slipped forward. Angrily, he yanked it from his head and threw it on the ground.

Pongo looked inquisitively at the helmet, as if to be sure it contained nothing edible.

"We have no more food," Slipher said as he dismounted and tied Pongo to a tree. "We'll be without supper tonight."

After striking a campfire, he took the pipe from his pocket, his hand shaking slightly as he packed it with tobacco from the pouch.

"No sentimentality tonight," he said. "We have work to do."

He lit the pipe and lay back against a log near the fire, and with thoughts of the shamalan boy in his head, he conjured a picture. But still the smoke showed him only the aerial view of the Southern edge of the forest.

What did this mean? Could the shamalan already be dead in the forest? Slipher tried again, and again the smoke showed him only the forest. But this time he saw something he had missed in the earlier picture: a grayfarer, flying in circles over a particular swatch of dense trees near the middle of the forest. Searching his thoughts, he realized that he had seen this grayfarer several times in the smoke, and always circling near the same area of the forest.

Closing his eyes, he concentrated on the figure and inhaled. It circled and circled, staring down into the forest, sometimes flying just above the treetops as it strained to see through the dense foliage.

Slipher conjured the pictures of the grayfarer over and over, trying to find some sort of clue to what the flying beast might know that he himself had not yet discovered.

Finally, after countless exhalations of the smoke, the gray-farer flew a straight line southward and landed near the scrub at the forest's southern edge. Slipher turned and looked to his right. The spot where it had just landed was only a short distance from where he now camped.

Hurriedly, he threw dirt on the fire. About three hundred paces away, campfire smoke curled upward.

Silently Slipher put on his armor and buckled on his sword. After throwing more dirt on the fire for good measure, he slunk toward the grayfarer's smoke, grateful for the loud droning of the cydonia bugs. He crawled on his belly, maneuvering under the thick brush.

Slipher had never been so close to a grayfarer. It was a massive creature indeed, though smaller than its estranged cousins the black darfoyles, the race of his former commander, Viscount Ecsar. It sat a few feet from the campfire and appeared to be talking to itself, though Slipher couldn't make out the words.

He wriggled closer, to within perhaps ten paces, and saw that the grayfarer was not talking to itself after all—it was conversing with, of all things, a large rat. He listened.

"Don't get short with me!" said the rat. "I have been trying to catch up to you for days. Do you have any idea what an effort it is to keep up with something that *flies*?"

"I have long remained in the same location, awaiting your arrival," said the grayfarer. "I need to know what you can tell me of the boy. The forest canopy is so dense, I cannot see anything on the ground. From time to time, I hear him down there, but I cannot discern why he moves so slowly."

Slipher grinned. So the boy was alive!

"He is in grave danger, Woolf," said the rat. As we speak, the salax hold him prisoner. I believe they mean to eat him. Earlier this evening, I spoke to a beaver who witnessed the horrible death of his mate at the hands of the salax. With his own eyes, he saw the boy carried off into the forest. Marvus and Jingo are also prisoners, and Marvus is said to be gravely wounded. As the male beaver chewed at the bindings of his three kittens, which were also captured, the salax king himself brought Elliott back to the scene. The gray salax were so agitated by the presence of the shamalan and the king salax that the beaver managed to free his kittens, and they fled into the forest. He does not know what happened to the boy."

"I have to go in there, Taldar," said Woolf. "Can you tell me his exact location?"

"I don't know if that's a good idea," said the rat. "With due respect, a single grayfarer wouldn't be much of a match for a colony of salax.

"Where is Councilman Fanta?" Woolf asked. "Perhaps he can assist me. We mustn't waste any time"

"I'm afraid Councilman Fanta won't be any help—he is many leagues north of here, far off the boy's scent." Taldar hesitated a moment before continuing. "And I don't think you would want his help anyway."

"And why is that?"

"This is a delicate topic, to be sure," said Taldar, "and I have no wish to insert myself into council politics."

"Out with it," said Woolf. "What do you know?"

"Well," said the rat, "it just so happens that one of my kindred was scavenging in the castle the evening before your departure. He sends word that . . . I can assure you, this news has reached my ears only recently—you know how long it can take for news to travel such a distance."

"Spit it out," Woolf snapped.

"Councilman Fanta has received direct orders from Chancellor Waldemariam to execute the boy on sight."

"This cannot be true."

"I'm afraid it is," said Taldar. "Vermin never lie."

"And your kinsman heard this with his own ears?"

"He heard Waldemariam issue the order himself."

"And Councilman Fanta agreed?"

"By my account, Councilman Fanta was in complete agreement." Taldar paused. "Councilman Oskar was present for this discussion as well."

"Unbelievable," Woolf growled. "Waldemariam and those two scheming fools want to *kill* the boy?" His eyes narrowed to slits. "How can the council be expected to govern during wartime when we act in secrecy and at cross-purposes to one another? No wonder we find ourselves in such a diminished position! Waldemariam and his two knaves should be publicly drawn and quartered, for their actions are nothing less than treason."

Taldar looked away. "As I said, I would prefer not to get involved in the council's doings."

Slipher listened intently, trying to process what he was hearing.

"We'll talk more about this later," said Woolf. "Tell me where the boy is."

"He is held in dense forest about one-quarter of the way in from where we sit. Word has it there was a raging bonfire at the site, which might help you locate it."

"I'll see what I can do," said Woolf, donning his armor.

"Before you go," said Taldar, "I have news that should interest you."

Woolf paused for a moment, then lifted off the ground and headed skyward. As he departed, he said, "Stay there—you'll tell me the rest when I return."

"Travel well," said Taldar. But Woolf was already gone.

Slipher listened intently, trying to
process what he was hearing.

Chapter 21

The Salax King
and the Satyral

Jingo watched in horror as the salax king jerked his head violently to and fro, sinking his teeth deeper into Elliott's side with each shake. The crown of bones fell from his head to the blood-soaked ground, and the blood he had slung across his smooth head gleamed in the moonlight.

Suddenly, Elliott vomited great gouts of water, and the webbing on his hands and feet shrank back.

The smaller, gray salax slunk closer to their frenzied king, pressing their oily flesh against him as they strove to get closer to the boy. Those who came within reach raised their claws and slashed at him, becoming further aroused with every fresh rivulet of blood.

As Jingo looked on in horror, Elliott struck feebly at the king's head, but his fists, finding no purchase on the smooth, blood-slick flesh, slipped off. In time, his futile defense weakened, and his breath grew shallow.

One of the salax leaped up from the ground and planted his teeth in Elliott's thigh. Another grasped his arm. One by one, they latched on to him, their collective weight slowly forcing him, along with their king, to the bloody soil below, where he disappeared under the backs and bobbing heads of the creatures encircling him.

From the treetops above came a long, low howl.

Jingo looked up, hoping against hope that the howl signaled the return of the wedjat. It was unlikely, he knew—any number of creatures might have made the noise. Moreover, he had no idea how a wedjat's presence might counter the actions of the colony of feeding salax, or whether it might save his friend.

But the sound had gotten the salax's attention, and they stopped and peered into the canopy.

Again came the long, low howl.

One by one, the salax stepped away from the boy, apparently fearful of the lonely howl, until only the king remained. Like a predator refusing to part with its kill, the king held the limp and bleeding boy in his jaws.

Just outside the camp, Jingo heard the crunch of leaves and sticks as something approached. He watched in disbelief as a creature even stranger than the salax entered the encampment. He had not believed such things were real, even though the ancient texts told of them. Their race was said to be among the oldest in Pangrelor, but never in his life had he thought he would see a living, breathing chimera.

It had the head and torso of a man, springing from the body of a simitar, with the tail of a scorpion. It was a satyral, a member of the legendary race of rulers from the very dawn of Pangrelorian history, from the age of Malgothar, when Valderon ruled the world. Its fur was sleek and of a deep lavender hue, giving it a regal appearance. Long horns swept back from its skull, and a segmented tail culminating in a row of thorny spikes rose over its back as if ready to strike.

Thunderstruck, Jingo forgot for the moment the dire peril he and his companions were in.

Another howl came from the treetops, and the satyral looked up. He nodded at the wedjat, which sat crouched on a branch not so far above.

The salax king jerked his head violently to and fro,
sinking his teeth deeper into Eliott's side, but stopped when
he heard the long, low howl of a wedjat from the treetops.

Jingo was staggered. *A wedjat and a satyral. Who would be-lieve it?*

The gray salax backed away from their king, leaving him to face the bizarre creature alone. Though the satyral looked formidable, the hulking salax king towered over him. The king released Elliott from his jaws, discarding him on the ground, and the two stared at each other in silence.

Behind the satyral, the foliage rustled, and to Jingo's mounting astonishment, a huge brown susquat rushed into the encampment and stood beside the satyral, growling and bar-ing his teeth at the salax king. It was Hooks, and the ghastly wounds on his legs were gone. Jingo had never been so happy to see someone.

The satyral nodded at Hooks without looking away from the salax king.

And just when Jingo had decided that things could get no stranger, from behind Hooks a fourth newcomer entered the clearing. An old man in a flowing green tunic stood leaning on a staff, beside the susquat. A hood concealed his face from view. Side by side, the three of them stood facing the salax king.

Overhead, the wedjat howled again. All the salax, except for their king, had retreated to the edge of the clearing, where they sat on their haunches, bobbing agitatedly up and down.

The satyral was first to speak, directing his comments to the group of salax at the edge of the camp. "Leave us now and I shall spare your lives," it said. "My business is with your king." The satyral's voice, alien, deep, and somehow musical, rever-berated through the forest.

One of the salax turned to the trees and leaped out of sight, and within seconds its comrades followed, until only the king remained. The clearing was now eerily quiet.

"This is not the time for agression, Kerberos," the satyral said. "If you value your life, you will remove that bracelet from your wrist, place in on the ground, and leave my sight at once. You know full well that your strength cannot match that of a grown satyral."

The salax king lifted his head and screeched, louder and longer than before, then reached to the ground and picked up his crown of bones, placing it defiantly on his head.

"I'll not warn you again." The satyral looked at Elliott, lying in a heap on the ground. "The boy has the favor of the wedjat, and you will do him no more harm." The satyral crossed his arms and raised his tail ominously behind him.

Slowly, the salax king squatted on his haunches, removed the bracelet of the nine clans from his wrist, and dropped it on the ground. He leaned forward, his eyes narrowed to slits.

"Leave us," boomed the satyral.

The salax king loosed an unearthly screech and, with claws outstretched, lunged at the satyral.

In the blink of an eye, the satyral's tail swung forward, hurling a poisonous dart, which sank into the salax king's throat. The salax king fell, dead even before he hit the ground with a wet thud.

The old man pulled back his hood and rushed to Elliott's side with surprising speed. Reaching into his sleeve, he took out a small vial and placed a single drop of silvery liquid from it on the boy's tongue.

Hooks scooped Elliott up and cradled him in his arms. "It's not working," he said to the old man. "We're too late."

The old man closed his eyes and stretched his arms over Elliott's body. "*Ga-no-du,*" he whispered. "*Uh-la-ne guh. Ga-no-du.*" His voice grew louder as he spoke the incantation.

Elliott didn't move.

Crosslyn looked up at Hooks and then to the satyral. His expression spoke volumes.

The satyral nodded. "Keep trying."

The old man closed his eyes and chanted the syllables again.

A brisk wind blew through the clearing, stirring up the fallen leaves. The wind strengthened, stirring the leaves into a dervish, and the leaves of the trees surrounding Elliott began to turn brown. A faint glow appeared between Elliott, still cradled in Hooks's arms, and the ground.

Overhead, the browning of the leaves progressed, as if the trees' entire life span had somehow sped up to play out in a matter of seconds. The trees themselves began to wither, and their bark grayed and turned white. As the trees wilted, the glow beneath Elliott intensified and seeped upward and around his body, like water flowing against gravity. Strands of the light trickled into his wounds, mixing with the blood, and the lacerations on his arms and legs began to close.

"It's working," Hooks said, staring back at the trees.

The wind blowing through the clearing gained force, blowing the crown of bones from the dead salax king's head and sending it tumbling into the forest.

"*Ga-no-du!*" the old man said.

Thunder tore through the sky.

With a palpable force, the remaining life force left the trees all at once, and a loud thunderclap filled Jingo's ears as they shriveled to wispy husks. The wind rose around them.

Before everyone's eyes, the wound in Elliott's side began to glow from within. A large chunk of flesh and ribs that had nearly separated from the torso knitted itself together, dividing the chutes of light that sprang forth from within as the wound began to close. New skin poured like slow-flowing honey over the sealed wound, until not even the tiniest cut was visible. Elliott was whole again, though his breath still came in quick, shallow pants.

Exhausted, the old man slumped to the ground.

After what seemed an eternity, Elliott stirred.

"Magnificent!" whispered Jingo, and Hooks bellowed triumphantly. He ran to Jingo and hugged him, embracing the tree that held him as well. A purring sound emanated from his throat.

Jingo laughed. "It is good to see you, too, Hooks. Now, get me down from here."

"I never thought I'd be so happy to see a gimlet," Hooks said as he took a dagger from his belt and cut through the silvery webbing.

Jingo fell to the ground and ran at once to the boy's side.

Slowly, Elliott opened his eyes. His hand ran along the length of his torso; then he held his arms out before him and inspected them, noticing that the tip of his right index finger was missing.

"What happened?" he asked, looking not entirely invested in the weight of the moment, as if he had just woken from a deep sleep.

"You have just been delivered from the brink of death," the satyral said. "No small feat, to be sure. Give thanks to the trees, who have sacrificed themselves so that you might live. And give thanks to this old warlock, without whom you would be dead." The satyral nodded at the old man, who sat on the ground, drenched with sweat.

Elliott looked at the satyral in confused disbelief. "I don't understand," he whispered.

"I am Jemtel the satyral. I have ruled over Golroc for more than an age." He looked to the treetops. "Your wedjat enlisted my aid."

"I knew it!" Jingo said.

"Indeed. And on the way here, I encountered these two." He nodded to Hooks and the old man. "And a good thing I did, for I have no knowledge of the old magic. If not for Crosslyn, this boy would be lost."

The old man stood up. He towered over the boy. "May I introduce myself?" he said, extending his hand. "I am Crosslyn of the swamplands, priest of Harwelden during the reign of King Dagnar. And I have been waiting a very long time to meet you."

Elliott stared at him. He was tall and tan, with a mane of white hair that was speckled with black. He wore a flowing green tunic, and deep wrinkles carved a map in his face. Purple birthmarks ran from between his fingers to the wrist. Elliott grasped his hand, and they looked into each other's eyes for what seemed a long time.

"Well . . . uh," Elliott said finally, "thank you for saving my life." He turned to the satyral. "And thanks to you, too, Jemtel." He couldn't take his eyes off of the strange creature.

Jemtel nodded. "I leave you now, but get out of this forest as quickly as you can. The salax will regroup." He paused for a moment, as if contemplating his next words. "And be warned that foul things are afoot at the bastion of Malgothar." He looked at them, perhaps gauging whether they grasped the import of his warning. "Valderon is in the forest."

And with that, he turned and left.

Jingo stepped toward Elliott. "I think the bastion of Malgothar is the stone fort we passed at dusk."

With the satyral gone, Hooks ran to Elliott and gave him a shaggy embrace. "It's so good to see you again!" he said. "I knew you would get yourself into trouble without me."

Elliott smiled, burying his face in the thick fur. "I'm glad to see you, too."

"And what shall we do about this one?" the old man asked, stepping over the carcass of the salax king toward Marvus, still glued fast to his tree trunk. "As I understand it, this unfortunate gimlet is the reason Hooks brought me here in the first place." The old man felt the sticky silvery webbing, then raised his fingertips to his nose. "Of course, we must do something about these other prisoners as well."

Jingo blushed. In all the excitement, he had forgotten his friend. With Hooks helping, he rushed to cut Marvus from the tree. "It's his neck, sir," he said as they gently laid him on the ground. "A wolf mauled him."

"Yes, I've heard the tale," Crosslyn said, kneeling over the deathly pale gimlet.

"Can you help him?"

Crosslyn looked slyly at Jingo. "We'll see. Remove the bandages."

The blood-soaked bandages were putrid, and the wound had turned black. Several maggots wriggled in the reeking, diseased flesh. Jingo recoiled, shocked at the wound's appearance, and rebuked himself for not giving it greater care.

"Don't worry," Crosslyn said. "We've got much more to work with than we had with the boy." Closing his eyes, he held his hands before him. "*Curatio menda,*" he said.

"You can use the new magic, too?" Jingo said in surprise.

Crosslyn looked at him dismissively, then closed his eyes. "*Curatio menda abundo.*" He held his hands before him, and a small glimmer of blue light appeared above his hands, growing to the size of a seer stone. It began to pulse at the rate of a beating heart.

Crosslyn opened his eyes and inspected the ball. Satisfied, he hurled it at Marvus. It struck him in the neck, and rivulets of blue light trickled the length of the wound. Like liquid, the light ran through every recess of the diseased tissue, then slowly diminished in brightness and was gone. The wound had vanished, leaving the flesh smooth and clean.

For the first time since the attack on the mountain, Marvus opened his eyes. "Where am I?" His voice was thick. "What in the name of Antilia is going on? And what is that terrible smell?" He pushed up onto his elbows and looked around. His face contorted into a grimace. Finally, his eyes settled on Hooks. "You smell as if you haven't bathed all season," he whispered, turning up his nose.

And then, slowly, as if still not awake, Marvus closed his eyes again and rolled onto his side. In seconds, he was sleeping.

Hooks grinned with relief. "Back to his old self already,"

"He'll sleep for a few days," said Crosslyn. "Gimlet reserves are small, and he will need some time to regain his strength, but he will be fine."

Hooks picked Marvus up and slung him over one shoulder. "Good. Now, let's get out of this accursed place."

"We have a few more things to attend to," Crosslyn said, turning to the remaining prisoners, which included a small, dark susquat and the wingless birds. The strange susquat looked back at him with a mixture of fear and awe.

"Of course," said Jingo. And flicking out his dagger with his good arm, he went to work freeing the prisoners.

"And I think we might want to hang on to this," Crosslyn said, kneeling to retrieve the bracelet of the nine clans. He inspected it before tossing it to Elliott. "Put this in your knapsack," he said. "It isn't safe for you to wear it. And the salax king—he wears something that I think will be of value to us."

Elliott followed him to the salax king's carcass.

The body was a glistening heap. Rolls of bloodstained blubber glimmered in the moonlight, and the short forelimbs stuck out comically before it, frozen in a last, futile defensive parry. Elliott looked repulsed. "It's gross. How did you kill it?"

"Not I," Crosslyn said, examining the dart in the creature's neck. "Few can survive the sting of a satyral. We're quite lucky to have come across Jemtel, for the salax are resistant to all forms of magic—my skills would have been of little use against the red king."

"It was the wedjat that summoned him," Jingo said, peering up into the canopy. But the strange tiger-striped monkey was gone.

Jingo finished cutting the prisoners loose. The last of them, the dark susquat, was smaller than Hooks and had a bright maroon splotch, like a birthmark, across its face. It was timid and seemed afraid of them. Once freed, it nodded at Jingo and walked to Crosslyn. It lowered its head, refusing to make eye contact with him. It was crying. After bowing to Crosslyn, it went to Hooks, who towered a foot above it. It knelt on the ground before him and bowed its head.

Unsure how to interpret the act, Hooks patted the dark susquat on the head.

The creature was trembling. In time, it stood and retreated to the clearing's edge. Before disappearing from view, it turned to face them. "*Aaank uuu*," it said, raising a hand. A tear rolled down its cheek. It then turned and vanished into the forest.

"What did he say?" asked Elliott.

"He was thanking us," Hooks said. "I had no idea those creatures could speak."

Crosslyn smiled. There was a twinkle in his eye. "Ah, Hooks," he said, "there is much you don't know about the susquats of Golroc."

Hooks looked at Crosslyn strangely.

"Yes," Crosslyn said, turning to Jingo. "It was the wedjat who summoned Jemtel to your defense. Baruna has smiled on us all tonight. Now we must return to the task at hand." He leaned over the dead salax king and ran his hand along the golden shirt that the beast wore. As he caressed the shirt, waves of motion pulsed across it, making it appear alive. "Vibrissae." He looked up. "This shirt is made from the fibers of the Primordial Tree. I'd recognize it anywhere." He carefully removed the shirt from the salax king's body. As soon as it was loose, it shrank to the size of an adult human male. "I can't imagine where he got it from. That is no doubt a tale unto itself."

"What's the Primordial Tree?" Elliott asked.

Jingo stared starry-eyed at the golden shirt. "It is the oldest tree in Pangrelor. It lies on the opposite side of the world. They say its roots stretch all the way to Hulgaar, and its upper limbs to Antilia."

"You are an apt student of the old lore," Crosslyn said. "I have seen these fibers used only a few times." He caressed the shirt, which responded to his touch as before, and then handed it to Elliott.

"You want me to take it?"

"Why, of course. Now, put it in your knapsack and let's get going."

Crosslyn reached up his sleeve and took out a round stone. "*Dilusesco*," he said, and the stone erupted in brilliant blue light. "My seer stone will help guide us out of the forest. I have a boat waiting at the banks of the river Tantasar—Hooks and I used it to travel here from the swamps. When we reach the forest's edge, we will board it and be off."

Jingo chuckled.

"What's so funny?" Elliott asked.

Crosslyn also looked at Jingo, making him blush.

"I've just never heard of a shamalan traveling by boat, that's all."

"Well," Crosslyn said, "in the coming days you will see many things you haven't seen before. Now, let's get going."

"Where are we going?" Elliott said, hanging on his every word.

"We will travel to Susquatania, where we will counsel with the beasts of the forest."

"Is it true?" Jingo whispered, turning to Hooks with concern in his voice.

Hooks nodded.

"Why are we going to Susquatania?" Elliott asked. "Shouldn't we be going back to Ondor or Harwelden or something?"

Crosslyn gazed at him. "There is no time to discuss it now," he said. We must get out of the forest before the salax regroup, and we must heed the satyral's warning against the bastion of Malgothar. Now, let's move."

With that, they marched out of the salax encampment and into the darkness of Golroc, guided by the light of Crosslyn's seer stone.

Chapter 22

Woolf Hears a Secret

Slipher lay motionless at the edge of Woolf's campsite, awaiting his return. After hiding in the brambles for hours, one arm was asleep and his feet were numb from the cold. But he was determined to learn the fate and whereabouts of the shamalan boy, and for that he would endure any hardship, no matter how irksome. He was also interested in learning the remaining bit of news that Taldar the rat had hinted at.

Several paces ahead of where Slipher hid, the rat slept by the fire. Dawn was nearly upon them. Slipher hadn't slept at all, and he struggled to stay awake. Over and over he dozed off, jerking awake repeatedly and fighting to keep his eyes open. Finally he decided, for just a moment, to rest his cheek on the prickly underbrush of his hiding spot.

Hours later, he jerked awake with the suns in his eyes. Cursing himself for the lapse and praying they hadn't discovered him during his unintended slumber, he peered tentatively into the campsite.

Woolf was sitting at the edge of the campfire, talking to Taldar. Breathing a sigh of relief, Slipher listened.

"Yes," Woolf said. "I found the salax camp. The bonfire was still burning, and the carnage reminded me of a battlefield, but the boy and the gimlets were nowhere to be seen."

"Did you see any of the fiends of Golroc?" Taldar asked.

"Yes. There was a dead one in the clearing, and it was still warm. I have never laid eyes on a more hideous thing. I've heard about them all of my days, but I had never seen one before. I didn't know they were red."

"The *red* salax is dead?" Taldar asked, perking up. "He is the king of those beasts. What was the manner of his death?"

"A bony dart protruded from his throat. I have no idea what type of weapon it came from. In any event, my only encounter was with a small black susquat, watching me from behind a ring of trees as I searched the area."

"Yes," Taldar said, "I am familiar with the strange susquats of Golroc. They are smaller and darker than those of the Valley of Susquatania. They are said to be dim-witted."

"His face was discolored with a large swatch of red," Woolf said. "Some sort of defect he was born with, I suppose. And his fur was covered in silvery webbing. It was similar to webbing that hung from the trees encircling the clearing. I had the impression that he was held prisoner there but managed to escape. I tried many times to speak with him, but he cowered and refused to speak. When he fled, I did not give chase."

Tucked away in the brambles, Slipher felt a tickle on his inner right calf, then the unmistakable sensation of something writhing against his skin inside his pant leg. Slowly, he turned his head, careful not to make a sound, just in time to see a thick black serpents tail disappear inside his pants. He suppressed the urge to scream.

"The growth of those susquats is stunted from so many generations in the dark forest," Taldar continued. "They are very strange beasts. Even I cannot find any creatures that communicate with them."

"After he fled, I noticed bone pile at the edge of the camp and searched it for bones of a gimlet or a shamalan," Woolf said. "No gimlet bones, but some in the pile may have belonged to the boy. I cannot be certain, though—they may have belonged to a smaller susquat. It is not time to give up the search, though

I have some doubts about the boy's survival. It was a ghastly scene back there."

The rat looked up into the eyes of his huge winged ally. "Because it is your wish that the boy remain alive, it is my wish as well."

Staying as still as he could, Slipher felt the serpent working its way up his right leg. But he couldn't allow himself to move a muscle. He imagined the sensation of the serpent's fangs piercing the tough hide of his thigh. He took a quiet, deep breath, steeling himself against whatever might come, and hoping he could avoid drawing the grayfarer's attention at such close range.

"Merely out of curiosity," Woolf continued, "what do you know of the condemned susquat that Marvus and Jingo freed from Harwelden? He does not seem to be traveling with them anymore."

"I know only that he parted company with the others before they entered the Forest of Golroc," Taldar said.

"Sounds like a wise beast. I still don't understand their connection to him. What other news?"

Taldar reached to the string around his neck, which bore the pendant Woolf had given him in the castle. A small pouch was tied to it. With his tiny pink forepaws, he opened the pouch and took out a gem, which he handed to the grayfarer.

"What's this?" Woolf asked.

"One of my kindred took this from Chancellor Waldemariam's bedchamber. As it turns out, the chancellor . . ."

Just then a morning breeze riffled through the campsite, stirring the dewy leaves and boughs and making just enough noise that Slipher missed the last words of the sentence. At the same time, he felt the snake against his lower belly. Without meaning to, he let out a yelp. Thankfully, the snake exited his pants at the waist and slithered into the prickly underbrush, but Slipher feared the damage was done. Holding his breath, he stared into the clearing to see if Woolf had heard his cry, or if the passing breeze had made just enough of a ruckus to save his skin.

Woolf stared into the brush, in his direction, for several seconds. Finally, he turned back to the rat. "Hmmph." Woolf pocketed the gem. "Is that your big news?"

"Not all of it. I also bring news of the serpans. They are preparing for an attack on Harwelden. By my last information, a vast army of serpan warriors gathers at the northern end of the Forest of Ondor. Malus Lothar has amassed his entire strength for an assault on the castle. The army is said to be larger than any seen in Pangrelor since the start of the war."

"Larger even than the army that took Prytania?" Woolf replied. "It defeated our finest troops, and our numbers have shrunk to one-tenth since the time of that battle."

Taldar sat silent for a moment. "The forces that overtook Prytania would make up a mere fraction of the army that gathers outside Ondor," he said, casting his eyes to the ground. "Their camp encircles Ondor's entire northern border and extends well into the desert. Serpan forces from Obsidia, Scopulus, and Prytania have traveled to the camp, and legions more are marching from Vengala. All four viscounts and Malus Lothar himself will be joining the army. They aim to take Harwelden and finish the war."

Incredulous, Woolf remained silent.

"I am told that for good measure, the malus has commissioned several clans of Haviru to join the assault on Harwelden."

"Haviru, you say! We have tried to enlist them in our cause, sending messengers as far as Zunis and Eburnea, but none would agree to help us. Perhaps this is the reason they would not join us—they believe the malus will prevail, and they have thrown in with the stronger side."

"Or perhaps he paid them more."

"Perhaps." Woolf scratched at the ground with a stick. "This is most devastating news. I am loath to admit it, Taldar, but my hope for the future of the empire is dying. Though you will not hear a member of the council say it, many share my fears."

Taldar seemed surprised by the intimacy of the remark and said nothing.

Woolf sighed. "In light of your news, I do not see how the boy changes the situation. It seems the war is already lost. After I rest, I will return to Harwelden and do what I can to prepare for the battle. I want you to come, too. You have been an invaluable resource."

"I have one more thing to tell," Taldar said.

"Alas," Woolf replied, "I cannot bear any more bad news."

"I received word that General Grimaldi and the princess have escaped from Mount Sitticus."

The news seemed to energize Woolf. "Can it be true?" he asked. "How did they do it? Where are they now?"

"Those things I know not," the rat replied.

"That is fine news indeed!" Woolf said. "But if what you have told me is true, I honestly cannot see how it changes anything."

"Keep faith. The future looks grim, but it is not yet lost." Taldar paused for a moment. "If I may offer an opinion, I think you should continue your search for the boy."

"Explain yourself," Woolf said, his ears perking up.

"The council is aware of the forces arising against it. Besides another crossbow, I do not see what you add to the effort by returning to Harwelden."

"The council is corrupted. It may be that Waldemariam himself is forging the nails for our coffins."

"Councilman Alasdar has the situation well in hand," Taldar said. "And Baucus and Landrew are with him."

"Alasdar," Woolf said fondly. "So he knows of the chancellor's plan to kill the boy?"

"He does."

"Does he also believe that this action signals the chancellor's infidelity?"

"He feels the same as you."

"Perhaps your suggestion makes sense," Woolf said. "I do not know what finding the boy at this late hour achieves, but my shamalan masters always believed in the scrolls and the prophecies. I will consider your suggestion."

"Your shamalan masters also understood that it is not the number of warriors that counts the most; it is the ardor with which they fight."

Woolf smiled. "You are a wise little creature, aren't you?"

"You told me yourself that high-ranking members of Harwelden think the war is already lost," Taldar said. "So what about the soldiers? Do you think they won't sense the council's ambivalence? How can a warrior be asked to sacrifice his life for a cause that his superiors have already given up? What is to keep him from throwing down his arms or joining the enemy?"

Woolf nodded. "These are the thoughts that fill my days and trouble my sleep."

"It is passion and zeal that motivates the soldier, and a belief that his cause is just," Taldar said. "That is the secret your shamalan masters have always known, and a key part of their success for so many generations. There can be no greater harbinger of passion than the appearance of the shamalan boy, as predicted by the scrolls, on the eve of the greatest of all battles. You say that finding the boy is of little consequence. I counter that finding him is of the *utmost* consequence and is the greatest contribution you can make. Fulfilling the prophecy will provide the spark that may ignite a blaze. It is our belief in something greater that motivates us all—whether grayfarers or rats of the field. At this late hour, after so many seasons of bitter defeat, I imagine the passions of your soldiers could use some fueling."

"How does a scurrying rodent speak such words of wisdom?" Woolf asked. "This sounds like a speech one might hear from a king in the great hall of Harwelden, not from the mouth of a rat." He smiled. "You are a remarkable creature, and my mind is a muddle with all you have told me. I must rest my wings and decide my next actions carefully, when my thoughts are sharper. Thank you for all you have done. Your services have been more valuable than I could ever have imagined. Indeed, I am beginning to understand why the shamalans put such stock in communicating with the beasts."

And with a weary groan, Woolf took off his armor and stretched out on the ground. Soon they both were fast asleep.

🔱 🔱 🔱

Relieved to have avoided capture, Slipher worked his way backward, careful not to make a sound. When he was far enough away, he got to his feet and hurried back to his campsite, where Pongo remained tied to a tree, lackadaisically surveying the surroundings.

"We have to move camp," Slipher said, "though we won't be traveling today. The boy is within sight. We will follow the grayfarer, and if we can't keep pace with him, we will follow the rat."

Pongo looked at him impassively.

Slipher packed his blankets and scattered the ashes of the campfire to make it look as if no one had been there. Then he led Pongo back along the animal trail skirting the mountain and went off in search of a better hiding place. He wanted to sleep for a few hours before stalking the grayfarer in earnest. And he wanted to smoke his pipe.

Slipher led Pongo back along the animal trail
skirting the mountain and went off in search
of a better hiding place.

A short time later, after moving farther away from Woolf's camp, he made camp below an outcropping of rocks that marked the gateway to the nearby Azure Mountains. Picking a tuft of dry grass, he frayed it between his hands and rolled it into a loose ball, then used his fire bow and socket to make a spark, igniting the ball of grass. After lighting his pipe with this, he stomped the flame out.

"There'll be no campfires for a while, Pongo," he said, leaning back against a log and inhaling deeply.

The smoke showed him his homeland. At the base of the wooden palisade, a large collection of scavenger birds pecked at a pair of bodies. His mother held Oort tightly to her frozen bosom. Though the smoke was silent, Slipher could almost hear the pecking of the scavenger birds as they worked on the corpses. The smoke hovered briefly over the grim scene and then disintegrated.

Pongo lowered his head and licked his master's cheek, as if appreciating his despair. Standing up, Slipher hugged the donkey's neck and wept.

Chapter 23

Escape to Mangrathea

Sarintha and Grimaldi flew toward the sea as fast as Grimaldi's battered wings could carry them. The trip eastward was an unlikely route given their desire to return to Harwelden, but it stood the best chance of getting them past Malus Lothar's forces undetected. Besides, neither of them possessed the strength to brave the blustery Toltugan wilderness, the most direct way, so they sought a night's refuge on the isle of Mangrathea.

The uninhabited atoll lay off the southern coast of Vengala, well past the basin of the salty river Tantasar, which paralleled the ocean shore. After a brief respite on Mangrathea, they would hasten to their homeland, following the Tantasar southward to Harwelden.

"I haven't seen any darfoyles, Sarintha said, craning her neck backward. "I think our escape is secure." She had to speak loudly to be heard over the wind rushing past as Grimaldi hurtled through the skies. "How are you feeling?"

"Better since you restored my voice," Grimaldi said, with surprising clarity given the suffering he had just endured.

"The fates have smiled on us," Sarintha yelled, her long hair streaming behind in the brilliant light of the full moon. The clouds she had seen from her prison window atop Mount Sitticus had vanished, and the night was crystal clear. "I expected that we would both meet our doom in that chamber."

For a moment, they flew onward in silence.

For a moment, Sarintha and Grimaldi
flew onward in silence.

"Despite all the seasons I have known you," Grimaldi said, "I was not aware that you possessed the magic to secure my escape. You are full of surprises, young one. Your father would be proud."

"It was not magic," she yelled. "And your assumptions are correct. I possess few skills in the art of magic. Nobles aren't practiced in such things." The cold night wind whipped against her face. "I am at my limit in restoring your voice—a simple hex to reverse. I wish I had the power to heal us, for the journey to Harwelden will be arduous." She lowered her hand and felt the wounds in her abdomen, reminders of how close she had come to death. "With holes in your limbs and my weight on your back, the journey will be particularly difficult for you," she yelled. "Perhaps when we reach the sea, I can travel by water and lighten your burden. I should be able to keep pace with you."

"With due respect, Your Highness," Grimaldi said, "that would be welcome."

"Then it is done," she yelled back, though she did not relish the idea of saltwater touching her wounds.

"If it was not magic that secured my release, then what?"

She smiled, recalling the events that led to their unlikely escape. "Of all things, it was a rat that saved us," she said. And on reflection, she could hardly believe it herself.

"A rat . . . I don't understand," said Grimaldi.

"Before his death, my father sent a rat to spy on the malus. I was not aware of his presence in the enemy's castle. He contacted me in my cell and then summoned his friends from their nest. It was the rats that released you from the rack," she yelled, recalling her hopelessness and the dire deed she had been contemplating at the time Grinjar made contact. "If not for those little vermin, our fate would have gone very differently."

"I will never understand the shamalans' fascination with

the animals," he said. "But if it was a rat that saved us, then thank the elders for his presence. I'm glad to be out of there."

"And I'm glad to be reunited with you, old friend," Sarintha yelled, leaning forward to hug him. "I feared you were long dead."

In the moonlight, she scouted the lands beneath them. They were fast approaching the basin of the river Tantasar. Soon they would be over the sea. She turned her head and scanned the sky behind them. No one followed.

"Wait until they see us soaring into the western tower," Grimaldi said. "It will be quite a homecoming, I'm sure. The princess and the general, both feared lost, triumphantly returning to the homeland. I may have to do some acrobatics for effect." He grinned. "The mead will flow like water."

She stiffened, recalling Grinjar's instruction about the enemy forces amassed at the edge of Ondor. She had not yet discussed this with her friend.

"We should reach Harwelden just before the equinox," Grimaldi said. "We will arrive in time to celebrate the harvest at the Festival of Opik. My fondest memories of Harwelden have always centered on the festival, and I feared I had seen my last. For once, it will be like the old days."

Sarintha furrowed her brow. "The rat brought tidings of Harwelden," she yelled, saddened that she must diminish her friend's joy. "He is privy to information back home. He communicates with other rats."

Grimaldi laughed. "So what did the rat tell you about Harwelden? I can't wait to see it again."

The malus prepares an assault," she yelled.

"Then let him come," said Grimaldi. "Harwelden is not some gimlet city in the hinterlands. It is unassailable. They will have to attack from the bottom of the mountain, with us firing down on them. And the suns will shine brightly behind us, dazzling their eyes. Not to mention the wall that encircles the place. It will be suicide for him to attack."

"The rat tells that Malus Lothar is assembling a large force at Ondor's edge. We didn't have time to discuss it at length, but I am left with the impression that legions of troops have amassed, with more on the way." The wind whipped at her face. "The malus plans to attack during the Festival of Opik."

"Are you confident of this communication?" he asked.

"He did save our lives. I don't know why he would lie."

"The impudence of that turncoat Lothar boils my blood," Grimaldi said. "I would not have imagined that even he would sink so low."

"I have little trouble imagining it," she yelled, staring blankly ahead as she envisioned the seminal event that started the latest cycle of the ancient war. "We have been attacked during the Festival of Opik before."

She gazed downward, inspecting the landscape again. They had crossed the basin of the river Tantasar and were about to pass into the skies over the sea. It would not be long before they reached the isle of Mangrathea. Again she turned and surveyed the skies behind them. As before, no one followed.

"We will be ready for them this time," Grimaldi said. "When we arrive at Harwelden, we will issue an order that no one must enter the Forest of Ondor during the festival. If they dare assault, we will rain the fire of the gods on them. With Baruna as my witness, we will not suffer another loss to those savages."

She paused before speaking, choosing her words carefully. Discussion of the impending serpan assault brought another topic to the forefront of her mind: the night Grimaldi was taken prisoner, when she first came face-to-face with Malus Lothar. "On the eve of our assault on Prytania," she yelled, "when we were ambushed by the forces of the malus and you were captured . . . Have you considered how the serpans might have learned of our plans? Our strategy was designed with great precision, with only eleven living souls, including you and me, knowing of the preparations."

"I have considered it at length," he said. "In my cell I had much time to think."

"I believe that a traitor was present at that meeting," she said. "It is the only plausible explanation."

Below them, the moonlit contours of the land had turned to black, empty sea.

"I have considered this, too," Grimaldi said. "But I can think of no one with the motivation to wreak such devastation as we suffered that night. I trust all the souls who were present in that room. I trust any of them with my life."

"But one of them betrayed us," said Sarintha. "And I believe I know who it was. I suspect Waldemariam."

"Such a thing is not possible!" scoffed Grimaldi.

She said nothing, allowing the weight of her accusation to sink in. "I do not make this claim casually," she said. "I know he is your friend."

Grimaldi flew on in silence.

"You have to admit," Sarintha said, "the chancellor's behavior has been erratic since my father's death. His leadership has weakened, and his decision making is flawed. He has not been himself since. There is conflict within him—I can feel it. Sometimes I fear he has gone mad."

Grimaldi remained silent.

"I am the rightful heir to the royal throne of Harwelden," she continued, "yet he has treated me with nothing but contempt. He prefers his own rule to my coronation, and he scoffs at my plans, offering instead to do nothing."

She knew that her words bit deeply, for Grimaldi and Waldemariam were like brothers.

"Since your capture," she continued, making her case, "Scopulus has fallen. Though an obvious target for aggression, it fell to the enemy unguarded. It took the serpans mere hours to capture, and thousands of gimlets paid with their lives."

"How do you know this?" he asked.

"Malus Lothar himself told me when I was with him in his sky chariot."

The grayfarer laughed. "Not exactly a reliable source, Princess."

"But what he said is true," she said. "Even as he told me, I could feel it in the Shama."

Grimaldi softened noticeably—shamalans were usually correct when it came to impressions given them by the Shama. "If what you say is true," he said, "it is troublesome news indeed."

"I cannot understand why the chancellor left the city unprotected," said Sarintha. "Unless . . ."

"I do not comprehend it, either," Grimaldi said, "but I am certain he has good reason. Waldemariam is no fool. I know he is difficult, and he is not the most devout adherent of the tenets of the Shama, but truthfully, Princess, what grayfarer is? Waldemariam has been a brother to me for many long seasons. He is no traitor. I would trust him with my life."

"You *have* trusted him with your life," Sarintha said, "and you nearly lost it."

"With due respect, Your Highness, you are wrong about Waldemariam. Another explanation will present itself."

"I ask you only to consider it," she said. "For I can draw no other conclusions. Harwelden has been betrayed by a trusted soul before."

"Yes," Grimaldi said, his voice softening, "it has."

Beneath them, the shimmering waters of the Ponchatoulan Ocean gleamed in the moonlight.

"I will take leave of you now," Sarintha said. "We will meet at the isle of Mangrathea at daybreak. There we will rest our tired limbs, get some food, and prepare for our journey to Harwelden. We must make haste if we are to get there in time."

"Agreed." Grimaldi tipped his wings slightly, and they sailed down, toward the surface of the water.

"And we must speak of Waldemariam again, before we return home."

Grimaldi nodded.

When the grayfarer was skimming only a few feet above the ocean, Sarintha balanced herself on his back and leaped off, into the icy waters below.

As Grimaldi again rose skyward, she inhaled a lungful of the icy seawater. Instantaneously, pale green membranes slipped over her eyes, and her hands and feet transformed into the familiar shamalan sculls. Her heart rate quickened perceptibly, counteracting the effects of the icy sea as warmed blood coursed through her vessels. In seconds, she was swimming as if born in the water, slipping through it like a porpoise.

Despite her pain, Sarintha felt invigorated by the transformation. Her mood improved. It was good to be in the water. League after league, she sliced through the ocean, keeping pace with Grimaldi, who soared through the moonlit skies above. Despite the great distance separating them, Sarintha sensed him above her, even though he, like all grayfarers, could not do the same. On and on they traveled through the night, determined to reach Mangrathea before daybreak.

After a time, to her consternation, she began to lose track of Grimaldi. He had moved higher into the skies. She reached out to him, straining her senses to maintain an impression of him, but eventually she could feel him no longer.

Alarmed, she slowed her pace. Why had he separated himself from her? Had the darfoyles given chase after all?

Just ahead of her, she saw a break in the ocean's surface. The unmistakable bulk of a massive ship's hull loomed ahead. Drawing nearer the ship, she decided this must be the cause of Grimaldi's evasive maneuvering. But what ship could be sailing so far from inhabited lands—and to what purpose? The ship bore toward her from the east. Grimaldi had no doubt spotted it and flown higher to avoid being seen, and she would do well to take similar evasive action.

Cautiously, she approached the massive vessel, looking for a clue to its identity. As she drew nearer, she saw a second hull in its wake . . . and behind it, another. A whole fleet was approaching from the east.

This could mean only one thing. But to confirm her suspicions, she was going to need help. With the moon shining so brightly above, she dare not break the surface. If she suspected aright, she was in danger of recapture if spotted. And the crew of a vessel this large would certainly know how to wield a harpoon. Even if she evaded capture, she did not want to reveal her location to a possible enemy. Both she and Grimaldi were vulnerable out here. Moving directly in front of the oncoming ship, she ejected the water from her lungs and, holding her breath, floated just beneath the surface. Soon the ship was almost on top of her, oars on either side of the hull slapping in rhythm at the water around her. A feeling of dread enveloped her. Grabbing on to the bottom of the ship, she inhaled water and felt relieved at her deliverance from the hunger for breath.

As the ship lumbered forward, pulling her along, she closed her eyes and sent a communication to any beast of the sea that might be close enough to hear her: *Who is available to me?* She cleared her thoughts and opened her mind wide, listening for any response. There was nothing.

Come to me now, she thought. *Anyone listening, a shamalan needs your assistance.*

Beneath her, a hulking black form rose from the depths—a sea creature so massive that its girth eclipsed that of the ship to which she clung. Sarintha had never seen such a creature. It frightened her.

I am here, shamalan, said a voice in her mind.

She looked at the giant black form in the dark water beneath her. A creature so large was not what she had in mind. She had hoped for a porpoise. *Who are you?* she thought.

I am Galego.

She waited for more, but it transmitted nothing else as it kept pace with the ship.

What are you? she thought.

I am an arctodon.

She had never heard of an arctodon. She let go of the boat and swam to it. As she approached, she saw that it had a massive triangular head, like that of a giant serpent. It had brilliant green eyes with diamond-shaped irises, like a simitar's, and narrow, pointy teeth interlocking just outside its clenched jaws.

I have not encountered a member of your species, she thought. *May I look you over?*

Why, of course, the creature responded. *You have no need to fear me, shamalan.*

Relieved, she swam closer and ran her hands along its back. Its skin was scaly and coarse, like the bark of a tree covered with wet moss. It had four short, webbed paddles that propelled it forward, and a long, scaly tail that served as a rudder.

Are you able to break the surface of the water? she thought.

Of course.

Then I would ask that you peek above the surface and take account of these ships. As you look at them, I would like to enter your mind and see through your eyes. I need to see what they look like, though I cannot risk surfacing myself.

The arctodon moved to the side of the ship and then rose toward the surface. With its tail swaying rhythmically behind it, it peeked above the water and looked at the ship.

Sarintha grabbed on to the creature's belly and closed her eyes. A brief flash of light filled her mind's eye, and she saw through its eyes.

Her decision to remain underwater had been a wise one. The sea creature, Galego, stared directly into the eyes of Viscount Erebus, who stood on the deck of the ship. He stared at the arctodon suspiciously. Erebus was a darfoyle from Mount Sitticus, who, under Malus Lothar's direction, had murdered hundreds of her shamalan brothers and sisters in the time since the Great Betrayal.

Sarintha was dismayed. How had he spotted them so quickly? And what was he doing on the deck of that ship? Instantly, she closed her connection with Galego and safeguarded her thoughts, returning her vision to the murky ocean depths. She chided herself for not recalling whether darfoyles had the ability to detect when a shamalan joined with the Shama, as she had done when she called out to Galego and looked through his eyes. From the speed with which the viscount had detected them, she feared so.

She peered up through the surface in time to see Viscount Erebus spread his wings and lift off the deck, rising lazily above the ship before descending to the water below. He hovered curiously just above the level of Galego's head.

Holding tight to the belly of the beast, Sarintha watched the viscount's moonlit shape circling above like a predator circling its prey.

Galego lurched, propelling himself out of the water with a swish of his tail, and the great, snakelike head whipped upward, snapping its jaws at the hovering darfoyle.

If Galego had warned Sarintha of his intentions, she hadn't heard it. He must feel threatened, she realized.

Again Galego surged upward, his snapping teeth just missing the talons of the black darfoyle. Hovering just out of reach, Viscount Erebus unslung a crossbow from his back and slotted an arrow as the arctodon lurched again and missed again.

Jarred, Sarintha let go of the beast and dived. She felt guilty for abandoning him, for it was she who had gotten him into this. But she had to get to safety. Suppressing her guilt, she plunged downward, ignoring the myriad strange predators that inhabited the depths. After many minutes, she reached the safety of the sea bottom. There was no way the darfoyle could reach her here. The weight of the water above bore down on her, straining her every movement. In slow motion, she anchored herself against the deep currents by holding on to a massive tree on the seafloor. The membranes that covered her eyes glowed fluourescent green, allowing her to see for a few feet in every direction.

She was in the midst of a great sea forest, not so different from the forests of Ondor or Susquatania on the surface, but with an otherworldly strangeness about it. The leaves of the trees were spindly and serpentine and writhed with the currents as if they were eels. The trunk of the tree she held had a thick, slimy coating in which small, tubular, transluscent creatures burrowed. Life teemed around her. Creatures great and small, of bizarre shapes and vibrant colors, moved through the sea forest in search of a meal. Though none of the creatures had eyes—for there was no light at this depth—many had fearsome-looking teeth. With the weight of the water pressing down on her, she was in a poor position to defend herself should one of these creatures fancy a taste of shamalan.

As she sat anchored against the sea currents, deciding her next move, a wall of flesh passed overhead. Thinking Galego had come to find her, she started to call out, then noticed the long, spindly tentacles trailing behind the beast. This was no arctodon. One of the tentacles dropped and inspected her, tentatively caressing her face.

She stood terrified, unsure what to do, when suddenly the tentacle encircled her body. She felt the gentle suction of the cups; it squeezed lightly, as if inspecting a piece of fruit.

With the tentacle squeezing against her, Sarintha had difficulty drawing in the water, and she began to fear for her life.

Then suddenly, the tentacle released her, and the beast went on its way.

Time to get out of here, she thought, straining against the weight of the ocean to propel herself upward. It was quite heavy going at first, but eventually, her ascent required less and less effort. When she had reached about half the distance to the surface, she came upon a frenzy of whipping, snapping sea creatures. A herd of voracious pleisadars, massive predators with teeth as long as a gimlet's arm, ripped at the body of something huge. Rolling in the midst of the feeding pleisadars was the carcass of an arctodon, with an arrow shaft still protruding from between its eyes. It was Galego.

Disheartened, she gave a blessing and continued upward, giving wide berth to the feeding pleisadars. When she reached the surface, the fleet of ships was out of sight.

With her heart heavy at the loss of Galego, and feeling guilt for her role in his slaughter, she continued toward Mangrathea, again reaching out with her mind for Grimaldi. He was nowhere to be found.

Chapter 24

Slipher's Shame

The suns were high in the sky when Slipher awoke in his clandestine campsite. Feeling groggy, he rolled onto his side and closed his eyes for just a bit longer. In his sleep-fogged mind, it occurred to him that he had something important to do this day, though for the life of him, he could not remember what.

He woke to something nudging at his back.

"Stop it, Pongo!" he grumbled, curling into a ball. "Sometimes your need for attention is maddening."

Again he felt the nudging at his back.

"I said stop it, you infernal beast! I'm not ready to get up." He squeezed his eyes defiantly against the sunlight.

The nudging came again, more forceful this time.

Enraged, he rolled toward the disturbance, raising his arm to slap the annoying beast on the nose. But Pongo was nowhere to be seen. Before him, in shining armor and with wings fully extended, stood Councilman Woolf.

Slipher gaped, unsure how to proceed. His mind spun.

"You should choose your moves wisely, grayfarer," he said, lying supine on the ground and feeling rather vulnerable. "You are in the presence of an emissary of Malus Lothar." Though he strove to sound forceful, his voice quivered.

"*You?*" Woolf snorted, looking him over. "An emissary of the malus? I would have thought he could do better."

"The Malus does not seek your counsel when making assignments," Slipher growled, pushing himself up into a sitting position. "You would be wise to take leave while you still can." Again his voice quivered. Surreptitiously he moved his arm to his side and then behind him, running his hand through the dirt in an attempt to locate his sword.

"On your feet, runt," Woolf said. "And show me your hands or I cut off your arms."

A sickening dismay overcame Slipher. One errant grayfarer threatened to end his pursuit of the boy and quash his hopes for redemption. He felt behind him for his sword.

Appearing angered by his refusal to obey, Woolf pulled a sword from his belt and whacked him on the side of the head with the flat, knocking him back to the ground.

Slipher now saw that it was his own sword Woolf used against him.

Walking over to him, Woolf put a foot on his back, pressing his weight into him and pinning him to the ground. Without a word, he leaned forward and stripped off the serpan armor piecemeal, discarding it on the rocks.

Feeling naked, Slipher lay quivering beneath the grayfarer's weight. "You will pay for this insult with your life!" he snarled, sounding even meeker than before. "Valderon will avenge the treachery of this ambush. My honor will be restored. I am an emissary of the malus."

Woolf shifted his weight, pressing harder against his chest. "Pathetic serpan," he said, "what honor have you to avenge? I was aware of your eavesdropping as you lay in the shadows last night. I have watched you throughout the night, sharpening my blade in preparation to face a worthy adversary, and instead I find only an ill-fitted, petulant runt. I should have taken my night's rest."

"I am an emissary of the malus!" Slipher insisted, tears building in the corners of his eyes. "Take leave of me at once!" He began to sob.

Woolf put a foot on his back, pressing his weight
into him and pinning Slipher to the ground.

Woolf took his foot off the serpan and took a step backward. "Stand up," he said.

The sobbing continued. Defeated, Slipher stood to face Woolf.

Woolf glared at him. "Stand up and dress yourself. Your demeanor is shameful."

I have no clothes," said Slipher, sounding like a child speaking to an angry parent. "All I have is my armor."

"Then get it. Dress yourself properly and behave like a warrior. I cannot bear your cringing and whining."

Humiliated, he got his armor on, and as he walked back to face Woolf, the helmet slipped forward over his eyes. As the grayfarer laughed, he adjusted his helmet and stood before him, staring at the ground.

Finally, Woolf stopped laughing and said, "Turn around."
Slipher complied.

Woolf lashed his hands behind him and fashioned a harness of rope with a loop in the back. When he was finished, he flew up off the ground, grasping the loop of the harness in his talons. To Slipher's dismay, they ascended.

"What about Pongo?" Slipher said, watching his donkey grow smaller beneath them.

"What in the name of Antilia is Pongo?" Woolf asked.

"My donkey," Slipher replied, his voice filled with panic.

Woolf looked over his shoulder at the donkey and continued his ascent. "You'd best worry about yourself," he said. "For your luck is far worse than his, to be sure. When we return to Harwelden, you will sit in a dungeon until the time of your execution, which, I promise, will not be a pleasant one."

Slipher gasped. This was something that he had not considered. "On what grounds will you hold me?"

"On the grounds that you are serpan."

Woolf flew to the eastern edge of Golroc and turned north, following the river Tantasar toward Harwelden.

Dangling beneath him, Slipher swayed in the wind created by his wings. The bindings tore welts in his skin. Over and over again, he cursed the day of his birth.

Chapter 25

Shadows of Golroc

"So where shall we begin?" Crosslyn asked, beaming.

Elliott had no idea what he should say. He didn't want to disappoint the old man, though he feared it was inevitable.

The crude boat that carried them upriver was long enough that the two shamalans could speak privately where they sat in the stern—which seemed to be what Crosslyn intended. Near the bow, Jingo and Hooks paddled quietly, with Hooks at the tiller, guiding the craft northward with the current. Between them, Marvus lay sleeping, curled up on a nest of blankets they had made for him. The night was quiet save for the occasional call of a night bird or some unknown animal, and the moon shone brightly overhead, casting shadows from the trees of Golroc onto the riverbank. The horrors of the dark forest had already begun to fade to memory.

On the riverbank, a raven stared from its perch, watching with unseemly interest as the boat drifted past.

Crosslyn nodded. "I'll begin, then," he said. "Remove the bracelet from your knapsack."

Elliott reached into the bottom of his knapsack and felt about until he found the cool metal of the bracelet.

It glimmered in the moonlight as Crosslyn held it close to his face. "A remarkable bit of craftsmanship, no? Tell me where you came across such a piece."

"I found it in my grandfather's basement," Elliott said. "Back home." He watched Crosslyn's reaction to the bracelet with interest, pleased that he was pleased.

"Interesting indeed," Crosslyn replied, holding the bracelet before him. "What do you know of it?"

"Nothing really," he mumbled, wishing he had something more to say. "I found it hidden in my grandfather's basement. It was in this knapsack with this other stuff." He dumped the contents of the knapsack onto the floor of the boat. Along with a lighter and a pair of pajamas—otherworldly remnants from his journey to the basement long ago—there were the sack of coins, the seer stone, and the slingshot.

Crosslyn examined each item, then then turned his attention back to the bracelet. "Tell me about your home," he said, "and about your family. Then we shall discuss the bracelet."

"Well," Elliott said, shifting in his seat, "back home I live in a place called New Orleans, with my mother and grandfather. My mother and I moved there because she's sick, so my grandfather could help take care of her." It felt strange to be speaking of New Orleans and his family in his current surroundings.

"New Orleans," Crosslyn said, forming the words slowly. "How many suns are there in New Orleans?"

"Just one."

"Fine," he said. He seemed pleased with the answer. "Is this place near water?"

"Yes. It is bordered on one side by a big river, one of the biggest rivers in the world, and it is bordered on the other side by a huge lake formed from an inlet of the ocean. It lies beneath sea level. In a way, it's a city beneath the sea."

"Perfect," Crosslyn said. "And tell me about your father."

"My father doesn't live with us. He and my mother aren't together anymore." It was a painful subject to discuss with a stranger.

Crosslyn's face was expressionless. "Do you bear a resemblance to your father?"

"Yes. When I was younger, my mother used to show me pictures of him when he was my age. We looked a lot alike."

Crosslyn continued studying the bracelet. "Does your father bear the markings of a shamalan?"

"No," he said, hoping this wouldn't disappoint the old man.

"All right," Crosslyn said quietly. "Now, tell me about your grandfather."

"There's not much to tell, really. I met him for the first time a few weeks before . . . before I came here. He's a little strange, to be honest. He's really tall and has white hair and a white beard. He wears the same clothes every day."

Crosslyn grinned. "Tall with white hair and a beard, you say?" His eyes twinkled. "And the knapsack was in his possession?"

"Yes."

"Good. That's very good. Tell me about your mother."

Elliott winced, thinking of his mother's illness. "Well," he said, searching for an appropriate description, "she has the birthmarks."

Crosslyn furrowed his brow, as if failing to understand the reference.

"The markings of a shamalan."

Crosslyn sat thinking for a moment. "I see," he said at last. "Are shamalans common where you come from?"

Elliott couldn't help smiling. "No," he said. "I didn't even know what it meant to have the markings of a shamalan until the grayfarers locked me in the testing chamber back at the castle."

Crosslyn's eyes widened. "You underwent the transformation for the first time only recently? How is that possible?"

Elliott shrugged. "I don't know." He looked at the floor of the boat.

"You have only just experienced your first transformation," Crosslyn marveled. "Well there is a great deal in store for you, then." He laughed. "Most of this makes sense, though I cannot imagine how one gets to be your age without ever having undergone the transformation. I find it astonishing."

Blood rushed to Elliott's cheeks.

"Other than yourself, your mother, and your grandfather, did you know of *any* shamalans in your daughterland?"

Daughterland . . . He had seen the word in the journal in his grandfather's basement, but he let it pass for the moment. "No," he said. "There were no other shamalans where I came from." He paused, wondering if he should continue. "In fact, my mother always taught me to stay away from the water." He cast his eyes downward. "I've always been afraid of the water."

Crosslyn erupted in laughter. "I've never heard of such a thing—a shamalan afraid of the water! Baruna help us! Don't worry," he said, regaining his composure at last. "We'll have you cured of your fear of the water in no time. I will take you beneath the surface soon. But now we need to talk about the bracelet.

"This bracelet is sacred to my people." Crosslyn had a more serious tone now. "It is an ancient relic, fashioned as a gift for King Griogair at the dawn of our history. Griogair was the first shamalan king. It was under his reign that the castle Harwelden was built. Under his leadership, primitive clans of nomadic shamalans from across the many lands of Pangrelor gathered together and formed a great empire."

He paused as if to gauge the boy's interest, then continued. "Griogair was the first to form an alliance with the grayfarers. Before joining the empire, the grayfarers were savages. They lived in caves and warred endlessly, clan against clan. Griogair unified the grayfarers and turned them into a great army, the protectors of Harwelden. After raising and training his grayfarer army, he formed treaties with the beasts of the wild and allied with the many clans of gimlets scattered across the continent, bringing them into the new empire. Under his leadership, the entire Carafayan continent assembled under one flag. His ascendancy was the most historic event in the history of our world. When his name is spoken, it is with reverence."

"It was the gimlets who presented Griogair with this bracelet," Crosslyn said. "At the signing of the Treaty of Harwelden, the chiefs of the nine gimlet clans collected and offered their solidarity with the new empire, disassembling the political structure they had embraced for more than an age, and vowing allegiance to King Griogair. It was a historic event. With all the grayfarers and shamalans of the new realm in attendance, the gimlet chiefs, one by one, signed the Treaty of Harwelden. When it was done, they presented Griogair with this bracelet." Crosslyn held it out before him. "The bracelet is fashioned from gimlet silver ore and encrusted with nine stones—one for each of the ancient gimlet tribes.

Engrossed in the tale, Elliott studied the bracelet.

"This was no small gift," Crosslyn said. "I haven't yet told you the best part." His voice dropped to a whisper. "The bracelet has passed from generation to generation, following the direct lineage of King Griogair himself. It is a relic of the kings." The twinkle in his eye brightened. "Imbued by ancient gimlet sorcery, it possesses great power—but only when worn by an heir of King Griogair. I imagine you made quite an impression when you showed up at Harwelden with this in your possession. It has been missing since the time of the Great Betrayal."

"Wow," Elliott said, trying to imagine the scene of King Griogair receiving the bracelet from the nine gimlet chiefs. He recalled the frescoes in Harwelden's great foyer—this event had been one of the scenes depicted. "But what's this Great Betrayal I keep hearing about?" he asked.

"An event that started this latest and most vicious cycle of war, and which threatens to put an end to us all," the old man said, shaking his head. "We will speak of the Great Betrayal in due time. It is supremely relevant, but not to our discussion tonight."

"What sort of powers does the bracelet have?" Elliott asked.

"When worn by the true heir of King Griogair, the bracelet allows one to mask himself."

"I don't understand."

"If the wearer wants to appear as a cave bear, for example, he need only think of a cave bear and command the bracelet to make him appear in that form. If the wearer wants to go unseen, he has but to wish for it."

"Wow," Elliott said, imagining the implications. "It's a little hard to believe."

"That is what it can do," Crosslyn replied, "but only for Griogair's rightful heir. To all others, the bracelet is a mere trinket."

"Is it hard to use?" Elliott asked.

There was a gleam in Crosslyn's eye. "Put it on and we shall see."

Elliott was confused. "But . . . it's not going to work for me."

"Put it on."

Elliott stared at Crosslyn, considering the fanciful proposition. This was silly. The whole story was a fairy tale, and the claims nothing short of fantastical. He placed the bracelet on his wrist and looked to Crosslyn, awaiting some sort of instruction, but the old man just stared at him. "What shall I try to become?" he finally asked.

"Surprise me."

Tentatively, Elliott nodded. Very well, he would put the legend to rest for good. He closed his eyes and envisioned a simitar, summoning all his imagination.

And, of course, nothing happened.

"Keep trying," said Crosslyn patiently. "It is a difficult skill to master. Clear your mind of all thought, and focus on what you wish to achieve."

He tried again, concentrating hard on the appearance of the simitar.

Still nothing.

After several seconds, he shucked the bracelet from his wrist and tossed it back to Crosslyn. "I can't do it," he sighed, ashamed to have disappointed the old man. "I knew it wouldn't work."

Crosslyn placed the bracelet beside him and stared at Elliott. His smile was gone.

On the riverbank, the raven stared at the boat. It was following them.

Crosslyn stared long at Elliott, though he said nothing. His behavior made Elliott self-conscious.

On the river's western bank, something stirred in the shadows of the huge trees. The raven cawed, breaking the silence of the night.

Crosslyn's head jerked sideways. And in the bow, Hooks and Jingo, too, were watching something on the riverbank.

Elliott scanned the trees and finally saw what they were looking at. A serpan warrior, riding a large reptilian creature, emerged from the trees. His mount looked like a smallish dinosaur, though like none he had ever studied in school. It walked on muscular hind limbs and held its small forelimbs before it, and its long neck culminated in a thick-jawed head. On the thick leather saddle strapped to its back sat a squat armored serpan warrior. As Elliott watched in horror, the serpan looked right at him and raised a spiraled ram's horn, sounding an alarm.

A second mounted serpan appeared alongside the first. And behind him, another. They pointed and murmured excitedly to one another, unslinging their crossbows.

Within seconds, the banks were crawling with serpan warriors astride more of the fearsome lizards. As one, they raised their crossbows and took aim at the defenseless vessel.

"A malevosaur brigade!" Jingo yelled. He reached for his dagger and scanned the length of the boat, as if searching for weapons of defense. Turning to face the serpans, he crouched below the railing. A moment later, an arrow thunked into the side of the boat.

On the riverbanks, the serpans slotted arrows in their crossbows and yelled taunts at the crew.

"Surrender or die, shamalan!" yelled one. "Come with us, boy, and we'll let your friends go."

Without waiting for instructions from Crosslyn, Jingo stood and flung his dagger. A heartbeat later, the taunting serpan fell backward off his mount, with the dagger planted in his forehead. Before the serpans could register the death of their fellow soldier, Jingo slipped Marvus's dagger from his belt and threw it as well. It felled another serpan, whose crossbow discharged as he fell, launching its bolt into the thigh of the malevosaur beside him. The great beast roared and bolted, trampling its rider.

"Elliott throw me your knapsack!" Jingo yelled.

Elliott grabbed the knapsack and scampered to the front of the boat as arrows zipped through the air all around them. It seemed that Jingo had angered the serpans.

Jingo reached into the knapsack and retrieved the slingshot. "What will we do for stones?" he asked. "We haven't a thing to launch at them."

Ducking to avoid the arrows, Elliott reached into the pack and took a handful of coins from the sack. "Try these," he said, thrusting a fistful toward Jingo. He hadn't appreciated their heaviness before.

More arrows flew as more and more serpans emerged from the forest on their great, lumbering beasts.

"I hope this works," Jingo said, loading a coin in the slingshot.

In the stern, Crosslyn stood facing the marauding army. He closed his eyes as the barrage of arrows thickened. The entire bank was lined with serpan warriors, and more poured in behind them, their malevosaurs pawing the ground and stamping, snarling at the boat.

While the others crouched below the rails, Crosslyn stood chanting with arms outstretched. "*Hah-lay-wee-sss-tah*," he intoned, standing in full view. Yet somehow, inexplicably, the hail of arrows never touched him.

The others had no such confidence. Holding the slingshot above the gunwale, Jingo Jingo took haphazard aim and launched a coin, and another mortally wounded serpan slumped to the ground, leaving his riderless lizard to run amok.

"Good one!" Hooks crowed. "Four down."

The ram's horn sounded again, and dozens more serpans appeared on the riverbank, shooting bolt after bolt at the vulnerable craft.

"*Hah-lay-wee-sss-tah*," Crosslyn chanted, and something strange began to happen on the riverbank.

In the full moon, the trees of Golroc cast dark shadows, which stretched across the riverbank toward the water. But as Elliott watched, those shadows began to move as if alive. At first, the movement was barely a rustle, a shimmer in the darkness. But then the movement grew more deliberate.

Disbelieving his eyes, Elliott blinked to force the shadows to their rightful places. But the faint shadows of the trees grew darker and coalesced into a sort of puddle on the riverbank. Then, like a slow, sticky liquid, they ran together, thickening and darkening, gaining strength.

The serpans, oblivious of the movement in the puddle of coalesced shadows beneath them, moved to the edge of the water and launched bolt after bolt from their crossbows, hooting and jeering at the boat. Meanwhile, thin, wispy tendrils bubbled out of the mass, curling and snaking along at the malevosaurs' feet.

"*Hah-lay-wee-sss-tah*," Crosslyn chanted, raising his hands as if conducting an orchestra.

The shadowy mass darkened and grew, and more of the smoky appendages sprang forth, grasping the malevosaurs by the hocks and clawing up to their torsos.

Panicked, the affected lizards reared and kicked upward, throwing their riders to the ground. The malevosaurs struggled to free themselves from the shadow tentacles but found themselves held fast.

The shadow mass engulfed the fallen serpans, too, bubbling around them as they fell to the ground, until they were enveloped in a roiling black mass. Soon the cries of the fallen serpans mixed with the screeches of their embattled lizards, and the arrows ceased.

"*Hah-lay-wee-sss-tah,*" Crosslyn repeated, his voice booming in anger.

Realizing that something was terribly wrong, the serpans behind the front line began to lower their bows. They looked to the shadowy mass with a mix of fear and awe. All around them, the shadows tugged their fellow soldiers to the ground, where they quickly succumbed to the smoky tentacles. As the affected serpans cried out, the smell of burning flesh filled the air. Somehow, the shadows were burning them.

As Elliott watched in horrified fascination, the shadow mass began to separate, reproducing itself as an amoeba might. With each separation, the newly cleaved shadows took shape in the form of the trees that fathered them. They were gaining strength. Although shaped like trees, they sprouted limblike legs where the trunks should be. Spindly branchlike arms reached out for the serpans, searing the flesh with their touch. More and more of these individual tree shadows broke off from the mass until they towered over the serpans like an army of demons from some nightmarish netherworld. And like living beings, they went for the soldiers and their lizards in earnest, embracing their victims with a fatal, searing hiss.

The shadowy mass darkened and grew, and more of
the smoky appendages sprang forth, grasping the panicked
lizards by the hocks and clawing up to their torsos.

As Crosslyn chanted on, the serpans continued to fall victim to the shadows.

"*Hah-lay-wee-sss-tah!*" Crosslyn yelled. "You shall not prevail!" He pushed outward with his hands against the air.

Following his cue, the tree shadows moved to engulf the remaining serpans, until every serpan and malevosaur was lost from sight, drowned in the welter of slinking shadows. Finally, even the screams were swallowed.

When the last of the serpans was gone, the shadow trees walked to the riverbank and lay down. Losing mass and the darkness of their shade, the phantoms became shadows once more, attached to the trees of Golroc. On the riverbank, the bones of felled serpans and malevosaurs, stripped of their flesh, showed pale in the moonlight.

Crosslyn looked over the riverbank, then sat down in the stern. He appeared shaken.

On the riverbank, a rabbit with oddly sharp-pointed teeth hopped into view. It stared at the boat and hopped along the riverbank, following them.

Jingo slotted a coin in the slingshot and killed the strange rabbit. Then he looked to Crosslyn with wide eyes. "How can we fight against this?" he asked. "Lothar knows where we are. The spies at his disposal are endless."

"Lothar has his limits," Crosslyn said, dripping with sweat. "Take the boat to shore."

Jingo stared at him. "I'll not go back into Golroc."

"Take us to shore," Crosslyn repeated. "Do it now."

Jingo grabbed the tiller to steer the boat to the riverbank, while Hooks paddled. Though everyone seemed nervous about going ashore, they seemed even less willing to disobey the wizard who had just conjured shadows to consume an army.

When the boat scraped over the gravel in the shallows, Crosslyn stepped out and walked over the field of serpan and malevosaur bones. Several times he turned and stared into the forest. At last, he knelt and retrieved the daggers Jingo had thrown at the serpans. He stepped back into the boat and handed the daggers to Jingo. "Let's get going," he said. "Keep the slingshot handy. We have to be on our guard."

Jingo nodded. Though he wasn't entirely clear on the plan, he was relieved they weren't setting off into Golroc afoot. As the boat pushed away from the riverbank, the distant screech of a salax filled his ears.

With Hooks at the tiller, Elliott moved forward to help paddle while Jingo, seated in the center of the boat, scanned the shore for animals, slingshot in hand and the coin sack at his feet. In the stern, Crosslyn, too, scanned the treeline.

Though dawn fast approached, no one had slept. For a while, they traveled downriver without incident. As the earliest rays of sunshine began to transform the darkness, however, a large simitar appeared on the riverbank. Black with silky fur, it sat on the bank and licked its massive paw, never taking its eyes off them.

Looking at it, Elliott was downright scared. He thought he saw movement in the trees behind it, but maybe it was just his tired eyes.

Quietly, Jingo took a coin from the sack and loaded it in the slingshot's pouch. But as he raised the weapon and squared his shot, he heard a bowstring release above him.

The simitar heard it, too, apparently, for it looked up just as an arrow plummeted down and struck it between the eyes. Without so much as a whimper, the great cat fell, pawing once at its forehead, then was still.

Elliott looked upward, but a thick fog obscured his view.

Something large was falling toward them from the sky. Whatever it was, it threatened to fall right on top of them.

The falling mass screamed, and Jingo scrambled out of the

way just before it landed in the center of the boat with such force that it nearly tipped them over.

It screamed again.

Something large flew overhead, though they couldn't make out anything but a dark shadow.

Hooks appeared shaken. He dropped the tiller and stood. He clenched his fists and stared into the sky, growling before joining the others in the center of the boat to gawk at the new arrival.

Lying in a heap, Slipher sobbed, "Don't hurt me." He looked up at the group collected around him.

Elliott was the first to respond. Though he had never seen a serpan up close, and found Slipher's appearance frightening, his first instinct was to help him. He noticed the bindings at the wrists and ankles, which were chafed and bleeding. But when he knelt to help him, Crosslyn held out his hand.

"Leave him as he is."

Above their heads, the air stirred again, and Councilman Woolf descended through the fog. "Quite a crew you have here," he said. He scanned the faces around him, studying Crosslyn for some time before finally turning to Elliott. "I've been searching for you, young one."

Hooks was first to speak. Taking a step backward, he growled, "Be aware, grayfarer, that you won't take me alive. I'm not going back to that dungeon."

"I've been searching for you, too, beast," he said. "Your presence is required before the council." He unsheathed his sword and took a step toward Hooks, who growled and looked as if he might lunge at Woolf.

"Calm down, both of you," Crosslyn said, stepping between them.

Woolf shifted his attention to Crosslyn. "You," he said. "This cannot be real."

"It's a pleasure to see you again, Woolf," Crosslyn replied. "The last time I laid eyes on you was at your ceremony of first flight. You were strong even as a fledgling. What a delight to learn that you have ascended to the ranks of the council!"

Woolf stared in shock. "This cannot be," he murmured.

"We must thank you for ridding us of the simitar," said Crosslyn, who seemed amused by Woolf's reaction. "We must make haste downriver, for Lothar seems to know our precise location. Surely you won't try to stop us from acting in the service of Harwelden." His demeanor indicated that he was instructing Councilman Woolf rather than beseeching him. "You've grown into a strong warrior," he said with undisguised admiration. "Saralyn and Phebos would be most proud, I'm sure, to see their eldest grandchild developed into such a fine warrior. They were great friends of mine—I was with them for your father's ceremony of first flight. Those were good days."

"But . . . how is this possible?" Woolf asked. "And where have you been for all these long seasons."

"None of that matters," Crosslyn said. "What matters is that I am here now and that we have found this boy—or, rather, he has found us." He beamed at Elliott.

Marvus awoke from his long slumber, looking as surprised as Woolf to see Crosslyn standing before them. He stood, steadying himself before approaching them.

"Councilman Woolf," Marvus said thickly, "may I inquire as to your intentions? Waldemariam has sent you to capture us, no doubt."

Elliott, Jingo, and Hooks, thrilled to see Marvus back among the living, rushed to his side. Jingo reached out and hugged him.

"Why, thank you, Jingo," Marvus said, "but I haven't any idea what all the fuss is about. My last recollection is of being attacked by a pack of dire wolves on the mountaintop. The lead wolf was an agent of Malus Lothar." A look of concern darkened his face. "Lothar is using the animals to spy on us." His eyes darted back and forth.

"It's all right, Marvus," Jingo said. "We know. You won't believe what we've been through. We'll tell you all about it later."

"So there really *was* a shamalan healer hiding in the swamps," Marvus said, turning to Crosslyn. "My head is spinning." Then, for the first time, he noticed Slipher.

Crosslyn extended a hand, drawing Marvus's attention before commenting on Slipher's presence. "I am Crosslyn, sorcerer under the reign of King Dagnar. It is a pleasure to meet you," he said, clasping hands with Marvus. "It is an important journey we embark on together. I, too, have much to learn, as I have been in hiding a very long time. We will learn together and will get to know one another in the bargain. We can fill you in on the rest of the details later," he said. "I believe you just asked a question of our friend Councilman Woolf."

"Hello, Marvus," Woolf said. "Your suspicion is true. Waldemariam has sent Councilman Fanta and me to find you. I have been instructed to return you to Harwelden. My sources tell me that Councilman Fanta has been instructed to execute the boy on sight and bring the rest of you to the dungeon. Like you, I have just learned of the presence of this old shamalan friend."

Elliott stiffened at the word "execute."

"Thank the elders I found you first," Woolf said. "You will be safe in my custody. I have no intention of complying with the chancellor's wishes."

Crosslyn furrowed his brow. "Things are worse than I thought," he said. "There is discord among the council, then. This is an unforeseen development."

"It is difficult for me to understand how I find myself standing before King Dagnar's alchemist," Woolf said to

Crosslyn. "But I behold you with my own eyes. As you are an esteemed member of the royal court, I may report to you on happenings at Harwelden, if you desire."

Crosslyn smiled. After so long a time in hiding, he seemed amused at Woolf's formality. "Then give me your report."

"The council is indeed in turmoil," Woolf said. "Every living shamalan, except for the princess and yourself, has been slaughtered."

Crosslyn looked at him with disbelief. "You forget our young friend here," he said, nodding to Elliott.

"True enough," said Woolf, "if things are as they appear."

"They are indeed," Crosslyn said. "The boy is shamalan. His presence is strong in the Shama.

"I will take you at your word," Woolf said.

"You say that all the shamalans have been killed," Crosslyn said. "What of King Gregorus?"

"Murdered by Viscount Ecsar more than a season ago."

And you referred to the princess—is she the offspring of Gregorus?"

"Indeed," Woolf replied. "She is the sole surviving noble. And she is still a child, barely fit to lead."

"What, then, of Galeren and Gaillart, and Julien and Isabella."

"All dead at the hands of the viscounts," Woolf said. "None remain."

Crosslyn slumped. His voice fell. "And Arnulf and Hugo, Dagnar and Mary?"

"Long since slaughtered. Only Princess Sarintha lives."

Crosslyn slumped to the floor of the boat. For the first time since his arrival among them, Elliott thought he looked fragile.

"Things have progressed much further than I imagined," Crosslyn said. "I had no idea . . . I have resisted joining with the Shama for all these many seasons. I did not want to be found."

"The serpans have captured Prytania, Obsidia, and Scopulus," Woolf said. "Under the direction of Lothar and Viscount Ecsar, an army amasses at the edge of the Forest of Ondor, preparing for an assault on Harwelden. My sources tell me it is the largest force that has congregated since the time of the written word."

"Go on," Crosslyn said.

"Valderon is rising."

Crosslyn raised an eyebrow. "Valderon. I have longed dreaded this day."

"And the council is in turmoil," Woolf continued. "Councilman Alasdar and I have no faith in Chancellor Waldemariam's leadership. And Waldemariam, Fanta, and Oskar have no faith in the princess's leadership. Baucus and Landrew occupy the middle ground. Our fate rides to and fro on every breeze that blows through our chambers."

"Troubling news indeed," Crosslyn said. "I never would have imagined that Harwelden could totter at the brink of the abyss as you describe."

"The attack on Harwelden is imminent," he said. "Our armies are much diminished. We are positioned to fall."

"You present a hopeless scenario," Crosslyn said.

On the riverbank, a raven appeared. Slipher laughed where he lay on the floor of the boat.

Chapter 26

The Isle of Mangrathea

After leaving the site of Galego's slaughter, Sarintha swam as fast as her sculls would carry her. She opened her mind and reached out to Grimaldi as she plunged ahead toward Mangrathea. Approaching the lonely atoll, the waters grew shallower, and a beach came in sight. In a single effort, she emptied her lungs of the frigid saltwater and propelled herself into the air above the surface. When her head broke the surface, she inhaled the night air and instantaneously transformed. Before her feet landed in the shallow waters, the membranes over her eyes retracted, and the webbing between her digits shrank back.

Grimaldi, where are you? she thought, stretching her mind in every direction as she walked onto the beach.

Ahead lay a dense patch of jungle, with a single trail leading from the sandy dunes of the beach into the dense wilderness. Moving quickly, she took the trail and was immediately swallowed up by the dark canopy, where little moonlight penetrated.

In the distance, she heard the growl of an unknown animal. The sound made her uneasy, and she slowed her pace, looking in every direction as she ghosted through the darkness.

Finally, she sensed something up ahead. Grimaldi was near. Following her instincts, she continued through the trail until she emerged in a clearing. A sandy plain stretched before her, surrounded on all sides by dense jungle. In the center of the clearing was a collection of dilapidated huts. Overgrown with moss, and with gaping holes in their thatch roofs, they appeared long since abandoned. Surrounding the huts was a circle of massive stone statues, each as tall as the wall surrounding Harwelden. The statues were long and rectangular, most standing upright, and each carved with a massive, leering face. The devilish images stared at her, sending a shiver down her spine, and she wondered who had labored to create these ghoulish monoliths.

What was this place? Cautiously she approached the ring of statues. Centered in the cluster of huts, which were enclosed in the ring of monoliths, was another, larger statue, which loomed above the crumbling village. It was crudely fashioned in the form of a warrior. A stony headdress rose from its head and cascaded down either side of its body to the waist. It held its arms oustretched over the village, as if in a protective gesture, though its face, too, was fashioned into a fiendish scowl. By the light of the moon, she saw shiny black serpents slithering in and out through crevices in the stone. At the base of the statue sat a stone table. Bones were scattered across its surface, and a skull stared back at her from the edge of the table. She had the impression that it was some type of altar, with the remains of its last offering still in place. The place unnerved her.

Atop the stone warrior sat a shadowy figure, and as Sarintha watched, it raised its wings and sailed down toward her.

Sarintha gasped, raising her arms in defense as the creature descended upon her.

It was Grimaldi.

"I thought you would never make it," he said.

"I ran into some trouble on the way," she replied, heaving an inner sigh of relief.

"Yes," he said, "I saw the ships. I'm relieved they didn't harm you."

Sarintha quickly related the tale of Galego and Viscount Erebus. Then she asked, "Whose ships were they, and why does the darfoyle Erebus travel with them?"

Sarintha had the impression that it was some type
of altar, with the remains of its last offering still in place.

"Let me show you something," Grimaldi said. He rose into the air and grasped Sarintha under the arms with his hindlimbs, carrying her over the treetops and into the sky.

"I'm happy to get away from that village," she said.

"And I."

"Who might have lived there?" she asked.

"You'll see in a moment."

Together they soared back to the edge of the sea. When they reached the beach, Grimaldi flew west along the shore for a short while and descended to the ground. A long, decaying stretch of docks ran along the beach. She had not seen these when she arrived. When they landed in front of the docks, Grimaldi swept his arm across them and looked at her, expecting her to understand.

"What is this?" she asked.

"This is the port that the ships departed from," he said. "Don't you see?"

"You'll have to explain," Sarintha said. "What does this mean?"

"Did you not recognize the figures in the statues?"

"No," she said meekly.

"This island was once inhabited by the Haviru. I assume that a clan of them lived here for a time before they migrated to Corythalia. The ships must have stopped at this old homestead for supplies before continuing toward Harwelden."

Recognition slowly dawned. "The darfoyle Erebus," she said. "He must have traveled to Corythalia to enlist their armies for the war against us."

"Exactly," said Grimaldi.

The blood rushed from her face. "I have heard of the Haviru," she said. "They are a little-known people, but with their weapons, they could stage a terrible assault on Harwelden. If I am correct, my father has tried to enlist their help before, but they come at a very high price."

"A price that, no doubt, Malus Lothar has met," Grimaldi replied. "If we assume correctly, our plight has just worsened substantially."

"We have to get to Harwelden to warn the others," she said. "We haven't time to convalesce on this abandoned island. We must head for home tonight."

"Agreed," Grimaldi said. "I have collected a bit of fruit from the jungle—and slain a few rodents for myself."

"I'm not hungry," she said.

"You must eat. We have a long journey ahead. And you will have to swim."

"You're right," she said, feeling the painful welts on her abdomen given her by Malus Lothar's spiders. "I can swim back to the basin of the river Tantasar, then upstream toward Harwelden. We can meet at the riverfront east of the castle."

"I'm sorry to ask you to swim, but it will be faster," Grimaldi said, looking at the holes in his wrists. "Now, eat.

They sat on the beach and ate in silence. Grimaldi chewed on the tough water rat meat while Sarintha gobbled down the tart fruit. When they had finished, she waded into the surf, and Grimaldi flapped his wings and was airborne. "Be careful," he called back. "Leave nothing to chance."

Chapter 27

The Prisoner

Elliott and Crosslyn stood peering down at Slipher, bound hand and foot and with an overlarge helmet half covering his eyes.

Improbably, he laughed at them.

"I am at a loss to understand what you find so humorous," Crosslyn said.

"You will all die like animals at the hands of the malus," he said. "And you don't even have the sense to realize it. Now, untie me at once and perhaps I will request a speedy death for you when my countrymen arrive."

"Let us understand who is the prisoner and who are his keepers," said Crosslyn. And pointing his index finger at the young serpan, he said, "*Acerbitas.*"

Slipher's face contorted, and he jumped as if bitten. "Stop it!" he shouted as if in pain.

"It is time you learned some manners," Crosslyn said, aiming his index finger again. "Now, let's start again. What is your name?"

No longer laughing, Slipher looked up at the finger.

"I will not ask you again."

Slipher looked like a child being scolded. "My name is Slipher."

"There's a start. Now, tell us how you came to be in Councilman Woolf's custody." He glanced up at Woolf, signaling to let the serpan tell the tale.

"I was hunting the shamalan boy. I have been following his trail for many days. I was spying on the grayfarer to learn what he knew of the boy, when he detected my presence and captured me. If he hadn't found me, this shamalan would already be dead."

"Who sent you to search for the boy?"

Slipher winced, and his eyes wandered. "Malus Lothar sent me," he croaked.

Crosslyn laughed. "You expect me to believe that Malus Lothar sent *you, alone,* to seek out the most dangerous enemy he has faced since acceding to the serpan throne? I have a hard time believing that." He aimed his finger at Slipher. "*Acerbitas.*"

Slipher howled in pain, and his body jerked up off the floor of the boat.

"Stop it!" Elliott protested, pushing Crosslyn's finger aside. "He's no danger to us. This is cruel."

Crosslyn looked annoyed.

"I mean it," said Elliott. "He's done nothing to hurt us." He turned and made his way aft, leaving Crosslyn alone with Hooks and the gimlets.

Soon after he sat down away from the others, Elliott felt a tap on his shoulder. He turned to find Marvus behind him. "Crosslyn does not mean to upset you," the gimlet said. "May I sit?"

Elliott nodded. Marvus scooted beside him on the narrow stern bench, and they sat staring upriver, with their backs to the others.

"That creature is a serpan, Elliott," Marvus said. "He would kill you without a moment's hesitation, and he may have information that is valuable to us. Crosslyn's actions will not cause him any lasting harm. He means only to protect you."

"That creature's done nothing to me," Elliott said. "And he's *pathetic.* He can't hurt anyone; just look at him."

"He himself said he was sent to kill you," Marvus countered. "You may have a difficult time understanding it, but he is a mortal foe. A serpan malevosaur brigade has just attacked us, and who knows what other dangers lie in wait for us."

Elliott turned to gaze at Slipher. "He looks like a child. I'm sure we can get him to talk without hurting him." He grimaced. "That thing Crosslyn's doing . . . it bothers me." He felt an unlikely compassion for Slipher, and perhaps even a kinship of sorts, for many times, he, too, had been tormented by those stronger than him.

"Come," Marvus said. "We will ask Crosslyn to let you speak to him. At least then you can see the kind of enemy we're dealing with."

With a sigh, Elliott stood up and went forward to join the others.

"Elliott would like to speak to the serpan in private," Marvus said. And before Woolf, Hooks, Crosslyn, and Jingo could protest, he put up his hand. "Woolf can check to see that his bindings are secure, but after that, let's leave them for a moment. Elliott won't be in any danger."

Crosslyn nodded and motioned for the others to follow him, leaving Elliott alone with Slipher.

Elliott looked the strange prisoner over from top to bottom. He looked like a member of the same brown race he had seen in his grandfather's painting. "My name is Elliott," he started.

Slipher sneered and turned away from him.

"Why would you want to kill me?" he asked. "I've never done anything to you."

Slipher ignored him.

"Come on," Elliott said. "I'm trying to help you. Answer my questions, and I'll give you something to eat."

Slipher remained silent, though he seemed to consider the proposition. "Do you have any meat?" he said finally.

Elliott took some dried meat from Crosslyn's knapsack, then returned to Slipher's side and sat, holding out a bit before him. "Tell me why you would want to kill me, and you can have it," he said.

Slipher glowered at him. "I want to kill you because you are a shamalan."

Elliott waited for more.

"I have answered your question," Slipher said. "Now, give me the meat."

"That's not good enough," Elliott said. "You don't know me, and I have never done anything to you. It makes no sense that you want to kill me. Now, make me understand."

Slipher rolled clumsily to face him. "My family is dead because of the war with the shamalan empire," he said. "My brothers and father died in battle against the tyrants who occupy Harwelden. While your people grow fat from the harvests of your lands, my people starve, grubbing roots from the stones to feed our young. Many times in our history, we have tried to settle on the Carafayan continent, and each time, we have been cast out of your paradise. You fight in the name of your elders and the Shama, but your every deed is selfish. At the point of your weapons, you take food from our mouths. But finally, my people have found hope. Malus Lothar has foreseen the death of every last shamalan. Lord Valderon is rising from the prison your gods have fashioned for him, and he has offered his blessing to the malus. I do not care what the prophecies say, but I know that I will kill you—and the old man who travels with you. To avenge my father and my brothers, I will kill you. For the miserable lives of my mother and her youngest child, I will drain the blood from your veins if it is my last act in this world." Slipher glared at Elliott. "Now, give me the meat."

Taken aback, Elliott gave him the meat, then stood and returned to the others.

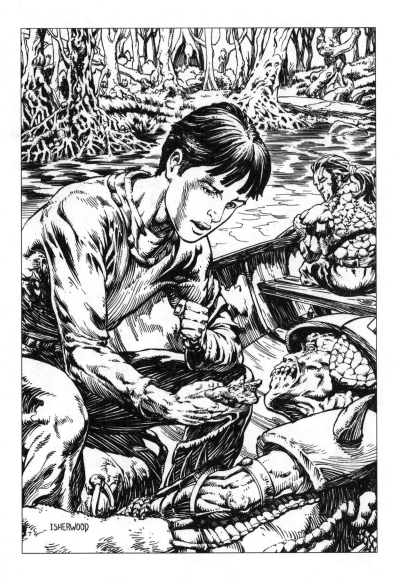

Elliott said, "You don't know me,
and I have never done anything to you.
It makes no sense that you want to kill me."

Crosslyn watched as he approached. "What have you learned from that exchange?" he asked.

Elliott thought for a moment. "Only that he hates me," he said. "And that he doesn't seem likely to change."

"Then you have just learned something useful."

Woolf, Hooks, and the gimlets looked at Elliott gently. Woolf was first to speak.

"That creature is a poor introduction to the serpans," he said. "They are a mighty foe, though he is hardly more than a child. He speaks as if he were powerful, though it only makes him look foolish. Do not be afraid of him. As long as I am with you, he poses no threat."

"I'm not afraid of him," Elliott said. "Come, I'm hungry. Can we have something to eat?"

Crosslyn broke apart a loaf and a wedge of hard cheese from his knapsack.

"We eat this dinner in honor of Marvus," Elliott said. "It's good to have you back."

"Hear, hear!" Jingo said. "I couldn't have said it better myself.

"To Marvus," Hooks said.

Marvus smiled.

In silence, they ate, heading ever northward down the river Tantasar.

Chapter 28

Waldemariam Prepares for Sarintha's Return

The suns shone brightly in the midday sky over Ondor, dulling the cool breeze that blew through the windows of the great hall. Waldemariam stood gazing over the forest as, behind and all around him, servants of the castle made ready for the upcoming celebration of the equinox and the harvest, to be marked in the usual fashion with the Festival of Opik.

Councilman Oskar joined him at the window. "The days are growing cooler," he said. "Winter approaches."

Waldemariam nodded.

"Have you given any more thought to our discussion last night?" Oskar asked.

The chancellor turned to face him. "I have considered it at length," he said. "I do not find the results of the census relevant. We will go forward as planned."

"I agree with you, of course," Oskar said. "But the others will not share my faith in your plan."

"It doesn't matter," Waldemariam said. "They must do as I say. I am chancellor." He caressed the gold amulet that hung from his neck.

"Do you believe the findings of the census?" Oskar asked. "Every boy in the village is accounted for. If the census is correct, the boy who fled with the gimlets and the susquat prisoner *must* be the boy from the forest. They have checked and re-checked and keep arriving at the same conclusion."

"It matters not. My feelings are unchanged. It does not mean he is shamalan."

"Then Fanta's orders regarding the boy are unchanged?" Oskar asked.

Waldemariam nodded. "They are unchanged."

For a moment, they stood in silence. Waldemariam stared out the window, as if deep in thought. A frown crossed his face.

"Have you received word from Fanta or Woolf?" Oskar asked.

"I've heard from neither of them," said Waldemariam. "Councilman Woolf is not reliable. I exercised poor judgment in allowing him to go. I am surprised, though, that I haven't heard from Councilman Fanta."

"As am I," Oskar said. "It is unlike him."

Waldemariam's frown deepened. "Can I confide in you, Oskar?"

"Always."

"I am troubled by the force that collects at the outskirts of Ondor. My scouts tell me that it grows larger with each passing day. We haven't the strength to repel such an army. "

Councilman Oskar sighed. "It troubles me, too. Our army is a skeleton of what it was even a few seasons ago. I fear they could defeat us with half the troops they have already amassed."

"Regardless of what the others think," Waldemariam said, "the appearance of the boy means nothing. It is time to discipline ourselves to face what lies ahead, whatever it shall be. It is not the time to be carried away with the fantasy that a child will deliver us from our enemies. We shall prepare ourselves with dignity for the fight that remains, and resist this false notion that a frightened young boy can turn the tide of this war. It is folly, Oskar."

For a moment, they stood in silence. Waldemariam
stared out the window, as if deep in thought.

Oskar said nothing.

Waldemariam sighed. "My only regret is that the Antiquitas Trident remains lost. If it were intact, then perhaps we might have a chance. At this moment in our history, I do not think that disassembling it and hiding its parts was wise."

"Galeren only wanted to protect it," Oskar replied. "It is what the shamalans deemed best. Besides, the Antiquitas is of little use unless wielded by a shamalan noble."

"By the time the Festival of Opik arrives, we will have our noble. I have recently received word that Grimaldi and Sarintha have escaped from Mount Sitticus. No doubt they travel to Harwelden even as we speak."

Oskar gasped. "That is wonderful news, Chancellor! They are alive! Why haven't you informed the council?"

"I learned of it only this morning."

Who sent word from Mount Sitticus? I did not know we had a contact there."

"That is not important," Waldemariam said, turning his gaze from Oskar. "What is important is that the princess will arrive soon, and we must develop a strategy for dealing with her. She will expect to take command when she arrives. We mustn't let that happen."

Oskar fidgeted. "I don't understand, Chancellor. It is her right to take command."

"She is a *child*," Waldemariam snapped. "What does she know of command? We are positioned for an assault by the full strength of Lothar's forces. Valderon is rising. In the face of all this, we fight without the protection of the Antiquitas. The Shama will fail us, Oskar. Its time draws to a close as surely as we both draw breath. Valderon gains strength each day. He is rising, just as foreseen by the prophecies. Our interests are not served by placing our faith in an untested girl or a frightened young boy."

"What you say makes sense," Oskar said. "But when she arrives, she will regain the full support of the people. Councilmen Alasdar, Baucus, and Landrew will side with her over you."

"I am considering our options," Waldemariam said. "Until she arrives, my word is the law. With the forces of the malus amassing against us, I am within my rights to declare myself the sole voice of the empire, and if anyone dares question me, I will punish him harshly. Under a state of emergency rule, I can place the princess in custody if she challenges our plans."

"The measures you suggest are drastic," Oskar said. "I am not sure the rest of the council will go along."

"They will go along," Waldemariam said, "as long as they do not know of her return. Later today, I will call a meeting of the council and declare a state of emergency rule. After that, my power cannot be challenged. With this decree in place, we will deal with Sarintha when she arrives. Call a meeting of the council tonight."

"I will do as you say." Oskar turned and left, leaving Waldemariam alone once more.

Waldemariam returned his gaze to the Forest of Ondor. As he stared out over the treescape, his ever-present frown deepened. All the while, he caressed the golden amulet that hung at his throat.

Chapter 29

The Bracelet and the Water

The dawn came unnoticed to most of the travelers aboard Crosslyn's boat. Except for Crosslyn and Slipher, everyone slept as they floated downstream, steadily northward. After the fight in Golroc, they all were exhausted, and they had been asleep for hours, waking only to take their turn at the tiller. It was not till midday that they arose, feeling mostly refreshed after the long rest.

After rising, Elliott went to Crosslyn, who worked the tiller while keeping watch over the captive serpan in the stern. It was the first time Elliott had seen a serpan in the full light of day, and he found the creature quite ugly, though he couldn't help but feel some compassion for it.

Slipher recognized the suggestion of sympathy in Elliott's expression. "Turn your eyes away from me," he said. "I do not need your pity."

Elliott was taken aback. "I don't pity you," he said. "And I'll look at you as long as I want." And he stared longer than he would have otherwise.

Slipher glared at him. "My time for revenge will come." He pulled against his restraints. "You'll get what's coming to you."

"Silence," Crosslyn said, pointing a finger at him in warning.

Slipher sneered and rolled to his side, turning his face away from them, again bringing his bindings to Elliott's notice.

Elliott turned to Crosslyn. "What are our plans for today?"

Crosslyn looked at Slipher and frowned, then turned to Elliott. "We have many things to discuss. After that, we will enter the water. It is time for you to learn a thing or two about your shamalan abilities."

Butterflies danced in Elliott's stomach. The prospect of entering the water with the old man excited him. But before he could respond, Woolf appeared behind them.

"Sorry to interrupt," he said, "but I have something I must share with Crosslyn."

When the old man nodded, Woolf stole a guilty glance at Elliott and squatted on his haunches and whispered to Crosslyn.

When Woolf finished, Crosslyn smiled broadly, almost laughing, and held out his hand. "Give it to me, then," he said.

Woolf took something from his pocket and handed it over. Elliott could not see what it was. Then Woolf nodded and returned to the bow, where Hooks and the two gimlets were preparing breakfast.

Crosslyn grinned as he reached into his sleeve and took out the bracelet of the nine clans. Using his dagger blade, he pried one of the stones from its fixture and held the solitary gem up to the sunlight. Then, to Elliott's astonishment, he threw the stone into the river.

Elliott was alarmed. "What are you doing!" he cried, peering over the edge of the boat.

Crosslyn smiled. He presented the object that Woolf had given him. It was another gemstone. He seated the stone in the empty fixture on the bracelet and again held the bracelet up to the sunlight. Satisfied, he turned to Elliott. "Put it on," he said, handing him the bracelet.

Confused, Elliott clasped the bracelet on his wrist.

"Try it," Crosslyn said, smiling.

Elliott looked at the bracelet, turning his arm so that the gems and the metal glistened in the sun. After several seconds, he looked up at Crosslyn and nodded. The butterflies in his stomach intensified. He closed his eyes and pictured a simitar: the massive paws, the thick brown coat, and, of course, the fearsome fangs. Despite his concentration, he felt nothing. Disheartened, he opened his eyes.

Crosslyn stared at him, but his expression was one Elliott couldn't put his finger on. He was grinning.

Elliott realized that his perspective was different from a few seconds ago. Now he stood above Crosslyn, looking down. He turned his head to the bow, where Hooks, Woolf, Marvus, and Jingo stared at him with mouths agape.

Hooks cocked his head sideways, then took a step toward Elliott but tripped, falling headfirst into the water.

Despite the commotion, all eyes remained fixed on Elliott.

With a strange realization dawning, Elliott looked down at himself. Instead of hands, he saw a massive pair of forepaws, though the tip of one digit was missing. He pawed at his face. His nose was cool and wet, and long tusks protruded downward from his jaws. *It worked!*

Elliott watched with amusement as Hooks tried clumsily to climb back aboard, falling repeatedly back into the river and, at one point, nearly tipping the vessel over.

"Help him," Elliott said. His voice was deep and gravelly.

The gimlets and Woolf did as they were bidden, and helped Hooks back onto the boat, barely taking their eyes off Elliott during the whole affair.

"Magnificent!" Marvus said.

"Most magnificent," Jingo parroted.

"You look fearsome," Woolf said. "I would not believe it had I not seen it with my own eyes."

Hooks cocked his head sideways, then took a step toward
Elliott but tripped, falling headfirst into the water.

"Praise Baruna," Jingo whispered. "An heir to King Griogair lives."

Elliott smiled, exposing a row of sharp teeth. "I don't understand, Crosslyn," he said. "Why didn't it work before?" He rather liked the sound of his simitar voice.

"Because the chancellor tried to make fools of us," he said. "Waldemariam substituted a worthless stone for one of the magical gems. The chancellor did not want you to be able to use the bracelet. Woolf has told me that the chancellor claims to believe you are not shamalan, and certainly not an heir to the great king, but he hedges his bets by removing the stone. Thankfully, one of Woolf's contacts became aware of the action and returned the proper stone to him."

"Are you sure the bracelet works only for the heirs to the king?" Elliott asked, again holding a paw in front of his face.

Crosslyn smiled. "I am sure," he said. "It would be wise for you to transform back into yourself, as this magic will exhaust you. Managing the energy required to perform feats of magic is a subject you and I shall have to spend some time on. It is a difficult skill to master. If you don't transform now, you will grow exhausted and I won't be able to take you into the water."

Elliott held the paw before his eyes for a little longer. He was having fun and was not eager to change back, though he acquiesced, nodding to Crosslyn. He closed his eyes and conjured a picture of himself, as a boy again, in his mind's eye. When he opened his eyes, he was back to normal.

Marvus and Jingo rushed to his side, smiling and clapping him on the back. Hooks and Woolf also congratulated him.

Crosslyn sat smiling. "There are few things that could bring such joy to my heart as seeing you able to use that bracelet," he said.

Elliott blushed. "I have a hard time believing it myself," he said. "And I still don't understand why it should work for me. I don't see how I can be related to your King Griogair. And there's another thing I don't understand."

"Yes?" Crosslyn said.

"If Waldemariam is the ruler of the Grayfarer Council, why is he so dead set against us? And why is he so against me in particular? I mean, why did he change the stone?"

"I am perhaps the best one to answer that," Woolf said.

"Please enlighten us," Crosslyn said.

"Waldemariam, like most of the grayfarers at Harwelden, does not believe in the tenets of the Shama. Grayfarers, as Crosslyn and the stewards know, are not known for their faith. With all the nobles murdered or captured, Waldemariam has grown comfortable expressing his disbelief in the ancient ways. When you arrived in the Forest of Ondor, Elliott, he regarded it as coincidence, not providence. He sees you not as an ally but as a threat—someone who has the ability to undermine his rule, because so many will be ready to follow you. He seeks to undermine you in every possible way so that he can maintain control of the troops and the castle. Though many disagree with him, his supporters counter that he is following his conscience, that his deeds will prove effective and have no sinister intent."

"What do you believe, Woolf?" Crosslyn asked. "Are Waldemariam's motivations as simple as that, or is something more baleful afoot?"

"Difficult to say," Woolf said. "Waldemariam has proved himself a powerful leader and a responsible steward of Harwelden, but his behavior upon Elliott's discovery was strange, as it has been for much of the past season. I've halfway come to believe that the chancellor is going mad."

Crosslyn looked surprised. "Continue, and please be candid. No one here sees your comments as treasonous in any way."

Woolf fidgeted. "The council believes, as did General Grimaldi and Princess Sarintha, that our plans are being leaked to the enemy. The question we all ask ourselves is, *who* might be leaking the plans?"

"What evidence have you that your secrets have been betrayed?" Crosslyn asked.

"There are many. The serpans seem to know our every move before we make it. They captured Prytania when our troops there were at their lowest strength. Though we were careful to hide our retreat, leaving many warriors along the front lines so as to appear strong, they attacked on the very day that we shifted our forces to Iracema, as if they were privy to our strategies. Later that night, Ecsar murdered King Gregorus as he lay in his bedclothes near the fire. Less than a season later, despite our most careful attempts, the sequence repeated itself. Princess Sarintha and her troops were ambushed in a nearly identical fashion. It was only by coincidence that the army from Iracema stumbled onto the ambush, allowing our forces to escape to Ondor."

"Yes," said Marvus. "Jingo and I accompanied the princess on that journey. After we fled from the outskirts of Prytania, they followed us into Ondor and ambushed again after nightfall. That is how the princess was recaptured. Jingo and I barely escaped with our lives."

"Then you found Elliott," Woolf said, recounting the story for Crosslyn, "and presented him to the Grayfarer Council upon your return to Harwelden."

"Yes," Marvus said. "I thought the council would receive him with joy, but instead they treated him as a prisoner. I have felt very badly about this, Elliott. I hope you will forgive Jingo and me. We did not intend to mislead you."

Elliott smiled. "Of course I forgive you, Marvus," he said, tousling the gimlet's hair. "You and Jingo have been my best friends since I got here. I don't know what I would have done if I hadn't found you guys."

"What about me?" Hooks snorted.

Woolf cut Elliott off before he could respond. "Yes," he said, pointing at Hooks. "Let's take a moment to talk about you."

Hooks bristled. He seemed caught off guard.

"You, too, have deepened the mystery at Harwelden," Woolf said. "Waldemariam believes that the gimlets rescued you only to inflame the forces at Harwelden so they would give chase to you, leaving the castle unprotected against a serpan assault. No one can understand why the stewards of the princess would sacrifice themselves to save a condemned prisoner—especially a susquat who stands accused of kidnapping grayfarer fledglings in an effort to extinguish them just as the shamalans have been brought to the brink of extinction. While we are on the topic, what have you to say for yourself in this matter."

"Not guilty," Hooks said. "Just as I told you before." His eyes narrowed.

"It is true, though, that you don't possess the most honorable of reputations," Woolf challenged.

"Hooks would never do anything like that," said Elliott, moving to Hooks's side. "He's saved my life twice. He's with us."

"Who, then, has taken so many of our fledglings over the past several seasons? And who would go to the trouble to implicate you as the criminal?"

"I haven't the slightest idea," Hooks replied. "Before I was captured in Ondor, I had never laid eyes on Harwelden."

Crosslyn watched the exchange between the susquat and the grayfarer with interest. "He speaks the truth, Woolf," he said. "I have known Hooks for many seasons. Whatever his transgressions, he didn't kidnap or kill any of your fledglings."

"Then the mystery deepens," Woolf said, glaring at Hooks. "In addition to a conspirator, we now must consider who has kidnapped so many fledglings, and who seeks to pin this grave crime on a wayward susquat."

"Choose your words carefully when you speak to me, flying dog," Hooks growled.

"Enough," Crosslyn said, raising his hand. "We will not travel this path. The fates have thrown us together, and we must act as one. I myself am unsure how Hooks figures in all this, but I have known him for many seasons, and I trust him. He is not the criminal you seek, Woolf. Now, let's focus our efforts on a more productive endeavor."

"But if I understand your plans," Woolf protested, we journey aboard this boat to Susquatania. How well do you think the susquats will receive us while we are in the company of the shame of their clans?" Woolf looked from Crosslyn to Hooks. "Are you aware of the reasons Hooks was banished from his kindred so many seasons ago? His past is far from honorable. If he can betray his own kind, then he is certainly capable of conspiring with the enemy against Harwelden. By his actions against his own people, we know that his motivation for money outweighs all other loyalties."

"You know nothing of my motivations," Hooks growled.

"I said enough of this, both of you," Crosslyn said. "If you honor my service to Harwelden, you will honor me on this matter. The armies at Harwelden are splintered. The Grayfarer Council is in disarray, and we prepare for the greatest battle in the history of the empire. If we are to have any good effect on the happenings around us and on the fate of Harwelden and the empire itself, you must let go of your suspicions, Woolf. We must act as one."

Elliott, still at Hooks's side, reached up and placed a hand on his back in a show of support. "You haven't got to know him yet, Woolf, but we wouldn't have survived this journey without him. He has saved us from wolves, Lothar, and the salax. He's the one who convinced us to flee Harwelden and find Crosslyn in the first place. If that doesn't convince you that he's with us, I don't know what will."

"Elliott speaks the truth, Woolf," Marvus said. "I saw the disappearance of the fledglings unfold just as you did, but I will speak on behalf of this susquat." Like Elliott, he moved to stand at Hooks's side.

"And I will speak for him, too," Jingo said. "No offense intended to you, but Hooks is one of us now."

Woolf surveyed the group as they stood in support of Hooks. "As a member of the council, I have heard the testimony offered against the beast, and I do not share your faith in his innocence. But I will do as Crosslyn asks. But I must ask, Crosslyn, about your plans upon our arrival in Susquatania. What is our purpose for traveling there? And how do you propose, on our journey to Susquatania, that we sail past Harwelden undetected? With the exception of you and me, everyone aboard this boat has been branded a fugitive and an enemy of Harwelden."

Crosslyn smiled. "As for the journey past the port of Harwelden, that will be simple. We will ask Elliott to use the bracelet. With my guidance, he will be able to mask our presence as we pass. No one will have any idea we are there—we will drift right past them."

"Wow," Elliott said, holding his arm before him so he could again look at the bracelet. "Will I really be able to do that?"

Crosslyn smiled. "Indeed. And as for the purpose of our trip to Susquatania, that will be revealed in due time. We must make haste, though. The Festival of Opik draws near. We shall have to travel to Susquatania, conduct our business there, and return to Harwelden before the festival begins. If we hope to foil the serpans' plans, all must be ready by the time we arrive. It will not be easy."

Marvus listened keenly. "And what are your plans for when we return to Harwelden from Susquatania?" he asked. "Waldemariam will be ready to throw us all in the dungeon. If things are as bad as Woolf says, even Woolf might not escape the chancellor's wrath."

Crosslyn stroked his beard. "We will cross that bridge when we come to it," he said. "But for now, I shall take Elliott into the water. We haven't much time for frolicking, for we should pass by the port of Harwelden tomorrow." He moved to the edge of the boat. "So let's get going, Elliott," he said. "I'll see you below. And doffing his robe, he dived into the salty river.

Elliott's throat went dry. He had expected some instruction from Crosslyn before they went under. He stared into the river, appreciating the speed of the current. He looked to Marvus for guidance.

Marvus smiled. "I guess you better get going."

Elliott nodded. Stoically he walked to the edge of the boat, and after stealing one last nervous glance at Marvus, he jumped feetfirst into the water.

Marvus and Jingo smiled as his head went under the rushing waters. Even Hooks and Woolf looked pleased.

⚓ ⚓ ⚓

Beneath the surface, Elliott held his breath and tried to orient himself in the darkness. The current pushed him relentlessly, and he soon found himself far from the boat. He couldn't see much, and the water was colder than he expected. The salt stung his eyes. Suppressing his panic, he willed himself to inhale the water.

But he couldn't do it. Memories of the awful sensation of drowning outmatched his desire to transform. Again and again he willed himself to breathe in the cold water, but he could not bring himself to do it. As his hunger for air grew, he couldn't take it any longer and kicked toward the surface.

But something grabbed his leg, pulling him down.

Panicking, he kicked with all his might, but to no avail. Whatever had clamped on to his leg drew him deeper into the murky waters. Beneath him, he could barely make out the glowing red eyes of his captor. The grip around his leg tightened, and whatever had grasped him pulled him deeper into the water.

Elliott's lungs felt as though they might burst. He kicked wildly, and his efforts grew more erratic as his air hunger worsened. And finally, he could resist no more. Reflexively, despite the inner battle, he blew out his breath and inhaled. Liters of saltwater filled the recesses of his lungs. It burned.

Again the thin yellow membranes descended over his eyes, and again the birthmarks between his fingers and toes tingled pleasantly. He felt the birthmarks pop as the tissues between his knuckles opened, and the thin membranes of webbing blossomed between them. His vision grew keener, and the stinging in his eyes abated as the landscape beneath the water materialized in shades of pale yellow.

The riverbed was deep and wide. Tree roots and streamers of aquatic vegetation reached inward from the submerged banks, oscillating with the currents that brought life to the strange underworld that teemed around him. All sorts of strange fish, some quite menacing in appearance, swam past, yet he was not afraid. Inexplicably, he felt confident under the water, and this was a feeling with which he had limited experience. With renewed vigor, he kicked again, striving to escape from whatever held him down. This time, the sculls of his hands and feet displaced larger quantities of water, propelling him upward and finally breaking the grasp on his leg. But he did not return to the surface. He swam a smooth arc above his pursuer and circled downward, diving to the level of the creature that held him. As he completed his dive, he found himself face to face with the glowing red eyes of his captor: Crosslyn.

Elliott smiled.

Welcome, young one, to the enchantments of the deep, said a voice in his mind. It was Crosslyn's voice.

How does he do that? Elliott thought.

The same way as you.

Wow, Elliott thought. *You can hear what I'm thinking.*

We communicate by telepathy. We can communicate this way on the surface as well, but it comes much less easily.

Elliott grinned. *Cool.*

Indeed, Crosslyn replied. *Now, follow me.* And he kicked, propelling himself with the current. His body gyrated as he gained speed, his sculls navigating the water like the feet of an otter. He moved like a creature born of the water.

Joyfully Elliott followed. To his surprise, he had no trouble keeping up with the old man. He moved to Crosslyn's side, and side by side they raced through the murky waters.

Your transformation lacked finesse, Crosslyn thought, *but your swimming is quite natural. Hard to believe this is your first full excursion under the water.*

I know, Elliott replied. *I feel like I've done this before. I want to go faster.* He kicked harder, accelerating past the old man.

Excellent, Crosslyn thought, striving to keep pace. *Now, follow me. I want to show you something.* And abruptly, Crosslyn dived straight down.

Elliott followed. They swam straight downward for what seemed several minutes. The darkness around them thickened, though Elliott could still see several feet in front of him. At last, they reached the river bottom. At the last possible moment, Crosslyn reversed his dive and arced upward. Upright again, he floated to the murky sediments of the riverbed, landing perfectly upright on his feet.

Elliott mimicked the action, landing next to him.

Impressive, Crosslyn thought. *You do quite well beneath the surface, especially for a Gayan.*

Elliott was perplexed. He had heard the term before. *What's a Gayan?*

Someone from the daughterworld Gaya, Crosslyn thought. *Specifically, if I am correct in my assumptions, you are a Gayan.*

Hmmm, Elliott thought. *Then what's a daughterworld?*

That is a difficult concept to grasp, Crosslyn thought, *and one that you will come to understand as you navigate your xcercio. That is the ancient word for cultivation.*

My grandfather spoke of a cultivation.

Did he? Crosslyn thought. *That does not entirely surprise me. So what is it?* Elliott thought.

The cultivation is a process that teaches a young one like you what it means to be shamalan. Everyone must undertake it. During the cultivation, a shamalan learns to unlock his power. He learns of his natural abilities, as well as shamalan culture and history. During the cultivation, the subject's caste in the shamalan world is decided. One can be fated to be a noble, a master, a priest, or a warrior. Once your fate is chosen, your cultivation is tailored accordingly.

Yes, Elliott replied, *Jingo spoke of this on the night before we entered the Forest of Golroc. When will my cultivation begin?*

It has already begun. Crosslyn smiled. *Now, follow me. I want to show you something.* Crosslyn walked along the riverbed in silence, leading Elliott farther upstream.

Elliott marveled at the array of strange creatures in the river. He felt life all around him. To his surprise, he caught glimpses of the thoughts of the creatures that swam by. Most of his impressions were of dull-witted creatures scanning the waters in search of a meal. On occasion, he felt the fear of an animal being chased by a predator. It was an unsettling sensation. Sometimes, the underwater creatures swam close enough that he could see them; invariably, they were strange to his eye. All around him, creatures great and small went about their activities, mostly oblivious to the presence of the two shamalans.

As they marched farther upstream, the sediment beneath their feet hardened, and the water cleared. They emerged into an underwater valley, surrounded on all sides by the wispy vegetation of the riverbed. In this section of the riverbed, more light from the surface penetrated. Crosslyn stopped and turned to Elliott.

Time for your first test, he thought.

What test?

You'll see. Crosslyn turned his back to Elliott and spread his arms.

Come to me, naiads, Crosslyn thought, still facing away from him.

What are you doing?

Crosslyn ignored him. *Come to me now,* he repeated.

To Elliott, it seemed that the riverbed had grown still. The chatter of thoughts and impressions that had filled his mind just moments ago ceased. Looking all around him, he saw vague shadows of creatures of the river suspended in the water. All motion had halted.

Crosslyn remained silent, standing on the river bottom, arms outstretched.

Then, in his mind, Elliott heard singing. A chorus of sweet, childlike voices from the distance filled his head, squeezing out his own thoughts.

We march to him to heed his call.
We march in search of the last to fall.
Onward, through the river's sprawl,
We march to him to heed his call.

Without realizing it, Elliott was entranced by the smooth, melodic voices, which grew louder as they approached.

The warlock's in the Phaestian pass,
He travels with the stranger cast

As shamalan for all to know.
The boy of lore, whose fame shall grow.

Crosslyn turned to Elliott. *That was easier than I expected.*
He smiled. *They're coming.*

Who's coming?

Crosslyn ignored him and turned in the direction of the
music. The singing grew louder.

The river shall flow red as blood.
The soil of Ondor turns to mud.
With plague of rats and death they'll see
The victor, who shall hold the key.

What plague? Elliott thought, alarmed. *Crosslyn, what's going on?*

Crosslyn continued to ignore him.

But no one knows who has the right
to claim the victory in the fight.
The elders watch from points on high
as Valderon brings the tempest nigh.

From a few paces ahead, a triad of small creatures approached, singing. They had the appearance of tiny, bearded
old men with large, pointed ears and flowing white hair. Wispy
appendages sprouted symmetrically from their backs and legs,
giving them the appearance of bizarre winged elves.

We come to him to heed his call.
The shamalan,
The last to fall.

The creatures hung suspended in the water before them. They stopped singing.

Greetings, warlock, said one of them.

Greetings, sprite, Crosslyn said. *I have a task I would like you to perform.*

We are at your service, shamalan.

As you can see, Crosslyn said, *I have a shamalan boy with me. We have only just begun his cultivation. We do not yet know how he is to be fated.*

The sprites looked at Elliott as if taking his measure. *I see,* said one. *We will be happy to pass judgment on him.*

That would be most welcome, Crosslyn said.

The sprites swam toward Elliott. Frightened and unsure what to do, he stood motionless as they swam all around him, inspecting him from head to foot. One by one, they hovered in front of his face, searching his eyes. After several seconds of this, one of the sprites addressed him. *There is tragedy in your future,* it said, staring at him. *But your enemy is not who you think. Your enemy is shamalan.*

He stared at the creature. *What do you mean?* he said. *What are you telling me?*

Things are not as you imagine, the sprite said. *The answer to the riddle is for you to discover.* It hovered a moment longer. *There is tragedy in your future,* it said again. *You will not achieve your goal.*

And with that, the creature left him and swam to Crosslyn. Cupping his hands over his mouth, one of the sprites whispered into Crosslyn's ear. The blood drained from the old man's face, and he turned to stare at Elliott. When the sprite finished whispering in his ear, the triad swam out of sight.

May the elders be with you, child, Elliott heard as they disappeared into the murk. *There is death in your future. Nothing can be done to change this. Be cautious with your power, and turn away from hubris.*

The sprites were gone, and Elliott stood alone again with Crosslyn on the river floor.

Whatever the naiads had said to Crosslyn had shaken him. Without offering an explanation, the old shamalan kicked toward the shallows. *Come on, boy,* he thought. *It's time to get back to the boat.*

Elliott followed. Crosslyn's reaction to the naiads, and their final admonishment to him, gave him a bad feeling.

Chapter 30

Sarintha's Homecoming

Sarintha plowed upstream, bucking the current of the Tantasar. Since leaving Mangrathea, she had not stopped for
food or rest for nearly two days, and the relentless exertion was
taking its toll. Her strength flagging, she willed herself forward,
ever closer to the port of Harwelden, at the edge of Mount Kalipharus and just east of the main castle complex.

Early in the journey from Mangrathea, she had sensed
Grimaldi above her, but shortly after entering the river from the
sea, they had caught up with the Haviru fleet, and he had to fly
higher while she dived deep. She had lost her awareness of the
grayfarer while passing beneath the fleet and had not regained
it since. But this was of minor consequence—Grimaldi could
take care of himself. With dogged determination, she had cir-
cumvented the Haviru fleet and homed in on Harwelden as fast
as her sculls could propel her. She would arrive a full day before
the Haviru reached their suspected destination: where the river
crossed the southern edge of Toltuga, and where the growing
serpan army camped at Ondor's edge. Now, on the final league
of her trek, she could at last see before her the familiar piers of
the port of Harwelden. She had made it home.

With renewed strength, she swam the final lengths to the
port and reached out to touch the submerged piers as if they
were old friends. Finally, thankfully, she kicked toward the
bank and gave a final thrust to propel herself out of the water.
The shamalan transformation reversed itself, and she walked

onto the riverbank and collapsed, relishing the feel of the grass between her fingers as she succumbed to exhaustion.

Not long after, she awoke. *Have to get to the castle,* she thought, willing herself upright. Her limbs felt like dense, heavy wood, but despite her exhaustion, she was overjoyed to be home.

Up the wharf from her, a grayfarer and two soldiers approached. Her heart leapt, and she ran toward them as they hastened toward her. Nearing them, she could see that the grayfarer was Councilman Oskar, accompanied by two grayshirts—a contingent of specialized soldiers assigned to the council.

"Dear Princess, Oskar said, "thank Baruna you are well! We learned of your escape and have been awaiting your return. There are teams throughout the territory searching for you."

She fell into his arms and hugged him. "It is wonderful to see you again, old friend! she said. "I didn't know if I would ever lay eyes on Harwelden again."

"How did you do it? When Marvus and Jingo informed the council of your abduction, we feared you were lost forever. Your resourcefulness and bravery are an example for us all."

"Thank you, dear Oskar," she said, "but the credit is not mine alone. Grimaldi and a friend of Harwelden played as great a role as I in our escape."

"Yes," Oskar said. "Grimaldi arrived a short while ago. We are so happy to see him alive. If I may inquire, who is this friend of Harwelden you speak of?"

She smiled, thinking of Grinjar. "That is not important right now. I must get to the castle."

"Yes, Highness," Oskar said. "Grimaldi is anxious to see you again."

"And I him," she replied. "Help me to the castle; then assemble the council. We have much to discuss."

Oskar fidgeted. "The council is assembled," he said. "But I have news I must share with you." He motioned to the grayshirts. They approached her, flanking her on either side, and took her by the arms.

"Please be more gentle," she said. "It has been a long journey—my limbs burn like fire."

The grayshirts looked to Oskar.

"Much has transpired since you left us," he said, the smile leaving his face. "I'm afraid you may not like what you find here."

"I don't understand," she said. She turned to the gray-shirts. "And as for you two, release me from your grip. I will walk to the castle under my own power. You jostle me as if I were a prisoner!"

"Forgive me, dear Princess, for what I am about to do," Oskar said.

Confused, she looked from Oskar to the grayshirts. "Release me at once!" she shouted, trying to jerk free from their grasp.

The grayshirts appeared uncomfortable but maintained their hold on her, looking to Oskar for guidance.

He nodded. "Do with her as we have discussed."

"What is the meaning of this!" she demanded, looking to Oskar with anger and confusion.

"I am afraid you will not be seated before the council," he said, appearing saddened. "Waldemariam has instituted a state of emergency rule. You will be held in protective custody until such time as he deems it appropriate for you to be released."

"He has no such right!" she yelled. "Release me!" She struggled against the grayshirts, who only tightened their hold.

"That is not possible," Oskar said. "The will of the chancellor is that you be restrained. It is for the best. In time, you will see that."

"I will see no such thing! Now, release me at once or suffer the wrath of the nobles."

Oskar motioned to the grayshirts, then looked to the ground. One of the men took a sack from the pouch at his waist

The grayshirts appeared uncomfortable but maintained their
hold on Sarintha, looking to Oskar for guidance.

and placed it over her head, tying it loosely at the neck. The other pulled her arms behind her and bound them. Finally, a cord was wrapped around her head and pulled taut so that it forced the sack into her mouth, gagging her.

Frowning, Oskar nodded to the grayshirts and set off for Harwelden Castle. The two soldiers, maintaining their hold on the princess, followed.

Despite Sarintha's vigorous protests, they led her along the trail around the back of Mount Kalipharus.

"We plan to make you comfortable," Oskar said. "You will be released in time, but Waldemariam wants no interference in his plans to defend Harwelden from the coming attack. A perilous time approaches. For the time being, you will remain under arrest while those versed in military strategy arrange for our defense. It is for the best."

She tried to retort, but the gag made her words incomprehensible. From the absence of sun and the many bird sounds, she deduced that they had come to the southern valley. There the grayshirts stopped, and she heard a sound of metal against stone, then a creak as if an ancient door or portcullis were opening. Feeling a draft of cool air, she deduced that they were entering some hidden passageway into the mountain. Then she heard the heavy door close behind them, sealing them under the mountain.

Someone struck a flint and lit a torch, and the musty chamber filled with light, though she saw little beneath her hood. The grayshirts pulled her along between them, following the light, only to stop a hundred paces later and start up a long flight of stairs. The stairs ended, then began again, winding and turning, taking them ever upward through a convoluted series of stairways and underground trails. In time, they stopped again, and again she heard the sound of metal, as if a key were being used on an ancient lock. Again a heavy door or gate creaked open, and the air grew warm and rank.

"You may remove her hood," Oskar said. "But replace the gag—I do not want her to raise an alarm."

The grayshirts loosened the rope and lifted the sack from her head.

"You will pay for this treachery, Oskar!" she hissed. "Do not believe that you will be forgiven this transgression against me— it matters not that you are following the chancellor's orders."

Oskar motioned for the grayshirts to finish their task.

One of them wadded the hood into a ball and shoved it into Sarintha's mouth. The other, standing behind her, placed the rope around her head and cinched the gag in place.

"Follow me to the cell I have prepared," said Oskar. "I have evacuated this wing of the dungeon. No one need know she is here."

The grayshirts walked her past rows of empty cells, stopping at one. It differed from the other cells only in the cloth drapes hanging from floor to ceiling across the front bars, preventing passersby from seeing inside.

"Shackle her," Oskar said. As she struggled in vain against her jailers, he said, "I told you, Princess, that we plan to keep you comfortable. I hope you understand that at this point, your accommodations cannot be improved on—we cannot let anyone learn of your presence here."

The grayshirts raised her arms above her head and shackled them as she screamed and jerked, her muffled protests echoing throughout the chamber.

"Leave the gag in place," Oskar said as the grayshirts shackled her feet. Then he turned and left the cell, stealing one last glance at her before releasing the cloth over the bars.

As the sound of their footsteps faded, she struggled again and tried to scream, but the gag muffled her protests. In time, her struggles weakened until she hung limp against the wall, resigned to captivity once again.

Chapter 31

The Masking

After hearing the revelation of the sprites, Crosslyn raced upward through the water, toward the boat. With Elliott watching from below, he kicked hard, propelling himself above the surface and out of sight.

From beneath the surface, Elliott saw the boat above him jostle, dipping deeper in the water as Crosslyn landed in it. The old man was acting strangely, to be sure, and Elliott had to wonder what the sprites could have whispered in his ear. Following Crosslyn's lead, he kicked to the surface and launched himself out of the water, aiming to land in the boat just as Crosslyn had. For a moment, he was fully out of the water, suspended in air, until gravity took over and he splashed clumsily back in the river. He kicked again, just enough to bring his head above the surface. With the boat just before him, he inhaled a lungful of air, displacing the water from his lungs and causing a violent fit of coughing. He began to sink back in the water, but as his head fell beneath the surface, a big hand grabbed the back of his shirt and hoisted him into the boat. It was Hooks.

"You're going to have to work on your transformations," Hooks said, laughing and setting him down in the center of the boat. "They're not very . . . shamalan."

Elliott coughed again as his body readjusted to the air, while Hooks, Marvus, and Jingo had a good laugh. After a moment, Marvus looked at Elliott's clothes. "What's this?" he asked, leaning down to examine a red splotch on his shirt. He ran his finger across the smudge, smearing the strange material. "Look," he said. "These red splotches are all over you."

Elliott looked at his clothes, and indeed he was covered with the red stains. "I have no idea what it is," he said. He said nothing of his and Crosslyn's strange experience on the river floor.

Marvus stole a glance at Jingo, and Jingo nodded.

"What's going on?" Elliott asked, sensing that they knew more than they were letting on.

"Nothing," Jingo blurted. His eyes darted back toward Marvus.

In the stern, Crosslyn, still dripping wet, sat talking to Woolf in hushed tones. Deep in conversation, they had missed the merriment provided by Elliott's attempts to reenter the boat.

Elliott excused himself from the others and went to them. "Can I talk to you?" he said to Crosslyn.

Crosslyn turned and raised an eyebrow. He didn't get up. He, too, was covered in the strange red stains.

"What were those creatures at the bottom of the river? And what did they tell you about me?"

Crosslyn's face had lost all color. "Don't trouble yourself with the sprites, Elliott," he said. "You did well under the surface. Your swimming is excellent, though you will need some practice with the transformation."

"But I want to know what they told you."

Crosslyn looked to the floor of the boat, collecting his thoughts. "The sprites can tell what the fate of a shamalan will be."

"Yes," Elliott said, trying to sound casual and mask the growing dread he felt.

Crosslyn paused, as if considering what to say. "In due time, Elliott, you will learn your fate," he said. "You did well beneath the surface, and you've much to be proud of. Don't allow the sprites to taint the beauty of your first excursion under the water." Crosslyn looked to the shore. "It is my right to decide when you shall learn your fate. Now is not the time."

Elliott didn't know how to respond. "But I'm going to be okay, aren't I?"

"In the end, I think you will be all right." The old man's eyes had a faraway look.

"I don't like the sound of that."

Finally, Crosslyn looked at him. He did not smile. "For now, it is the best response I can offer."

Elliott frowned but let the subject drop. He wasn't sure he wanted to hear more. Turning his attention again to his clothes, he ran a finger through a splotch on his chest, leaving a streak in the material. The tip of his finger came away scarlet.

"What is this?" he asked.

Crosslyn continued to look melancholy and uninterested in talking to him. "It's nothing to be concerned about," he said. "The red material is the waste product of a community of very small creatures that inhabit the river. Their numbers become great from time to time, depending on conditions in the river. By the look of the amount of residue we find deposited on ourselves, I suppose they are thriving this season. It's called the red tide."

Elliott stared at him. He hadn't seen the old man act this way before.

"Now, listen to me closely," Crosslyn said, changing the subject. "Tomorrow we will pass by the port of Harwelden on our journey to Susquatania. It is imperative that we go past undetected, and for safe passage we must rely on you. You will need to use the bracelet of the nine clans to mask us as we pass. Later in the day, as we journey northward, we will cross the borders of the Forest of Ondor. At the northern edge of the forest, the trees turn to scrub, then desert. It is at this border that the serpan army prepares its assault against Harwelden. Though it will not be easy for you, you will have to mask us a second time as we pass through these territories."

He paused for a moment, looking pensive. "For these acts of magic," he said. "You will need to find an input of energy. All magic requires the channeling of energy, and the old magic is hardest to manage. You are not strong enough to do it without help, so I will assist you, but the task you face will be difficult for both of us. Now, we must practice the use of the bracelet if you are to be successful. Masking all of us will be much more difficult than turning yourself into a simitar."

"Okay," Elliott said. "I'll do whatever you tell me, but I still want to know what the sprites said about me."

"In due time. Now, let's begin practicing with the brace-let. Today you will practice without my aid. Tomorrow you will have to draw energy from me. This will preserve you so that you can mask us twice tomorrow."

Elliott looked at the bracelet. "Just tell me what to do."

"Close your eyes. "We'll try it now."

Elliott closed his eyes.

"Now, picture the boat in your mind, with all of us aboard. You will have to picture the vessel itself and each of us individually. Try to form the image with as much detail as possible."

Elliott pictured the boat, trying to recall it in detail, down to the individual reeds and lashings with which it was made. While holding the picture in his mind, he envisioned Marvus, Jingo, Hooks, Woolf, and finally Crosslyn. He called up the images in his mind with as much detail as he could recall. "Okay," he said.

"Now, bring forth in your mind an image of the river, with the boat sailing downstream, just as we are doing right now."

In his vision, the boat sailed downstream, following the currents and drifting past the trees lining the riverbanks. Again he pictured each of his companions individually. "I've got it," he said.

"Now imagine that the entire vision of the boat and its passengers has vanished into thin air," Crosslyn said.

Elliott did this, holding a vague impression of the boat in his mind while he envisioned only the river and the vegetation on the banks.

"Wonderful. You've done it. Now open your eyes."

Opening his eyes, Elliott was startled to find that he, the boat, and all the passengers were, well, not there. He looked down at his feet, and all he saw was the moving surface of the water beneath him, as if he were floating on air above the river. He held his hand in front of his face but couldn't see it. "We're invisible!" he cried.

"Almost," Crosslyn said. "Look to where my feet should be."

Elliott did as instructed. Suspended in midair over the water, in full view, was Slipher, lying supine with his hands bound behind him, just as he had been before Elliott began the exercise.

"You forgot to envision the serpan."

"I see that," Elliott said. "I almost forgot he was here."

"Well," Slipher said, "I'm still here. Now, make the boat reappear. I don't like this game."

With Slipher's words, the boat flickered. Elliott's concentration was broken, and it did not take long for the vessel and all its passengers to become fully visible again.

Crosslyn looked at Slipher with some annoyance, then at Elliott. "That will have to do," he said. "We can't risk you overdoing it before our big day tomorrow."

"I see what you mean," Elliott said, slumping to the floor of the boat. "I feel like my arms and legs are made of lead. I just want to sleep."

"Rest now," Crosslyn said. Night approaches. You will sleep well tonight. Let yourself succumb to the exhaustion brought on by your practice of the old magic, and do not stir until morning. We are counting on you to be fresh."

"That sounds good." Elliott yawned. "I feel so tired . . ." He stretched out on the floor of the boat and closed his eyes.

Hours later, with the moon bright in the sky, he stirred. Something had woken him from his deep sleep. Sitting up, he looked around to find everyone asleep except for Marvus, at the tiller, and Slipher, who lay on his back, staring at the sky.

As if sensing Elliott's wakefulness, Slipher turned and looked at him. "Greetings, shamalan," he said.

Elliott stared back at him, afraid to respond.

"It is quite late," said Slipher. "I believe your instructions are to be asleep."

"Don't worry about my instructions," Elliott snapped. He looked up to see Marvus watching with interest from the stern.

"Well, then, since you are awake, perhaps you could get me something to eat. I haven't had anything since last night."

Elliott considered the request. He looked back to the tiller again, and Marvus returned his gaze with a look of concern, though he said nothing. Elliott got up, went to Crosslyn's knapsack, and took out two strips of dried meat. Creeping over to Slipher, he sat cross-legged on the floor next to him and dangled a bit of meat over his mouth. "Go on," he said. "Eat it." He looked over his shoulder. Marvus, still watching, did not intervene.

"I don't need your pity," Slipher said. "I can go without food for as long as I must." He stared at the meat.

"Just eat it," Elliott said. "And don't call me 'shamalan.' My name is Elliott."

"All right, Elliott," he sneered. "If you insist." He chomped at the meat, pulling it from Elliott's hand with his teeth.

Elliott gave him the other piece, which he also devoured.

"That's all, Elliott whispered. If I give you any more, Crosslyn will notice it's gone."

"I don't need any more," Slipher said, stealing a glance at

the knapsack. "I am a highly trained warrior. I can go without food for a long time without feeling it."

"I see that," Elliott said.

"You mock me at your peril."

"All right, I get it. You don't need my help. Can I ask you something?"

"Ask whatever you wish, but I do not promise an answer."

"What are they going to do with you when we get to Harwelden?"

"You assume that I will remain in captivity that long," Slipher said. "I will not. But what concern of yours is it?"

"Just curious, that's all."

Slipher stared at him. "If the warlock and his ilk were to succeed in getting me to Harwelden," he said, "then I suppose I would be executed." His voice trailed off. "But that will not happen."

Elliott looked to the bindings that held Slipher's hands and feet. They looked distressingly tight. "I'm not trying to mock you, but it doesn't look like you have much chance of escaping."

"My countrymen will come to my aid," he said. "Just wait and see. I am an emissary of Malus Lothar; they will come looking for me."

"If you say so."

"I say so."

"But if Crosslyn and Woolf did successfully get you to Harwelden, would you really be killed?"

"Without a doubt," Slipher said, rolling over and staring at the moon. "But even if that were to happen, I would travel to a glorious afterlife and stand beside my fathers. In death, I will become a god."

"Is that so," Elliott chuckled.

"It is so. I will stand with my ancestors in the afterlife. I will rejoin my father and brothers. I will be reunited with my mother. We will rejoice together and continue our struggle from our new home in Antilia."

"So your family really is dead?" Elliott thought of his mother.

Slipher winced. He seemed to have weakened visibly in the short time aboard the boat.

"Look," Elliott said, "I don't mean to upset you. If you want, I can leave you alone and you can go back to sleep." He started to scoot away.

"No," Slipher replied. "It's all right. You don't have to leave." Elliott stayed seated.

"My family is dead," Slipher said. "My father and brothers were killed in the battles for Scopulus and Prytania. After their deaths, my mother and youngest brother were banished from their home in Vengala. They died soon after, unable to withstand the winter without shelter."

"That's horrible!" said Elliott. "Why were they banished?"

Slipher looked away. "One of my brothers conducted himself shamefully during the conquest of Scopulus. My mother and brother were banished because of his actions. It was a terrible burden for him to bear, I'm sure."

"I'm sure it was," Elliott said. "I'm sorry about your family."

"Do not pity me, shamalan."

"Because you are an emissary of Malus Lothar," Elliott finished.

Slipher blushed.

"I'm going back to bed now," Elliott said.

"Wait," Slipher said. "May I ask for one more small favor?"

"You can ask," Elliott said, mimicking the serpan's voice, "but I do not promise to comply."

Perhaps unintentionally, Slipher smiled at the teasing. "There is a pipe in my pocket," he said. "It calms me to smoke from it. I would like it very much if you could fill it with tobacco and strike it up with the flint in my tinderbox. Just a few puffs are all I ask."

Elliott considered the proposition. "I guess it can't hurt," he said, looking to Marvus, who sat in silence at the tiller. Elliott felt along Slipher's shirt pocket until he located the pipe and tobacco. After packing the pipe, he went to his knapsack and got out the lighter he had taken from his grandfather's kitchen. He placed the pipe to his lips and lit it, and the tobacco flared. He coughed and put the pipe to Slipher's lips.

Slipher inhaled, and his body relaxed visibly. He exhaled and turned to Elliott, making an O with his mouth, indicating that he wanted another puff.

Elliott held the pipe to his lips again.

He held the smoke in his lungs for a second and exhaled. "One more," he said in a voice grown suddenly mellow.

"One more," Elliott said. "Then I have to get back to bed." He held the pipe up, and again Slipher inhaled and held it.

Elliott stood and tapped out the contents of the pipe over the side of the boat. He was careful not to wake anyone. Returning the pipe to Slipher's shirt pocket, he said, "I'm going now."

Still holding his breath, Slipher nodded.

After lying down, Elliott rolled and peeked back at Slipher from under the blanket. To his astonishment, when Slipher exhaled, the smoke hovered above his head for a moment before forming a picture of a donkey grazing in the moonlight. As if it knew someone was watching, the beast looked upward. The smoke disintegrated.

Elliott could have sworn he heard Slipher chuckle. He watched for a moment longer, wondering by what magic the serpan had shaped the smoke into a picture of a donkey, though he knew he was less amazed than he would have been just a few days ago. He supposed he was getting used to magic. After lying on the floor of the boat for a moment, Elliott stood and walked to the stern, where Marvus glared at him disapprovingly. "Not a word of this to anyone, Marvus. Do me this one favor."

⚓ ⚓ ⚓

Early the next morning, Crosslyn, now at the tiller, gazed out at the deep woods on either side of the boat and at the Azure Mountains in the distance. Except for Woolf, everyone was still asleep.

Woolf came astern and said, "We are nearing Harwelden."

Crosslyn nodded, still looking into the distance.

"Are you certain this plan of yours is wise?" Woolf asked. "I cannot help but feel that we should go directly to Harwelden. I'm not sure what you have in mind, but if you expect to engage the susquats and rally them to our cause, it is a fool's errand."

A faint smile lit the corners of Crosslyn's mouth. "Your suspicion of my motivation is correct," he said. "I will try to persuade the chieftain of the susquats to rally his clans to our defense. This is our one and only hope against Malus Lothar's forces. If things at Harwelden are as dire as you describe, then we need a large and powerful army. The only such army on the Carafayan continent is that of the susquats."

"They will not join us, old man, but I will follow you."

Crosslyn stared wistfully at the mountains, as if he hadn't heard Woolf. "We must persuade them that *now* is the time to join us, for it is only a matter of time before they, too, become targets of aggression. Lothar's goal is to exterminate the entire Carafayan continent and claim it for the serpans. This was the will of Valderon in the olden times, and it is the will of Malus Lothar in these times."

Woolf shook his head. "The idea of recruiting the susquats comes up season after season. I don't know specifically what type of dialogue Waldemariam has held with them, but he is in contact with their chieftan. Waldemariam spoke with Chieftan Keats when we were hunting for your friend over there." He motioned to Hooks, who was just rising in the bow of the boat. "They have been painstaking in their efforts to remain neutral as the war has progressed. I am certain they have had contact with Malus Lothar as well as with us. You will never persuade them to join us."

Crosslyn remained silent.

"Besides," Woolf said, "where in the scrolls does it say that Harwelden will be delivered by the beasts of the forest? If I am to believe we are living in the days foretold by the scrolls, how can I justify that with a plea to the susquats? The scrolls speak extensively about the final days of the war. They fortell the rise of a powerful servant of Valderon, and the appearance of a Gayan. The forest beasts are never mentioned. You are a *priest*, Crosslyn. Of all learned beings, what causes you to believe the empire might be saved by a band of susquats? If the scrolls are correct, it is the *boy*, not the susquats, who will turn the tide of the war. We are wasting valuable time. The Festival of Opik draws near."

Crosslyn placed his hands on the top rail and stared out at the crags, wreathed in mist. "Your knowledge of the ancient scrolls is thorough," he said. "And, indeed, I am a priest of the Shama." He turned to face him. "But I am also a pragmatist. The elders will help us, but we must also be savvy. The xcercio instructs that we must use wisdom when confronting a problem. Wisdom tells me that a fractured army, a corrupt council, and a shamalan child are a poor defense against the greatest assault force ever assembled on the Carafayan continent. Wisdom says we are doomed if we do not open our minds to a strategy for success. The susquats are our only hope. If they will not join us, Harwelden will be forever lost. The scrolls may predict a shamalan victory, but shamalans *wrote* those scrolls.

The serpans worship their own gods, and the texts of Malgothar and Valderon undoubtedly predict a different outcome entirely. I trust in the scrolls, Woolf. The foreknowledge of their authors is manifest all around us." He looked to Elliott, who had woken and was near the bow, talking with Hooks and the gimlets. "But I also believe we must make our own best effort to defeat our enemies. Right or wrong, I am taking this boat to Susquatania."

Woolf stared long at him. "I will follow your lead, warlock. But my misgivings remain. The susquats will not join us—especially if we approach them with *him* in our midst." He motioned to Hooks. "Do you have any idea of the betrayal he brought to them? You may contest his role in kidnapping the grayfarer fledglings, but his actions against his own clan are a matter of record. There is no honor in him. He will bring shame to your mission."

"I disagree with your assessment of Hooks," said Crosslyn. "But I am pleased that you will continue with us to Susquatania." He looked downstream. "Harwelden approaches. We must ready the boy for his task."

Elliott was watching Hooks and the gimlets use the slingshot on fruit hanging from trees along the riverbanks. Hooks raised the weapon and fired, knocking a piece of fruit from a distant tree.

"If I had one of these," he mused, "I would never go hungry again."

Marvus, Jingo, and Elliott laughed, then fell silent on seeing Crosslyn's serious expression.

Crosslyn nodded to them. "The port of Harwelden approaches. I must speak to Elliott in private."

"Of course," said Marvus, sidling past him toward the stern.

The others followed. As Hooks walked past, the old man reached out and touched his arm. "You and I must speak later," he said.

Hooks nodded, then followed the gimlets.

"Are you ready?" Crosslyn said when he and Elliott were alone. "Today we begin to depend on you in ways we haven't had to before."

Elliott nodded. Looking at the bracelet on his wrist, he said, "I think I'm ready."

"It is important for you to maintain concentration at all times. You saw what happened when the serpan distracted you yesterday. If your concentration is broken, we will become visible for all to see, and our whole journey will be in jeopardy. You must prepare yourself to blot out all other thoughts while you mask our presence. You will have to be fully immersed to do it."

"I'm going to do my best," Elliott said.

Crosslyn nodded. "Eat something, he said, "and spend the morning alone. Focus on the task ahead, and prepare yourself mentally for it."

"How?" Elliott asked.

"Picture in your mind what is going to happen. Focus on the details of the boat so that the image will be familiar to you. This will make it easy to hold the picture in your mind. Do the same with the images of each of us, and don't forget the serpan this time. Practicing the old magic—or any kind of magic—is largely a mental task. Do as I have said, and your mind will be prepared."

"I won't let you down," the boy replied.

"Good." Crosslyn patted him on the back and walked away. *Focus. Learn to strengthen your mind.*

I will, Elliott responded. He passed the morning forming mental images of the boat and his fellow travelers, repeating the task over and over until he could stand it no longer. After what seemed like several hours of practice, Marvus approached, breaking his concentration. The suns were at their zenith, signaling midday.

"It is almost time," Marvus said. "Look ahead and to the west."

The castle Harwelden loomed in the distance, looking just as Elliott remembered. In the sky above the castle, grayfarers flew in lazy circles, keeping watch over the grounds below. They looked like specks in the distance. "How will I know when to mask us?" he asked.

"Crosslyn will tell you," Marvus said. "Just relax. He will help you. We all know you will not fail us." He smiled.

"Thanks," Elliott said. "I haven't said it that much, but I don't know what I would do without you guys. When the wolves attacked and you got so sick . . ."

"It's all right," Marvus said, cutting him off. "Everything happens for a reason. It was fate that brought you here, and I am honored to travel with you on this journey. I am the lucky one."

"I won't let you down."

"I know you won't." Marvus left, and Crosslyn approached. "Are you ready?" he asked.

Elliott thought the old man looked nervous. "I think so."

"I will let you know when to begin. Our timing has to be flawless. I will sit with you while we approach. I have put the serpan to sleep so he cannot interfere. Be prepared to begin at my command."

Elliott closed his eyes, again calling up images of the boat and its passengers. His heart began to beat faster.

With Woolf at the tiller, the boat drifted northward in silence as Harwelden loomed in the middle distance. Elliott sat with eyes closed while Crosslyn kept a keen watch on the grayfarers circling the castle. He waited until the last possible moment, hoping to preserve Elliott's strength, when one of the grayfarers swung toward them overhead. Crosslyn was sure they'd been spotted.

With Woolf at the tiller . . . Elliott sat with eyes
closed while Crosslyn kept a keen watch on
the grayfarers circling the castle.

"Mask us," he whispered. "Do it now!"

Instantly, they disappeared from sight.

Good, thought Crosslyn. *Now, hold it.*

To their left, a grayfarer emerged from behind a copse of trees, flying low to the ground. His crossbow was drawn, and his eyes scanned up and down the river. Undoubtedly, he had seen them. Rising just above the treetops and looking to his left, he motioned at someone to join him.

Two more grayfarers joined him in the air just over the boat, flying so low, Crosslyn could have stood up and touched them.

"I saw a boat," said one of the grayfarers. "It was right here; I'm sure of it."

"That's impossible, Falkar," said another. "Our line of sight extends almost to the Phaestian pass. There's nothing here."

"But I'm sure I saw a boat," Falkar said. "Spread out. There's something amiss here."

On their leader's command, the grayfarers fanned out over the river while Falkar hovered just over the boat, sniffing at the air. "I know there's something here," he said quietly, scanning the waters beneath him.

Crosslyn and the others held their breath as the grayfarer hovered just above them, scanning the river and sniffing. Over and over, he turned his attention to their location. Though they remained successfully masked, the grayfarer appeared hesitant to leave the spot. After what seemed an eternity, he gazed in their direction a final time and headed southward down the river.

Suddenly, out of the blue, Elliott sneezed. For a split second, the boat and its passengers fully materialized. Elliott cursed himself and concentrated as hard as he could, masking them once more.

Hearing the sneeze, Falkar turned toward them. "Who goes there?" he demanded, brandishing his crossbow. He flew close again, stopping to hover just above them once more. "I know someone is here." In the distance, his two grayfarer companions looked his way. He beckoned them with his arm.

To everyone's surprise, Woolf spoke. "Go away, Falkar," he whispered. "For the sake of Harwelden, leave us in peace."

A look of shock dawned on Falkar's face. "Is that you, Woolf?" he asked, scanning up and down the river, trying to locate the source of the voice. "What treachery is this? Where are you?"

"For all you hold dear, Falkar, leave us," said Woolf. "Do not inform the others of our presence. Trust me, old friend. Let us pass here in peace."

Hovering above them, Falkar looked flummoxed. His two companions flew to his side. "What's going on?" asked one of them, scanning the riverbanks. "What's gotten into you?"

"Yes," said the other. "You look as if you'd seen a phantom."

While Falkar remained speechless, one of the other grayfarers sniffed at the air, seeming to sense something. "Is that a susquat I smell?" he asked. Still sniffing at the air, he looked in the direction of the boat. "The smell is very strong right here," he said, pointing at where Hooks sat masked on the floor of the boat.

Bewildered, Falkar flew higher in the sky, holding his gaze in the direction of the boat. "I was mistaken," he said. "There's nothing here. We should return to the castle."

"But wait," said the grayfarer above Hooks. "I smell susquat right here, in the middle of the river." He, too, looked perplexed. "I'm certain of it." He poked with his crossbow at the air above Hooks's head. "The scent is as strong as if one of the beasts were right here."

Hooks ducked the crossbow, making the boat list to the side and nearly breaking Elliott's concentration.

"There's nothing here," Falkar said. "Now, return to the castle. That's an order."

The grayfarer sighed and flew higher to join his comrades overhead. "You're acting strange, Falkar," he said. "I don't know what's gotten into you."

Ignoring him, Falkar flew toward the castle, and the other two grayfarers followed. As they flew northward, Falkar stole a final glance in the direction of the boat, then flapped his wings in earnest, picking up speed.

Elliott, still holding the impression of the vanished boat in his mind, sighed heavily as the grayfarers departed.

Don't let your guard down, son. We've a ways to go yet, thought Crosslyn. *Draw the energy you need from me.*

Elliott kept focused on the masking, all the while drawing energy from Crosslyn. *I can hold it,* he replied. The communication passed easily. The boat remained masked.

You're getting stronger, thought Crosslyn, *but don't overdo it. You have much work left to do, and my energy is a limited resource.*

Following Crosslyn's admonition, Elliott remained silent. They drifted northward.

Mount Kalipharus materialized to their left, rising at a steep, almost sheer angle from their vantage point on the river. Near its top, the majestic castle Harwelden loomed above the splendid stone enclosure that encircled the mountaintop. Just above them, the eastern tower was abuzz with grayfarers, flying in and out of the tower windows, their armor gleaming in the sunlight, making it difficult to look directly at them. Others wore cloth frocks and carried satchels on their backs. Though the boat passed directly beneath the eastern tower, the grayfarers appeared as gnats in the sky. From within the stone enclosure far above, music blared as if the festivities were already under way. Given the circumstances, it seemed strange to Elliott. The juxtaposition of revelry within the walls, and the grayfarers patrolling the grounds around the mountain was difficult to make sense of.

The boat drifted past, silent and unseen.

Warriors and grayfarers canvassed the many trails hewn into the mountainside, as well as the riverbanks and the valleys surrounding the base of the mountain. The area was on full alert. As the boat crossed the eastern base of Mount Kalipharus, the port of Harwelden materialized. Magnificently hewn wooden piers rose up from the riverbed, supporting rows of docks, between which dozens of small ships stood moored. Crews worked at polishing the hulls of the ships while sailors mopped and scrubbed their decks.

All the while, the little boat drifted past, so close to the docks that anyone could have reached out with a barge pole and touched it. And the distant sounds of revelry continued to drift down from above.

Sitting next to Elliott, Crosslyn frowned. He cocked his head to the side, listening for something. As his concentration gained focus, his frown deepened.

He sensed Princess Sarintha. From somewhere close by, Sarintha was fanning out with her mind, attempting to make contact with anyone who might listen. Her feeling was one of distress.

For fear that Elliott might lose focus on his task, Crosslyn closed off his thoughts. He did not want to risk communicating with the princess and disrupting Elliott's concentration. Her calls for help vexed him, and he hoped Elliott did not pick up a sense of her.

In time, the boat drifted past the strange scene of Harwelden, and the castle and its inhabitants receded into the background. When it seemed safe, Crosslyn communicated to Elliott that the boat could become visible again.

At once, the little craft and its passengers materialized. In the same instant, Elliott slumped to the floor of the boat. He was soaking wet with sweat, and the blood was drained from his face. He crawled to the edge of the boat and retched into the water.

Crosslyn frowned. He, too, felt the strain of the magic, and they had much left to do. Ignoring Elliott for the moment, he turned and looked back at Harwelden, trying to make sense of the fact that the princess was apparently being held prisoner within her own castle.

The others, sensing something grave in Crosslyn's expression and watching Elliott retch overboard, lost the victorious feeling over their safe passage past Harwelden.

Finally, Hooks broke the uncomfortable silence. "What's the matter, Crosslyn?" he asked. "Everything worked fine. They didn't see us."

"And you did wonderfully, Elliott," Marvus said. "I knew you wouldn't let us down."

"Thanks," Elliott replied, looking gray and slumping against the side of the boat. He wiped at his mouth. "I did it," he said, looking to Crosslyn. Before Crosslyn could respond, he turned and vomited over the side of the boat again.

Crosslyn patted the boy on the back and eased him back into the boat. "Yes, son, you did wonderfully," he said. "Now, I want you to lie down and rest. You will have to mask us again in a very short while. You have been substantially weakened by this last endeavor, and you'll need energy to do it again. But don't worry, I'll be with you."

Elliott smiled. "I can do it," he said quietly. And he slumped to his side and slept.

Crosslyn's expression became grave once more, and he motioned for Woolf to sit beside him. After asking Hooks and the gimlets to excuse them, he said to Woolf, "The daughter of Gregorus is held prisoner at Harwelden. What madness is this?"

Woolf looked stunned. "I haven't any idea," he said. "I've been away from the castle for much of the past season, searching for Elliott. My last word on Princess Sarintha was that she escaped from her cell at Mount Sitticus, along with General Grimaldi."

"Well, she obviously made it home," Crosslyn said. "But who would imprison a shamalan princess in her own dungeon? I cannot conceive of such a thing." He stared into the distance. "When we met, you said the chancellor is someone named Waldemariam. You also referred to the other councilmen: Baucus, Landrew, Alasdar, Fanta, and Oskar. I know of Oskar and Alasdar; both come from old families. I do not know the others. And I have never heard of a name such as Waldemariam. Tell me again about the dynamics of the council. And tell me about Waldemariam."

Woolf nodded. "Waldemariam ascended to the council under the reign of King Fahroy, who succeeded Julien."

"Yes," Crosslyn said. "Julien's accession was expected after the fall of Dagnar."

"Julien was murdered by a darfoyle viscount not long after his accession. His son, Fahroy, took the throne but had a relatively short reign as well—he, too, was murdered by a darfoyle. Back then we could not foresee how quickly everyone would fall."

"This is the first time I've heard the story firsthand," Crosslyn said.

"Waldemariam was not born of Harwelden," Woolf continued. "He is from the unknown lands across the eastern sea. He arrived at Harwelden near the beginning of Fahroy's reign. He was quite odd to us at first, for his customs were different from our own. But he was loyal and fierce. Waldemariam said he had heard of the betrayal from the other side of the world, and he wanted to fight. He entered the training and performed so magnificently, his strength and prowess soon became legend. He grew close to Grimaldi, who commanded the training camps in those days."

"Yes," Crosslyn said, "I remember Grimaldi well. I knew him when he was a fledgling."

"Anyway," Woolf continued, "Waldemariam proved himself without equal on the battlefield. His instincts were uncanny, and he fought with the strength of ten ordinary grayfarers. When the war began to go badly, the people of Harwelden used to joke that we should go across the sea and find more of Waldemariam's clan. With a few more like him, they said, we could turn the war in short order."

"He sounds impressive as a warrior," Crosslyn said.

"Indeed. His fame quickly eclipsed that of all other grayfarers, including Grimaldi. In only a few seasons, he rose from the training camps to the ranks of the council. King Fahroy appointed him. So impressive were his skills, no one questioned such a fast appointment. It seemed a natural thing to place him on the council.

"As a councilman, he continued to excel. During the battle of Laborteaux, Chancellor Vistar was slain, and King Fahroy was nearly taken. Waldemariam singlehandedly rescued the king by fighting off two darfoyles at once. When Waldemariam returned Fahroy to Harwelden, Fahroy summarily appointed him the new chancellor of the Grayfarer Council, and he has sat at its helm ever since. Most of the other councilmen were already seated at the time Waldemariam joined. Baucus, Landrew, Alasdar, and I were all looked over for the leadership position. Waldemariam appointed Oskar and Fanta to the council later. Those two are eternally loyal to him. They will go along with anything he says." Woolf paused and looked into Crosslyn's eyes. "And I mean *anything*," he said. "Baucus and Landrew are older and a little more contemplative. But they are by no means against Waldemariam. Alasdar and I are wary of the chancellor. Speaking only for myself, he makes me uneasy."

"Why is that?" Crosslyn asked.

"The real problems began after the death of King Gregorus, who ascended to the throne after Fahroy's death. Princess Sarintha is young and unsure of herself. Waldemariam, perhaps because he is not born of Harwelden, has mostly been unwilling to acquiesce to her wishes. Behind closed doors, he argues that she is naive and unfit to lead. He has never supported her, never granted her the reins of power that are her birthright. Were it not for Grimaldi's standing up for her, she would have no voice at all."

"So it is in this fashion that this peculiar dynamic has taken foot," Crosslyn said. "That a grayfarer sits in command of the throne while a shamalan noble languishes in the dungeon. I can scarcely conceive of it." His voice was filled with contempt. "It is no mystery that Harwelden is set to fall when such a bizarre scenario unfolds within its walls. Rest assured, Woolf, this situation will be remedied upon my return. I am hardly a noble, but neither am I to be trifled with by the likes of an arrogant councilman."

Woolf bowed his head in deference. "I am with you," he said. "We must right things at Harwelden. And if Princess Sarintha sits in the dungeon as you say, then an unforgivable treason has been committed."

"The problem," Crosslyn said, "is that on the eve of an attack by our enemies, our own house is in disarray. It will not be a simple task to deal with Waldemariam, especially if he is as powerful as you say, while also planning to defend what is indefensible." Crosslyn shook his head in disbelief.

"There is one more thing," Woolf said.

"Yes, I know. You mentioned that someone at Harwelden is in league with the enemy. There is a conspirator within the castle walls."

"And I believe it is a member of the Grayfarer Council," Woolf said. "It has to be Waldemariam."

Crosslyn nodded. "Then it would all make sense," he said. He turned to gaze upon Elliott, who lay sleeping at his feet. "It is hard for even me to believe, but the scrolls tell us that our hope lies with him. This poor lad who knows nothing of this war and who has to try so hard to accomplish even small things. It is hard to imagine how he might deliver us from all this, isn't it?"

"Indeed," Woolf said. "If I may ask, what did the river sprites tell you of the boy's fate?"

Crosslyn frowned and shook his head. He leaned forward and whispered into Woolf's ear.

Chapter 32

Let the Music Play

From a podium overlooking Harwelden's central square, Waldemariam looked out into the sea of cheering faces. Music filled the square, adding to the noise of the revelers, as the court band played "The Majesty of Home," the castle's unofficial anthem since the days of King Griogair. It was always a crowd-pleaser. Wearing his finest dress armor, Waldemariam grasped the podium and extended his wings behind him, preening for the crowd and presenting a formidable presence to the multitude of admirers filling the square. Behind him in a formal row sat the full council except for Woolf and Fanta. At either end of the row, empty chairs filled with floral bouquets represented the two absent councilmen. Councilman Alasdar sat next to the empty chair of his missing friend Woolf, ready to hear Waldemariam's speech. All around the dais, the seven flags of Harwelden flapped majestically in the cool evening breeze. Waldemariam lifted his head and addressed the crowd. His voice boomed across the square, signaling the band to fade out as a hush fell over the crowd.

"Greetings to all on this glorious night," he said, raising his hands to the sky. "And welcome to the beginning of one of the most historic festivals in recent memory." An easy grin spread across his face.

The crowd roared its approval.

"It is an honor to stand before you on such a night," he continued. "And it is with great joy that I announce the commencement of this year's events. At the rising of the next full moon, the Festival of Opik will be upon us."

The crowd bellowed its approval.

"And despite recent setbacks, I want to assure you that this year's festival will be one to stand out in the memory of Harweldenites for generations to come. We are well positioned for what the fates may bring, and we won't let a few angry serpans disrupt this year's ritual."

At the mention of the serpan threat, the raucous cheers of the crowd grew in fervor.

"As is customary," Waldemariam said, quieting the crowd, "we will begin tonight with an update on the state of the empire. The empire is in sound health, and the brotherhood and leadership of the Grayfarer Council is stronger than ever."

The crowd cheered again, though less fervently, for many were anxious to hear the comments Waldemariam had prepared. An uneasy hush fell over the square.

"First," Waldemariam said, "an update on Princess Sarintha."

The crowd grew deathly silent. Word of the princess had been scarce for many days, and rumors even circulated that she had been killed.

"Our beautiful princess is alive and well and travels to Harwelden to join us in this year's festival. Even as we speak, her chambermaids are preparing her quarters for her return."

Gasps of relief erupted from the throng, gradually coalescing into chants of rejoicing.

"And our beloved General Grimaldi, my closest of personal friends, travels with her," the chancellor added. "We are expecting the two of them to arrive any day now. We have posted warriors throughout the lands surrounding the castle to escort them back to the castle once they reach the safety of our sacred lands."

At the mention of the serpan threat, the raucous
cheers of the crowd grew in fervor.

The crowd cheered.

"Many of you know," Waldemariam said, lowering his voice, "that the enemy gathers at the edge of Ondor."

The crowd grew quiet again, hanging on his every word.

"I offer you my personal assurance that we are prepared to repel the enemy should he grow bold enough to attack. Our armies have painstakingly prepared for every scenario. If the enemy chooses to engage us, we will make him rue the day he dared make so bold." He paused and surveyed the crowd. "We are the empire of the sages," he said, pounding the podium with his fist. "We are the empire of Griogair, and we have much fight in us. So let them come and experience the hammer of Harwelden. We will send them back to their rock once and forever!"

The crowd cheered, and chants of "Wal-de-mariam! Wal-de-mariam!" began in the back of the square.

Speaking over the exuberant crowd, he continued. "And we have received word from Councilmen Fanta and Woolf. As many of you know, they were dispatched at the end of last season to arrest the fugitive susquat who stands convicted of kidnapping our grayfarer fledglings. The fugitive has proved cunning, but the council is here to assure you that the beast will be brought back within our walls before the beginning of the festival. He shall not escape justice!"

Again the crowd cheered.

"But what of the princess's stewards, Marvus and Jingo?" a voice near the front of the crowd called out.

"Yes," Waldemariam said. "What of Marvus and Jingo?" He lowered his head for a moment, as if preparing his thoughts. Raising his head again, he continued. "Marvus and Jingo have been engaged in a clandestine operation, conceived by me personally, to assist in the capture of the susquat and bring him to justice. Many of you have heard that the stewards played a role in freeing the beast, but this is not the case." He scanned the crowd to gauge its response.

The crowd remained quiet.

"Marvus and Jingo show loyalty to the empire in their willingness to engage in this dangerous task against the susquat, who is a treacherous agent of the malus. We mustn't let the beast's crimes go unpunished. We will establish for all that a crime against our grayfarer fledglings is a crime that we will not let stand. In these days, our meting out of punishment must be firm." He paused and looked out over the crowd. "But there is more afoot than just the capture of the susquat. In accordance with the prophecies laid out in the ancient Scrolls of Ondor, a shamalan boy has presented himself to the council. I have sent the boy to the testing chamber myself, and he has proved himself outright. It is my belief that the boy is Gayan, as was foreseen in the scrolls, and that the prophecies of the elders are unfolding all around us."

Again the crowd gasped. "I knew it!" yelled someone in the back.

"And our beloved stewards Marvus and Jingo are with the boy as we speak. With his guidance, the susquat will be brought back to us, and we will win a victory against the treacherous tactics of Malus Lothar. This victory will prove to be a turning point. With the Gayan on one flank and myself on the other, Princess Sarintha will lead us to the sweetest of victories against our ancient foe. I can tell you tonight that the turning point of the war draws near and that the serpan army, with its diseased and shameful emperor, will fall if it chooses to engage us. The war will turn, just as foreseen in the prophecies."

A wave of triumphant cheers erupted from the crowd.

"So let us drink and be joyful tonight. To each of you here, let your heart be light. From this night forward, we shall commence with the merriments leading up to the festival. We are and shall continue to be the mighty empire of Griogair. May the fates be with all of us."

The crowd cheered as Waldemariam motioned for the band to begin again. In the central square, the revelers began dancing and tossing back cups of mead, turning their collective attention to celebrating the commencement of the upcoming Festival of Opik.

On the dais, Councilman Alasdar noticed that a frown had replaced the sunny smile on Waldemariam's face. He watched as the chancellor turned and left the stage, nodding to the other members of the council, who then stood and followed him off the stage.

A short time later, with the noise of the celebrating crowd filtering into the great hall, the councilmen filed into the torchlit chamber. At the head of the table, Waldemariam unstrapped his dress armor and laid it on the floor beside him. He wore a cotton frock beneath it and appeared relieved to be free of the armor. The rest of the Council, except for Oskar, did the same. When everyone was more comfortable, they sat around the table, preparing for the meeting that Waldemariam had arranged in advance of the night's speech.

Waldemariam laid his head in his hands and stared at the table while the rest of the council sat patiently, waiting for him to speak. Finally, he looked up.

"I do not relish the position of chancellor," he said. "I know what you are all thinking. But what was I to tell them?"

The councilmen remained quiet, staring at their leader.

"Should I have told them to savor their final days with their loved ones?" he asked. "And that we haven't a strategy to repel the forces assembled against us? Or that they may all soon die horrible deaths at the hands of their most feared enemies?"

"Listen to them out there," Baucus said. "They have no idea what lies ahead."

Waldemariam frowned. "It is for the best."

"Are we giving up, then?" Alasdar asked. "Perhaps we should march to the edge of the forest and bare our necks to the malus. Is that, in essence, what you propose, Waldemariam? I, for one, believe in the prophecies. They do not tell us that we will be overcome. Rather, they say we will be victorious in any assault against Harwelden. Why must we assume such a defeatist posture?"

Seeing that he had the attention of all and hearing no objection, Alasdar continued. "Just days ago, I received word that you entertained the idea of usurping the throne upon the princess's return. So confident were you in your military strategies that you did not want her interfering with your plans. Though this approach is one that the council would never let stand, I must confess my confusion in your latest epiphany. Why have you now decided that the battle is lost before it is fought? Your tenure as chancellor has not been characterized by the lies, treachery, and indecision apparent in your actions of late. What in the name of Antilia is going on?"

Music blared through the windows, louder now, as the merriment outside grew.

Waldemariam fingered the gold amulet around his neck. "I received word today that a fleet of Haviru ships has docked on the river Tantasar, near the base camp of the serpans."

Alasdar sat stunned, and several of the councilmen groaned.

"I would never have believed it so," Landrew said, lowering his head. "I shall witness firsthand the fall of Harwelden and, with it, the fall of the Shamalan Empire." He scanned the faces of his colleagues. Dejection surrounded him.

"What will we do?" Baucus asked.

Waldemariam sighed. "We will be defeated. It is true that I considered subduing the princess upon her return. Perhaps that was a wise plan, and perhaps not." He paused and looked at Oskar. "In any event, none of that matters anymore. When and if the princess returns, I will gladly pass the mantle of leadership. If the boy from the forest materializes, I will hand him my sword. None of it matters anymore. I desire to lead us with wisdom. I have desired to lead us to victory. As things are now, I can only conclude that we are already defeated. I have studied the tactics of warfare all my days, and I have considered our plight from every conceivable angle. Again and again, one certainty arises in my mind."

"And what is that?" Alasdar asked.

"The certainty that we all shall die when the serpans lay siege to the castle," he said, placing his head in his hands. "The taking of Harwelden is but an aftershock of a war already lost."

"So you have no faith in the prophecies," Alasdar said, "and you take no comfort whatever in the appearance of the boy from Gaya, though he has appeared on the eve of the greatest battle of the whole war, just as foreseen by our elders generations ago."

Waldemariam stared at the table. "That is correct, Alasdar. I haven't any faith. The boy's presence changes nothing. And while we are on the topic, it is my belief that the princess and General Grimaldi will not be returning to the castle. The same messenger that brought news of the Haviru also delivered reports about the princess and the general. They have been recaptured."

The councilmen groaned almost as one.

"I must confess, this news does not truly surprise me," Oskar said. "The princess behaves rashly, and the loyalty shown her by the general degrades his efficacy as a warrior. If they truly escaped in the first place, it was a matter of time before their recapture."

"So that is why you gave the speech you did tonight, Waldemariam?" Baucus asked. "You believe our situation is hopeless, and you want our people to be joyful in their final days?"

"That is correct," the chancellor replied. "I am open to each of your thoughts on the matter, but not tonight." He stood up. "I go to my bedchamber. We may reconvene at the request of any member of this council, at any future date. But tonight we adjourn. I apologize to each of you for the state we find ourselves in. If my leadership were more capable, perhaps our situation would be different. Please know that I have endeavored only to succeed and to be faithful to the memories of our lost nobles." He bowed his head and turned to leave.

"One last thing before you go," Alasdar said. "What word have you received from Fanta and Woolf?"

"There has been no word from either," Waldemariam said quietly. "That, too, was a lie." He turned and left the great hall.

The council sat and watched his exit in silence while the sounds of the evening's celebrations filled the room. After a long pause, Alasdar surveyed his fellow councilmen, each of whom appeared disconsolate. "What do you make of the chancellor's behavior?" he said to no one in particular. "It is unlike him to concede defeat so easily. Am I the only one to find his behavior strange?"

"I agree," Baucus said. "It is unlike him to declare our situation hopeless, though I cannot say I entirely disagree."

"Nor can I," Landrew said. "I would be the first on this council to advocate a strategy for victory, but I know none to suggest. Honestly, Alasdar, do his words not ring true? We haven't the strength to repel even the serpans. If a whole fleet of Haviru has joined them, what would you have us do?"

"I would have us fight," Alasdar said, "just as anyone loyal to this council should." He glared at them. "In the morning, I will speak to Waldemariam. I do not approve of this plan to *do nothing* while we await our slaughter. I will not go willingly to my grave, and I expect better from each of you. A whole city—a whole *empire*—depends on our leadership. I confess that I do not understand what infests the heart of the mighty Waldemariam, but I do not accept his lies and acquiescence. He is failing us. Somewhere out there walks a shamalan, a Gayan, who has appeared on the eve of the greatest battle of the war. The prophecies have foreseen this, just as they have foreseen our victory in the coming assault on Harwelden. Like each of you, I do not know how a boy can turn the tide of this war, but if our shamalan nobles were with us, they would see the fates differently than does Waldemariam. I will trust in the faith of the nobles, and I will stand against this enemy who seeks to annihilate us. One thing is for certain: we cannot win this fight if we do not stand and face it with aggression."

"We do not know that the boy is Gayan," Oskar said. "We do not even know if he is truly shamalan."

"What has gotten into you!" Alasdar demanded, beating his fist against the table. "We must stand as one. At no time in our history has the leadership of the council been more important. We must stand together and fight. We must prepare for battle. It is a time for urgency, not for moaning and equivocating."

Oskar frowned. "I'm going to bed, Alasdar, to enjoy the comforts of my chamber. I am not a fool and I am not a coward. I am, however, a realist. You have no right to question Waldemariam. He is the lawful ruler of the council—and, in the absence of the nobles, of the entire empire. You would do well to avoid comments that may be construed as treasonous." He glared at Alasdar. "Good night."

The remaining councilmen followed Oskar from the great hall, leaving Alasdar alone at last in the chamber. He walked to the window and gazed out over the Forest of Ondor as, outside, the music and revelry continued.

Chapter 33

Slipher's Bid for Freedom

After slipping past Harwelden, the boat continued north-ward to Susquatania. As the day faded to dusk, the trees of Ondor grew smaller, heralding the approach to the forest's edge. Past the trees lay the borderlands between Ondor and the Toltugan desert, and the place where the massive serpan army camped as it prepared its assault.

In the bow, Crosslyn, outraged by the princess's confinement at Harwelden, and weakened from aiding in Elliott's magic, gazed quietly into the distance.

Elliott remained asleep like a log at his feet. The boy still looked ill, almost feverish. Masking the boat for such a long period had taken a toll on him, though the time for his next performance was fast approaching.

The touch of a hand on Crosslyn's shoulder jarred him from his reverie. He turned to find Hooks standing beside him, and nodded. The two sat down next to Elliott on the floor.

Hooks said, "Is this journey to Susquatania really a good idea? Even if I did not travel with you, your chances of swaying the chieftan would be small. But with me alongside you . . ." His voice trailed off, and he stared at the jute-and-tar caulking between the floorboards. "I just don't want to be the source of any conflict between you and the clan of beasts in Susquatania. Woolf is right about me—I will not be well received there."

I am no fool, Hooks," Crosslyn said. "I have known you a long time. I have trusted you with the knowledge of my presence in the swamps, and during all those seasons you never once betrayed me. I do not know the details of your situation with your people, but I know you have honor. We will approach the chieftan cautiously. With you at my side, we will ask for his help. I do not know the role you are set to play as this scenario unfolds, but the Shama has placed you with us for a reason."

Hooks fidgeted. "I trust you as well," he said. "But you should reconsider whether you want me to come with you."

"May I ask you," Crosslyn said, "what is the nature of your disagreement with your clan?"

Uncomfortable seconds passed, and Hooks lowered his head. "I can't talk about it."

"Undoubtedly, we are going to learn about the circumstances of your banishment when we reach Susquatania. Why not tell me about it now, so that we may plan a proper approach to the leaders of your clan."

Hooks snorted and stared at the floor. "There is no plan we can make that will lessen the hatred for me in Susquatania," he said. "I am guilty of the gravest of crimes against my people." He raised his gaze to Crosslyn's. "It is important for you to know what you bring upon yourself by traveling alongside me. I will go with you to Susquatania if that is your wish. I have nothing more to lose. But understand that by showing up with me, you make a difficult task impossible. My kindred are not naive to the circumstances of the war. They have carefully crafted friendships with serpans and the Shamalan Empire alike. It is my estimation that if they were to choose sides now, it would be with the serpans, because they are more likely to win. If you show up with me at your side, you will go a long way toward helping them choose their side in this fight, and it won't be the outcome you hope for."

Crosslyn looked at him with no discernible expression. "You have reinforced my notion that you are honorable," he said. "Your humility and honesty are commendable, but they do not change my mind. You will travel with us to Susquatania. We must trust in the Shama, and the Shama tells me that you are to stand at my side when we meet with the chieftan." He stood. "It is time for me to wake Elliott. The base camp of the serpans draws near."

"And I will trust in you, sorcerer," Hooks said, turning away. "But know that soon comes a day I have long dreaded. When you learn of my crimes, you may regret your friendship with me. Do not say you haven't been warned."

The shrill screech of a bone horn shattered the silence— a sure sign that the serpans were nearby, waiting somewhere ahead in the encroaching darkness. Crosslyn's head turned this way and that, trying to pinpoint the sound of the horn. With great urgency, he leaned over and shook Elliott. "Wake up, boy," he said. "It is time."

Elliott snorted but didn't wake.

The bone horn sounded again.

At that moment, a malevosaur brigade, atop their fearsome lizards, materialized on the western banks of the river. Within seconds, waves of arrows pelted the side of the boat and whizzed past their ears.

"We've got them!" yelled one of the serpans. "Over here."

Despite the commotion, Elliott remained unconscious.

In the stern, Woolf returned fire with his crossbow, though his arrows were a poor match for the dozens of serpans on the riverbank. "Protect yourselves!" he shouted to the others, frantically slotting another arrow.

The boat had reached the edge of the forest, and the majestic trees had given way to scrub. Unlike in Golroc, there could be no shadow allies here, and moreover, Crosslyn had lost much strength in his efforts to supply Elliott with the needed energy to mask the boat at Harwelden. He knew they were in real trouble.

Jingo and Marvus scrambled for the slingshot and the coins.

As they ducked behind the wooden hull, a second malevo-saur brigade arrived, across the river from the first. Just ahead, barely visible in the growing moonlight, the massive hulls of the moored Haviru ships blocked the river. The little boat was surrounded. Arrows whizzed through the air all around them.

Jingo launched coins at the serpans while Woolf loosed arrow after arrow against them.

Hooks dropped to Elliott's side and shook him roughly. "You've got to wake up!" he yelled. "We need you!"

Finally, Elliott stirred, appearing sluggish and confused. "Wha . . . what's going on?" he asked thickly, looking around the boat and to the shore.

Understanding slowly dawned, and suddenly, he was wide-awake. He closed his eyes, and an instant later, the boat disappeared from sight.

For a moment, the serpans on either side of the river looked perplexed. A warlord from the eastern bank tentatively loosed an arrow in the direction where the boat was last seen. The arrow struck the hull with a hollow thud before disappearing. "They're still here!" the warlord yelled. "Keep shooting!" With that, the rain of arrows resumed. All the while, the hulls of the Haviru ships blocking their passage downriver loomed larger.

Crosslyn was surprised by Elliott's strength. He would not have guessed that the boy could effect the masking so suddenly and so completely. Even the arrows disappeared as they sank into the boat. *He is getting stronger,* Crosslyn thought. *There is more to this child than meets the eye.*

Overhead, the dark forms of two darfoyles appeared in the sky. They were well and truly trapped. In his mind, Crosslyn heard Elliott speak.

Stay with me, Crosslyn. The boy's voice was surprisingly confident.

Again Crosslyn surveyed their surroundings, looking for any means of escape. They were about to plunge headfirst into the hull of the nearest Haviru ship. There was no path to freedom. From above and around them, arrows rained forth. He knew they would not be able to withstand the assault indefinitely, but he could think of no recourse. As they neared the hull of the nearest Haviru ship, he braced himself for the collision.

From the banks, the hail of serpan arrows continued.

Stay with me.

Though Crosslyn could not see Elliott, he had an image of the boy standing at the prow of the boat. He seemed intent on the hull of the Haviru vessel just ahead. He was leaning forward, as if ready to strike at the massive ship with his bare hands.

Suddenly, Crosslyn felt energy flood out of him.

Hold on, old man, he heard faintly. The confident tone remained. Again, in a rush of images, he saw Elliott standing in the prow. As Crosslyn struggled to remain on his feet, his mind's eye saw Elliott's forehead make contact with the hull of the ship. Crosslyn felt as though he might vomit. His legs wobbled beneath him. As the image continued in his thoughts, he saw Elliott's head pass *into* the hull of the ship, and a heartbeat later, the hull of the ship was upon him. Flinching, he felt his body make contact with the vessel's waterlogged timbers. He felt the barnacles of the hull press against his clothes and then against his bare skin. And without warning, he was *inside* the dank lower decks of the ship. His boat was somehow moving *through* the ship itself. What magic was this? All the while, the smaller craft moved forward as if nothing were there to impede its motion downstream. Crosslyn felt a new wave of nausea, and then it passed altogether. Just ahead of him, Elliott beamed. Though he could not see the boy, he could feel him.

All around them, the mundane goings-on inside the ship's hull played out. Crewmen lay on narrow planks of bedding while rats scurried to and fro across the floor. Even to the rats, the interlopers' physical presence inside of the ship went un-noticed. As the boat edged forward, Crosslyn caught snippets of conversation from the crew. It seemed the enemy—Crosslyn and his companions—were trapped just outside the ship and were about to be captured.

Astounded, he surveyed the inside of the ship as they passed through it. Far to one side of the hull, away from the sleeping quarters, lay the disassembled parts of the Haviru's most feared weapons. Sections of siege towers and pieces of great trebuchets were stored neatly belowdecks. Large wood-en barrels seeping black oil were stacked against another wall. Rows of giant catapults, stacked one upon another, lined the wall in some sections from floor to ceiling. Crosslyn shuddered at the thought of such formidable weaponry. This was what the Haviru were known for. This was what caused one to shudder at the mention of their name. All around him, the hold of the ship buzzed with the preparations for war.

Slowly, the boat traversed the first ship until, briefly, Crosslyn found himself over the water again as they crossed the gap between the first and second ships in the fleet. Then, as before, he felt the wet timbers touch him as he passed into the hull of the second ship. As in the first ship, the lower deck was filled with conversation about the capture presumed to be taking place on the river. Little did the crewmen know that the party they sought was traveling, quite literally, *through* them.

The boat continued, passing through a third ship and into a fourth. All was going well until, without warning, a scream shattered the silence. It was Slipher. Forgotten by the others, he had woken on the floor of the boat. "HELP ME!" he screeched. "We are here! HELP ME!"

The crew of the fourth Haviru vessel, confused by the scream, jumped to their feet. They scanned the hull of the ship for the source and looked to one another for guidance as Slipher kept up his caterwauling. Then, before their eyes, the boat and its crew flashed back into existence.

Slipher's screams had provided enough distraction to break Elliott's concentration. The boat, squarely in the center of the Haviru ship, came into full view. With the unmasking, timbers from Crosslyn's boat fused with the timbers of the Haviru ship's floor. Crosslyn's and his companions' legs stuck through the floor of the Haviru ship, encased by the floorboards. The crew was trapped within the confines of the Haviru ship, completely immobile.

Crosslyn, severely weakened by Elliott's use of the magic, thought, *Do something, Elliott. I haven't the strength.*

All around them, Haviru crewmen drew their swords and descended on the boat.

Slipher screamed.

Woolf drew his sword. Behind him, Marvus and Jingo struggled for the slingshot, but it was encased in the ship's floorboards. They drew the daggers from their belts and prepared to fight. Hooks, caught unarmed, raised his fists.

In the prow of the boat, Elliott squeezed his eyes shut. And in an eyeblink, Slipher's screams were squelched, and the boat flashed out of sight.

As the boat disappeared, a Haviru warrior swung his sword, slicing the air where Elliott's neck had been just a split second before.

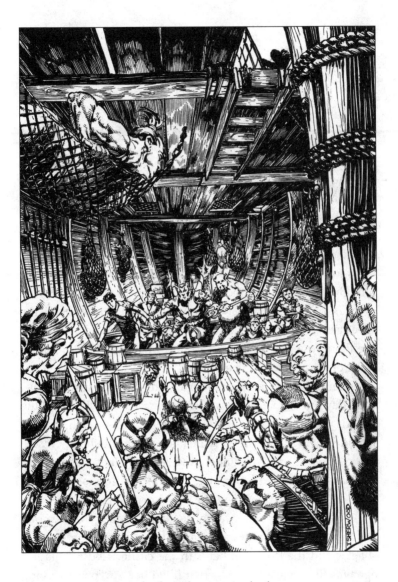

Then, before their eyes, the boat
and its crew flashed back into existence.

Chapter 34

A Savior in the Dungeon

It was useless, Sarintha finally decided. No one could hear her. She didn't know how long she had been in the dungeon, though she knew that the time ran to days rather than hours. She spent the days calling out with her mind in the hope that someone, anyone, might pick up a trace of her thoughts. Her arms and legs were bound by the shackles, and no one had brought water or food since her arrival. In fact, she had not seen or heard a living soul since Councilman Oskar dropped the sheet across her cell. Even the serpans had treated her better, she thought wryly, pushing herself up with her legs to relieve some of the pressure on her wrists.

Periodically, she listened for sounds from the castle above. Any day now, the siege would begin. Would she hear the sounds of war? Or was the dungeon insulated enough that she would hear none of the carnage above? For all she knew, the battle might already be under way. Perhaps that was why no one had brought food or water. Perhaps her grayfarer captors were dead and no one knew she was down here.

With nothing better to do, she decided to try once more. Squeezing her eyes shut, she transmitted an image of herself, shackled in the dungeon beneath the castle. Tied to this image was the sense of despair that filled her. Anyone receiving the message would get the idea she was trying to convey: the shamalan princess was held prisoner in the dungeons of her own castle.

As she sat concentrating on her message, to her utter amazement, there it was: the glimmer of a response.

I hear you, Princess.

She sat upright. *Who is listening?*

A friend, came the reply.

Despite the pain and the terrible thirst, she smiled. She could not help but think of Grinjar, the rat who had saved her from Malus Lothar at Mount Sitticus. He had responded the same way.

Who are you? she called out.

I am Taldar, citizen of Harwelden and friend of the grayfarer Woolf.

She stiffened. *Then are you friend or foe?*

I am a friend, of course, Taldar replied.

I have no confidence in the council, she thought. *It is thanks to them that I find myself here.*

That is not quite right, Taldar thought. *It is because of Waldemariam, and his henchman Oskar, that you sit here in shackles. The rest of the council has no idea of your presence here, nor does anyone else in the castle or the entire city.*

She waited a moment before responding. *How do I know that you can be trusted?*

With all due respect, Princess, your alternatives are meager.

She strained her eyes against the darkness but couldn't see a thing. *What are you?* she thought.

A rat. And I am here to help you.

Again she smiled. Before meeting Grinjar, she would not have given much credence to a communication from a rat. But she had learned better. *Do you know where Grimaldi is?*

He is in the next wing of the dungeon. This whole section has been emptied of its prisoners. You are the only two down here.

Is he all right?

If by that you mean "Is he alive?" then yes. But he has endured much.

To Sarintha's utter amazement, there it was:
the glimmer of a response.

Thank Baruna! she thought. *Where are you?*

I am here.

Do not speak to me in riddles! she scolded. *Where are you?*

Right here, at your foot.

What can you possibly do to help me? she thought. Then, realizing how dismissive this sounded, she added, *Thank you for answering.*

You are most welcome, Highness. And I can do much to help you. I can report on the happenings in the castle above, and I have stolen a key to free you from your shackles. I have it between my teeth.

She was overjoyed, though she guarded her emotions against the rodent. *And what do you ask in return for your services?*

I am in the employ of Councilman Woolf. I require nothing from you for my services.

Does he know I am here? she responded.

Except for me, Waldemariam, and Oskar and the two grayshirts who locked you up, no one knows you are here. Woolf is away from the castle. I am not at liberty to say anything more, except that he acts in the true service of Harwelden.

I will take you at your word, she thought. *Now, what can we do to get me free of these shackles?*

No sooner had the thoughts left her mind than she felt the rat scurry across her leg and up her body. She shuddered at the sensation of tiny paws on her, running up her arm to her wrist, and despite her thankfulness, she struggled to remain calm as the little claws found purchase in her skin. The days in darkness and solitude had taken their toll.

Taldar struggled with the key for several minutes, nearly dropping it twice, but eventually, he managed to turn the key in the lock, and the manacle snapped open.

Praise Baruna! she thought. *And thank you, my little friend. I shall never forget your service to me and the empire.* She lowered her arm to her side, her muscles and joints rejoicing at the change of position.

I will give you the key now, Taldar thought. *With one hand free, you can open the other shackles much easier than I.* And scurrying down her arm, he dropped the key in her free hand. When the feeling returned to her hand, she leaned across herself and managed to find the keyholes of the other shackles. Free at last, she stood and stretched, careful not to move her feet lest she step on her little savior. *Thank you again,* she thought. *When the time comes, I will see that you and yours are richly rewarded for your efforts.* After stretching, she sat back down. *Now, come and tell me what you know. Together we shall devise a plan.*

I am at your service, Highness, he thought, scurrying onto her lap.

Chapter 35

Into the Deep

Elliott felt the whoosh of the Haviru sword just over his head. Thankfully, he had managed to silence Slipher and mask their presence again. He had further managed to get the boat moving, though how he ever moved it through a physical obstacle of wood and iron, he had no clue. Crosslyn had never mentioned anything like this.

With all these sword-slinging Haviru about, he felt unsafe continuing forward, so he willed the boat down. Drawing on instinct—*shamalan* instinct, he supposed—he planned to descend beneath the surface of the river and complete the passage underwater, as deep as he could make them go. He did not know how he was doing such a patently impossible thing; he only knew, somehow, that he could make it happen.

On the deck of the Haviru ship, the call of a bone horn heralded the discovery of the boat and its crew. Above, confused Haviru crewmen scrambled to regain control of the situation. Wielding their swords, they poked the air where the boat had been, hoping to strike flesh and bone with their blades.

Amid all the chaos, Elliott willed the boat downward. It dropped through and beneath the lower deck of the ship and, finally, into the icy waters of the river.

Water rushed all around them, and the shock of the cold water on his body nearly caused him to lose his concentration. Though he had no concept of the magic he was performing, he understood that any lapse of his focus could prove deadly to them all. Focusing his thoughts, he felt the strange sensation of water rushing *through* him. The sensation was oddly pleasing, though he had no time to dwell on it. As the icy water enveloped them, Elliott prepared to breathe it in, effecting the transformation, when he heard an outcry of distress somewhere in his mind. The coldness of the water gripped him. Vague impressions of many voices screamed out to him. He focused on the outcry, trying to sharpen it in his mind, while willing the boat deeper, out of the reach of the Haviru.

The submerged hull of the nearest Haviru ship was now well above them, and he felt the growing weight of the water on them as they descended. Focusing on the outcry, he was able to sharpen the voices in his head. They revealed themselves in a flood. The voices were those of his friends—Marvus, Jingo, Hooks, and Woolf couldn't breathe. With all his heroic efforts, he was drowning them. He had been so entranced in performing the strange act of diving, he had failed to realize that no one but he and Crosslyn would be safe under the water.

Rattled, he improvised, imagining a protective cocoon around the ship. Focusing on detail, he imagined the boat and its crew surrounded by a bubble. When the bubble was in place in his mind's eye, he willed all the water out of it and imagined it filled with air. To pull it off, he needed power. He drew on Crosslyn as before, pulling what he needed as if it were water from a reservoir.

He pulled and pulled from the well of energy, conscious of the need to keep himself strong for the safety of his patrons and to maintain the integrity of the makeshift escape. Drawing such vast stores of energy, he grew exhilarated. Water lurched outward from the center of his cocoon and bubbled to the surface, and fresh air replaced it, filling the space. All the while, the boat dived deeper.

They were now several meters below the Haviru fleet and still moving northward in the bizarre improvised transport.

Elated, Elliott reached out with his mind, searching for a sensation of the others. He wanted to make sure they were all right, and he couldn't wait to discuss this amazing development with them the moment they were clear of the Haviru. All the while, he held the impression of the bubble in his mind. He sensed each of his companions in turn, gaining an impression of their relief. Feeling self-satisfied, he reached out to Crosslyn, ready to be congratulated on his rare and wondrous deed.

The old man didn't answer.

Surprised by the lack of response, Elliott reached out again. *Crosslyn, where are you? Answer me.*

Again he got no response.

At that moment, a hand reached out for him in the darkness. Though he could see very little, he knew it was Marvus—with these latest feats of magic, his mental sense of his surroundings had grown keener.

"We have to get back to the surface," Marvus said. His voice sounded hollow inside the bubble, but Elliott could tell he was worried.

"That's crazy," he said, craning his head to see the ships' hulls overhead. "Look at all of them up there."

Marvus gripped his arm. "Listen to me. No matter what the cost, we must return to the surface." He squeezed Elliott's arm so tightly, his fingernails cut into the skin.

Elliott was confused. "We need to talk to Crosslyn before we—"

Marvus cut him off. "I don't know what you did, Elliott, but you used some very potent magic to effect our escape."

"Yes, I did," Elliott said, smiling.

"Somehow you have harmed Crosslyn," Marvus said. "He is lying in the middle of the boat, and I can't arouse him. We must return to the surface at once so you can stop whatever you're doing to him."

Panic surged through Elliott as he thought of all the energy he had sucked from Crosslyn to achieve the escape. Again he looked up at the ships. If they returned to the surface, they would face danger. If he kept them safe below, it would harm Crosslyn even more. In short order, he knew what he must do, and he concentrated on returning the boat to the surface—all the while, to his growing dismay, drawing on Crosslyn for the magic needed to maintain the bubble and protect the others.

By the time they reached the surface, they had passed beneath seven ships. He chose a spot between two more hulking vessels and maneuvered the boat to the surface. As soon as they were topside, he ceased all efforts to protect the boat, thereby releasing Crosslyn from the steady drain of energy. And though yet unnoticed by the Haviru, the small boat was now plainly visible.

By this time, Woolf, Hooks, and Jingo seemed to understand what was happening. They rushed to the center of the boat, offering all their attention to Crosslyn, who wasn't moving.

Elliott watched the awful scene unfold. Crosslyn wasn't moving at all. Elliott's head felt thick and fuzzy, as if all were happening in a dream. He surveyed the boat and saw Slipher struggling against his bindings. Slipher turned and opened his mouth to scream, and realizing the potential danger, Elliott silenced him with a thought—though for this magic, too, he drew from Crosslyn. Cursing Slipher for causing the whole mess, he joined the others at the old man's side.

Crosslyn was ashen and looked even more aged than before. Elliott was horrified. He couldn't believe how frail and withered his old mentor looked.

As the group hovered around Crosslyn, pleading with him to stay alive, the old man opened his eyes. Even this seemed to take great effort. Straining to focus, he looked at Elliott. "Get us out of the water," he whispered.

Determined to right the situation, Elliott scanned the surroundings to ensure that no one had spotted them. Then he reached out and placed his hands against the hull of the nearest Haviru ship, pushing against it to maneuver their little craft to the shore. The rest of the crew quickly joined in. When they reached the eastern bank, Elliott stepped out of the boat, careful to make as little noise as possible. Hooks hoisted Crosslyn over his shoulder, and, one at a time, they got out of the boat and began wading to shore, all the while scanning the riverbank to be sure they hadn't been spotted.

When everyone was ashore, Woolf grabbed the boat, which still held the struggling Slipher, and pulled it onto land. "Go," he whispered, motioning to the crew to head inland as he yanked Slipher up and tossed him over his shoulder. They scampered into the cover of the scrub trees, making as little noise as possible.

The night was quiet, and they managed to get away from the river safely. With the moonlight guiding them, and the chirping of the cydonias covering the sound of their flight, they walked for several minutes under the cover of scrub forest until they emerged into a clearing. After a cautious look around, Woolf dropped Slipher to the ground with a thud, and Hooks laid Crosslyn gently down. Hooks stroked the side of the old man's cheek and peered into his face as the others knelt around him.

Hooks looked up at Elliott. "You did this," he growled.

Elliott was frightened beyond words. He had never seen Hooks this angry.

"He has the smell of death on him," Hooks snarled, glaring at him. "You did this." He looked as if he wanted to lunge at Elliott.

Elliott didn't know what to say. He hadn't meant to hurt anyone. He scanned the faces of his fellow travelers, looking for support.

Hooks looked up at Elliott.
"You did this," he growled.

Woolf glared at him. "You went too far with it, Elliott."

Elliott opened his mouth to say something, then closed it again. He leaned over Crosslyn and jostled him. *Wake up*, he thought. *You have to wake up.*

Marvus scooted next to Elliott and put a hand on his shoulder. When Elliott looked up, he saw that Marvus had tears in his eyes. "We know you didn't mean to do it, Elliott, but you should have been more careful."

Please wake up, Elliott thought.

"What did you do to him?" Jingo asked, wide-eyed. "Why would you want to hurt Crosslyn?"

"He didn't mean to do it," Marvus sobbed. "It's the magic. He was using the old magic and doesn't know what he's doing yet. He took the energy from Crosslyn, and the stronger the magic became, the more he took."

Please, please, please wake up, Elliott thought.

Slowly Crosslyn opened his eyes. His face was so withered, it was almost unrecognizable. He looked at Elliott, holding his gaze for several seconds without speaking.

I'm so sorry, thought Elliott. He felt as if he might cry.

Crosslyn stared at him with an inscrutable expression, causing Elliott to wonder if he had rendered the old man vacant. After a time, Crosslyn said to Marvus, "Come closer to me."

Marvus leaned forward and grasped Crosslyn's hand. "I am here, sir."

With great effort, moving as if his limbs were made of lead, Crosslyn reached into his tunic and brought forth a dagger. Holding it out to Marvus, he croaked, "Do you know what this is?"

Marvus took the dagger and looked at it. It was a fine piece of craftsmanship. He studied the markings on the hilt, and the flawless curve of the blade. After what seemed a long time, he looked at Crosslyn. "I know what it is," he said.

"Good," Crosslyn said. "Protect it at all costs. You will know what to do with it when the time comes."

Marvus nodded and tucked the dagger in his belt.

"Now, Hooks," he whispered. "Come closer."

"I am here, old friend," Hooks said, his voice breaking as he spoke. He stroked the old man's cheek.

"It is you who must make our case to the chieftan," Crosslyn said. "*You* are the key to persuading the forest beasts. Atone for your misdeeds and rejoin with your kindred."

"I will do as you ask."

"Good," the old man whispered, and his eyes closed again.

Tears formed in Hooks's eyes, and he caressed the withered cheek.

Elliott, Crosslyn thought.

I'm here, Elliott responded. *Tell me what to do for you.* Though he could hear Crosslyn in his mind, the old man's body lay still. *I'm so sorry.*

Stop whimpering, Crosslyn replied. *They need you to be strong.*

Elliott stared at him, desperately wishing he could undo the events that led to this awful pass.

You are the one, Crosslyn thought.

I don't know if I can go on without you, Elliott replied.

Crosslyn seemed to grow paler by the second. *Hold these friends dear, Elliott. If you are to succeed, it will be with them at your side. . . . And, Elliott . . .*

Yes.

Next time use the trees.

In his final thoughts, Crosslyn offered a lesson: if you need to draw power from a living being, use the trees.

Without warning, an arrow whizzed through the clearing. In the distance, the shrill call of a bone horn filled the air.

The terrible roar of a malevosaur pounded their eardrums as a contingent of the fearsome lizards and their riders smashed into the clearing.

As the first malevosaur cleared the tree line, Elliott and his crew remained huddled around Crosslyn.

For the last time, Crosslyn opened his eyes. "Run, fools!" he whispered. It was the last they would hear him speak.

Stealing a final glance at Crosslyn, Woolf nodded to Elliott and lit into the air, taking to the skies with Slipher in tow.

Elliott reached out for the others, and in a flash, they vanished.

Overhead, the leaves of the trees browned imperceptibly.

Chapter 36

Stranded

Hidden by Elliott's magic, they ran deeper and deeper into the scrub forest. With Hooks in the lead, they trekked northward for a league or more before finally stopping to rest. For the moment, they had escaped the Haviru and the malevosaurs, though Crosslyn's loss left them reeling, and their boat lay beached on the banks of the river, with hopes of reclaiming it growing ever dimmer. In a few days' time, the Festival of Opik would begin, and the prospects for reaching Susquatania or Harwelden seemed all but gone.

Inland, the trees had grown thinner and the ground sandier. The landscape offered little cover or concealment from pursuers. Struggling to catch their breath, the invisible group huddled behind a copse of thornbushes, where Elliott unmasked them. The burden of Crosslyn's loss showed in each inconsolable face.

"What now?" Elliott asked. His words were as meek as the day he arrived in Pangrelor.

Hooks glared but said nothing.

In the distance, the grunting cries of the malevosaurs served as sobering reminders of their plight.

Elliott struggled to digest the unfathomable tragedy of the past few hours.

Crosslyn was gone.

A disturbance overhead relieved the awkward silence as Woolf descended into their midst. Dangling beneath him, looking more dazed and frightened than ever, was Slipher.

Woolf dropped his captive onto the ground as if he were a sack of rotten fruit, and looked at the sullen faces around him. He scowled in disapproval. "It is time for action," he said. "Abandon melancholy." He turned to Elliott. "And decide your next actions carefully, shamalan. We can afford no more mistakes. We have to keep moving."

Woolf's words stung. Elliott searched his mind for the right response. Whatever was going to happen, he didn't share Woolf's zeal for continuing the quest. More than ever, he wanted to be away from this whole affair. *I didn't ask for any of this,* he thought.

"We must continue to Susquatania," Woolf said. "Crosslyn was certain that it is the right course of action."

Elliott remained silent. Overcome with shame over what he had done, he felt unworthy to participate in planning their next move.

Apparently feeling a modicum of compassion, Woolf softened his tone. "It goes without saying that you must be more careful, Elliott," he started. "But what shall we do if we do not follow the path Crosslyn laid out for us?" He scanned each of their faces. "Shall we sit here and wish these things had not happened, and await the claws of the malevosaurs? Or perhaps flee to the eastern lands while Harwelden falls? The wisest among us believed that our fate lies in Susquatania, and we should see his wishes to their fruition, even now that he is lost. Search your hearts, and you will see that I am right."

Marvus looked up from the ground. "He's right."

Jingo nodded.

Elliott put his face in his hands and wept.

Softening at last, Hooks went to him and comforted him.

In time, Elliott collected himself. "All right," he mumbled. "We go to Susquatania."

Woolf cracked a thin smile. "Hooks," he said. "You had better start working on the plea we will make to your kindred when we arrive. The hopes of the empire—and all of us—rest on your shoulders."

Hooks nodded, though all could see that his trepidation at the thought of returning to Susquatania was even greater with the loss of Crosslyn.

"How are we going to get to Susquatania without the boat?" Elliott said.

Marvus nodded. "The Festival of Opik and the assault on Harwelden are fast approaching. We haven't a chance of making it in time on foot."

"Right," Woolf said. "If we are to succeed, we must have the boat."

"But how?" Elliott asked. "The whole place is swarming with serpans."

As if to punctuate those words, a bone horn sounded in the distance.

"Well, whatever we do," Jingo said, "we'd better hop to it."

Woolf nodded. "Hooks and I will go back for the boat," he said. "The rest of you can meet us downriver after we have secured it."

Elliott was confused. "Why don't we *all* go?" he asked. I can mask us so they'll never even see us."

"No," Woolf said, shaking his head. "The lands that way are full of serpans, as is the riverbank. It is madness to consider placing you back in harm's way, Elliott. Hooks and I will get the boat. The rest of you must stay as far away from the serpans as you can."

"He's right, Elliott," Hooks said. "Traveling back to the river will be dangerous. As few of us as possible should go."

Woolf nodded soberly. "Hooks can use his natural-born ability to go unnoticed in the forest, and I will fly. When the opportunity arises, we will get the boat and carry it northward. Once at the riverbank, if we can escape detection by the Haviru, we should be all right. The serpans will be occupied searching the forest. As for the rest of you," he said, "Elliott can mask you if they get too close."

"But what about him?" Marvus asked, motioning to Slipher.

"Elliott will have to find a way to deal with him," Woolf said, already inspecting his crossbow and arrows. "Hooks, we've no time to spare. We must get away with the boat before daylight."

"But wait," Elliott said. "How will we know how to find you? How will we know when you're ready for us to join you? I'm not even sure we can find our way back to the river."

"You will have to use your seer stone," Woolf replied.

Elliott's face flushed bright red. "I don't have it," he mumbled. "My knapsack is still on the boat."

Woolf glowered at him. "All right, then," he said. "You'll have to devise another strategy."

In the distance, the bone horn blared again. Slipher squealed into his gag.

"There's no time to discuss it," Woolf said. "Hooks and I will get the boat and meet you on the shore downriver. Look for us about a league downstream from the Haviru fleet. We've got to get going now, Hooks," he said. "They'll soon be here looking for us, and daylight approaches." He flapped his great wings and took flight. "I'll meet you at the boat, beast," he said as he flew into the night sky. "The rest of you, get out of here."

The bone horn sounded again, closer.

"Take care of yourself, Elliott," Hooks said, grasping his hand. The rancor over Crosslyn's loss was gone from his face. "Be careful. And that goes for you two as well, he said, placing a hand over Jingo's entire head. "I'll see you at the other end." With that, he headed back into the scrub, in the direction of the horn calls. When he had gone a few paces, he used piloerection and disappeared from their sight even amid the sparse brush.

Elliott stared after them. He had no idea what to do.

In the distance, they heard the crunch of twigs beneath malevosaur feet.

Elliott stood. "Unbind Slipher's feet," he said. "He'll have to walk."

After the gimlets got their captive's feet free, Elliott masked them all, and they set off to the north as quietly as possible.

Slipher, thankfully, followed without incident.

The plan was simple: they would walk northward for a league or more, parallel to the river, then cut west. Once back at the river, they would search the shoreline for Hooks and Woolf in the boat. With their plan decided, on they trekked.

Soon enough they found themselves out of the scrub forest and in the windblown sands of the Toltugan desert, where the night air held a noticeable bite. With no living trees to draw from in the barren wasteland of dunes, Elliott was obliged to unmask them all.

The moon provided ample light, though the relentless monotony of endless rows of dunes began to play tricks on the mind. After what seemed like hours of walking straight northward, they encountered footsteps in the sand.

"Someone has been here," Marvus whispered, kneeling to inspect the footsteps. "There are four travelers." He scanned the line of footprints stretching across the infinity of sand, making a direct line eastward. "Anyone might be lurking out here. We have no protection whatever."

"At least there are no malevosaur tracks," Elliott said.

Jingo crouched to inspect the footprints. After a time, he looked up. "No one else is out here," he said. "We needn't fear the makers of these tracks."

"Whatever do you mean?" Marvus said. "Of course someone has been here!" The tracks are as plain as your nose."

Elliott looked again at the tracks, considering Jingo's

After what seemed like hours of walking straight northward,
they encountered footsteps in the sand.

words. "Jingo's right," he said. No one else has been here. Those are *our* tracks."

"Understanding dawned on Marvus's face.

"We must have walked in a circle," Elliott said. He looked up to the stars, trying to glean an impression of their location. The moonlight was fading as dawn approached. "We're lost."

"Oh, no," Marvus said again, wrapping his arms around himself against the cold as he stared at the tracks.

"Yes," Jingo said. "Lost . . . in the Toltugan desert . . . with daybreak approaching."

Marvus and Jingo stared wide-eyed at each other while Jingo scanned the fading stars, trying to get a handle on their location.

Beneath his gag, Slipher squealed.

Chapter 37

Hooks, Woolf, and the Boat

Hooks stood stock-still as a patrol of malevosaur-mounted warriors walked near enough for him to reach out and touch the nearest lizard's scaly hide. The creatures were everywhere in the scrub forest. Word of Elliott's presence in the forest had spread, and Hooks had never dreamed there would be so many serpans to contend with.

He had made it nearly to the river, but not yet close enough to spot the boat. Nor did he have any idea where Woolf was. In the distance, he saw the hulking shapes of the Haviru ships shrouded in the morning fog. Full daylight was not far away. Hooks wondered about Woolf. The grayfarer had the greater challenge, for without the cover of darkness, he would be easily spotted. If they wanted to grab the boat, it was now or never.

Another group of malevosaurs snorted past him, responding to the call of a bone horn in the distance. Using the usual method, Hooks hid himself, hoping the horn was making a routine call and not announcing the discovery of his friends.

As the malevosaurs passed, he froze. The next tree was several paces away, and small at that. After scanning his surroundings without moving his head, he went for it.

In three great strides, he reached the tree and piloerected, standing perfectly still. Before moving again, he would wait a moment to make sure no one had spotted his movement.

Near the shore, a mounted serpan pointed in his direction. Two other serpans rode to the side of the first, whispering, and Hooks felt exposed to the world. All three sauntered toward him, eyes fixed on the tree that disguised him.

Hooks tensed. He closed his eyes so the whites would not betray his presence.

"Are you sure you saw something?" said one of the serpans.

"I thought I did," the first replied. "From the corner of my eye . . . something was moving."

They walked around the tree, inspecting it.

Hooks held his breath as one of the malevosaurs stepped on his foot. The trio of Serpans circled the tree, looking it up and down. One reached out and touched it, caressing the bark inches from Hooks's chest, which blended seamlessly into the pattern of the bark.

"There's nothing here," said the first to have spoken.

"Agreed, said the one who had first pointed. "The warlock's use of the old magic has got my mind to spinning tales."

The others chuckled. "But there'll be no more of that!" said another, and the two laughed outright.

"No," the first snapped, "I suppose not. Come on." He reined his malevosaur back to the shoreline, and the others followed.

In the distance, Hooks heard yet another patrol of galloping malevosaurs headed his way. He had to move now. Slipping to the next tree, he glanced about, then darted to the next.

The lizards' thundering footfalls behind him grew louder as he floated silently from tree to tree, keeping pace with the trio of serpans that had almost found him. Panic crowded the corners of his mind as, bracing himself, he stepped to the next tree. A few more strides, and he was crouching at the shoreline, with the flotilla of Haviru ships before him. In the forest behind him, the galloping malevosaurs grew ever closer as the first sun began to crest the horizon, washing the landscape in the serene glow of dawn.

The trio of Serpans circled the tree,
looking it up and down.

The trio of serpans he had followed out of the forest headed south, upriver. He scanned the shoreline without moving anything but his eyes.

On the decks of the Haviru ships, the crews were waking and beginning their morning tasks. The place would soon be teeming with the mercenaries.

Several paces downriver, to the north, he spotted it, tucked under a curtain of vines, just as they'd left it. His heart pounded. This was it.

In several cautious strides, he made his way to the boat, following the tree line, staying in the shadows.

The approaching malevosaurs grew ever louder, and he could make out serpan voices. He wondered if Elliott and the gimlets had gotten away safely. There was no sign of Woolf.

With day breaking in earnest, he had to move now. He reached out from beneath the trailing vines and grabbed the prow, dragging it farther up the bank, into the tree line. Surprised at its weight, he dragged it along, barely trying to be secretive. Adrenaline coursed through his veins. He was ready to be away from the enemy camp.

They had left the boat beached near the eighth ship in the Haviru flotilla, and now he must pull it past six or seven more ships before reaching the end of the flotilla. As he pulled the boat between the eighth and ninth ships, the gap between the vessels allowed him to see across the river. Beyond the ships, on the western side of the river, the serpan base camp ran as far as the eye could see—row after row of tents, reaching to infinity. Hooks gasped. He had had no idea there would be so many. Already warriors were peeking out of their tents, squinting into the brightness of the rising suns.

Hooks broke into a run. Pulling the boat behind him, he ran as fast as the dead weight would allow. In a surge of adrenaline and fear, he broke into a sprint.

The crewmen aboard the Haviru ships, oblivious of the running susquat, multiplied on the decks above him. The day had begun.

Out of nowhere, Woolf hit the ground running beside him and grabbed on to the boat, and without a word, they sprinted for safety.

They reached the end of the flotilla without incident, despite the numbers of serpans and Haviru moving about. In broad daylight, they sprinted pell-mell along the shoreline, hidden from view only by the hulking mass of ships, praying they wouldn't be spotted.

From the scrub forest, the company of mounted serpans that Hooks had been hearing emerged near the seventh ship in the flotilla. The commander rode to the riverbank.

In full sprint, Hooks turned his head to assess the situation. With no protection from the trees, and in the full light of day, they were anyone's prey.

Without turning in Hooks's direction, the mounted serpan rode southward, away from them. Several of his company followed him out of the tree line. To Hooks's unbounded relief, none looked back.

After passing the final Haviru ship, Hooks and Woolf ran as long as they could. Across the river, the serpans on the periphery of the camp, perhaps because of their remoteness from their leadership in Ondor, had not yet begun to stir.

At last, the susquat and the grayfarer could run no more, though their proximity to the enemy still placed them at great risk. Exhausted, they pushed the boat into the water and, entering it, lay on their bellies so their silhouettes would not show in the distance. Had they peeked over the side, they would have seen that the river had a deep red tinge.

Chapter 38

The Deal with Slipher in the Desert

The suns blasted the four travelers both from above and from the blazing sands below them. With each windswept dune they crested, they found only more dunes, indistinguishable from those they had already traversed.

"Are you sure this is the right way?" Marvus asked.

Jingo lowered his head and trudged onward. "Just keep walking."

Behind them, Elliott kept a close watch on Slipher, who struggled to keep up. Elliott had removed his gag earlier in the day, but the serpan had little enough to say.

Though loath to admit it, Elliott sensed they were in real danger. Compounding his fears of the heat and the serpan army, the wind was gaining force, and he worried that a full-blown sandstorm might bury them. Yet on they walked, slowing gradually as the day wore on.

Slipher was the first to fall.

"Wait, guys!" Elliott yelled. "We've got to take a break."

Jingo paused at the dune's crest, as if weighing the advantages of continuing without the serpan, but finally returned to Elliott and Slipher in the sand. Scowling, Marvus followed.

"We can't take a break," Jingo said. "If the serpan can't make it, then we leave him here."

The wind was gaining force, and Elliott worried
that a full-blown sandstorm might bury them.
Wait, guys!" he yelled. "We've got to take a break."

Elliott turned to Slipher, considering Jingo's ultimatum. "I can't do it," he said finally. "Slipher, you have to get up."

Even as they paused, the wind whipped over the dune, stinging their faces with the sharp spicules of sand.

"Elliott," Jingo said, "we will die if we don't get out of the desert."

Elliott had drawn the same conclusion much earlier. He looked at Slipher, hunkered down in the sand. "I can't just leave him," he yelled to be heard over the coming storm. "You have to get up, Slipher."

Slipher looked up at Elliott and spat the sand out of his parched mouth. "Go with them," he said. "Leave me. There is no place for me."

Elliott looked at Jingo, then finally said, "I just can't do it."

"Then we are at an impasse," Marvus said. "Because we cannot leave you."

Gusts of wind scoured them, and though it was not yet noon, the sky seemed to grow darker.

"Go with them, Elliott," Slipher groaned. "Don't forfeit your life to stay with me."

Elliott searched his mind for a solution to the dilemma. He looked to Marvus and Jingo, praying for them to come up with something, as they had so many times before. But the gimlets seemed merely angry, or at least very afraid. They knew no way out of the situation.

"Get up, Slipher," Elliott pleaded.

Slipher ignored him. "I want to smoke my pipe," he said.

"This is madness!" Jingo shouted. "We can't sit here any longer. We have to leave him."

Slipher pulled out his pipe. "Can you help me light it, Elliott?" he asked. "Like you did on the boat?"

Elliott winced, embarrassed for Jingo to know that he had

helped Slipher. He patted his trouser pocket and felt the lump made by the lighter.

"Elliott," Jingo said, "our chances are running out. We have to go now."

Taking out the lighter, Elliott squatted with his back to the wind, cupping his hand around the lighter as he flicked the wheel. It ignited, and he held the tenuous flame to Slipher's pipe.

Slipher inhaled, and the tobacco glowed red. After pulling deeply, he exhaled. The wind buffeted their faces with granules of sand, but Slipher's smoke, unaffected by the gusts, hovered peacefully over his head, then dissipated.

"Did you see that?" Marvus gasped, yelling to be heard over the howling wind. "The wind has no effect on the smoke! How in the name of Antilia is that possible?"

Slipher smiled.

"Elliott!" Jingo yelled. "Leave him! Time is running out."

Inexplicably, Slipher grinned. "What if I could show us the way out of here?" he asked. "Would you then speak for me at Harwelden, Elliott?"

Elliott didn't understand.

"If I help save your life today, will you promise to try to save mine upon our return to the castle?"

Elliott gave him a bewildered nod.

Slipher pulled deeply from the pipe and closed his eyes, concentrating on an image of Hooks and Woolf, then exhaled.

As Elliott and the gimlets looked on in amazement, the smoke coalesced into an image above his head. It showed the four of them huddled in the sand, then pulled back to show the edge of the Toltugan desert, where it met the scrub forest. As they watched in disbelief, it pulled back farther to show the entirety of the scrub forest and the river itself. Finally, it zoomed down to the edge of the river to show Hooks and Woolf with the boat. Both of them stared nervously into the scrub, awaiting the return of their friends. Then the smoke dissipated.

"Unbelievable," Jingo whispered.

Marvus turned and looked west. He pointed in the direction of the river.

Jingo nodded.

Without a word, Elliott and the gimlets helped Slipher to his feet, and he set out with renewed strength against the headwind.

The trek through the sands was arduous, and as Elliott feared, the sandstorm worsened. But Jingo, determined not to get lost again, watched the suns as they marched, using them to reference his position.

In time, they reached the scrub forest, and finally, there was the boat, beached at the river's edge. An overjoyed Hooks rushed out to receive them, lifting Elliott off the ground in a tight embrace.

Chapter 39

Susquatania

For two days and a night they floated downriver, taking turns at the tiller and watching for animals on the shoreline. At dusk of the second day, the trees bordering the river grew larger, then larger still. Elliott looked to Hooks, who nodded. At last, they had reached the wooded valley of Susquatania.

The forest was eerily quiet. Unlike Ondor and Golroc, the stillness of the Susquatanian night was unbroken by the sounds of wild creatures. The only sound was the babbling of the river and the occasional slap of a paddle against the water. As the vegetation grew denser, the limbs of the Susquatanian forest stretched farther and farther over the water, eventually enveloping the river Tantasar in a cocoon of ancient woodland, offering the impression that the boat traveled ever deeper into the recesses of a great, green tunnel. The silence was unnerving, and the bright light of the moon grew ever dimmer, masked by the dense triple canopy. The other travelers turned their attention to Hooks, who guided them down the middle of the channel with subtle, effortless movements of his paddle. Though it did not show in his face, they knew this was his home, the birthplace from which he had been banished almost a generation ago. Despite his connection to the foreboding place, he surveyed the lands around him with no discernible emotion.

"Where do they live, Hooks?" Elliott asked out of the blue. "How are we going to find them?"

Hooks turned his gaze toward the riverbank, staring deep

into the forest. "We won't have to look hard," he said softly. "They are all around us."

Elliott scanned the riverbank. There was no sign of a living thing.

"They're everywhere," Hooks said dreamily. "Watching from every nook and shadow."

He steered to a quiet eddy. "This is as good a place as any," he said, stepping out of the boat and pulling it up onto the shore. As the others stepped cautiously onto land, he said, "Prepare yourselves. And stay calm. Whatever happens, mine is not a violent race."

"What do you mean?" Elliott whispered. "The place is un-inhabited." As soon as the words left his mouth, he turned to see a strange susquat hulking beside him.

And more followed. All around them, susquats appeared as if conjured out of thin air. Hooks had been right: the beasts were indeed everywhere, though they had hidden themselves so well that no one but he had any idea of their presence. In the space of a few seconds, the travelers were surrounded.

The susquats carried wooden spears tipped with sharpened bits of stone. The beast nearest Elliott turned to give Hooks a long look. "I knew that one day you would return," he said.

Elliott had trouble discerning the tone of the strange susquat's comment, though it seemed tinged with sadness.

"You will face justice here," said the susquat.

Hooks stared at him. The tension was palpable. "My friends and I request an audience with the chieftan."

"No doubt you do," the susquat growled. With gentle force, he pointed his spear at Hooks. "Come," he said. "All of you."

Holding his head high, Hooks fell in line behind one of the beasts. The others followed. The gaggle of susquats formed a tight formation around them, dispelling any notion in the travelers' minds that they could do anything or go anywhere without their hosts' consent.

All around them, susquats appeared
as if conjured out of thin air.

Chapter 40

The Wand of Griogair

In the time since Taldar came to the princess's cell, the two of them had accomplished a great deal. Taldar managed to drag a key to the cell door from the unmanned guard station, and Sarintha was now moving freely about the dungeon. She tended to Grimaldi's healing wounds daily but had elected to leave him in his cell, for she did not want to raise any suspicions should Waldemariam or Oskar venture into the dungeons to check on them. With each foray out of her cell, she carefully replaced the sheet and locked the cell door behind her. For Grimaldi's cell, she did the same. She, Grimaldi, and Taldar had agreed to stay in hiding for the time being and to hide their early successes in the dungeon. They were surviving on scraps of food provided by the rats, who foraged at Taldar's behest. Sarintha had placed a chamber bucket in a corner of the dungeon to collect the condensation that fell there in a steady drip. Then, using a fireplace in the deserted guards' chamber, she meticulously boiled each bucket of water to ensure its potability. Thankfully, despite her fears, no one noticed the smoke billowing from the chimney that rose from this particular part of the castle. In this fashion, though not thriving, they were surviving. More importantly, with Taldar's help, Sarintha had begun to make a plan for how she might regain her throne, though the plan was risky and fraught with opportunities for failure. It was this plan that Sarintha discussed with Grimaldi as she made her evening visit to his cell.

They were surviving on scraps of food provided
by the rats, and Sarintha used a chamber bucket to collect
condensation that fell there in a steady drip.

"It looks as though your wounds are improving," she said, swabbing his forehead with tepid water from a bucket boiled earlier in the day.

"I am not ready to fly," he said, "but I can stretch my wings a little farther with each passing day. I can feel my strength returning. . . . I want to get out of here."

"Soon," she said. "Taldar has presented an option that we have not considered."

"Oh?" he said, raising an eyebrow.

"He has devised a way to get rid of Waldemariam so that I might regain the throne."

"You know how I feel about that," Grimaldi replied. "Waldemariam is not the enemy we seek."

"Don't be a fool," she said gently. "He feigns fidelity to you, but look where we find ourselves while the castle is under his charge. You must give up this misguided loyalty. Dealing decisively with Waldemariam is our only option. And thanks to Taldar, I believe I have found a way to do just that."

"I'm listening," he said, "but I make no commitment."

"Good," she said. "My proposal is straightforward and will not have been considered by Waldemariam or any members of the council. In the shamalan temple are many artifacts from ages past. Among those artifacts, Taldar reminded me, are weapons."

Waldemariam interrupted her. "If you speak of the components of the Trident . . ."

"No," she said. "Of course I do not speak of the Trident. I refer to the Wand of Griogair. It lies unguarded amid the relics, forgotten in the stacks at the rear of the building. My father once showed it to me during my xcercio. Taldar suggested that it might be of use, and I am dismayed that I did not think of it myself."

"I am not familiar with this artifact," said Grimaldi.

"Exactly. And Waldemariam won't be familiar with it, either. It is little known, but it holds great power. If we can apprise Taldar and the rats of its exact location, and if they can deliver it to us, we can use it to thwart Waldemariam."

"How does it work?" the grayfarer asked.

"It is imbued with the power to subdue a single enemy. At the dawn of empire, it was crafted by Griogair's sorceror, Merkelo, to be used in battle against Valderon himself, though Griogair never made use of it. My father told me that the bearer of the wand has only one chance to use the magic it holds, and that if the magic is used improperly, there will be dire consequences for the wielder."

"But what does it *do*?"

She shifted uncomfortably in her seat. "The specifics are not well known to me. I know only that it can be used but once. And if it wields enough power to subdue Valderon, then surely it will suffice in holding Waldemariam at bay."

Grimaldi was skeptical. "You must have some idea of the nature of its power," he said.

"I don't know what it does, but I trust what my father told me."

Grimaldi sat in silence in the darkness, absorbing the princess's words.

"I know that you feel allegiance to Waldemariam," she said, "but it is my conviction that the Wand of Griogair is our only hope."

Grimaldi hesitated. "But, Your Highness," he pleaded, "What if he is not the one?"

"He is the one. Going all the way back to the first battle for Prytania, it is Waldemariam who betrayed us. With every new hope, he alerted our enemy. I feel it in my marrow."

Grimaldi shifted and looked at her for a long time. His face grew sad. "All right," he said at last. "I will trust you."

"Then it is decided," she said. "We must plan carefully. Getting myself in front of Waldemariam will be no small feat. We must consider every possibility of how it may play out. I will summon Taldar and make arrangements for the wand to be delivered to me. I will return later so that we may work out the details."

She left Grimaldi's cell, carefully replacing the sheet, and locked the door. Before she had reached her cell, she called out with her mind for Taldar.

Chapter 41

An Audience with the Chieftan

In silence, the six travelers marched through the dark forest, surrounded by their escort of susquats. If their pace slowed, the prod of a spear reminded them to keep moving and that, on this night, they were not the masters of their own fate. The susquats didn't speak, nor did anyone else. After walking for what seemed a very long time, they reached the outskirts of a settlement. Though the vegetation remained lush and dense, the landscape grew hillier, and the hillsides were pocked with caves. On occasion, despite the late hour, susquats squatted on their haunches outside their caves, tending campfires or doing other mundane tasks. The beasts watched them pass, then returned to whatever they were doing. Farther along, the caves clustered more densely, heralding their arrival in a more populated area. Finally, after a time, they came upon a palisade of thick wooden poles lashed together with ropes twisted from vines and aerial roots. The escort stopped at the gate, indicating that they would pass the rest of the night outside the palisade.

Following the prompts of his fellow susquats, Hooks sat. He scanned the length of the palisade with apparent surprise, as if it had not been there in the days when Susquatania was his home.

Elliott and the others, following their hosts' bidding, stretched out on the ground. Just then two susquats approached Woolf. One held lengths of rope; the other pointed his spear at him.

"Fold your wings behind you," said the one with the spear.

Woolf glowered at the susquat and stood, extending his wings—the opposite of what he had been instructed to do.

The susquat raised his voice. "Fold your wings behind you," he said, "or we will do it for you." Several others closed in around Woolf, raising their spears.

Angered, Woolf turned to Hooks. It was clear that he was struggling to contain his rage.

Hooks shook his head, and after a few tense moments, Woolf acquiesced. He folded his wings behind him and turned his back to the susquats, though his eyes told the tale: he was *letting* them tie him.

When they finished tying his wings, the travelers lay down and prepared to sleep, eventually succumbing to the soothing chirp of the cydonias.

⚚ ⚚ ⚚

Early the next morning, the susquats roused them. With the suns shining brightly in the morning sky, they stood and stretched, preparing, Elliott presumed, to pass through the palisade gate. It had been a long journey to Susquatania, and they had sacrificed much to get here. If they were to realize Crosslyn's plan to save Harwelden, they would do so today.

Inside the gate, the settlement buzzed with activity. Elliott marveled at the beasts, some of whom were larger even than Hooks, though he also noticed a scattering of infant and toddler susquats. Most were unclothed save for their long, matted fur, though some wore armor of bone, tortoiseshell, and animal hides. Despite the primitive components of the armor, it looked durable, and the warrior susquats struck Elliott as both elegant and fearsome.

And he marveled at how gracefully they moved. Despite their size and girth—some were larger than a grown grizzly bear—they moved like ghosts through the trees. He had observed this same trait in Hooks, though to see so many of the beasts moving around so quietly seemed almost dreamlike. Just beyond the fence, a gateway marked the passage to the inner settlement. To Elliott's wonderment, a pair of woolly mammoths sat guard on either side of the entrance, and like the susquats, the enormous creatures made implausibly little noise. The mammoths were fitted at the withers with leather saddles, and susquat warriors sat astride them. Quivers of arrows and spears hung behind the saddles, within easy reach of the riders.

As they approached the gateway, one of the guards recognized Hooks. A look of surprise dawned on his face. "You!" he growled, pointing his crossbow at Hooks, his eyes narrowing to slits.

"Good morning, Trap," Hooks said sheepishly, nodding to the guard. "Good to see you again."

The guard glowered back. "You should not have come here."

Hooks nodded demurely. "It looks like you've made something of yourself," he said. "I knew they were wrong about you."

The guard bristled. "You should have stayed away," he growled, waving them through. "You'll get what's coming to you."

With a solemn nod, Hooks marched through the gate with the others in tow.

Relieved to be away from the tense exchange with the guard, Elliott looked about him at the forest. It was like nothing he had seen before. The trees had been altered into something approaching architecture. The six travelers walked with their escort down a central trail, lined on either side by uniform rows of the massive trees. The treetops, however, unlike those in

Ondor and Golroc, did not reach upward toward the sky but bent unnaturally inward, merging into a uniform, cathedral-like archway high overhead. Ivy, orchids, and other flowering plants adorned the ceiling of the wooded archway, enhancing the strange artistry of the architecture.

Between the massive trunks on either side of him, Elliott glimpsed other structures, all created by manipulating the natural growth of the trees. Striding past the huge tree-buildings, he gaped in wonder, trying to understand how they had been made. Each was formed from the limbs and outgrowths of the trees themselves, bent and shaped to fit together in interlocking, living creations of ingenious design. In shape and function, the buildings were like those at Harwelden, with windows, doors, steps, and porches, but the tree-buildings were grander in scale. Even the steps of the buildings were part of the living trees, formed from trained networks of roots.

Elliott reasoned that the plans for these structures must have been laid down centuries ago, the manipulation of the limbs necessarily begun when they were saplings. He pictured the landscape as it might have been before the growth of the living city, and envisioned ancient susquats planting the trees and artfully molding their young limbs and roots to form the designs. The planning of such a feat must have been impeccably precise. In a very real sense, the susquats had *built* the forest of Susquatania, eons before it would ever be habitable in its current form.

The looks of disbelief on the gimlets and Woolf surprised Elliott. Indeed, they seemed as amazed as he.

Eventually, they reached the end of the walkway and stood in a clearing that housed the most splendid of all the tree-buildings. The structure lay just beyond a city square, with a courtyard in front. Here a pair of susquat warriors sat majestically astride their wooly mammoths, and just beyond, between the central square and the tree-building, stood a full rank of mounted guards. The spectacle of two dozen caparisoned mammoths in front of the immense tree-fortress made Elliott feel small, and he wondered how his motley band of friends might have any impact on the dealings of such a civilization. Encircling the square before him, huge flowers undulated like anemones in the absence of any breeze. The colorful, undulating flowers were both beautiful and frightening and looked as though they might become fierce if one got too close.

The building beyond the square was an otherworldly castle, with the higher limbs of its trees stretching skyward like towers. And indeed, turrets along the highest limbs housed guards, who watched over the entire city from such lofty heights that Elliott could scarcely make out their features.

A robed susquat emerged from the castle. Never taking his eyes off them, he walked through the flower-laden square toward them. Behind him, a group of warriors emerged from the fortress carrying large wooden chairs, which they placed in front of the mammoths, in two facing rows. Apparently, the meeting with the susquat elders was to be an outdoor affair. Finally, a line of robed and ornamented older susquats emerged from the building and seated themselves in the chairs. Then a guard motioned for the newcomers to follow him and take their seats before the susquat tribunal.

The chair in the middle of the row of susquats was larger than the others and held an august, carefully groomed susquat in a flowing robe of fine purple cloth. Flecks of gray peppered the mane about his head. Like the other susquats, he held a spear in his right hand, though his was of shiny gold. When everyone had taken their seats, the susquat in the center addressed Hooks directly. "I am disappointed to see you here among us again," he said, sounding genuinely saddened. "Your return presents me with a dilemma I had hoped never to face."

"I do not come for selfish motives," Hooks said.

The chieftan chuckled. "I have known you for all my seasons in this world, Hooks," he said. "And I have never known you to make a decision *not* born of a selfish motive." He paused before continuing. "I can think of few things that saddened me as deeply as the day you were led away from our home." The chieftan's voice grew melancholy. "The vision of you trussed and bound to a mountain horse, blindfolded, humiliated, and led to the outskirts of the forest was as painful to behold as anything I have witnessed. That vision has haunted my dreams since the day it occurred."

Hooks listened quietly and bowed his head as if burdened by the memory.

"Many times I have wondered what became of you," the chieftan said. "Many times I have wondered if you were still alive . . . and if you were happy." The intensity of his gaze deepened. "But coupled to these torments was an abiding wish that you never return." The chieftan sighed. "With all my being, I hoped this day would never come."

Hooks appeared to be trying to maintain his composure.

"You once held such promise," the chieftan said, speaking as if no one else were present. "We looked up to you. Despite your shortcomings, we *all* looked up to you. But rather than realize the promise of your birthright, and the potential for the great things that might be, you shook the very foundations of our civilization. You betrayed us in a way that cannot be forgiven." He raised his head. "You recall, no doubt, the penalty suggested at your trial in the event you ever returned to Susquatania."

"I remember it well," Hooks replied.

"Then what would you have me do, older brother, to my own flesh and blood, and to the onetime heir to the rule of all Susquatania?"

The chieftan said, "You recall, no doubt, the penalty suggested at your trial in the event you ever returned to Susquatania."
"I remember it well," Hooks replied.

Elliott's jaw dropped at the revelation.

Hooks grew uncharacteristically emotional. "I would have you listen," he said, still holding his brother's gaze, "to the susquat whom you once held in such high regard. And I would ask you and the elders, all of whom I once saw as brethren, to consider my sorrow for the events that happened so long ago. And I would have you listen to the reason I have returned to you." He raised his head, and a gleam brightened his eye. "And I will ask you, younger brother, to be the leader that I know you are capable of being."

Elliott sat in disbelief. He looked to Marvus and Jingo, who also appeared transfixed by the revelation. Even Woolf appeared to be at a loss.

The chieftan bowed his head. The members of the council began to speak in whispers, and the awkwardness of the situation showed on their faces. As the whispers of the Council increased, Chieftan Keats held up his hand. "The Council of Elders will convene in private," he said.

With a swirl of his robe, he turned and walked back toward the castle, and the elders followed in procession between the ranked mammoths and disappeared into the fortress.

Eventually, Hooks and the others sat facing an empty row of chairs. The flowers in the square, oblivious to the revelation, continued their dysrhythmic undulations. Guards convened around them, clearly implying that they were expected to stay put while the council convened.

Elliott looked at Hooks with amazement. "Why didn't you tell us?"

"Because it was none of your business," he said quietly.

Woolf looked at Hooks without discernible expression. "What was the cause of your banishment?" he asked.

"That is none of your business, either."

"But it has *become* our business," said Woolf, glancing over his shoulder at his lashed wings. "Our fates are irreversibly tied to yours. It is time for you to share the reason for the animosity and sadness we see directed at you."

Hooks looked at him pleadingly, but Woolf's eyes insisted.

"I was banished for the crime of . . ." Hooks's voice trailed off.

Woolf stared, waiting.

"It was for the crime of murder," he blurted. "I was banished for murdering the chieftan of the susquats—who was my uncle." His chest heaved. "He raised my brother and me from the time we were young children. He was beloved to me."

Woolf reached over and placed a hand on Hooks's shoulder. His face remained expressionless. "We will support you, whatever happens, he said. "As a sitting member of the Grayfarer Council, and on behalf of Harwelden, I shall offer whatever support I can."

Hooks looked at him skeptically.

"The matter of the grayfarer fledglings is an issue for Harwelden," said Woolf, "and will be addressed later. But in this time and place, for the deeds you have done, I will support you." He looked at Hooks, seeming to organize his thoughts. "Tell us, though, what is to be your penalty for defying your banishment and returning to your homeland?"

Hooks stared at the ground. "There is only one punishment," he whispered. "Execution."

Elliott gasped.

The susquat guards surrounding them nodded. "Execution," affirmed one.

Chapter 42

Harwelden's Last Days

Councilman Baucus slammed his fist on the table. "Where in the name of Antilia are Fanta and Woolf?" he demanded.

A cool breeze blew through the window in the great hall, stirring the leaves in the Forest of Ondor below and heralding the emergence of the cooler season celebrated with the Festival of Opik. Inside the hall, the remnants of the Grayfarer Council, save for Waldemariam, were convened.

Councilman Baucus led the discussion, and his frustrations with the preparations for defense were apparent. "Why is Waldemariam spending so much time cloistered in his room?" he asked. "Has he gone mad?" Baucus glared at Councilman Oskar. "The Festival of Opik is upon us, and the equinox is two days away," he said. "Our scouts inform me that the serpan forces have fanned out along the perimeter of the mountain, holding back only far enough so that we can't see them from the city. The assembly of the Haviru siege weapons is nearly complete. Their trebuchets and catapults will soon be ready to roll against us. Before the next full moon, they will rain fire and stone upon our city."

No one else spoke.

"The river Tantasar has been blockaded by the Haviru both north and south of the mountain," continued Baucus, "lest the army of men from Abarynthia, or the Iracemans or susquats try to come to our rescue. All around us, the grip of the vise tightens, and our council sits divided, with two of its members missing for more than a season. And while the winds of war threaten to engulf us, our chancellor won't so much as leave his bedchamber!"

Again he glowered at Oskar. "Our princess and her general haven't returned, and Marvus and Jingo remain missing, as well as the boy who travels with them." Baucus turned to the window, as if looking for them in the distance. "We have no chance of prevailing over the forces assembled against us, and the people of Harwelden celebrate as they did in the times before the Great Betrayal, as if the muse of death were not knocking at our door. What in the name of Baruna has become of us? Where is the great Waldemariam? The great Harwelden?" He slumped in his chair.

Outside the window, music filled the air as a parade marched across the flagstones beneath the castle. The voices of the revelers rose and fell with the pitch of the music. The joyous sounds from the courtyard played out in sharp contrast to the council's mood.

"I remain in close contact with Chancellor Waldemariam," said Oskar, who sat polishing his sword at the end of the table. Sunlight glinted off his shimmering breastplate. "The plans for our defense proceed unencumbered. The chancellor spends these days diagramming strategies for battle, preparing for every eventuality. He keeps close council with his generals, and it is not your place to question him." His eyes narrowed.

"It is beyond me, then, why he does not keep council with us," said Landrew, who sat next to Baucus. "I have seen the troops preparing, though they assemble at night, when the city sleeps. I do not understand the need for such secrecy. At this point, I believe we are scarcely more informed than the towns-people themselves."

"We have all seen the troops preparing for battle at night," Alasdar said. "I confess, though, I do not understand

Waldemariam's insistence that the townspeople should know nothing of the threat we face. I suppose it is his obsessive fear that someone in the village is sending word to the serpans— that the conspirator we have feared does not hold a position of power but rather walks among the commoners. Last season, Waldemariam insisted that Marvus and Jingo were the traitors. It seems that he is not as certain as he professed."

"Perhaps Waldemariam is to be taken at his word," Landrew said, "and he believes the villagers should enjoy their final carnival in oblivion. But why do we not shore up our defenses as a community, rather than operating in secret and denying what comes at us?"

"You have answered your own question, Alasdar," Oskar sneered, caressing his sword. "The chancellor will be sure our plans are not betrayed again. Though Marvus and Jingo remain the most likely suspects, there is no room for error. If these are to be the final days of Harwelden, they will come at the hands of our foe, not those of a traitor. That is why the chancellor eschews our council and why he doesn't want the villagers to know how far things have advanced."

"He keeps you informed of his plans, then?" Baucus said, raising an eyebrow.

"Of course," Oskar said cryptically. "And I keep him informed of mine."

"This is an outrage!" cried Baucus, standing up. "I will not sit idly by while Waldemariam plans our fate in secret. I have sat on this council for a long time." He narrowed his eyes at Oskar.

"Sit down, Baucus," Alasdar said. "We have no reason to mistrust Waldemariam, and no cause to further the chaos that envelops us by warring with one another."

"Are you certain of that?" Baucus said. "Because questions have stirred in my thoughts for quite some time now."

"Sit down, Baucus," Alasdar repeated. "We have no cause to mistrust Waldemariam."

Grudgingly Baucus retook his seat. "I do not wish to create conflict within the council, but the chancellor is obligated to inform us of his plans," Baucus said. "We need to know—*I* need to know—what he is up to. I need to know that he still merits our trust. He holds the position of chancellor, but he is not empowered to act without our knowledge and consent."

"We shall see about that," Oskar mumbled.

"What did you say?" Baucus challenged. "Why don't you speak more clearly, so that we all may have your meaning?"

"Enough of this," Alasdar said. "I will go to Waldemariam tonight. Baucus is correct in this much: Waldemariam is obligated to tell us of his plans. But we must work to avoid conflict among ourselves."

Outside, on the flagstones below, the merriment continued.

"And if we can hold on to reason for a little longer," Alasdar said, "there is more I would like to discuss. First, what are we to make of the absence of Fanta and Woolf? Are we to assume them dead? Assume them traitors? Both?" He scanned the faces of his colleagues, trying to glean their thoughts.

"I can assure you that Councilman Fanta is no traitor to our cause," Oskar said. "Of Councilman Woolf, I am less sure."

"Ridiculous!" Baucus snapped. "Where do you dredge up this poison?"

"Stop it!" Alasdar shouted. "I have spent a great deal of time pondering the whereabouts of Fanta and Woolf. We asked that they find the strange boy and recapture the susquat lest the beast make fools of the council of Harwelden. What seemed so important at the time seems folly to me now." He lowered his voice. "What I would give to have Fanta and Woolf with us now. They both knew that the assault was inevitable."

Baucus bowed his head. "I fear that they are lost."

"So what if they are?" Oskar said. "Shall we sit here and mourn, or face reality? They won't be returning to us, and I move that we act accordingly. The chancellor agrees with me on this point. I don't see what difference it makes, anyway."

Baucus lunged at Oskar. "You are entirely without honor!" he said, grasping at him as Alasdar and Landrew moved to restrain him. "If only we had sent you instead of them!"

"Sit down, Baucus!" Alasdar barked. "We must control ourselves—all of us. If the princess does not find her way back here by tomorrow—and it appears that she will not—then the fate of Harwelden, and of the empire, rests in our hands. There are five of us now. We must engage Waldemariam and address our plight in a way that confronts reality. In two days' time, I expect the attack on Harwelden to begin. We must stop the revelry in the city and plot the escape of our women and children. We must discuss our military strategies in depth. I cannot believe we have failed to respond to the enormity of the threat we face. We are failing our people and ourselves."

Baucus and Landrew nodded.

At the end of the table, Oskar, still absorbed in polishing his sword, said nothing.

"Has anyone taken notice of the river recently?" Alasdar said.

"What of it?" Oskar replied.

"It turns red, like blood."

"Do not start with this nonsense, Alasdar," Oskar scoffed.

"*At the end of the third age,*" Alasdar began, citing a passage from the scrolls, "*the necromancer, son of Malgothar, shall rise from the abyss, selecting a proxy from the ranks of his enemy.*" Disregarding his own appeal for civility, he glared at Oskar as he recalled each word of the verse. "*In his quest for resurgence, Valderon will guide his chosen one to unprecedented success, and the ferocity of the armies to the north shall grow beyond measure. As it was in the Age of Malgothar,*" Alasdar continued, his voice growing louder

Baucus lunged at Oskar.
"You are entirely without honor! ...
If only we had sent you instead of them!"

and more pointed, *"the armies from Angrelar will flourish across Vassalia, reclaiming for Valderon that which was taken from him, and Valderon's power shall blossom once more."*

Oskar glared at him.

"In the final days, the towers of the white city shall fall," Alasdar continued, in a lower voice now. *"And a great plague shall unleash itself within the walls of the city. In these times, the River Tantasar shall turn to blood."* Upon completing the verse, Alasdar stared at Oskar. "I quote from the eighty-third chapter of the Scrolls of Ondor."

"Do not presume to lecture me from the scrolls of the shamalans," Oskar said. I do not predicate my plans on shamalan fables. The color of the river is brought by the red tide, nothing more."

Like Alasdar, Landrew glared at Oskar. He continued quoting the verse, picking up where Alasdar left off. *"But in these final days, the heir to the great king shall rise up. Like his forefather, the Gayan will achieve impossible feats and will lead the armies of the white city to victory, repelling the hordes and restoring order to Vassalia. The new Gayan shall strive to unite the mighty Antiquitas. To the corners of the world shall he travel, though his success will not be certain until Valderon is banished to Hulgaar, never to return."*

"The heir to the great king," scoffed Oskar. "There *is no* heir to the great king. The shamalans are dead, fools. Though the assault against us is set to begin, the river has not turned to blood, and there is no plague within the walls of our city." Oskar scanned the other faces at the table. "Sarintha is dead. No doubt the boy is, too."

Baucus lunged at Oskar again. "What do you know of the princess?" he demanded, as Landrew and Alasdar dragged him back to his seat. Baucus was seething.

"Sarintha is dead," Oskar said. "In her failure to return to Harwelden, that fact has become clear."

"I do not believe it," Landrew said, bowing his head, the language of his body less certain than that of his claim.

"Believe what you want," Oskar replied. "But the time of the shamalans has passed, and the fate of Harwelden rests in our hands. For my part, I will fight. When the time comes, I will prepare myself for battle, and I will enter the fray. Until then, I will celebrate my final days in this world." And he stood and left the great hall.

$$\text{\ding{62} \ding{62} \ding{62}}$$

Outside, day turned to night, and the drunken laughter of the townspeople rang through the great hall. On and on, the music played.

Later that night, after the villagers had cleared the square, Alasdar, Baucus, and Landrew stole out into the courtyard beneath the castle. Hiding behind a corner of the edifice, they watched as Waldemariam assembled the troops. Under the cover of night, legions of grayfarers, gimlets, and men, warriors all, assembled to practice their maneuvers. Throughout the village, the army of Harwelden came forth. With steely eyes and sharpened blades, they entered their formations, prepared to receive instruction from their leader. Above them, Waldemariam hovered in the night sky, directing his generals, inspiring his troops.

From their hiding place, Baucus, Landrew, and Alasdar looked on with a mixture of hope and unease. Who was this grayfarer Waldemariam, from the unseen lands to the east? And what did they really know of him?

Chapter 43

The Susquat Council Decides

Elliott sat in stunned silence, scarcely able to believe the revelation that Hooks had risked execution by returning to his homeland. A thousand questions rushed through his mind. The surly arrogance that had characterized Hooks's every action since they first met was gone, and the great beast looked as exposed and vulnerable as a child. "What happened back then?" Elliott asked, laying a hand on his shaggy arm, "when your uncle died."

Hooks slumped in his chair, staring at his feet.

"Tell us what happened," Elliott urged. "When the elders come back, maybe there's something we can say to defend you."

"There is nothing you can say to defend me," Hooks whispered. "They can do nothing to me that I do not deserve." He looked up at him. "I loved my uncle deeply. He was strong, wise, and kind, beloved by all Susquatania. He was a stronger chieftan even than my father," he said quietly, as if ashamed to admit it. "After my parents' death, my uncle took Keats and me to raise. He reared us with a capable hand, and he loved us as much as we loved him. Because I was the slain chieftan's eldest son, I, not Keats, was next in line for the position of chieftan. But the murder of my parents filled me with rage. I never recovered from these wounds. As I grew into adulthood, I remained embittered in a way that Keats was not." He looked to Elliott, pleading for understanding.

"How were your parents killed?" Elliott asked softly.

"Keats was much younger than I," Hooks said, as if he hadn't heard the question. "As we grew into adulthood, Keats didn't remember them the way I did. All the while, the war between the shamalans and the serpans escalated. Gimlets in the surrounding villages were slain in droves, and the shameful acts of the serpan warlords went unpunished. Everything was out of control. But the serpans, who fear almost nothing, are afraid of the susquats." His eyes narrowed. "Then and now, they strive to appease us— to keep us either on their side or at least unengaged. In the days before my banishment, many of my race did not wish to become entangled in the escalating war—that is, until the day three members of the susquat ruling family were brutally slain. On that day, my parents and my aunt rode outside the forest. As they hunted in the valley just beyond the settlement, a band of young serpans, up to no good, stumbled across them. No one is sure exactly what transpired when the serpans accosted my family, but from what was pieced together at the time, they were captured and held prisoner for hours before their murder." He paused, looking up to the skies as if seeking a sign. The anguish reawakened by telling the story threatened to consume him. "The serpans who killed my family had nothing to do with the armies that crossed over into Lon Carafay. They were criminals, up to their own mischief, and they killed my family for sport. They tortured, murdered, and desecrated the bodies of my loved ones for no discernible reason. By that act, an entire civilization was thrown into chaos." His voice trailed off. "From that day forward, my race was torn. For me, that is the day everything changed."

Slipher, who had sat unnoticed at the end of the row, was suddenly animated. "I remember something about this," he said. "It happened before I was born, but I have heard the tale of the murder of your family. All this time I've traveled with you, I had no idea . . ."

"What do you know about it?" Woolf asked.

"It is as he describes," Slipher said. "Our leaders have always worked diligently to keep the susquats out of the conflict. It's clear to me that our leaders fear their involvement in the war. When the susquat chieftan was murdered, as the story goes, there was a cry of anger throughout all Vengala. The warlords who ruled in the days before the rise of Malus Lothar offered rewards to anyone with information about the murder. And they threatened dire punishments. In the end, it was the families of the murderers who gave up their whereabouts. Each of the serpans responsible was held accountable. In the end, they were killed for their crime. To make the lesson clear, their families were also killed. Indeed, the warlords killed the very serpans who turned in their kindred. Because of these events, my people remain wary of susquats. To this day, Malus Lothar is said to keep council with the beasts, if only to keep them out of the war."

Hooks nodded. "After the murder of my family, a group of warlords came to Susquatania and met with my uncle." His eyes narrowed as he told the tale. "Though my uncle was heartbroken at the loss of his wife and family, he was no fool. He struck an unholy bargain with them. In secret, they crafted an agreement that the susquats would not retaliate. In return, the warlords promised never to threaten the Susquatanian Valley. And in all the seasons since the drafting of that agreement, it has been well honored. The susquats have remained free of any entanglements and have lived here in the forest, untouched by the war."

Marvus spoke up. "I have never heard this before, but it makes sense. On many occasions, our shamalan nobles have met with the susquats in secret to discuss the war. Among others, King Gregorus himself once rode to Susquatania to plead with Keats, but to no avail. The susquats have always been firm in their neutrality."

"And that is the problem," Hooks said. "I was a child when the warlords came to meet with my uncle. But I remember it as if it were yesterday. I hid beneath a table in that very building," he said, pointing to the tree-castle, "and listened to the negotiations. I know it was a sacrifice for my uncle to forgo avenging his wife, and that he believed he served a greater good, but I held this against him all his days. I vowed that when I became chieftan, my parents would be avenged with the full wrath of the susquat army. As I grew into adulthood, the fire of revenge still smoldered within me. It was this disagreement that led to my uncle's death and separated me forever from my people. Then and now, I have vowed revenge on the serpans for their crimes. And before I go to my grave, even if I am to go soon, somehow I will have it."

"But if the serpans did not sanction the murder of your family," Elliott said, "and they punished those who committed the act, how can you be angry with them?"

Hooks glared at him. "The serpans do not value life. The whole of their culture celebrates the brutality that led to the murder of my parents. The warlords didn't punish the murderers because it was just; they punished them because they feared our involvement—solely to appease us." He gnashed his teeth. "Susquats know that life is a gift. *I* know that life is a gift and that each life is to be cherished. In our culture, we honor even the lives of the beasts of prey. We do not kill that which we don't need to survive. We do not tarnish the soil of our lands with the blood of innocents." He stopped and looked at Woolf. "This is what your Grayfarer Council has failed to understand about me, Woolf." I confess to the crimes I have committed over the many seasons since I was banished. But I have not caused the death of a single grayfarer. On the grave of my father, I am not guilty of the crimes you ascribe to me. Other than the prey that I must kill to survive, I do not have it within me to cause the death of another unjustly. I am a susquat. That is what it means to be susquat."

Woolf returned his gaze. "You're not making sense," he said. "You tell us you are not capable of murder. But in the next breath, you tell us you killed your uncle, who was beloved to you. And in yet another, you voice the desire for war. I myself harbor no such neutralities. I am a grayfarer. We are a warring race; I will fight whom I must to survive. If someone brings a battle to me, I will take a war to them. But you, Hooks, speak in vagaries. So which is it? You are responsible for taking the life of your chieftan, who was your own blood, or you are a pacifist, incapable of killing another. Either you cherish life or you pine for war."

A gleam filled Hooks's eyes. "Again you fail to listen. We susquats value life, and I will not take the life of an innocent. But the serpans are not innocents. They murder their own over a matter of pride and murder others for the sport of it. They are a vile foe that must be met with force. This is what I argued to my people in the days before my uncle's death. This is the issue we struggled with communally. Our reverence toward life is what has led to our pacifism. But not taking action against the serpans will lead to our downfall. A war with the serpans is not incongruent. In warring against murderers, we protect the lives of our innocents. And that is a noble pursuit."

"Then why did you kill your uncle?" Woolf asked.

"The issue of my uncle's death is between my people and me." He turned and looked to the castle. "Had I not been the eldest son of the ruling family, I would have received harsher treatment. My banishment was allowed only because my brother, who had always placed me on the highest pedestal, became the chieftan and because he and the Elder Council were heartbroken over what came about."

Just then the band of guards around them came to attention. "They're returning," said Woolf.

"You have heard the message we must take to them," Hooks said as the council approached. "It is the only message they might hear. To protect the lives of our innocents and yours, we must stand together to face the serpan threat. This is the argument I shall make to the Council of Elders. The empire will soon fall. When the serpans begin to build their settlements in Lon Carafay, my forest and my people will be next. They may fear us now, but the time of our war approaches." Hooks sat tall in his chair, buoyed by his own words.

With silent grace and a melancholy face, Chieftan Keats led the elders to their seats. As before, Keats and Hooks looked at each other as if no one else were present. Several seconds ticked by before Keats spoke.

"For the second time in my life, Hooks," he said, "you have broken my heart."

Hooks stared back at him.

"We are all in agreement," Keats said, motioning to the Council of Elders. "We will not hear your plea."

Hooks opened his mouth to protest. "If only you will listen, brother—"

"Silence!" boomed the chieftan, nodding to the guards as his eyes grew wet.

"You have to listen to me," Hooks pleaded.

Keats motioned for the guards to restrain him. "We have allowed you to tear us apart once before, and it will not happen again." His voice began to break. "Why must you keep wrenching us apart?" Guards flanked Hooks on three sides. "Take him," said Keats, motioning feebly with his hand as he stared at the ground. "Get him out of my sight."

Elliott winced as two guards took hold of his arms. One grabbed him by the throat, silencing him, while others grabbed his arms and legs and bound him. After subduing him, they pulled him away, into the castle.

In time, the square grew quiet, and Keats addressed Elliott. "I want to thank you for your friendship to my brother,"
he said. His voice shook. "We have heard of your presence in
these lands, and we wish you well, though a daunting task lies
before you."

Elliott gave him an uncomprehending look.

"It is no secret that the siege of Harwelden is about to
take place," the chieftan said. "To be honest, I do not see a path
to victory for you. But your presence has raised hope in some
quarters, and you must not tarry here."

"Then you will let us go?" Elliott asked.

"Yes, you may go."

Elliott struggled to find the right words. "Can you let
Hooks go, too?" he pleaded. "We need him, sir. We *really*
need him."

"Do not tempt your fate. Hooks has unfinished business
here. Today we have agreed, we must finish that business and
write an end to the chapter that he began long ago. These are
things that do not concern you."

"But—" Elliott started.

"No. And do not speak of him again. The equinox is approaching fast," Keats said in a softer tone, "and I do not see
how you have time to travel to Harwelden before it arrives."

For the first time since arriving in Susquatania, Jingo
spoke up. "Can you provide us with horses?" he asked.

"I can," Keats said, "if that is what you desire. I can provide you with the fastest mountain horses in all Lon Carafay,
but I do not think you will be able to get to Harwelden by horse.
The serpans and the Haviru have fanned out around Mount
Kalipharus as they prepare to assault your castle, and the surrounding territory is thick with malevosaur cavalry."

"Then what shall we do?" Jingo asked. "We have to get
back before the equinox."

Keats looked at each member of the group in turn. When his eyes fell on Slipher, he nodded to him. Nervously, as if unsure why the chieftan had nodded to him, Slipher nodded back.

Once again, Jingo was the one to break the silence. "We cannot push a boat upriver, and if we cannot go on horseback, how do you recommend we get back to Harwelden in time?"

Keats turned to one of his fellow elders. "Jarius," he said, "do we have any means to assist them in their return to Harwelden?"

"Perhaps," said the elder called Jarius, and he took a small bag from his pocket.

"Many seasons ago," Keats said, "the shamalan king Gregorus paid me a visit." He turned to Elliott. "He left a gift I have never made use of but that may benefit you."

Marvus stared eagerly at the bag. "If I may ask," he said, "is that a percurro you have in the bag?"

"Ah," Keats said. "I was hoping you might be familiar with the device. So you know how to use it, then?"

Marvus's voice rose in pitch. "I've never used one before, but I think I can work it out."

"What is it?" Elliott asked.

"In a moment, you shall find out," Keats replied. "I am pleased to offer it as a gift. I told King Gregorus at the time that he need not leave it, but he insisted." He leaned toward Elliott. "Now, if I may offer you some advice . . ."

"Yes."

"I do not know why you are here or where you came from, but it seems that you are unique in a way that most of us hope never to be."

"What way is that?"

"It appears that you are the last of your kind," he said. "Truly, the last of the shamalans." The elders nodded in agreement. "You have not come here seeking my advice, but before I offer this gift, I shall offer my opinion."

Elliott nodded.

"Though you surely do not realize the gravity of your own presence here, creatures throughout the whole of Lon Carafay have taken notice of you in the short time since your arrival. I do not claim to know everything that happens on this continent, but many things reach my ears. Your arrival has given birth to a buzzing of rumors, arising from the smallest living creatures to the most powerful figures in our world. Some say you are a savior, that your very appearance heralds something . . . important. They say that in you lies the hope of Harwelden and that through your strength, the tide of war shall turn."

Jingo spoke. "What say you, Chieftan?"

Keats narrowed his eyes. "Do not believe it, young shamalan. For the sake of your very life, do not believe it."

Elliott stared wide-eyed at the chieftan.

"Each life holds a promise," Keats continued. "Your life is no different in that regard. Do not waste that promise. Whatever it entails, you should get as far away from this place as you can, for it will only devour you. Go back to your home. Your life holds a promise for you to find, but you will not find it in this place."

"You know nothing of the promise of his life," Jingo growled. "And if you believe your own words, you will not execute Hooks. His life holds more promise than that of any susquat I see here."

Keats scowled at him. "I will let that comment pass," he said. "These times are charged with the emotions of war. But do not disrespect me, gimlet. As my brother Hooks shall find out, there are few second chances in Susquatania."

Despite his growing fury, Jingo remained quiet.

"Consider my advice," Keats said to Elliott. "I, alone among your counselors, have nothing to gain from you." Again he studied the group of prisoners, halting his gaze on Slipher. "Now, before I offer you my gift, I have one condition."

"And what is that, sir?" Marvus asked, clearly anxious to get his hands on the percurro.

"You will release this serpan into my custody."

"We will do no such thing," Woolf said. "The serpan will return with us to Harwelden."

"Choose your words carefully, grayfarer," Keats said. "It is a generous gift I offer. Without it, you have no chance of returning to Harwelden to stand by your brethren in their final days. Perhaps this is what you desire," he said, raising an eyebrow. "But if you wish to make use of this percurro, you will leave the serpan with me."

Slipher wriggled in his seat, obviously uncomfortable to be the topic of discussion. He looked from Woolf to Keats, then back to Woolf again, perhaps thinking of the pledge he had extracted from Elliott in the desert, or worried that the susquats would release him back to the serpans. "I want to go with them," he blurted. "I want to travel to Harwelden with the shamalan boy and the grayfarer."

Keats peered down at him for several seconds. "So be it," he said at last. "Jarius, take them to the edge of the forest and give them the percurro."

Then, with a swirl of his robe, he stood and walked away and, without a backward look, disappeared into the castle. One by one, the susquat elders, save for Jarius, stood and followed him. At last, Elliott, Woolf, Slipher, and the gimlets sat facing Jarius.

"Release the grayfarer's wings," Jarius said, directing his comments to one of the dozen guards who remained. A guard took out a flint knife and cut the bindings that held Woolf's wings.

"Now, follow me," Jarius said, standing. "All of you."

They followed as Jarius led them past the mammoths, into the living green cathedral of trees, and through the passage to the outer gate. The whole time, no one spoke. They had not even been given the opportunity to ask the susquats for help, and they had lost Hooks in the bargain. They followed Jarius through the entry and past the palisade gate to the outer forest.

When they were well outside the settlement, Jarius held out the sack containing the percurro in his massive hand. "I know you are saddened by the detention of your friend and our kinsman Hooks," he said. "No doubt you are disappointed by our refusal to let you plead your case. But this is an argument we have considered many times over. In some ways, it has come to define our culture. Had we let you make your argument, you would not have offered any persuasions we have not already considered. Chieftan Keats has a kind heart and a difficult task. He is heartbroken over his brother, Hooks, and has been since the day we forced Hooks from the settlement. I think, in some ways, Keats still sees in Hooks the strong older brother whom he adored as a child. However, Keats and the council are responsible for the welfare of all the susquats in the valley. Our numbers are greater than anyone might imagine, and his responsibilities to preserve life and civilization weigh heavily on him. Our decision to stay out of the war is well considered and final. Please do not think ill of us, for we wish none of you any harm, and we have no hidden motive. Keats has offered this percurro in a gesture of kindness, and in the hope that it will help you to achieve your aims, even though we will not be able to join you in war against the serpans. That is the real reason you came here, is it not?"

"Indeed," Woolf said, "that is the reason."

"Take this percurro, then, and rejoin your brethren. We are honored to host a member of the Grayfarer Council, despite the precaution of lashing your wings. We are also honored to host this young shamalan, who has been the cause of so much excitement during this past season. We will keep all of you in our thoughts." Jarius bowed his head, then turned and disappeared into the forest, leaving Elliott holding the sack that contained the percurro.

Inside the smooth cloth of the sack, Elliott felt a firm, flat, lenticular object that could have been a river pebble. He looked to Marvus. "What is it?" he asked. "And how is it going to help us?"

Marvus rushed to his side. "Take it out of the bag."

Slipher, too, moved closer. Eyeing Slipher suspiciously, Woolf grabbed him by the shoulder. "Before Elliott opens the bag," he said, "tell us why you didn't wish to remain with the susquats when Keats offered you the chance."

Slipher recoiled at his captor's touch. "If I stayed with the susquats," he said, "they would have turned me over to the warlords."

"Why would that be a problem?" Woolf asked. "When I captured you, were you not on a mission for Malus Lothar?"

Realizing his error, Slipher bowed his head. "I am an emissary of the malus," he said feebly.

"Stop it!" Jingo snapped, moving to Woolf's side. "Tell us the truth about what you were doing when he found you."

"I am . . ." Slipher looked around him, tears filling the corners of his eyes.

"Yes?" Woolf said.

"I deserted my regiment," he mumbled. Tears streamed down his face. "I did not mean to. I am no coward." His whole body shook. "I partook of the pipe and became besotted with it," he sobbed, "and when I awoke the next morning, my regiment was gone." His words came in gasps. "They . . . left me. I had no choice but to . . ." Overcome with emotion, he searched for the right words. "When they realized I was gone, they killed my family." He fell to his knees. "I thought, if I could capture Elliott for the malus, I could regain my status and return safely home. I thought it would save me from punishment. But then you found me . . ." Tears streamed down his face as great gasps for air replaced his sobs. "I had no choice but to come with you," he said. "I thought if I helped you, you might show me mercy. I thought Harwelden might show me mercy." He slumped, heaving as the tears streamed down his face.

Elliott knelt at his side. "It's all right," he said gently. "You've been a big help." He searched the faces of the others, seeking their support. "We will do what we can to help you."

"I didn't mean to do it," Slipher whispered.

"Enough of this," Woolf said. "Get up, serpan. I am ashamed for you."

Elliott glared at Woolf. "We'll do what we can for you, Slipher," he said, helping him stand. "I'm glad you decided to come with us." With Slipher back on his feet, Elliott untied the purse string and slid the percurro out onto his palm.

It was the size of a small seer stone, though flattened. The sunlight cascaded off its opalescent surface. Though no bigger than a dried apricot, it was surprisingly heavy. Elliott looked up at Marvus, who glowed with excitement.

Marvus couldn't take his eyes off it. "A percurro is a means of transport," he said. "A very rare device indeed. I am surprised that King Gregorus left it behind. He must have thought Keats would be willing to come to Harwelden. Perhaps he saw a chance to advance his negotiations."

"An object of transport?" Elliott asked. "How does it work?"

"Well," said Marvus, moving in closer, "I've never used one before, but I think we must all be touching it for the magic to work. If you are not in physical contact with the percurro, you will be left behind." He leaned in closer, inspecting the strange stone, though keeping his hands at his side as if he were afraid to touch it.

"What else?" Elliott asked. "We touch it and then what?"

Marvus's brow crinkled. "After that, I'm not sure."

"What do you mean, you're not sure?" Elliott replied. "You told the chieftan you knew how to use it."

"Think, Marvus," Woolf said. "If we don't know how to use it, then we are in a terrible plight indeed. I do not wish to reenter the susquat settlement to ask for instruction. Despite their kind words, we are lucky to have come away from there unscathed. If we can't figure out how to use the percurro, it will be many days' hard journey before we can reach Harwelden by land, and we haven't the time for that. The equinox comes the day after tomorrow."

Marvus stared at the pearly stone, concentrating.

Jingo moved in closer, staring at it. "What are those indentations on the surface?" he asked. "Is that some type of writing beneath your thumb, Elliott?"

Elliott held his palm flat. They had failed to notice the markings on the surface.

"They are instructions," Marvus said, "inscribed in Albian, the ancient tongue of the Exterus."

"What's it say?" Elliott asked.

"Give me a moment." Marvus's lips moved silently as he tried to translate the writing. He leaned over and studied the markings. Finally, he straightened up, beaming. "The journey begins in the heart of the traveler," he said.

Elliott was shaken. *The journey begins in the heart of the traveler.* It was a phrase his mother used to use. "So we touch the stone and make a wish for where we want to go?"

"Sounds easy enough," Woolf said, stepping closer. "Let's get on with it."

Marvus nodded. With Elliott holding the percurro in the palm of his hand, the others gathered around him and each touched the stone.

"Everybody ready?" Marvus asked. He closed his eyes, and the others did the same. "We wish to travel to Harwelden."

With Elliott holding the percurro in the palm of his hand, the others gathered around him and each touched the stone.

Nothing happened.

Marvus opened his eyes. "I don't understand."

"The journey begins in the heart of the traveler," Jingo repeated. "If there is more than one traveler, then the journey must begin in the *hearts* of the *travelers*. If there is one among us who does not wish to go, it may affect the magic." He looked to Woolf, Marvus, then Elliott. One by one, they nodded. When Jingo's eyes fell on Slipher, he looked away.

Woolf looked ready to strangle him. "What is it you want, serpan?" he demanded. "We haven't time for this." Woolf shook his fist in the air, causing Slipher to flinch. "Either you want to stay here or you want to go with us. Either will suffice. Which is it?"

Slipher sobbed.

Elliott stepped between Slipher and Woolf. "What is it that you want, Slipher?"

Slipher's body shook. He stood hunched before him, wringing his hands. In that moment, he looked old. "I just don't want to die," he said meekly. "If I stay here, I will be recaptured by the susquats and returned to my people, where I will die a shameful death. If I go with you, I will be tried and executed—Woolf has said so himself. It is over for me."

Woolf shrugged. "We need to use the percurro," he said. "With or without him."

"It is true, Elliott," Marvus said. "We need to get going."

Unsatisfied, Elliott looked again at Slipher, searching for a way to comfort him, though he knew that his concerns were valid.

"If you don't go with us, Slipher," he said, "what would you do?"

"I have nowhere to go. There is nowhere I will be safe."

"Then you should go with us, Elliott said, but you must decide that is the course of action you want to take. If you are not in agreement, then we have to leave without you." He searched his mind for something else to say to him. "Each life is a gift," he started, repeating the words of Keats. "And each life has promise. Your life has promise as well, Slipher. You just need to find out what that promise is. I know that somehow, there is more you have to offer. I want you to return with us to Harwelden." He looked again to the others for support. "I am sure your knowledge of the serpan military will have some value at Harwelden. From my heart, I promise to take up your cause if you come with us. So I am offering to take a chance on you, but you must decide to take a chance on us as well."

Slipher sobbed. Woolf glared.

"I will go with you to Harwelden," Slipher whispered.

"Enough, then," Elliott said. "Let's try it again." For the second time, he held the percurro in his palm, and the others encircled him, each reaching out to touch it. Standing in a tightly huddled circle, with the trees of Susquatania whispering in the breeze all around them, they squeezed their eyes shut. "We wish to travel to Harwelden."

Without warning, a cold breeze blew, chilling him to the bone. From behind his eyelids, he sensed darkness. Then he was falling. End over end, he tumbled through the blackness. Coldness washed over him. Then, as quickly as it had come, the sensation evaporated. Finally, he fell to the ground with a thud, striking his shoulder hard against the ground.

Slowly he opened his eyes. The sound of music filled his ears. He looked up to see the others lying all around him. Before them stood the gate to Harwelden. After a season of traveling the continent, they had returned to the very spot where he once stood, contrived bandages covering his birthmarks, while Marvus negotiated their entrance to the village.

Chapter 44

The Vise Tightens

"Ready the trebuchets," Viscount Ecsar barked. He sat at a table in his makeshift command center in the heart of the Forest of Ondor, not far from where Princess Sarintha had been captured barely a season ago. "Inform the troops that the day is upon us. In the morning, we march to the base of Mount Kalipharus and begin, at long last, the siege of Harwelden."

The warlord seated across from him grinned and nodded. The tension that arose between them when Ecsar took command of the troops had vanished as the warlord, like his troops, basked in the presence of the legendary commander.

Ecsar drank from his horn of mead, relishing it. All around him, officers of the serpan forces made their final preparations. "Tomorrow," he continued, "the assault on the castle begins, and there is nothing the grayfarer dogs can do to stop us."

The warlord stood. "I will see that the troops are ready." With a bow of his head, he ducked under the tent flap and was gone.

Viscount Erebus remained at the table with Ecsar, sharpening his blade. "The river is blockaded from both north and south. The Haviru siege weapons are assembled. Our troops have surrounded the mountain, and we are three legions deep on all sides. Everything is in place, my friend. All they await is your command."

Ecsar smiled. "The malus will arrive by sky chariot later tonight," he said. "We must make sure all is in order." Taking another draft of mead, he said, "And what of the matter in Susquatania? Has that been handled?"

Erebus nodded. "The susquat threat, as you like to call it, is no threat at all. The chieftan has been well recompensed for his loyalty." A toothy grin stole over his face. "If you want my opinion, he has been overpaid. With Harwelden in the state she is in, the susquats are not fools enough to side with her forces."

"What do we know of the princess and Grimaldi?" Ecsar asked. "Has she been seen since you spotted her in the river?"

"What difference does it make?" Erebus sneered. "She is a child. She poses no threat."

"I did not ask your opinion."

Erebus bowed his head. "She has not been seen, though we believe she and the grayfarer captain made it to the castle."

Ecsar scowled. "And what about this boy on everyone's lips?"

Erebus shifted uncomfortably in his seat. "The susquats have sent word that they released him. The news has just reached my ears."

"Curse those beasts!" Ecsar snarled. "The malus will be furious."

"The chieftan accepts our payments but plays it right down the middle."

"I assume, then, that you have sent a party to find the boy?"

"Well," Erebus said, "the thing is . . ."

"The thing is what?"

"The chieftan provided the boy with a percurro." Erebus looked at Ecsar, trying to assess his level of rage. "So I did not send a party to search for him. The boy has surely used the talisman to go wherever it is he wanted to go."

"The malus wants him dead."

"With due respect to the malus, the boy does not matter. No matter if he stands from the highest tower of Harwelden, waving the very Scrolls of Ondor, he will be mowed down like the rest of them."

"I agree," Ecsar said, "but it is a failure on our part that the princess—and perhaps the boy, too—have returned safely to Harwelden."

"More rats in the trap."

"All right, then." Ecsar got to his feet. "I want to inspect the trebuchets."

Erebus pushed back from the table and stood, and together the darfoyle commanders marched into the forest.

A short time later, they arrived at the riverfront. Dozens of the fearsome trebuchets, heavy war engines for hurling large stones, lined the riverbanks. Behind them, the massive hulls of the Haviru fleet jammed the river. Haviru crews scuttled about the siege engines, readying them for transport to the base of the mountain.

The bustle of the war preparations pleased Ecsar. He turned his gaze northward, toward Toltuga, where the camps of his warriors filled the horizon. A grin stole across his face. "This is better than I imagined," he said. He turned back toward the river and approached the line of trebuchets as the Haviru crewmen nearly fell over one another to clear a path. "Will they be ready?" he asked a crewman greasing the huge wheels that would soon roll his trebuchet within reach of the castle wall.

"Yes sir!" the crewman said. "We await your command."

"Excellent," Ecsar said, caressing the massive catapult's huge wooden bucket. Side by side, Erebus and Ecsar strolled down the riverbank. Walking southward, they encountered several rows of smaller catapults, platforms of stones large and small, and several rows of wallflies—smaller, more precise weapons that would be used to assault Harwelden's wall at close range.

In the distance, Malus Lothar's sky chariot approached. Dangling from thick hawsers carried by four soaring golgomites, the chariot grew larger on the horizon. As it passed over the massive base camp, a chorus of cheers greeted it. Still grinning, Ecsar turned to Erebus. We will meet with the malus tonight," he said. "It won't be long now."

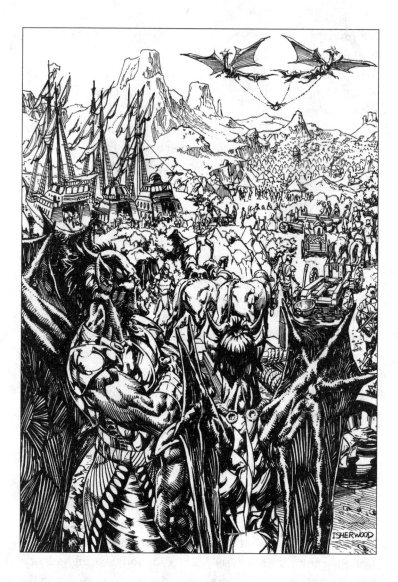

We will meet with the malus tonight," he said.
"It won't be long now."

Chapter 45

A Cold Reception

Elliott looked around them and quietly pocketed the percurro. He marveled at how quickly they had returned to Mount Kalipharus after so many weeks of arduous travel. The others brushed themselves off and clustered near him as the final rays of daylight trickled down the mountaintop. Harwelden's massive drawbridge loomed ahead, and on either side of the gate, the guards chatted casually. A titter of laughter filtered down. Meanwhile, almost imperceptibly, the topmost leaves of the surrounding trees shriveled as Elliott and his friends, still unseen by the guards, vanished.

"How are we going to get inside?" Elliott whispered. Before anyone could reply, the ratcheting mechanism of the drawbridge creaked, making him jump, and the drawbridge began to descend. "Someone from the village is leaving," he whispered. It was an unbelievable stroke of luck. Grinning, he grabbed Marvus's sleeve and pulled him out of the way.

When the drawbridge was down, a platoon of armored warriors bearing swords and axes galloped through the gate and thundered down the trail. When the last of them was through, the ratcheting mechanism once again started up and the drawbridge began to rise.

"Quick!" Elliott hissed, and they rushed through, with Jingo only barely managing to shinny up onto the rising drawbridge.

With the final rays of sunlight filtering down, gimlets, men, women, and the occasional grayfarer scurried about the cobbled walkways. Music played in the distance, and sounds of gaiety filled the streets. Before him, the Gateway Plaza was abuzz. The central fountain, lit by torches at the edges of the square, arced its streams high into the air as merchants down below peddled sweetmeats and strong drink, and children frolicked under the watchful eyes of their nursemaids. The city's festive air struck Elliott as strange in light of the impending assault. He looked to the far end of the square, where the entrance to the Boulevard of Kings led toward the castle, when a clamor arose from one of the guard towers.

"Over there!" yelled a guard. "It's the boy and the gimlets. There's a serpan with them, and they've got Councilman Woolf! Seize them!"

Looking up at the accusing guard, Elliott realized that in letting himself get caught up in the sights, he had unwittingly let his attention stray and allowed them all to become unmasked. As the leaves of the trees surrounding the square shriveled, again he and his friends disappeared. Chiding himself for letting his focus wander, he whispered, "Run to the Boulevard of Kings!"

At the entrance to the boulevard, the statue of King Gregorus was now complete. The likeness of Sarintha's father wielded a weapon that, Elliott supposed, must be the Antiquitas Trident of lore. Behind them, the north end of the city filled with warriors, and a wave of guards rushed past them toward the square. In the distance, a horn call signaled the city to a state of vigilance.

Dodging merrymakers and guards, Elliott, the two gimlets, Woolf, and Slipher pelted down the boulevard. With the spires of the castle looming ahead, the cobbled road widened, and various shops and meeting halls appeared on either side. To the left was a tailor shop, to the right a shop that sold ancient maps. Farther down the road, a tavern's sign hung over the boulevard. Torches lit the door of the pub, which was carved from a heavy, dark wood.

Marvus grasped Elliott's sleeve. "Follow me."

"And pay attention, Elliott," Woolf growled. "No more mistakes."

The interior was dark, illuminated only by the candles that flickered on every table. The barkeeper was a grizzled old man with a patch over one eye. In the corner, a band played on lutes and horns, animating the darkened space with a lilting air that seemed out of place.

The clientele here seemed different from the people Elliott had seen in the square or on the boulevard. They were rougher and gruffer and less genteel. In one corner, a tall, weathered grayfarer muttered to himself, periodically slurping from a pitcher. He seemed to be well into his cups, and it was not clear to whom he addressed his occasional remarks.

Elliott was suddenly struck with an idea. He squeezed his eyes shut and concentrated. The lights of the candles flickered, and as the candlelight regained force, Elliott appeared as a withered old man leading a crew of miscreants to the empty booth. Though well disguised, each member of the party retained a hint of his own appearance. Marvus, who appeared as a one-eyed gimlet of advanced years and boorish demeanor, was the first to speak. "Over here," he said, nodding to Elliott. In ones and twos, they went over to an empty table in the far corner and sat. Even Slipher, disguised as a toothless black rat, scurried up onto the windowsill by the table. When all were seated, Woolf spoke, and the others leaned in closely.

"I cannot understand what I see before me," he whispered. He appeared as a rather rough-looking sailor. "The equinox will occur on the day after tomorrow. According to the susquats and my sources in the trail," he said, referring obliquely to Taldar, "that is when the serpans will begin their assault. I expected fortifications and evacuations of the women and children. I expected militia on the towers and in the streets. I do not comprehend why the buildup to the festival is under way as if everything were normal. Do they not know that the war of the ages awaits them in a matter of hours?"

"I, too, find it strange," Marvus said, his voice uncharacteristically gruff. "It is almost as if they are being led quietly to the slaughter."

"Or their hubris is too great to anticipate the defeat that awaits them," said Jingo, who appeared as a peasant youth. "They fritter away their last hours celebrating because they cannot believe they will be defeated. Such is the weakness of an empire that has been so great for so long."

"Perhaps," Marvus replied, "but what can we do about it?"

"We must make contact with the council and the princess," said Woolf. "We must find a way to present ourselves without being treated as fugitives, and we must restore the princess to power if she still lives. If the council has made some manner of preparation for the attack, then we can fight for Harwelden as the shamalans would have wanted it."

"But how can we present ourselves to the council?" Elliott asked.

"There is only one way," Woolf replied. "We sneak into the castle, unmask ourselves before the council, and demand to see the princess."

"Easy as that?" Marvus mumbled skeptically.

"Then you make a suggestion," Woolf growled, loudly enough to draw stares from the nearest tables.

"I see no other path than the one Woolf suggests," Jingo whispered as the nearby customers returned to their own conversations. "And we have one thing on our side."

"What's that?" Marvus asked.

I do not comprehend why the buildup to the festival is under way as if everything were normal. Do they not know that the war of the ages awaits them in a matter of hours?"

"Elliott, of course," Jingo replied, beaming. "He has mastered the bracelet of the nine clans. He can appear in whatever form he likes. All he has to do is use the bracelet to prove that he is the heir to King Griogair."

Woolf raised an eyebrow, as if he had not considered this.

"And have any of you contemplated the feats that Elliott performed when he caused us to pass through the Haviru ships as if we were spirits?" Jingo continued excitedly. "I'll bet that took even Crosslyn by surprise."

"What about it?" Elliott asked.

Jingo closed his eyes and cited a verse from the Scrolls of Ondor: *"In the final days, as the towers of the white city fall, they will watch for his return. At last, the heir to the great king shall arrive. Though many will shun him, his actions will declare his true name. In battle, they will know him as Shadowcaster."* Jingo shivered after completing the verse. "Don't tell me you haven't thought about it," he said to Marvus.

"If only those words could be true," Marvus said wistfully. "I am not saying it's impossible, but it *is* a bit of a leap."

"What in the world is a Shadowcaster?" Elliott asked.

Before anyone could answer, something hit him hard in the side of the head, knocking him to the ground. This broke his concentration, causing them to appear in their true forms. Standing above Elliott was the giant grayfarer they had seen on their way in. He had removed his cloak to reveal himself as an officer of the grayfarer army.

Before Elliott could regain his composure, the grayfarer reached down and snapped the bracelet of the nine clans from his wrist. He barked a series of orders, and three patrons at a nearby table hurried over. Removing their robes, they, too, revealed themselves to be warriors.

"It is true, then," said one of them, standing above Elliott. The boy has returned, and he travels with the gimlets and a serpan."

And if I am not mistaken," said the leathery grayfarer, "Councilman Woolf keeps his company as well." His words dripped with contempt. "Bind them all."

Woolf spread his wings. "You will do no such thing!" His booming voice drew every eye in the tavern. "I am an officer of the court, and I travel with the stewards of the princess and a true shamalan. Step away from us and call off your henchmen."

The old grayfarer stood his ground, though seeming unsure what to do.

"Step away!" Woolf bellowed.

The grayfarer looked to his three soldiers as if searching for guidance, though they offered none. He turned to Woolf. "It is true that you outrank me," he said, "but I insist that you accompany me to the castle. You are not above reproach." He glared at Woolf. The soldiers moved to his side, hands on their sword hilts.

"I would not be so quick to challenge a member of the council if I were you."

"Much has changed in the past season," the grayfarer officer said. "What you find here may surprise you. Now, will you come peacefully?"

"We will accompany you, but you will treat my companions and me with the respect I have earned."

The grayfarer motioned to the door. Woolf marched down the center of the boulevard, with Elliott and the others following close behind, and the grayfarer from the pub and his soldiers bringing up the rear.

Slipher, visibly frightened, moved next to Elliott. "Will you keep your word and speak on my behalf when we go before the council?"

"Of course," Elliott said.

"They are going to kill me, you know."

Elliott was unsure what to say, for he might well have little influence on Slipher's fate.

"In exchange for helping me," Slipher said, "will you accept a gift?" He reached into his pocket. "Take these possessions and keep them safe," he said, taking the pipe, tobacco pouch, and mirror from his pockets. "They are the most valuable things I own." He stuffed them into Elliott's pocket.

Townspeople crowded the boulevard. Some of them shouted encouragement, though others reviled them. All around, skirmishes arose as the people argued over whether the gimlets were traitors and whether Elliott was shamalan. And from all quarters, merry music played.

Like an improbable pied piper, Woolf led the way to the castle with a growing mob behind him. The soldiers elbowed nearer them as the chaos surrounding their discovery grew. Soon they reached the courtyard outside the castle, and right away they were led inside and up to the great hall, where the Grayfarer Council, save for Waldemariam, Fanta, and Woolf, was assembled.

Councilman Oskar was the first to see them. Upon seeing Woolf, the blood drained from his face. Without a word, he shifted his gaze to Elliott.

Alasdar smiled warmly at Woolf, who then locked eyes with Oskar.

"Summon Chancellor Waldemariam," Oskar said.

Chapter 46

Marvus Makes His Case

M oments later, Waldemariam lurched into the hall, looking dazed and unkempt and presenting a countenance uncharacteristic of his regimented personality. His thick hair flew wildly in all directions, and he was shirtless, looking the part of a mead-addled patron from the tavern rather than the chancellor of the empire. By smell and appearance, it appeared that he had not bathed in weeks.

"What is this about?" he demanded, staring at Woolf as he took his seat.

"Greetings, Chancellor," Woolf said, though he appeared confused by the brusque greeting. "I return today to report on my mission and to join my brothers in the fight for our home."

Waldemariam's eyes narrowed as if he strove to recall some distant memory. "Give your report."

"As you know," Woolf said, "I departed last season, with Councilman Fanta at my side and at your behest, to capture the gimlet stewards, locate this shamalan boy, and capture the fugitive susquat. I am pleased to report that I succeeded on all counts."

"Where is Councilman Fanta," barked Waldemariam, his eyes darting across the room.

"I have not seen him since the days after we departed the castle," Woolf replied.

"Nor do I see the fugitive susquat," said Waldemariam, leaning back in his chair. "So I do not understand your claim of success on this count."

Unsettled by the chancellor's odd behavior, Woolf surveyed the rest of the councilmen. They, too, appeared confused by Waldemariam's erratic tone.

Oskar put a hand on Waldemariam's shoulder. "Yes, Councilman," he said. "Please do tell us of your journey."

Over the next several minutes, Woolf recounted his early separation from Councilman Fanta, his capture of Slipher, and his tracking and ultimate success in locating Elliott, Marvus, Jingo, and Crosslyn. After mentioning Crosslyn's name, Oskar stopped him.

"You say you met a shamalan named Crosslyn?" Oskar queried, leaning forward.

"We did," Woolf said. "Crosslyn was priest to the court of King Dagnar and has been in hiding since the time of the Great Betrayal."

"I know who Crosslyn is," Oskar huffed. "Where is he now? Why isn't he with you?"

Woolf looked sideways at Elliott. "Crosslyn did not survive our journey. He died at the border of Ondor and Toltuga. We were under assault by a serpan malevosaur brigade."

Oskar stared at Woolf. "A true shame," he said finally, turning his glare to Elliott. "I have sat on this court for many years, yet I had no idea that a powerful sorcerer—from the court of Dagnar, no less—remained alive." He tapped his fingers on the table. "We have always believed that Dagnar and his court perished during the Great Betrayal." He raised an eyebrow as if considering it. "Curious, though, that we have not heard from this shamalan priest in three generations. How do you explain it?"

"I will ask Marvus to address your question."

Oskar slammed his fist on the table. "It is *you* I have addressed my question to, Councilman," he said. Now, answer me."

Without a word, Woolf walked toward Oskar, stepping up on the dais and towering over him.

The onlookers gasped.

Woolf leaned forward, putting his face just inches from Oskar's. "While you may feel comfortable speaking to me like that in private," he said, "remember always that you shall not take such license when we are in public."

Oskar glared but kept silent.

Still standing on the dais, Woolf turned his attention to the befuddled Waldemariam. "You need to get your council in order, Chancellor." With that, Woolf jumped behind the dais. As he took his seat at the table, he placed a hand on Alasdar's shoulder.

"Good to have you back," whispered Alasdar.

Woolf nodded. "Now, Marvus," he said, "please tell Councilman Oskar and the rest of us of the events that led to your meeting with Crosslyn, and of your understanding of his motivation for hiding in the wilderness all this time."

Marvus recounted the night Jingo came to his room after meeting Hooks. In great detail, he told how this meeting eventually led to his own decision to free Hooks and Elliott and go in search of Crosslyn—all in the service of the empire, he was careful to point out. The room grew quiet as he told of the attack by the dire wolves in the Azure Mountains, and the group's realization that Malus Lothar was tracking them through the eyes of the beasts. To everyone's astonishment, he told of their journey through the Forest of Golroc, their capture by the salax, and how Hooks returned with Crosslyn and the satyral to rescue them. He never mentioned the wedjat, though he discussed Crosslyn at length, making the point that Crosslyn believed Elliott to be the shamalan forecast in the Scrolls of Ondor. He told of Elliott's success with the bracelet of the nine clans, making Elliott blush.

Finally, Marvus told of their meeting with Woolf and Slipher, the journey to Susquatania, and their encounter with

Marvus told of Elliott's success with the
bracelet of the nine clans, making Elliott blush.

the Haviru and the malevosaur brigades just north of the castle. During this part of the story, he glossed over the details regarding Crosslyn's death, to avoid putting Elliott in an awkward position. As he neared the end of his stirring tale, he told of their meeting with the susquats, and the revelation that Hooks was the brother of the chieftan. He recounted the imprisonment of Hooks, and the gift of King Gregorus's percurro.

"And that," he concluded, "is the whole remarkable tale. It was not long after reaching Harwelden that we were captured in the tavern by the grayfarer who stands at my side. I am aware that we took grave license with the decisions we made during our journey, but please judge us by our intentions. Jingo and I have served the shamalan nobles nearly all our days, and we acted in a manner they would have supported." Finished, he bowed his head, and stepped back.

Woolf smiled, obviously thinking that Marvus had done well.

Oskar leaned forward. "This story you tell paints you and your companions in a much different light than you were seen in after your flight. But who knows if what you say is true?"

"*I* know that what he says is true," Woolf said. "And this council should require nothing more."

"Oh, but we *do* require more," Oskar said. "We require a great deal more." He leaned back in his chair, adopting a sinister tone. "Each of us was present at the trial of the susquat, and the evidence against him was indisputable." He turned to Woolf. "You yourself were quick to assign blame after hearing the evidence."

At this, Baucus, Landrew, and Alasdar nodded. And slowly, as if considering the notion, Waldemariam nodded as well.

From somewhere in the back of the room, a hooded figure approached and stood next to Elliott.

"And for the past seasons," Oskar continued, seeming not to notice the hooded newcomer, "we have pondered the identity of the traitor who tells our secrets to the enemy." He glared at Marvus. "Why should I believe the tale spun before me today, when reason dictates that the traitors are those who fled the inquiries of the empire and have returned to this hall only under threat of force? If we are to consider this idea that you and Jingo are not the traitors," he said, "then whom might we suspect?" His eyes narrowed. "And please explain to me, Woolf, why I should not suspect you as well? The mighty Woolf, who has gone missing all this time, only to return with those who stand accused of high treason—and a *serpan*, of all things."

Slipher recoiled, moving closer to Elliott.

Baucus, Landrew, and Alasdar turned to Woolf. Following their lead, Waldemariam did the same.

"The answer to your question is simplicity itself," Woolf said. "Our veracity can be determined right here and now."

"Please share with us how," Oskar smirked.

"Give Elliott the bracelet," Woolf said. "If we believe the shamalan lore—and we have no reason not to—only an heir to King Griogair can use the magic of the bracelet. If what we say is true, then a simple demonstration should suffice."

All eyes turned to Elliott, who suddenly felt very small. Then the hooded figure next to him stepped forward.

Oskar seethed. "Who dares to place himself before me as I deal with these matters!" he demanded. "Who dares!"

The guards in the back of the room sank back, frightened by Oskar's tone. And as everyone in the room looked on in astonishment, the hooded figure threw back the robe. It was Princess Sarintha.

Chapter 47

The Wand

As if on cue, a gust of autumn wind blew through the window. Oskar sat in stunned silence, staring at the princess.

Sarintha reached inside her frock and withdrew the fabled Wand of Griogair. And as quickly as it had come, the breeze abated, and the hall fell deathly silent.

"Princess!" Oskar said. "How wonderful to see you after all this time!" He looked nervously at the other councilmen.

Sarintha's face was ice. She raised the wand.

"What is it you have there?"

Without a word, she held the wand before her, aiming it at Oskar. Despite the tension in the room, her hand remained rock steady. The trials she had borne during the past season showed now in her face. She glared at Oskar, oozing an almost palpable abhorrence.

Oskar raised his hand, holding it between himself and Sarintha in a feeble gesture of defense. "What is it you have there?" he asked again.

Without answering, Sarintha shifted her gaze from Oskar to Waldemariam. Though the chancellor returned her gaze, his expression was odd, as if he failed to comprehend the significance of her return, or the source of her aggression toward them. She aimed the wand at him.

Marvus reached toward her and placed a hand on her shoulder. "I am overjoyed to see you," he whispered. "Jingo and I have long feared you dead."

Sarintha's icy glare went unbroken.

"I don't know what you have in mind," Marvus said, "but now is a time for reconciliation."

She brandished the wand at Waldemariam. After several long seconds, she spoke. "I hold in my hand the Wand of Griogair, Chancellor. Are you familiar with this artifact?"

Waldemarian nodded. Then, perhaps thinking better of it, he shook his head.

"The wand was fashioned by the shamalan priest Merkelo, for his master, King Griogair, to be used in battle against Valderon himself. The wand holds a terrible power—a power that has never been used."

Waldemariam snorted, shifting in his seat. He seemed to sense that he was in danger.

"I have watched as our empire fell from lofty heights to historic depths," she continued, "all during your tenure as chancellor." Her hand never wavered. "I followed you blindly through the reign of my beloved father, who believed you infallible. And I witnessed your failure firsthand when his position in Prytania was betrayed, ending in his slaughter at the hands of a darfoyle as he prepared his attack on the city."

Just a few feet from her, Slipher shifted his weight uncomfortably. His eyes darted between the council and the princess.

"I wanted to believe in you, Waldemariam," she said wistfully. "In all my life, I have never known a more capable warrior. During your rise, you inspired no one more than me. But a chill wind accompanied your ascendance. Despite your magnificent skills and your majestic gift for oratory . . ." She paused for a moment, her stony gaze fixed on the befuddled Waldemariam. "And despite those who believed you to be the harbinger of all things good to Harwelden, look where we find ourselves now. Very soon we shall suffer an attack from the deadliest force ever assembled against our home. We are threatened with loss not only of life and property but of our very soul—of what it means to be of Harwelden. Over the ages, our civilization has blossomed into a beacon of goodness and light. Our justice and culture is renowned over the globe. Travel to any corner of this greatest of worlds, and you will find those who know the glory of Harwelden. But it is no more. Our descent into chaos has been swift and complete. And it has happened under your inept leadership."

Many of the spectators in the hall nodded in agreement.

"Though the chaos began in earnest with the murder of my father, it has simmered throughout your seasons as chancellor. Not since the Great Betrayal has Harwelden endured such cataclysmic betrayal as it has under your tenure." Her voice gained strength as, all the while, she brandished the wand, giving the sense that her lecture represented the final words of a judge before execution of a sentence.

"Now, see here, Your Highness!" Oskar shouted. "You have no—"

"Silence!" she roared, shaking the wand at him and holding her gaze on Waldemariam. "Since the death of my father," she said, "I have known of your misdeeds. And I have reached an awful realization over the past season, during which I was captured by the serpan lord, marched through the burning sands of Toltuga, and tortured in the chambers of Mount Sitticus. I have seen my armies slaughtered as they fought to defend our once-mighty empire, their lives have been needlessly snuffed—countless lives extinguished so that one terrible soul may live in comfort despite the horrors surrounding us. And when my general and I escaped the confines of the enemy's castle and suffered the insult of his chase, we returned, finally, to our beloved home." She paused to cast her baleful gaze across the row of seated councilmen, accusing them. "Though I am the undisputed heir to the throne of this empire, I was met as a fugitive.

My general and I were placed in the bowels of the dungeons, where the foulest of criminals have been imprisoned during my family's long dynasty, and we were left there to die of thirst and hunger. Let it be known that this was perpetrated by your own hand and through your primary henchman, Councilman Oskar." She glared at Oskar. "Over the seasons, Harweldenites have asked themselves many times, 'Who is the terrible soul who moves against us?' Today, before all who will listen, and as the true and rightful heir to the shamalan throne, I declare that the traitor to Harwelden is Waldemariam himself!"

Gasps of disbelief erupted throughout the chamber.

"So I stand before you now as judge and jury, Chancellor," she said. "Today is the day we begin to right the wrongs you have heaped upon us. Though I fear that justice has come too late, it has come nonetheless. Offer your prayers to the elders, Waldemariam. When I shake this wand before me, justice will come to you. And a terrible justice it will be."

Slowly Waldemariam stood. The befuddled expression was gone from his face, and for the first time in a great while, his eyes shone with understanding.

Sarintha raised her wand.

Slipher, who had gone unnoticed throughout the entire affair, suddenly lunged at the princess. In an instant, he closed the ground between them, and before anyone could grasp what was happening, he dived, snatching the wand from her outstretched hand and tumbling to the floor with it in his grasp. From the spectators—Sarintha, Elliott, and the gimlets included—hardly a muscle moved as the scrawny serpan rolled across the floor with the stolen wand and nimbly got to his feet. He stood before them, grinning, and raised the wand.

Sarintha roared, "When I shake this wand before me,
justice will come to you. And a terrible justice it will be."

Chapter 48

Slipher's Revenge

As Sarintha stood speechless, glaring at Slipher, a gleam of understanding brightened Waldemariam's eyes, and it seemed that whatever spell had entranced him was at last broken.

A crooked grin stole across Slipher's lips as he brandished the wand, realizing that at last he had the upper hand.

"What are you doing, Slipher?" Elliott asked. His tone was measured, as if trying to coax a bone from a growling dog.

Slipher straightened his back and turned to face Elliott, pointing the wand at him.

Sarintha stepped toward him. "Give me the wand," she said, holding out her hand. "I don't know who you are, but give it to me now or you will meet severe justice."

"Stay away from me!" he shrieked, pointing the wand at her. "My quarrel is not with you."

Flummoxed, she stepped back. "Do not shake the wand," she said carefully. "It holds power you cannot possibly control."

Slipher glared at her, shaking the wand just enough to make her flinch. "It seems you are in no position to give orders," he replied.

She stepped back to stand at Elliott's side.

Waldemariam, Woolf, and the gimlets looked on in impotent horror, for no one knew what the ancient relic might do.

Elliott looked at Sarintha, seeing her for the first time, and realized that she was the young woman he had dreamed of outside Golroc. "Don't do this, Slipher," he said. He turned to face the council.

Unmoved, Slipher pointed the wand at him.

"This serpan helped us return to Harwelden," Elliott said, turning to address the council. "The testimony given by Councilman Woolf and Marvus is true. We encountered the shamalan priest Crosslyn in the Forest of Golroc. After Crosslyn saved us from the salax, we set out by boat to Susquatania. During our journey, we encountered the Haviru." His voice was strong. "During this encounter, Crosslyn fell gravely ill. We came under heavy fire from the serpans. In the scrub forest at the outskirts of Ondor, Crosslyn succumbed to his illness and was lost to us." Telling of Crosslyn's death was hard. He felt blood rush to his face, but he was determined to continue. All the while, Slipher aimed the wand at him.

"Though we escaped the serpans," he continued, "we got lost in the desert. For hours we struggled to find our way out, but a sandstorm came up, and we were hopelessly lost." He turned to face Slipher. "It was with this serpan's help that we got out of the desert. Because of him, we escaped certain death and completed our journey to Susquatania. Whatever grievances you have with his race notwithstanding, he helped us."

Waldemariam nodded. "Go on," he said.

"When we arrived in Susquatania, Slipher—for that is his name—was offered release by the susquats." The timbre of Elliott's voice changed to something very close to fondness. "But he chose to continue with us. He told me that he had no place with the serpans and that he would take his chances at Harwelden. When he made this decision, I assured him that I would speak for him. I assured him that I would try to repay the kindness he showed us after Crosslyn's death, and that the authorities at Harwelden would know of his acts."

Waldemariam nodded. "Put down the wand, Slipher," he commanded. "And we will discuss your case." His voice was not threatening. "Your good deeds will be considered."

Slipher sneered at him. "I have no illusions about what my fate here will be," he said. "This boy who stands in front of you . . ." Slipher fixed his gaze on Elliott. "I have seen with my own eyes what he is capable of. This boy is the shamalan who is written of in your scrolls. "But Malus Lothar wants him dead, and that is enough for me."

The maniacal grin on Slipher's face held. "My family is dead," he said, his tone turning lugubrious in contrast to his toothy grin. "And my name has been shamed. But today I will undo the wrongs that have been done against my people. I will kill the boy, and the last hope of Harwelden will be taken. When he is dead, it doesn't matter what you do to me. My name will be known throughout Vengala. Now, step away from him. Harwelden's justice has come."

Sarintha straightened her back. She turned toward Elliott, and their eyes met. She reached out and took his arm.

Marvus and Jingo moved next to him as well. And Woolf walked down from the dais to stand at Elliott's side.

"I was right about you, serpan," Woolf said. "You are a woeful, pitiful little creature."

A gust of wind blew through the room, rumpling Slipher's hair. He said, "For all the wrongs that have been perpetrated against me, and for all of the injustice that has come from this wretched place . . ." He raised the wand. "Today, at long last, justice comes." He shook the wand at Elliott, throwing his full weight into it.

A howling wind surged through the window, filling the air with a strange dust, so that no one could see, and the great hall shook as if in the midst of a mighty storm. Water jars and drinking cups shattered on the floor, and the heavy furniture in the room swirled as if caught in a cyclone, while the howling of the wind rose to a deafening shriek. Then, as quickly as it had come, the wind abated. The hall fell silent once again, and the wand's magic showed itself.

Waldemariam stood alone at the dais. The councilmen got to their feet, sobered by what they had just witnessed, and gathered around him.

Slipher had not moved an inch. He stood with the wand still in his outstretched arm, a menacing grin still etched on his face. But something about him was different. The dark hue of his skin had turned, and the texture of his hair was unusual. Slipher remained deathly still.

Slowly a grin spread across Waldemariam's face.

Standing across from Slipher, Elliott held his hands before him, inspecting them to satisfy himself that he was still alive and whole. For several seconds, he stared at Slipher, trying to comprehend what had happened.

Slipher didn't move.

Elliott stepped toward him and reached out to touch him. He was cold . . . gray and hard. For the first time in several seconds, Elliott exhaled.

Sarintha walked up behind him, looking oddly at Slipher. Gingerly she touched him. "He has turned to stone!" she exclaimed. She turned to Elliott and embraced him, laughing. "I am Sarintha," she said. "It is wonderful to meet you."

"I'm Elliott," he stammered. She was even more beautiful than his old flame, Lisa Hastings. "It's nice to meet you as well."

Marvus and Jingo hugged them both, laughing in great whoops and gasps as the tension left them.

Woolf clapped him on the back. "Now you have seen," he said, turning to the council. "There is more to this boy than meets the eye."

Elliott stepped toward Slipher and reached out to touch him.
He was cold . . . gray and hard.

"And you have made me a believer, Woolf," Waldemariam said. "It is a pleasure to see you again, Elliott. And I hope you will find your second meeting at Harwelden more hospitable than the first."

Elliott grinned outright.

Despite the joyousness of the moment, Sarintha turned sharply to Waldemariam. "This changes nothing between you and me."

Waldemariam nodded. "We have many things to discuss."

"I relieve you of your position as chancellor." She scanned the room. A row of guards stood against the wall. "Guards," she said, "take him into custody."

The room fell silent. The guards did not move.

"Do it at once!"

"Guards, stand your ground," Waldemariam countered, raising his hand, though he did not bother to turn and face them.

Before she could respond, a deafening crash shattered the relative quiet. The castle shook, and mortar fell from between the stones.

"We are under attack!" Woolf yelled. "The siege against Harwelden has begun!"

Amid the chaos, Waldemariam walked to the window looking out over the Forest of Ondor. A sea of serpan warriors filled every bit of ground as far as the eye could see. The Haviru trebuchets formed a uniform row at the base of the mountain, stretching around it. As he watched, the great catapults fired, sending stones and flaming pitch arcing toward the outer wall.

With great sadness, Waldemariam turned to Sarintha, holding her gaze for a moment before turning his attention to Oskar. "It has begun."

Chapter 49

Under Siege

Sarintha and Waldemariam glared at one another. More chinks of mortar fell from the ceiling as flaming stones from the trebuchets slammed into the outer wall.

Waldemariam took charge. "Councilman Oskar!" he yelled, straining to be heard above the crash of stone against stone. "Dispatch the archers to the northern wall and assemble the generals."

Oskar nodded and rushed out of the room. He appeared shaken by the force of the assault.

"Councilman Baucus," Waldemariam continued, "take a brigade of soldiers and assemble the townspeople. I want everyone who is not of fighting age assembled in the courtyard before nightfall."

Baucus nodded solemnly and set about his task.

"And Councilman Woolf!" he yelled. "Go to the barracks at the south end of the town and take command of the army. Instruct them to take up their assault positions. They will know what to do."

Woolf nodded and took flight out the western window.

"And, General Grimaldi," Waldemariam said, looking to the ceiling, "come down from the rafters where you hide, and stand before me!"

At these words, everyone within earshot looked to the rafters, where Grimaldi sat perched. Despite Sarintha's command that he remain in the dungeon, he had stolen into the room ahead of everyone. With graceful ease, he descended to the floor and stood before his one-time protégé.

"Old friend," Waldemariam said, grasping Grimaldi's forearm, "what a comfort it is to see you among the living."

"I am at your service," Grimaldi replied, stealing a sideways glance at Sarintha, indicating with his eyes that this was a time to follow the chancellor.

"I need you to rally the grayfarer army to our defense," said Waldemariam. "Lead them in whatever tactics you deem necessary against the serpans. They will follow wherever you lead them."

"It is an honor to serve Harwelden," said Grimaldi, bowing his head.

"And take with you the grayfarer Arbusto," Waldemariam added, pointing to the old officer who had brought them from the tavern. "He is the new leader of the grayfarer elites, who have been well trained to begin our defense. He will be invaluable to you."

Grimaldi looked to Arbusto and nodded.

"But before you take leave of us, Arbusto," said Waldemariam, "bring me the bracelet of the nine clans."

As the assault continued outside, Arbusto reached up to the council table, where the bracelet still sat, and gave it to Waldemariam. He spoke briefly with him, then took flight out the western window.

Finally, Waldemariam turned his attention to Sarintha and Elliott. "Come with me."

Elliott started toward Waldemariam but paused when he realized Sarintha wasn't following. He turned and held out his hand. "Come," he said. "Let's hear what he has to say."

Hesitantly, Sarintha took his hand.

Waldemariam turned and left the great hall, pausing only to whisper some instruction to the guards at the exit. Then he hurried out of the hall, with Elliott and Sarintha in tow.

With graceful ease, Grimaldi descended to the floor
and stood before his one-time protégé.

Chapter 50

Harwelden Fights Back

By nightfall, the defense of Harwelden was well under way. The grayfarers flew in pairs high over the lines of Haviru siege engines, pouring vats of burning oil onto them and setting them and their crews ablaze. Soon the serpan front lines, too, were in shambles, engulfed in flame. Despite the simplicity of the defense, the Haviru had proved unable to counter it, and for the moment, the onslaught of the trebuchets was contained. Meanwhile, Harweldenite archers rained torrents of arrows into the endless mass of enemy warriors, whereupon others poured in from the rear to replace them. Already the enemy warriors filling the space at the base of the mountain stood higher and higher atop the growing mounds of corpses that sprang up like tickweed beneath them.

Under the guidance of Woolf and Oskar, the generals assembled in the plaza, and by midnight, brigades were positioned all along the encompassing wall, ready to defend the city should the walls be breached. Two especially brave brigades volunteered to patrol the mountainside, to combat the inevitable progression of the smaller siege weapons—the catapults and wallflies—to the outer wall. Woolf volunteered to serve as commander in this particularly risky endeavor.

Meanwhile, Councilman Baucus and his brigade of soldiers presided over the growing assemblage of Harweldenites in the courtyards outside the castle. A legion of cold and frightened townspeople, carrying their most precious effects, huddled

Harweldenite archers rained torrents of arrows into the
endless mass of enemy warriors, whereupon others
poured in from the rear to replace them.

together awaiting some promise of hope against the grisly fate that loomed over them. Crying children clung to their mothers and grandparents, for by now all males of fighting age, appreciating at last the magnitude of the threat, had finally taken up arms. Though the trebuchet onslaught was drastically diminished, the few not in flames still sent the panicked crowd huddling together under the spectral light of the moon.

High above the square, in the castle war room, Waldemariam, Elliott, and Sarintha were alone. Waldemariam spoke to the last of the shamalans. "We will address your concerns, Princess, at the appropriate time," he said. "But now you must join me, for we cannot succeed divided."

"Do not put me off!" she hissed. "Explain how my general and I came to be held prisoner after our homecoming and were left without food, water, or the medical attention Grimaldi so desperately needed."

Waldemariam winced. "I cannot explain right now, Your Highness, other than to tell you that you were safer in the dungeon than anywhere else. You believe you were left to die, though that isn't the case."

She glared at him. "And, pray tell, how did you know we were surviving, locked down there for days on end without food or water? Do you know the depths to which we sank to survive?"

"These have been difficult times," he growled. "For everyone. This is the last chance for Harwelden, and the fate of the empire depends on you"—he turned to Elliott—"and upon this poor boy." And reaching into his robe, he held out the bracelet of the nine clans. "Put it on," he said. "Your use of it is the key to everything."

Elliott took the bracelet and snapped it on his wrist, then said to Sarintha, "I think we should trust him."

"Against my better judgment," she said, "I am going to do as you ask, and join Waldemariam in the defense of Harwelden."

"Then let's get to it," Waldemariam said. "If my plan is going to work, it will have to be executed flawlessly."

Elliott and Sarintha looked at each other, communicating without the need for words.

"But before we begin, I already owe you a deep debt of gratitude, Elliott."

"For what?"

Waldemariam laughed. "For releasing me."

Elliott had no idea what the chancellor was talking about. But putting his confusion aside, he listened with Sarintha as Waldemariam laid out his plan for the defense of Harwelden.

They hurried down to the square to join Baucus and the growing mass of townspeople in the courtyard. Just as they arrived, a bloodied middle-aged man stumbled, sword in hand, from the Boulevard of Kings into the courtyard. "The grayfarers are doing all they can," he gasped, "but the trebuchets keep firing." Nervously he looked to Waldemariam. "The wall is beginning to crumble."

Chapter 51

Councilman Fanta's Return

In the courtyard below the castle, Elliott stood with Sarintha at his side, looking over the throng of terrified townspeople. He had not thought there could be so many. What could Waldemariam possibly do to save them once the Haviru's siege engines breached the wall?

In the distance, a steady barrage of hurtling boulders crashed against the wall, shaking the ground beneath him and feeding the townspeople's growing sense of dread.

Waldemariam walked to the center of the courtyard, preparing to address the huddled citizens, when, in a pause between the crashes of stone on stone, they heard the unmistakable sound of a flinging trebuchet—this one closer than the others.

From the west, a flaming projectile reached the zenith of its trajectory and started its downward arc, directly toward the center of the plaza, where they were standing. The serpans were expanding their assault to the western part of the city.

The crowd panicked, and women and children and doddering oldsters scattered in every direction, taking refuge behind crumbling statues of long-dead nobles, or whatever they could find, though Waldemariam and Sarintha stood unmoved, watching the shot plummet toward them. Though Elliott's first impulse was to run for cover with the others, he decided to trust Waldemariam's instincts and stay by the princess's side.

The fireball hit the paving stones with a wet splat.

Waldemariam's face fell as he looked upon the flaming heap, for he seemed to know at once what it was. The flaming mass, though broken and burned, was unmistakably a corpse. A pair of shattered wings jutted from the heap like broken lengths of wire, and the stench of burning flesh filled their nostrils as flaming sockets peered out at them from the skull of the fire-haloed, half-disintegrated body.

Waldemariam's mouth contorted with grief, then anger, as he looked to the west and said, "At last we know what has become of Councilman Fanta." Clenching his fists, he turned his face skyward and screamed out in a wordless, wrenching howl, at once grief-stricken and defiant. Then he turned to Elliott and Sarintha and said through clenched teeth, "I will avenge him." He turned to the townspeople gathering around the burning remains of their lost councilman.

"Do as I say," said Waldemariam, addressing the crowd, "and you will live." Completely gone from his presence was the harried disarray that he had displayed during the buildup to the attack. "Form lines and follow me."

And with the townspeople behind him, and Sarintha and Elliott at his side, Waldemariam turned and entered the castle.

He led them through the entrance and down a chain of stairways, deep into the belly of the castle. Pausing to wrest a torch from its wall mount, he entered the dungeons, wending his way through the many corridors until he reached a stone wall. Squatting, he worked a large iron key into a crevice in the stone and turned it. Slowly the wall turned, revealing the passage to the labyrinth beneath the mountain.

Holding the torch before him, Waldemariam led the townspeople into the passage.

Down they traveled through the twists and turns of the mountain's interior until they reached the bottom, where

Waldemariam defiantly screamed, "I will avenge him."

they continued southward down a long, winding path. At last, they reached a wall, where again Waldemariam knelt and fitted the key into a chink between the stones. Moments later, they were looking out at a valley filled with legions of serpans.

In every direction they stretched, wielding torches, crossbows, swords, axes, pikes. The nearest of them stood not a hundred feet away. There seemed no escape here.

Waldemariam turned to Elliott. "It is on you now."

Elliott stared, horror-struck. "What do I do?"

Waldemariam nodded at the bracelet.

The nearby serpans stared at them with a mix of amusement and curiosity.

"*This* is your plan?" Elliott gasped.

"It is time to show us the wonderful secret of the bracelet."

Elliott felt a flash of anger. He was in no way prepared for this.

Waldemariam drew his sword and lifted off the ground. "March forward!"

The serpans, looking to one another in puzzled disbelief, raised their weapons.

Sarintha turned to the townspeople behind her. "Trust in the chancellor!" she yelled. "And in our deliverer, Elliott of Ondor!"

An old man stepped forward, leaning against his cane for support. With Waldemariam hovering above him, he hobbled toward the wall of serpans ahead. Horrified, Elliott watched him walk toward certain death. Then the old man's wife, withered and bent, followed him into the valley, praying aloud as she went.

The serpans raised their crossbows, and an incredulous warlord grinned and raised his arm, signaling his subordinates to shoot on his mark.

Out walked the Harweldenites. The old man in the lead joined his wife in her prayer as Elliott looked on, frantic, unsure what to do.

He cleared his mind and drew a mental image of the townspeople, striving to recall every detail he could. Then he closed his eyes and rubbed the bracelet.

Chapter 52

Breach

Just outside the northern wall, Grimaldi and Arbusto stood shoulder to shoulder against a patrol of serpan warriors. Behind them, a section of the wall had succumbed to the pounding of the trebuchets, and a narrow breach offered passage to any who could fight their way past the pair of battling grayfarers. Glistening with sweat and blood, they stood in the moonlight, swinging their swords in deadly rhythm against the oncoming serpans. From farther down the mountain, another serpan patrol approached.

The bellow of a serpan horn called out, inviting others to join the fight, and Grimaldi knew they couldn't hold the breach for long. Standing amid the corpses of their slain enemies, their strength flagging, they parried and hacked as an endless stream of fresh serpans appeared.

The pain of exhaustion and loss showed on Arbusto's face, and he began losing ground against the leader of the serpan patrol, who was nearly as big as he. "It has been a pleasure to serve with the mighty General Grimaldi," he yelled.

Grimaldi slashed at the serpan leader, driving him back down the mountain. "Don't speak like that!" he yelled. "Just keep fighting. Reinforcements will arrive."

But Arbusto was tapping his last reserves. The serpan leader sidestepped Grimaldi's thrust and swung his sword at Arbusto, cleaving a great gash in his upper arm. Stunned, Arbusto fell to his knees as gouts of blood spurted from the wound.

The bellow of a serpan horn called out,
inviting others to join the fight, and Grimaldi knew
they couldn't hold the breach for long.

Clutching at the lifeless arm, he looked sadly at Grimaldi and made no effort to pick up his weapon from the ground, even as the serpan raised his sword for the deathblow.

Grimaldi swung, catching the enemy sword near the hilt and knocking the serpan back. But now the second serpan patrol had arrived, and more were pouring up the mountain. Grasping Arbusto around the chest, Grimaldi dodged a blade thrust and leaped into the air, towing Arbusto beneath him, as a wall of serpan warriors rushed through the breach.

At the eastern face, the sound of smashing boulders filled the air as the latest battlefront opened. Inside the village, serpan warriors fanned out like cockroaches, searching every recess of the village for surviving Harweldenites.

Chapter 53

Shadowcaster

At the base of the mountain, the old man leading the townspeople took his wife's hand and bowed his head. Clutching his cane, he walked toward the waiting serpan army as the commanding warlord dropped his arm, signaling his troops to open fire.

Waves of energy crashed into Elliott, and his breath quickened. The force of the energy he drew was unlike anything he had yet encountered. His skin tingled. The more he concentrated, the more readily it came, further sharpening his focus. The serpans and the townspeople seemed to exist on different planes. He drew in more and more of the energy, becoming drunk with it, though at the same time it soothed him, making him somehow more aware. He felt the air entering his lungs, felt his hair growing. The sensory overload was euphoric in a way he had never experienced. He squeezed his eyes and focused. In that moment, he didn't want it to end.

A hand reached out for his shoulder, interrupting his concentration. Against his will, the touch pulled him back, offsetting the influx that brought him such pleasure. His mind screamed against the disturbance.

It was Sarintha. "It is enough," she said. "Open your eyes."

A voice from deep in his thoughts told him to listen. He opened his eyes. Shaking off the effects of the magic, he struggled to interpret the scene before him.

He was alone. Where the serpans had been, there now stretched an empty valley beneath a starry Pangrelorian night sky. He looked left and right. Far in the distance, at either edge of the field, he could see more serpan troops, though the nearest were so far away, they appeared as ants in the distance. The valley that stretched before him was empty. Confused, he turned to Sarintha, but she wasn't there. He didn't know what to do.

"Do not be afraid," Sarintha said. "We are masked."

He stared into empty space. He was no longer trying to mask them, but there wasn't a soul in sight. The entire population of Harwelden had vanished.

"Look to the floor of the valley before us," said Sarintha.

The vast space where the serpan army had stood was covered in a layer of ash.

"You have stolen the enemy's energy and used it to mask the Harweldenites, and in so doing, you have reduced them to a layer of ash. . . . You have rescued us, Elliott!"

But his giddy elation was gone. "Sarintha," he mumbled, falling to his knees. He intended to say more, but his eyes closed and he tumbled to the ash before the next thought could form in his head.

Sarintha said, "You have stolen the enemy's energy and used it
to mask the Harweldenites, and in so doing, you have reduced
them to a layer of ash. . . . You have rescued us, Elliott!"

Chapter 54

Flight of the Golgomites

In the eastern tower of the castle, Elliott lay sleeping while Jingo and Marvus kept anxious watch over him. He hadn't moved a muscle since Waldemariam returned him to the castle a full day ago, after his collapse in the field.

Near the door, Marvus sat smoking his pipe, denying entrance to nearly all who came to see the boy. Jingo sat at the bedside.

"No one has heard from the princess," Marvus said. "I expected to see her by now."

"She will come," Jingo said.

Marvus twitched in his chair and drew on the pipe. "I don't know where it goes from here," he said. "It was a marvelous display in the field, but there are *so many* of them."

Jingo turned to him. "He is a proven shadowcaster," he said, "the true heir to King Griogair. Why do you doubt him so?"

Marvus stood and walked to the window. Hands clasped behind his back, he scanned the ash-covered valley, which was already filling with a new throng of serpans. He ignored Jingo's question. "No one has heard from the princess," he repeated, looking down into the courtyard. Serpan warriors, with no one to resist them, rolled their catapults into position around the castle.

"She will come," Jingo said.

In the city below, Sarintha moved about freely. No one could see her. After Elliott's collapse, she had led the frightened Harweldenites through the valley and directed them to travel to Abarynthia, a city just a few days south of Harwelden. It was reachable on foot, though the expedition was certain to be arduous, particularly since they had made no preparation for the sudden exodus. After setting the thankful townspeople on their difficult path, she had reentered the secret passage at the base of the mountain. But reaching the tunnels beneath the dungeons, she altered her route. Relishing the silence, she trekked through the subterranean darkness to the underground spring that the city used for water. There she entered the water and, falling beneath the surface, inhaled. Her fingers and toes tingled as the shamalan membranes popped through the skin, widening her hands and feet into the familiar sculls, and her vision sharpened as the geography of the spring took shape in shades of green.

She swam until she found a slim ray of daylight, glimmering down through one of the many wells that communicated with the surface. After verifying that she was still masked, she surfaced in a well near the Grand Plaza and expelled the water from her lungs, then crawled up out of the well and into the midst of the city. So powerful was the magic Elliott had conjured, she felt that she could remain safely masked for quite some time.

Harwelden was in utter disarray. The bodies of slain Harweldenite warriors sprawled across the roads, markets, and courtyards as far as the eye could see. Just north of her, a giant breach in the wall invited passage to the interior. Even as she watched, regiments of serpan warriors, marching shoulder to shoulder fifteen across, flooded into the city. Beside the breach, the drawbridge was lowered, and a line of catapults stretched from the base of the mountain into the streets. Not a single defender was present. Steeling herself, she examined the eastern end of the city, which overlooked the river. Though she could not imagine how the craggy terrain on the eastern face permitted it, Haviru siege towers had sprung up all along the wall. With unnerving discipline, rank after rank of serpan warriors lowered themselves into the city. At the western face, a similar scene unfolded. All around her, Harwelden burned, filling the air with acrid smoke.

She headed down the Boulevard of Kings, careful to avoid contact with the innumerable serpan troops around her, when an ear-shattering screech filled the air, freezing her in her tracks. Instantly recognizing the otherwordly sound, she looked skyward to see a quartet of fire-breathing golgomites approaching from the north. Their massive serpentine heads darted back and forth, scanning the battlefield, and their mighty wings cast shadows over the serpan warriors in the valley. Malus Lothar's sky chariot dangled beneath them.

With pounding heart, she set off toward the castle. Chastising herself for entering the city, she walked directly into a serpan warlord. As if to punctuate the moment, another screech filled the air as one of the beasts spat a stream of fire at the shamalan temple, engulfing it in flames.

The warlord didn't see her at first. Believing herself still masked, she held her breath and stood stock-still.

He squinted and seemed to be peering past her. But slowly his eyes seemed to make sense of her shape, and a look of realization dawned on his face.

Realizing that the masking must have begun to subside, and seeing no other options, she charged, barging him hard in the pit of the stomach with her shoulder, then raced down the Boulevard of Kings toward the castle, knowing that she ran for her very life.

The warlord bellowed, pointing after her, and gave chase. The warriors on the boulevard, confused at first, soon realized

But slowly the warlord's eyes seemed to make sense of
Sarintha's shape, and a look of realization dawned on his face.

the source of their commander's excitement and set out after her, crossbows raised.

Panic-stricken, she hurtled down the boulevard, ducking and dodging confused serpan warriors one after another. An arrow whizzed past her head, and she looked at her hands, aghast to see that they were almost completely visible. All around her, serpans joined in the chase. Behind her, a deafening golgomite screech shook the city.

The arrows zipped past her one after another, and suddenly the castle seemed a long way away. She had no idea how she would get inside even if she made it to the entrance, and the serpans were fast closing on her. Knowing that her chances were dwindling, she sprinted all out—until an arrow struck her in the calf, hobbling her. With a shriek, she fell to the boulevard. They descended on her.

Chapter 55

The Shadowcaster Awakens

In the eastern tower, after a day and a night of deep slumber, Elliott sat bolt upright in bed. He had been dreaming. Where was the princess?

Marvus dropped his pipe and rushed to the bedside, reaching out to take his hand. "Thank Baruna you have awakened," he breathed.

Elliott struggled to clear the cobwebs from his thoughts. "We must find her," he said, leaping from the bed. "We must go to her."

"But, Elliott," Marvus said, "we have no idea where she is."

"She's in the city, and she's in trouble." He pulled his shirt over his head, shucked his pants on, and started toward the door.

"Slow down," Marvus urged. "You can't just leave the castle. Harwelden is overrun. The wall has been breached."

Elliott stopped.

"It is true," said a voice from the doorway. He turned to see Councilman Alasdar. "Calm down, Elliott. If we are to consider leaving the safety of the castle, we must have a plan. If the princess is out there, there is little we can do for her."

"It can't be," Elliott said.

A frown darkened the corners of Alasdar's mouth. "Waldemariam and the grayfarers are scheming in the war room. Arbusto is direly wounded. Legions of our own forces have been slain, and the remnants of our army are congregated within the castle walls. Even as we speak, Haviru catapults fire on the castle itself."

Elliott stared at him, noting the lines of stress in his face.

"The princess has not been seen since she left your side in the valley," Alasdar continued. "We don't even know for certain that the townspeople escaped, for no one could see them after your magnificent feat." Alasdar moved toward him, clasping his arm gently. "Wait and see what plan Waldemariam devises. On this day, though I am loath to say it, the battle for Harwelden is lost. Even with your powers, it is not safe for you to enter the city."

Elliott shouldered past him and went for the door. "The three of you can do as you please, but I'm going to find her."

Smiling, Jingo hurried after him, checking the dagger at his belt.

Marvus sighed and followed, hurrying to catch up.

As they emerged from the staircase into the foyer, the din of nervous chatter filling the lower halls stopped. Soldiers throughout the ground floor turned to look at him. Blood-stained archers, cataphracts, and dragoons—the remnants of the Harweldenite army—gathered at the base of the stairs, staring up at him.

Elliott paused to look at the exhausted and broken warriors. Behind him, the golden tapestries of Harwelden decorated every inch of the wall, bearing magnificent testimony to all that was lost. After a moment, he started again down the stairs, and the sound of his footsteps echoed throughout the hushed foyer.

At the foot of the stairs, the warriors parted, making a path. The warrior nearest him looked reverently up at him, then bowed and knelt. The other soldiers also dropped to one knee.

In silence, with the remnants of Harwelden's army kneeling before him, Elliott walked to the door. When he reached it, two soldiers stood and lifted the crossbar, and he walked out into the courtyard.

In silence, with the remnants of Harwelden's army
kneeling before him, Elliott walked to the door.

Chapter 56

Fallen

As he heard the crossbar being fitted back into place on the other side of the door, Elliott took a deep breath and looked out at the smoking ruins of the city. Nervously the two gimlets flanked him. Serpans moved about unchallenged, setting torches to buildings and robbing corpses.

Elliott and the gimlets stepped into the courtyard, where spires of black smoke billowed toward the darkened sky, adding to the overwhelming sense of apocalypse. In the boulevard ahead, hundreds of agitated serpans had gathered to watch some spectacle there. With their backs to Elliott and the gimlets, they waved their fists and cheered. Hearing an ungodly screech, Elliott turned to see a giant flying lizard spit a stream of fire on a building near the northern wall.

In the center of the castle courtyard, he closed his eyes and raised his face toward the sky, listening. And in his mind, he heard Sarintha cry out. He opened his eyes.

Another screech tore through the city, and Elliott looked up in time to see the soaring black devil descending on him. Smoke streamed from its flaring nostrils. Its shiny black scales glistened as if oiled, and its great wings cast shadows over the boulevard. As the horrific beast descended, the rabble of serpans on the boulevard looked up, seeming to wonder what it was doing. As they turned to face him, surprise dawning on their faces, he saw the princess, bloody and hobbled, lying at their feet.

The demonic lizard spat a stream of fire, barely missing Elliott, and pumped its massive wings, retreating for the moment into the sky, where it circled like a carrion bird.

Marvus and Jingo closed ranks beside him. Methodically, the serpans abandoned Sarintha and inched toward him, seeming to build confidence with each step.

Elliott faced them, communicating with his eyes that he would not be cowed.

From the north, a trio of the fire-breathing lizards flew in to join the first, and bellowing smoke and flame, they slithered through the air in intertwining circles, preparing to strike.

The stench of sulfur filled Elliott's nostrils as he stood against the advancing serpans. Stone-faced, he said, "Release the princess to me."

For a moment they stopped, perhaps unsure whether to be fearful or amused. Some near the front laughed nervously. Gradually, they resumed their cautious march, leaving Sarintha forgotten behind them. One of the serpans raised his ax, and from somewhere within the advancing throng, an arrow streaked toward Elliott.

Searing pain exploded across his chest, stopping his breath. The serpans continued their advance, axes raised. Grasping at his chest, Elliott fell.

Stone-faced, Elliott said, "Release the princess to me."

Chapter 57

An Unwelcome Surprise

He must have passed out, though for how long, he didn't know. The pain in his chest made breathing torture. The stench of burning wood and flesh filled his nostrils as he slowly opened his eyes.

A circle of fiendish faces stared down at him, and ax bits glinted in the moonlight above them. Marvus and Jingo lay next to him, bloodied but conscious. The putrid whiff of serpan breath replaced the smell of smoke and char as the enemy warriors leaned in to finish him. Unable at first to pull his eyes from the shiny ax blades, he grew confused again. He closed his eyes and thought, for some reason, of his mother.

But before the axes could fall, a voice, deep and commanding, pulled Elliott back from his delirium. "Stand down!" it bellowed. "His life is not yours to take."

The serpans turned.

"Out of my way!" the voice boomed. "I want to see him."

Like turf before a plow, the crowd peeled back before Malus Lothar's steel mask, glistening in the light of many fires. His robe fluttered behind him in the wispy breeze. As he approached, they fell silent until the only sound was the click of his boots against the paving stones. Sneering, he sidestepped Sarintha and walked toward Elliott.

Marvus began to shake, though Jingo bristled, appearing somehow ready to fight.

Above them, a golgomite spat a stream of fire at the castle, and the eastern tower erupted in flames.

With the malus just a few paces away, Elliott's hands went to his chest. A shattered arrow lay beside him. He slipped a hand underneath his shirt, feeling for the wound, but instead felt the smooth fiber of the golden shirt he had stolen from the salax king. "Vibrissae from the Primordial Tree," Crosslyn had called the fiber. And somehow, it had stopped the arrow's penetration.

Slowly, clumsily, Elliott got to his feet. "I'm not afraid of you," he said. The words had come with hardly a thought, surprising him.

For a moment, Malus Lothar was quiet. Then, his expression hidden by the mask, he laughed. "Then that is your mistake. I have followed your progress since the day you set foot in this world," he said, unsheathing his broad curved sword. "And I have known, since you first appeared in Ondor, that this day would come."

"And what day is this?"

"It is the day Harwelden passes forever into memory, and the day its savior pays in blood for the sins of his fathers." Lothar raised his sword and seemed to savor its sheen in the firelight, whipped it through the air, then rested it on his shoulder.

"The River Tantasar has turned red." Lothar seemed to be mocking him. "It flows as dark as blood, just as the scrolls prophesy. Soon we will add more yet to its hue."

"But that is where the accuracy of the shamalan prophecies ends," he continued, for there will be no deliverance for Harwelden." He swung his sword again, this time within an inch of Elliott's face, before resting it again on his shoulder. "The shamalan scrolls tell only half the story. Omitted are the passages about mighty Malgothar and his apprentice, Valderon. Theirs is the part of the tale that no shamalan dare discuss, but they are the most important. Lord Valderon rises from the

Elliott slipped a hand underneath his shirt, feeling for
the wound, but instead felt the smooth fiber of the
golden shirt he had stolen from the salax king.

prison fashioned for him by your fathers, and grows strong again in this world. This, too, your scrolls prophesied, though this knowledge fell from the shamalan cultivation long ago."

Elliott stared at him, feeling more puzzled than scared. Memories of Crosslyn swam through his head, and he recalled when they went beneath the waters of the River Tantasar. *Your enemy is shamalan,* the sprites had said, though he hadn't understood their meaning. Seconds ticked by as they stared at one another.

"And what did you learn during your cultivation, Lothar?" Elliott said finally. "Did you learn that you would be the shame of your shamalan fathers?"

Lothar tensed, but only briefly, and then chuckled. "You think you know me, child. But do you know Lord Valderon?" The pitch of his voice changed, sounding more conversational than sinister. "It is his hand that guides me. As his power grows, so does mine."

"I'm not afraid of you."

Lothar raised his sword.

"I will defeat you."

Lothar loosed a full-throated laugh, seeming to enjoy himself. He raised the sword above his head.

Elliott closed his eyes, summoning the magic of the bracelet, knowing that this moment would require everything he had learned about its power.

From down the boulevard, Sarintha screamed, and Elliott opened his eyes to see her standing in the street, forgotten, watching.

Lothar swung the sword in a downward arc, aiming to cleave him in two.

With a shout, Jingo tackled Elliott, pushing him out of the way, so that the sword caught Jingo's leg below the knee, severing it from his body. He screamed, grasping for his severed leg.

Elliott reached for the bracelet, but it was gone.

Chapter 58

The Dagger and
the Plague

Grunting, Lothar raised the heavy sword again and brought it smashing down toward Elliott. Elliott rolled, finding himself nearly on top of Marvus, as the sword clattered against the stones of the boulevard in a shower of sparks.

"Here!" Marvus said, thrusting out a bejeweled dagger. "Crosslyn said I'd know what to do with it when the time comes—and I think the time has come!"

Elliott grabbed Crosslyn's dagger and rolled, thrusting it into Lothar's calf. It penetrated the armor as if stabbing butter. With a howl, Lothar fell.

The surroundings erupted in chaos as the serpans in the boulevard charged Sarintha, and the serpans surrounding Elliott came at him with renewed vigor.

From a crack in the boulevard, Taldar the rat emerged, twitching his pink nose and baring his four chisellike teeth. "The plague of rats has arrived, Lothar!" he yelled. "You will rue the day you crossed the vermin clan of the field!" Behind him, rats poured out of every darkened crack and crevice in the broad boulevard, from drains, and from beneath the stones of the fountain. In a twinkling they were everywhere, rippling like a furry wave over the city's streets and squares and walkways. As one, they attacked, squealing and biting at every inch of exposed serpan flesh. And though the serpans tried to fight back, their fearsome weapons were of little use against something as small and agile as a rat.

In the distance, Elliott spotted Sarintha. He wanted to go to her, but embattled serpans surrounded him, blocking him. They clawed at their faces and arms, trying to stop the onslaught of sharp little yellow teeth. With Malus Lothar writhing at his feet, Elliott strained to see what was happening to Sarintha. Amid the confusion of jumping, writhing fur-covered serpans, he caught glimpses of her, fighting with her hands. She appeared to be without any weapon.

Determined to go to her, Elliott tried to force his way through the crush of bodies, but he made it only a few feet. Crying out, he finally managed to get her attention, and she looked at him. She was beautiful.

Reaching into his pocket, he pulled out the slingshot—the only thing he could think of that might help her—and threw it to her. Remarkably, amid the howling, clamoring chaos, she reached up and plucked it from the air before a serpan with a face full of rats fell on him.

From behind him, a horn sounded, and he craned his neck upward in time to see Waldemariam, Grimaldi, and Woolf soar out of the castle's western tower. Behind them, the remaining grayfarers followed, their polished armor sparkling in the firelight as they streaked through the sky. The main door of the castle flew open, and Harweldenite soldiers poured into the square. A storm of arrows flew against the serpans from both ground and sky, while ever more rats poured into the streets.

From above, the fire-breathing golgomites descended, raining sheets of sulfur-reeking fire on the surging Harweldenites. Between fire-charged belches, they screeched louder and louder, so that Elliott had to cover his ears.

Above him, one of the creatures lowered its head and descended with talons outstretched. Like a hawk stooping on a

The serpans fearsome weapons were of little use
against something as small and agile as a rat.

rabbit, it took aim, shrieking as it smashed into the boulevard, scooping up two great handfuls of Harweldenite warriors. Then, with its claws full of screaming victims, it climbed back to the sky, belching fire, and gained speed as it hurtled toward the castle, its victims squirming helplessly in its grasp. Just before it flew headlong into the wall, it flared its wings and pulled up, releasing them. Still screaming, they tumbled through the air, high above the courtyard, and smashed against the castle wall.

In the streets, the rats bit and clawed at the serpans as the Harweldenite army pushed northward, pinning the enemy against the wall, near the breach.

And Elliott, who had barely avoided being scooped up by the golgomite, realized that Lothar was gone. Frantically, he pushed his way down the boulevard, searching for Sarintha. In the center of the Boulevard of Kings, just outside the tavern, he found her. She appeared badly injured and could barely stand under her own weight. Seeing the broken shaft of an arrow protruding from her calf, he counted her lucky that the rats had come when they did. Pulling her to him, he looped her arm around his neck to take some of her weight and tried to push back toward the castle.

In the sky, Woolf unleashed a guttural roar, and Elliott looked over his shoulder to see him land on the fiendish black lizard's neck. Either oblivious of the grayfarer on its back or simply unconcerned, it turned for another run at the boulevard and descended, spitting a long stream of fire. With his thighs and calves clinging to the huge, scaly neck, barely keeping hold, Woolf drew his sword as the golgomite stretched out its claws toward a company of Harweldenite pikemen. Plummeting toward the boulevard, Woolf plunged his sword into the beast's eye.

Unfazed, the lizard flung Woolf away with a shake of its neck and kept coming, with the sword still buried in its eye. Elliott had no time to get Sarintha to safety, and the bracelet was gone. Frantically, he cast about for the nearest weapon, only to be elbowed out of the way. Hobbling in front of him, Sarintha drew back the slingshot and launched a shard of paving stone at the golgomite.

The rough, angular stone struck it squarely between the eyes, and with a confused bellow, the golgomite listed sideways and crashed headlong into the row of buildings opposite the tavern. Sliding at last to a stop, the carcass lay still, with smoke still rising from its nostrils. From above, Woolf nodded to the two shamalans, smiling his approval, and went to rejoin the other grayfarers as they fought against the remaining three golgomites.

On the ground, thanks to Taldar and the rats, the momentum had turned against the serpans. In full retreat, they poured out of Harwelden, clambering through the breach or over the open drawbridge.

Though the Harweldenite army was spread thin, its remaining warriors mounted the wall, knocking the serpan ladders to the ground and toppling siege towers.

In the sky, the grayfarers swarmed against the remaining three golgomites. Perhaps sensing the change of fortune, the fiendish lizards retreated for now, leaving the grayfarers alone in the sky over the burning city.

Sarintha and Elliott walked side by side to the northern wall, where exultant soldiers hoisted them to the top. But when they looked down into the northern valley, a sense of foreboding froze their budding jubilation. In the moonlight, they could see enemy warriors filling the valley from the north as far as they could see. Some of them rolled fresh trebuchets before them, untouched by violence and ready to wreak fresh havoc. Elliott saw the dread in Sarintha's face as they descended the wall and began the short walk back to the castle, the fires of the burning city lighting their way. They did not speak of the vanished malus or Jingo's severed leg, or how they would deal with the coming onslaught.

Chapter 59

A Traitor Revealed

"They will attack again at first light," Waldemariam said, somberly addressing the remaining officers and councilmen, whose expressions were barely discernible in the war room's dim torchlight. No one had slept since the retreat, and sunrise was not far away.

"We must take the fight to them," Woolf said. "Our chances our better if we meet them on the mountainside, with the suns behind us."

"That is madness," Councilman Baucus said. "Have you seen their numbers?"

"What, then?" Woolf said. "Shall we hide in the castle while they burn the rest of Harwelden to the ground and desecrate our dead? Or perhaps flee our home to scrabble an existence in lands untouched by war?"

Baucus lowered his head. "If you present us with a viable solution, I will be the first to follow, but for a force of a few hundred to mount an offensive against ten thousand is sheer folly."

Woolf stared out the window at the sea of enemy warriors. Oskar joined him, placing a hand on his shoulder.

"I agree with Woolf," he said. "We cannot defeat them all, but we can make some of them pay for what they have done to us."

Woolf nodded to Oskar, and for the moment, the tension between them was gone. "We will be defeated," Woolf said softly. "In a few hours' time, whether on the mountain or within the battered city walls, we will face the full power of their army, and it seems that there are more of them than stars in the sky. From the mountainside, with the suns at our backs, we can at least fight as warriors. I do not wish to meet my end cowering in a castle."

Waldemariam nodded. "I agree."

The remaining grayfarers, including Baucus, nodded their heads.

"But let us explore another topic as well," Waldemariam said, turning to Elliott. "When is the last time you remember wearing the bracelet?"

Elliott reflected for a moment before answering. "I was wearing it at the base of the mountain, during the townspeople's flight. When I woke up, I didn't look for it until Malus Lothar came, and I didn't realize it was gone until I tried to use it against him." He lowered his eyes, thinking of Jingo, blaming himself for what had happened.

"Who were you in contact with after your awakening?"

"Only Marvus and Jingo."

Marvus sat nearby, slumped in his chair. "Don't forget Alasdar," he said absently. "He visited just before you left to find Sarintha."

Waldemariam tensed, as did Oskar. They looked at each other.

"Yes," Elliott said. "I spoke briefly with Alasdar before leaving the castle. He urged me not to go."

Waldemariam scanned the war room. "Did Alasdar come into actual physical contact with you?"

"I don't remember."

Marvus sat bolt upright in his chair. "He did! He grasped you by the arm and implored you to stay in the castle."

Waldemariam and Oskar locked eyes again. Waldemariam stood. "Has anyone in this room seen Alasdar since the serpan retreat?"

Waldemariam said, turning to Elliott,
"When is the last time you remember wearing the bracelet?"

The grayfarers and soldiers looked about them, waiting for someone to speak up. No one said anything.

Waldemariam's face grew stern. "All right, then," he said. "The bracelet is lost, and a long-pondered mystery is solved. Alasdar is Harwelden's traitor."

"You can't be serious!" Woolf said.

"Deadly serious. Oskar and I have suspected him, but we had no proof."

"But why suspect him?" Woolf replied. "He is the purest among us."

"You have noticed, no doubt, my strange behavior during the past season?"

"Yes. What does that have to do with Alasdar?"

"It has *everything* to do with him. My erratic behavior—my madness, if you will—was his doing."

"That's ridiculous! How can Alasdar have had anything to do with the things you've done?"

"Let me explain. At the beginning of last season, I knew something was wrong with me. My thoughts became jumbled and my mood erratic, but I didn't understand what was happening. I feared I was going mad or had contracted the Leshwart disease. Over time, my problems intensified, and I struggled to concentrate even on simple tasks. Oskar deduced that I was being bewitched. Determined to help me, he went to the temple and found a book of dark arts. He concocted a potion to release me from the bewitching, but it was only partly successful. As my madness grew, he pretended to agree with my strange decisions, to placate me, so that I would listen to him and succumb to his influence. From the outset, he covered for me, hiding my sickness and fulfilling my responsibilities, hoping to prevent me from causing too much harm. During all this time, he searched for the culprit, confiding in no one, for the traitor could be anyone."

Waldemariam turned to Sarintha. "That is why he imprisoned you when you returned: so you would not be targeted as I was, and so you would be safe from my erratic decisions. Since Grimaldi knew of your presence, it was necessary to restrain him as well. It was all done to protect you." He turned back to Woolf. "In any event, the hex was somehow broken when Elliott returned, and we have at last determined its cause. The source is the amulet I have worn around my neck for the past two seasons." He touched his neck, where the amulet had been. "It was a gift from Alasdar, given me to befuddle me and speed our demise. It was only through the return of Griogair's heir that the amulet's magic against me was broken." He nodded to Elliott. "With my thoughts clear again, Oskar and I have tested it and verified that it was the cause of my troubles. The only thing we didn't know was whether Alasdar knew of its influence when he gave it to me. We thought it possible that he, too, had been duped."

Sarintha's face lit up. "Somehow, Valderon's magic never fully worked on Griogair, and it is possible that the amulet's magic might be countered by Griogair's heir. But this implies Valderon's direct involvement with the amulet or with Alasdar. To consider it chills me to the core."

"Exactly," Waldemariam said. "This morning I went to destroy the amulet, but it has gone missing."

"But if the amulet was the only cause for your behavior, then why didn't Elliott's initial appearance end the hex?" Woolf asked.

"Because my intial treatment of Elliott was born of my own prejudice and arrogance and not a result of the spell," said Waldemariam. "When the gimlets rescued him and took him away, the hex continued unfettered. But when he returned, his lasting presence broke the spell."

"I don't believe it," Woolf said.

Waldemariam spread his arms, palms exposed. "At this late hour, all of us are here with you," he said. "Your friend Alasdar is not. What further proof do you require?"

The war room erupted in loud clamor.

"Now is not the time for this!" Woolf growled. "The question before us is straightforward: do we stay in the castle or go out to face them? I vote that we take the fight to them."

"I agree," Waldemariam said, turning to Sarintha. "I say we fight."

"In the names of our fathers," she said, "we fight!"

"Without hesitation," said Grimaldi. "We fight."

Landrew, Oskar, and Baucus nodded.

All eyes turned to Elliott. "I will follow whatever path you lead me to," he said, thinking suddenly of his grandfather's vague warnings on the evening before his journey into Pangrelor. *I fear that you have a terrible job you must fulfill.*

"It is decided, then, Woolf said. "Now, down to business."

In earnest, they huddled at the table, planning every facet of their strategy until the early morning hours, taking account of every advantage they might have in the final battle for their home.

Chapter 60

The Final Battle Begins

They gathered in the Grand Plaza just before dawn. Their breath plumed white in the chill air, though the coming sunrise promised to bring a temperate morning. All around them, Harwelden smoldered. After a night of preparation, they had perhaps an hour to rest. Upon rising, the grayfarers carefully bathed and oiled themselves, as was their custom before war. Soldiers sharpened their blades and checked their crossbows. Now, standing in the Grand Plaza, under the great statue of Griogair, which glimmered in the fading moonlight, the army appeared formidable despite its small size. No one said much, though they sought out their friends, shaking hands and embracing each other.

After a time, Waldemariam raised his arm, signaling them to their positions. Archers mounted the wall, and the cataphracts and dragoons, astride their chargers, assembled in ranks before the breach. The drawbridge was closed and sealed, making the gaping hole in the wall the only viable passage in or out of the city. With everyone in place, the grayfarers lifted off the ground and flew to their positions.

In the center of the Grand Plaza, Elliott and Sarintha stood side by side under the statue of Griogair. They, too, wore suits of shining armor, emblazoned with the crest of shamalan royalty. Sarintha's injured leg could bear more weight now that Waldemariam and Oskar had personally attended to it, removing the arrow before bandaging and splinting it for support. With the sunrise before them, she turned to Elliott and looked deeply into his eyes. "It is an honor to stand next to you on this day, Elliott of Ondor."

He looked into her eyes, fighting the urge to tell her how beautiful she looked. He also wanted to tell her that this wasn't his home and it wasn't his fight. He wanted to say that he didn't care enough about Harwelden to sacrifice his life for it, and that he wanted only to go back home. Instead, he said nothing, thinking only of how beautiful she looked with the morning sun spilling over her shoulders. He registered the thought that facing certain death, he didn't have the nerve to try to avoid it because he was standing next to a beautiful woman.

She kissed him on the cheek. "May Baruna be with you."

"And with you."

She drew her sword and left him. On the mountainside, a row of serpans appeared. Astride their frightful malevosaurs, they rode upward until they stood facing the Harweldenites across the breach. For several seconds, the two groups faced each other.

From behind the malevosaur brigade, Viscount Ecsar ascended. Like a dark angel, he hovered in the sky with his armor glistening under the light of the morning suns. "Today ends the long cycle of war!" he bellowed, sounding almost as if he were offering an olive branch. "And today the serpans of Vengala retake what has been stolen from them. To all born of Harwelden, prepare to meet your end, for today it comes with a vengeance."

From somewhere down the mountainside, a horn sounded. And in a crash of flesh and metal, the two groups slammed into each other.

Sarintha said, "It is an honor to stand next
to you on this day, Elliott of Ondor."

Chapter 61

Defense

A t first, it seemed that the flimsy defense could not hold. The snarling malevosaurs charged, threatening to crash through despite the best efforts of the outnumbered Harweldenites. In the Boulevard of Kings, soldiers pulled Haviru catapults, scavenged from the courtyards around the castle, into position behind the besieged warriors. They ignited stones wrapped in oiled cloth and lobbed them over the breach as rapidly as the catapults could fire, raining a hail of flaming projectiles down on the assailing serpans, clearing great swaths of the mountainside.

Cheering, the cataphracts surged through the gap, and the Harweldenites seemed buoyed—until a golgomite's shadow passed over them. Four black darfoyles flanked the fearsome lizard, each darfoyle carrying beneath him a large vat. Descending, the darfoyles released their cargo, drenching the soldiers on the front line. When the vats were emptied, the golgomite shrieked, bellowing a stream of fire that ignited the sludge, and the foremost Harweldenites disappeared in a wall of flame. Choking on black smoke and the smell of charring flesh, the survivors retreated.

From the castle, Woolf, Waldemariam, and Grimaldi flew into the sky, swarming against the darfoyles as the golgomite slapped at them with its tail, bellowing bursts of flame. Near the breach, Sarintha closed with a serpan warlord. Though she favored her good leg, the sun was at her back, and her swordsmanship impeccable. She landed a blow to his breastplate, knocking him back as, in the distance, two more golgomites approached from the north.

Elliott watched from the Grand Plaza, alone and terrified. Wishing to summon the courage to join Sarintha on the mountain, he drew his sword from its scabbard and gave it a practice swing. He had never wielded a sword, and it felt heavy. The inertia of the swing took his balance, and he fell. Dread knotted in his belly as he stared through the breach, watching Sarintha hack at the stunned warlord, and he remained as if welded in place, at the foot of Griogair's statue, afraid to enter the battlefield.

Above him, Waldemariam fought alone against the darfoyles while Woolf and the others battled the golgomite. The darfoyles tried to coordinate against Waldemariam but couldn't seem to get near him. In a flash of glinting armor, he zipped around and between them, slashing at their wing tendons so that their flying grew clumsy. As far as Elliott could see, they had yet to lay a sword on him. Though larger than Waldemariam, and though four to his one, they were outmatched, and with Waldemariam in hot pursuit, they fled.

Meanwhile, Woolf and Grimaldi swarmed about the golgomite's head, dodging the streams of sulfurous flame and slashing at its eyes. Beneath it, Baucus and Landrew stabbed at its belly, while Oskar slashed at the great leathern wings. Listing sideways, it gave a guttural croak and began losing altitude. Oskar kept at its wings, tattering them until they could no longer keep it aloft. Finally, it crashed headlong into the mountain, crushing a broad swath of advancing serpans in the bargain.

For a moment, Elliott was exultant, though the dread in his belly renewed itself when he looked up to see the remaining two golgomites above him. He looked for the grayfarers, only to find that they had left. The two golgomites wheeled in the air and came at him.

Dropping his sword, he turned and ran.

The golgomites spat their fire, igniting the ground behind him. Throwing off his helmet, he ran as fast as he could toward the castle. He felt the heat behind him, then *on* him, scorching his back. He tried to run faster and would have thrown off his heavy armor, too, if only he could. He felt fire on the backs of his legs, then against his neck. The smell of burning hair filled his nostrils as flames licked the back of his head. And there in the middle of the Boulevard of Kings, he fell beneath a curtain of sulfurous flame. A terrible screech shook the ground as he gagged on the smoke. With his heart pounding frantically, he tried to roll over and extinguish the flames, but they seemed unquenchable. With his consciousness dimming, he looked toward the breach, hoping for a final glimpse of Sarintha. Then, amid the flame, a shadow appeared. Like a dream, it came for him.

The next thing he knew, he was airborne. Talons dug into his shoulders, and his feet dangled high over the boulevard. He had lost half his armor, and his clothes were on fire. Certain that he was about to be smashed against the wall of the castle, he looked into the face of the creature that had snatched him up. It was Woolf.

From the north, Viscount Ecsar flew toward them, drawing his sword. Woolf hurtled at him, and they collided over the Grand Plaza. As they wrestled in the sky, Woolf's talons dug deeper, flinging Elliott from side to side as the winged warriors ducked and darted, until he felt that his bones would be jerked apart. Making an upward feint, Woolf grabbed Ecsar by the neck and maneuvered on top of him, until Ecsar and Elliott hung beneath him, far above the courtyard, staring into each other's eyes. Ecsar's eyes bulged, and glaring at Elliott through the pain of strangulation, he pulled back his sword and thrust.

With Ecsar's sword only inches from Elliott's breast, Woolf had no choice but to drop Elliott. End over end, he tumbled

The golgomites spat their fire,
igniting the ground behind him.

through the air, screaming as the ground spun up at him with dizzying speed.

But Woolf had aimed well. Without even touching the circular walls of the well in the Grand Plaza, Elliott fell directly into it, all the way to the underground stream that fed it.

The water quenched his burning clothes, and he inhaled. When he opened his eyes, the yellow hue again colored his vision, and the webbed spaces between his fingers and toes tingled and popped, releasing the membranes on his hands and feet.

⚓ ⚓ ⚓

Sarintha had fallen back to the boulevard, where only a handful of Harweldenites remained. Serpans poured through the breach, filling the city just as they had before. Swords flashed and clanged all around, and three serpans came at her. She stepped back, parrying their thrusts as best she could. With her injured leg screaming beneath her weight, she yelled for the Harweldenites with her to circle. Shoulder to shoulder, they linked to form a defensive ring of flashing swords. Over and over, she looked to the sky, wondering what had happened to the grayfarers, but only the golgomites were there, spitting fire at the castle. With so many against her, her swordplay diminished to a series of defensive parries, and it was all she could do to block the sword and ax blows assailing her. Desperate, she looked to the castle, praying for the truant grayfarers to rejoin the battle, when at last she saw one of them.

Rising from behind the parapets like an avenging angel, Arbusto ascended, raising his sword with his good arm. His oiled skin glistened, and his armor shone against the backdrop of black smoke. Instantly, the golgomites plunged toward him, spewing their fire. Hovering above the castle, he pointed his sword tip skyward and closed his eyes. The golgomites screeched, spitting streams of fire, singeing his flesh, yet he did not budge as the great lizards hurtled toward him with open jaws.

With only a few feet remaining before they crashed into him, Grimaldi, Baucus, Landrew, and Oskar shot upward from the roof, where they had been hiding behind the parapets. Soaring upward, they drove their blades into the golgomites' bellies. At the last second before impact, Arbusto dived backward while his fellow grayfarers struck at the beasts again and again.

⚱ ⚱ ⚱

In the subterranean spring, Elliott struggled to focus. Darkness surrounded him, and the soothing warmth of the underground channel beckoned him to sleep.

As he drifted, the sensations of the water against his body intermingled with memories from his past, and for a moment, he was with his mother. The babbling of the underground stream became the water of a running bath as his mother knelt over him. In his mind, she sang sweetly, comforting him, caressing him. The sickness he had grown accustomed to was gone from her. He looked at her and smiled. In the bathtub was his toy monkey—a windup plastic toy with a flipping tail that propelled it. While his mother sang to him, he wound the toy, sending its tail into action, and released it into the bath.

He relished the sound of the bathwater filling his tub while, at his feet, the toy stalled. Its flicking tail slapped against his heel over and over as he listened to the tones of his mother's soothing voice.

With the rhythmic slapping sensation still at his heel, Elliott opened his eyes. The sound of his mother's voice faded to nothing. In shades of yellow, he saw the moss-covered stones of the subterranean well, and in the distance, he heard the crash of boulders and the clang of metal. And still the slapping at his heel continued. He squeezed his eyes shut, straining to focus.

Back in the present, he turned, squinting. In the water behind him, a small creature tapped at his foot. It was a monkey, orange with black stripes, like a tiger. And it held something shiny between its teeth. Fully alert now, Elliott marveled at the wedjat, with the lost bracelet of the nine clans in its mouth. Reaching out, Elliott took the bracelet and snapped it onto his wrist. The wedjat chattered, then turned and dogpaddled down the stream, barely keeping its head above the water.

With renewed vigor, Elliott swam toward the mouth of the well. And with a final thrust of his sculls, he shot himself out of the water, leaping through the long opening onto the Boulevard of Kings, where he landed on his feet.

Chapter 62

Valderon

The devastation of the city struck Elliott like a physical blow. A small band of Harweldenites battled on in the middle of the boulevard, but when he searched for the rest of the army, it was, quite simply, gone. Turning toward the breach, he saw serpans freely entering the city. The brave cataphracts and dragoons fighting there not an hour ago were nowhere to be seen, though soon enough he found their mangled remains scattered about the Grand Plaza. Near the well, he recognized the pallid face of the soldier who had knelt before him in the castle. He had been run through and now stared into the suns with blank eyes. A quick look to the skies confirmed the absence of the grayfarers. Except for the small, barely surviving band of defenders in the boulevard, he was alone against the might of thousands of serpans now sacking the city.

With rising fear, he purged his lungs of water and looked to the circle of embattled defenders—all that was left of Harwelden's army. Sarintha stood shoulder to shoulder with the few remaining soldiers, defending herself as best she could against the attacking horde. She was beginning to buckle beneath the furious blows, and Elliott could see that she would not last much longer. Frantic, he called out to her, but she couldn't hear him over the din of battle.

He had scarcely collected himself when they saw him. From the boulevard and the breach, serpan warriors came at him. Shrieking in mortal terror, Elliott grasped the bracelet and wished himself home.

But the bracelet didn't take him home. When he looked up, a score of serpans not ten paces away lunged at him, screaming. Sunlight glinted off their grim weapons as they fell on him with ax and sword. Closing his eyes, he readied himself for a grisly end, wondering how long it would take. All around him, wind blew through the city, stirring the smoke of a hundred fires into a great, whirling vortex.

And in an instant, the clanging of swords stopped, and the screams fell silent.

Gripping the bracelet so tightly that his knuckles were white, he cracked one eye open, feeling almost too terrified to look . . .

He gaped in disbelief. The serpans hung frozen in midair, as if captured in a snapshot. The nearest of them, thrusting his still sword with maniacal zeal, was suspended in mid leap, the sword mere inches from Elliott's face.

For the first time in seconds, he breathed. He looked at the bracelet. It was glowing, its stones seeming to pulsate with cool fire.

In a circle around him, like pictures from the tapestries of Harwelden, the serpans remained frozen in action, their faces lit with premature satisfaction at the kill.

Gingerly, Elliott stepped out of the circle. In the sky, birds were frozen in flight, and all around, serpans hung suspended in whatever act they were performing at the moment of the bracelet's magic. The entire city was silent. Except for Elliott, time stood still.

In disbelief, he started down the boulevard as, in his mind, a voice spoke out. *You are the Shadowcaster*. It was Crosslyn. *The power lies within you*.

"I can hear you!" he screamed, looking up, searching for the voice. "Talk to me! Tell me what to do!" But his pleas met only silence.

Down the boulevard, Sarintha was on her knees, frozen like the rest, her hands held above her. She had at last dropped her sword, and a serpan had already swung his sword to a point in the air inches from her scalp.

In his mind, Elliott heard the childlike song of the sprites:

The river shall flow red as blood,
The soil of Ondor turns to mud.
With plague of rats and death, they'll see
The victor, who shall hold the key.
A shamalan, for all to know,
The boy of lore, whose fame shall grow.

He walked up to Sarintha. Standing next to where she knelt, he reached out and touched her. His skin tingled as if an electric current coursed through him. His heart rate ramped up. He looked into the eyes of the frozen serpan above her, caught in the split second before killing her, and he was overcome with rage.

He closed his eyes and let the energy crash into him. But now, unlike in the valley, he controlled it, allowing his rage to fuel it. He opened his eyes and stared at the frozen serpan above Sarintha, studied the lines in his face, and the sword that had stopped the instant before cleaving her head in two. Glaring at the serpan, Elliott pushed out with his mind.

A cracking sound filled his ears, and he watched the serpan turn gray.

Elliott pushed out with his mind again, wielding the strange power as if by second nature, commanding it, directing it. The serpan began to crack, as if it were ancient stone succumbing to the elemental ravages of eons.

Elliott pushed again, and it desiccated further. Its gray skin wrinkled, and its eyes sank into the recesses of their sockets. Fault lines crazed its surface, like fissures in a sere desert, until finally the figure crumbled to shards and dust. Like a ripple, the effect spread outward, and the serpans nearest Sarintha's would-be killer also turned gray.

Elliott realized that he was doing just what he had done in the valley. But this time, he was in control of it. The energy coursed through him, and he had never felt so invigorated or so powerful. As if flexing a once paralyzed muscle, he pushed again, and the effect spread through the city in a radiating wave, causing the serpans to wither and fall away into dust.

In that moment, he realized that the battle was won. He walked toward the breach, preparing to target the serpans on the mountain, when he heard a whoosh above his head, and a shadow fell over him. Amid the stillness, Alasdar approached from the north.

In stunned silence, Elliott watched as Alasdar touched down gently in front of him. The grayfarer's wolfish eyes burned like red coals, and Waldemariam's amulet hung from his neck. For the first time, Elliott noticed its detail. It was made of gold metal and fashioned in the shape of a tree.

Standing in front of him, Alasdar threw back his head and laughed. "You didn't really think it would be that easy, did you?"

Elliott pushed out with his mind, but against this foe the effort was fruitless, and the force doubled back on him, knocking him down.

"Your tricks are of no use against me, boy." Alasdar extended his wings in the usual grayfarer show of aggression. "Do you know who stands before you?"

Elliott got to his feet and dusted himself off.

Alasdar gave a sinister grin. "I have returned to claim what rightfully belongs to my master, Malgothar, the dark lord," he said in a raspy voice clearly not his own. "And with the help of my chosen one, Lothar, we shall end these last brief days of Shamalan Empire and return Pangrelor, and all her daughterlands, to him. It will be as Malgothar intended at the dawn of the ages, when he struck out with me against our creator, Baruna. Your feeble efforts today have done nothing to change that."

Still grasping the bracelet, Elliott straightened his back. "You have betrayed your people," he said. "You will pay the price."

Alasdar laughed. "Naive boy, through me, Malgothar's faithful servants shall return from their exile in Mantua and from the realm of the Shadow Mountain. The ancient battle between Baruna and Malgothar will be renewed, and the Antiquitas Trident rebuilt. The fallen angels who joined with Malgothar will be reborn on the sacred soil of Lon Carafay, which belonged only to them in the days before the shamalans slithered out of the seas. For I have discovered the secret to overcoming death. With the help of the dark lord, from the Forest of Golroc and the bastion at Angrelar, I am reborn. I have returned to my home for the reckoning. Though I have chosen this mortal body, I am Valderon."

The scene before Elliott blurred, and the images in his view distorted, as if the very fabric of the world were being stretched and pulled. Everything fell dark, and for a moment, he lost consciousness.

The next thing he knew, he was on his back. He opened his eyes to find himself in a different place, alone with Valderon. Still inhabiting the form of Alasdar, Valderon flew circles above him, laughing. Elliott looked around and found himself on the narrow, flat surface of a craggy stone spire, which rose high above a sea of molten lava. In the distance, a volcano bellowed. Lava rolled down the side of the mountain and into a hellish sea of red. The sea of lava covered the strange world as far as he could see.

He had dreamed of this desolate place in the Forest of Golroc. The sky above was gray and empty except for Valderon, who circled, laughing maniacally.

"What is this place?" Elliott asked. He tried to push himself up and very nearly fell off the narrow stone ledge. With a gasp, he lay flat again, terrified to move lest he plunge into the sea of lava, as he had in his dream.

"It is the sad daughterworld of Er, and it is the last place you will ever see."

Before Valderon had even finished speaking, chains snaked up the side of the spire, wrapping around Elliott's wrists, ankles, and torso. They felt hot against his skin as they pulled at him, holding him fast to the spire.

"You are not the only one with a command of the old magic," Valderon laughed.

Elliott wanted to use the power of the bracelet, but for that he would need a source of energy. His eyes darted back and forth, looking for something, anything, from which to draw the energy he needed to fight Valderon. But perhaps his enemy had anticipated this, because the world to which he had been transported was entirely barren.

Slowly Valderon approached. Flaring his great wings, he landed on the edge of the spire and walked toward Elliott, drawing his sword.

"I expected a great deal more from Griogair's heir," he said. "Your ancestor was a mighty foe." He slashed the air with his sword, as if testing its weight. "But you have not proved nearly so formidable." He stood over him, staring down, brandishing his sword. "Still," he said, "you have proved yourself capable with the bracelet. Perhaps there are things you can offer."

Helpless against the chains, Elliott stared up at him. Valderon looked to the sky and held up his sword. And in that second, Elliott went blind.

"There is something I want to show you," Valderon said.

Though Elliott's vision was gone, a familiar scene appeared in his mind's eye. A world away, he saw his mother, lying in her bed.

"There is a choice you must make."

Like a movie, the scene in his mind played out. His grandfather walked into the room and knelt over his mother's bed, grasping her hand. The old man stroked her forehead and laid his head on her chest. "Mary," he whispered. His voice broke, and he began to cry. The old man wept for several minutes, stroking her forehead, but she didn't move.

After a time, his grandfather stood. Slowly, with great sadness, he tugged at her bedsheet, pulling it up over her face until she was covered. Then, hanging his head, he turned and left the room.

Elliott screamed out. There was a flash beneath his eyelids. In an instant, the maudlin tableau gave way to different scene. His mother sat upright, reading a book, laughing. Her color had returned. In the background, "The Girl from Ipanema" streamed from the tinny speakers of her record player. She looked happy. As before, his grandfather entered the room, but this time he carried a vase of flowers. He set the flowers on the bedside table and knelt, taking her hand.

Tilting her head to the side, she smiled at him. "Thank you, Father," she said.

"The news . . . it's wonderful!" the old man said.

"Yes," she said, glowing. "It is."

The old man beamed at her. "Elliott," he said. "He must have done this."

She looked toward the window as if searching for him. "I knew he would."

The scene flashed out of Elliott's mind, and his eyesight returned. He lay on the craggy mountain spire, with Valderon standing over him.

"Through Valderon, all things are possible," he said. "Lothar is weak. Join me, and I will banish him to Hulgaar. With the dark lord Malgothar guiding us, you will stand at my side, and we will choose for ourselves the future of all worlds. Anything you desire will be given you, and your mother's life will be spared. Choose against me, and it is you who will be banished to eternal torment, your mother's fate sealed."

The hot chains pulled tighter against Elliott. In the distance, the volcano spewed another fountain of molten stone into the sky. Rivulets of sweat poured off him. He thought of the possibilities. *"Anything you desire will be given you."* The prospect was dizzying, and his mind flooded with all the things he might take, the people in his life whose fate he might control or destroy. But the whole thing felt wrong. Regardless of the consequences, he knew what his answer must be.

"I will never join you," he said.

"So be it." Valderon crouched over Elliott. Grasping the hilt of his sword in both hands, he pointed its tip at Elliott's chest and raised it high. The golden amulet dangled from his neck and seemed the only bright spot against the vast gray backdrop. With a gleeful laugh, he plunged the sword downward.

In his final seconds, Elliott heard Crosslyn's voice in his mind, though Crosslyn was not speaking to him directly. Rather, his voice was like an echo, repeating the last words he ever spoke: *"Use the trees."*

The realization washed over Elliott in a flood. He closed his eyes and concentrated on Valderon's amulet, which was fashioned in the shape of a tree and endowed with the power to bewitch a foe or transport its wielder between worlds. He sucked the power he needed from the amulet, and the chains binding him shattered like glass. With Valderon's sword grazing his chest, he rolled and jumped to his feet.

A look of astonishment replaced the smug leer on Valderon's face, and he reached for the amulet. But he pulled his hand away from it at once, as if it had burned him. For a moment, he stared at Elliott; then the sinister grin returned. He raised his sword. "Your tricks will not save you this time!" he bellowed. And he lunged, thrusting with the sword.

Elliott ducked and drew from his belt the dagger that Marvus had given him. He slashed in an upward arc, slicing a long gash in Valderon's wing.

Stunned, Valderon dropped the sword. In a rage, he dived for Elliott, arms outstretched.

Elliott fell backward onto the ledge. Below him, he could hear the thick sound of lava lapping against the base of the craggy outcropping. Valderon was on top of him, strangling him. Struggling to breathe, he tried to roll from underneath him, but Valderon's grip was like steel as he pushed Elliott closer to the precipice.

Elliott beat at him with his fist and tried to get at him with the dagger, but he was no match for Valderon's strength. He tried to use the power of the bracelet, but before he could act, Valderon lifted him off the ground and heaved him over the edge. Just as in his dream, he plummeted toward the lava sea.

⚓ ⚓ ⚓

In the boulevard, Sarintha's eyes fluttered. Time recommenced, and she yelped, holding her arms up against the attacking serpans. But they were gone. Everywhere, the serpans had vanished, leaving only a thick coating of ash on the ground. Her mind raced, and she struggled to comprehend what had happened. In front of the castle, something flashed, and she watched in bewildered silence as Elliott and Alasdar materialized. Elliott was falling, and above him, Alasdar descended, flying clumsily with a gash in one of his wings. In the shadow of the castle, they landed in the courtyard, and Elliott stood. Appearing confused, he grasped the bracelet and brushed himself off to face Alasdar.

Alasdar unleashed a wrenching, otherworldly scream. And as she looked on in horror, he began to change. His grayfarer skin grew dark, and he gained mass, growing taller until he towered over Elliott, dwarfing him. His eyes burned like bright coals. No longer recognizable as Alasdar, he raised a scaly arm with clenched fist. With his eyes locked on Elliott, as if no one else were present, Alasdar pointed a spindly forefinger at him and threw back his head to shriek out a bloodcurdling cry. Black smoke poured from his maw. His outstretched finger glowed red. The sky above the city darkened as the smoke formed into a whirlwind, blocking the light of the suns. Elliott struggled, and it looked as though a great wind would blow him away.

Thinking of the ash covering the city, and remembering Elliott's sleep after his earlier feat in the valley, Sarintha guessed that he must be greatly weakened. She prayed for Baruna to give him strength.

In the courtyard, Alasdar, no longer Alasdar at all, had grown to nearly half the height of the castle's highest tower. Horns sprouted from his head, and his scaly skin glowed red. A wispy halo of fire surrounded him, and his voice boomed so deeply that the ground beneath Sarintha's feet shook.

"It is time for you to go, boy," he roared. Beneath the flames, his face contorted in a hideous smile, and a stream of fire shot from his outstretched finger toward Elliott.

On his knees against the invisible force of the wind, Elliott looked up. As the fire came at him, he grasped the bracelet and croaked a single word: "Baruna."

Lightning ripped through the sky, and the city began to shake. Elliott glowed with a beautiful white light. With her breath catching in her throat, Sarintha watched as he, too, began to grow. The stream of fire glanced off him, and his dazzling light intensified as he grew. The light enveloped him, changed him. His face elongated and widened, and a long, crooked nose

Alasdar unleashed a wrenching, otherworldly scream. And began to change. His grayfarer skin grew dark, and he gained mass, growing taller until he towered over Elliott, dwarfing him.

sprouted, though it seemed that these features were as much from the dazzling, coalesced light as from any physical substance. The suggestion of a beard formed on his chin, and a glowing white robe flowed around him. All the while, his light intensified until the entire city was awash and it was hard to look upon him.

At last the two behemoths stood facing each other—a bearded old man bathed in white light, against the scaly red demon—evoking the most ancient images from Pangrelorian lore: Baruna the creator against his favorite son, the traitor Valderon.

Valderon's terrible cry continued until Sarintha thought her ears would shatter. Black smoke poured from his maw, joining the dervish in the sky.

An otherworldly voice came forth from the figure of light, whom she recognized as the father of all worlds. "Leave us, fallen son."

Screaming, Valderon fell to his knees, holding his hands over his face. He began to shrink, as if melting.

"This is not the end of it," he howled. He shriveled and sank until, in a matter of seconds, he was Alasdar again, lying broken at the old man's feet. With Baruna staring down at him, he thrashed as if in great agony, then grew still. At the moment his life left him, a shadow emerged from his body. The shadow was without form. Like a crippled black wind, it slithered down the boulevard. She thought she heard it shriek. And as she watched wide-eyed, it blew through the breach and was gone. Elliott's bright light dimmed, and the old man he personified fell to the ground.

In an instant, it was over, and Elliott lay still on the ground. With a yelp, Sarintha ran to him, kneeling over him. Crying, she shook him.

"Wake up, Elliott!" she sobbed. "You've got to wake up!"

Pale and limp, he lay there and didn't respond. She cradled him like a child, brushing the hair out of his face. Desperately she called to the other Harweldenites who had fought beside her in the street, and they, too, rushed to his side. As she held him, with the others hovered in a circle above them, she heard a noise at the breach. Beneath her, the ground began to tremble.

From the mountainside and the valley, the serpan army had awakened. At the far end of the boulevard, again they marched through the breach and into the city.

Chapter 63

Redemption

Sarintha stared at the breach as the horrible realization soaked in: they were coming again. With her senses in overload, she yelled to the Harweldenite soldiers around her. "Help me!" We have to get him into the castle!"

Through the breach the serpans came, looking as if they had just woken from a dream. As before, their numbers seemed endless. They saw the princess struggling to pull Elliott to the safety of the castle, and their expressions sharpened. From the end of the boulevard, they raised their weapons and broke into a run. Harwelden's few remaining soldiers rushed to her side, and together they lifted Elliott. With the serpans coming at a dead run, they lugged his lifeless body toward the castle.

All through the city, the ground quaked as if the mountain were about to crumble. The Harweldenites had made it through the courtyard to the castle door. Behind them, the serpans had covered half the distance and were gaining fast. Again the ground shook violently beneath Sarintha, and remants of the city's burned buildings crashed down into the streets. She couldn't understand what was causing the quake.

When they reached the door of the castle, she let go of Elliott and pushed, fearing that the door might be locked. But it creaked open, and they managed to pull him inside and drop the heavy crossbar into place.

Outside, the enemy smashed into the door. Sarintha stood in the foyer, listening as a dozen serpan axes bit into it. In perhaps a minute, the tip of an ax peeped through, and splinters flew around her. The ground continued to tremble.

"Upstairs!" she yelled. "Get him to the roof!"

With the castle door already giving way, they pulled Elliott up the stairs. He remained in a swoon, a dead weight. Reaching the roof, Sarintha looked to the breach and down into the valley. It was as if the serpans hadn't lost a soldier. Legions entered the city and ran for the castle. In the courtyard below, they pushed against each other, trying to get at the windows, or joined the others in their efforts to crash through the door. Beneath her feet, the castle shivered and quaked.

She knelt beside Elliott and shook him frantically. "Please wake up!" she yelled. "You have to do something!"

He didn't twitch a muscle, and she leaned over him, her face next to his, to see if he was breathing.

From the edge of the roof, one of her soldiers approached. "Your Highness, they've crashed through the door," he said.

From behind the western tower, the grayfarers emerged. Like the serpans on the mountainside a few moments earlier, they appeared to have just awakened. Except for Waldemariam, they were battered and bloody. Grimaldi's and Woolf's tattered wings dripped trails of blood behind them. Baucus and Landrew, burned from the golgomite fires, stood covered in black soot. Together, Sarintha, the few remaining soldiers, and the grayfarers huddled over Elliott.

"He's done all he could," Waldemariam said, kneeling over him. "We've all done all that we could."

"So what now?" Sarintha asked.

"We wait for them."

"So that's it?"

Waldemariam looked at her for several seconds. "That's it."

Straightening her back, she took a deep breath and looked out over her burning city. The roof shook beneath their feet. As her eyes fell over the breach, she saw something that stole her breath. For several seconds, she stared. "Look to the breach," she said.

It was Hooks, riding a mammoth over the stones where the wall had given way, swinging a club and knocking serpans down as if they were scarecrows. Behind him, scores of mounted susquats rampaged into the city atop bellowing mammoths. In a sea of swinging clubs and ivory tusks, serpan warriors flew through the air or were trampled underfoot by the monstrous beasts. From the edge of the desert, in the Forest of Ondor, to the valley and mountainside, the susquats rampaged, unleashing at last the might of their fury. Never before had Sarintha seen such a glorious sight.

Beside her, Waldemariam looked thunderstruck. "Our fugitive susquat has returned at last," he said.

Sarintha's grin widened. "It is . . . unbelievable."

Woolf looked as if he, too, were struggling to make sense of this strange turn of events. "And look to the southern valley."

From the base of the Azure Mountains, more susquats poured onto the battlefield. But they were different: smaller and darker than the others.

"What in the name of Antilia is happening?" Waldemariam asked.

Woolf stared into the distance. "The susquats of Golroc."

At the forefront of the army of dark susquats, their leader stormed onto the battlefield swinging a crudely made sword. He was small and had a red splotch across his face that looked like a birthmark. Fire burned in his eyes. Behind him, a wave of black poured into the valley, crashing into the serpan army, as the susquats of Golroc spilled out of the mountains in unfathomable numbers.

In both valleys, the serpans floundered, and by the time Sarintha had fully digested the magnitude of what was going on, they were scrambling away in disorderly retreat.

From the edge of the desert, in the Forest of Ondor,
to the valley and mountainside, the susquats rampaged,
unleashing at last the might of their fury.

Chapter 64

Victory

Sarintha smiled. "He wakes," she breathed, dabbing Elliott's forehead with a damp cloth. Sunlight streamed in through the window of Marvus's bedchamber, and birdsong filtered in through the open window.

"It's good to see him again," Hooks said, kneeling over him. With a great furry paw, he caressed Elliott's cheek.

"He's opening his eyes," Jingo said. His wooden leg clacked against the floorboards as he went to the bedside and knelt beside Hooks.

Standing at the foot of the bed, Woolf and Marvus smiled. "Indeed, he is awakening," Woolf said." And what a glorious sight to behold."

Outside in the village, the army of men from Abarynthia was busy at work, and sounds of sawing and hammering filled the bedchamber. At the breach, susquat mammoths were delivering quarried stone to the masons repairing the wall, working side by side with the men from Abarynthia and the gimlets of Iracema, who had arrived only yesterday. Outside, the streets bustled as they had in the days before the assault, and a sense of calm at last replaced the frenzy and confusion that had consumed the city since the serpans first arrived in the Valley of Ondor.

Slowly Elliott sat up, with Hooks gently supporting him. "What happened?" he asked, rubbing the sleep from his eyes and stretching. "I don't remember."

"Don't worry, friend, Sarintha said, smiling as she grasped his hand. "We will tell you everything."

Standing at the foot of the bed, Woolf and Marvus smiled.
"Indeed, he is awakening," Woolf said.

Chapter 65

Harwelden Returns

Some days later, with much of the town rebuilt, Waldemariam decided that the time had come for Sarintha's coronation. As in the days before the festival, the village took on new life, though this time without the serpan threat and the sense of impending doom. These were the happiest days Harwelden had seen in many seasons, and all gave thanks to its deliverer, Elliott of Ondor.

On the eve of her coronation, Sarintha knocked on the door to Elliott's bedchamber. Outside, he could hear the comforting chirps of the cydonias. The mood was overwhelmingly happy, and everyone, it seemed, felt the sense of renewal and return to order that the victory had ushered in. In the throne room of the castle, above the main complex, preparations were complete. Tomorrow Sarintha, Queen of the Shamalan Empire, was to be crowned at last.

When Elliott heard the knock at his door, he rose from the bed Marvus had given him, and opened the door. Seeing Sarintha, he smiled. She smiled back. Despite the brevity of their friendship, the events of the past season had bonded them in a way that few ever experienced. And their status as the last shamalans cemented the bond.

"Take a walk with me," she said.

Elliott's grin widened. "It would be my pleasure, Your Highness," he said, taking her arm.

Together they walked through the castle and out into the courtyards, simply enjoying being together. At first, neither spoke. They just strolled, arm in arm, out onto the Boulevard of Kings. Above them, the moon shone brightly, bathing the village in a pleasant glow.

Elliott said, "Where are we going?"

"To the temple," she replied. "There is something there I want to show you."

Sarintha giggled as she quickened her pace, pulling him along to the Shamalan Temple, just inside the drawbridge. When they arrived, she took out a key and opened the heavy, creaking wooden door. Once inside, she produced a seer stone, the very one that Marvus had stolen from her bedchamber soon after finding Elliott in the forest, and beckoned its light.

By the light of the stone, she led Elliott up the stairs to the upper chamber. At the top of the stairs, she opened a door and led him past dusty crates of ancient relics, all the way to the yellowed stacks of books at the rear, grinning mischievously all the while. After a brief search of the many volumes lining the shelves, she pulled down one entitled *The Book of Valderon*. By the light of the stone, she bade Elliott sit next to her as she opened the yellowed tome.

"What are you looking for?" Elliott asked as she thumbed through the ancient leaves.

"Here," she said. "Let me read this to you."

He nodded.

"From the shores of Gaya," she began, tracing the lines with her finger, "the new king will arise to thwart Malgothar's plan." She paused a moment, gauging his response to her words. "From his distant homeland, a daughter of the parent to all the stars in the sky, he will find passage to Pangrelor, the great mother of the stars. Upon his arrival, the new king will perform feats never before dreamed possible. From humble beginnings, he will rise to great heights, and the great warring factions of the world will unite under his banner, and the mightiest of all kingdoms will spring forth as the product of his will. When his kingdom is risen, it will fall to Malgothar's liege, mighty Valderon, to rise up against it and take back what has been lost."

She closed the book and gazed at Elliott in the thin light of the seer stone. Elliott returned her gaze, confused, sensing that he was missing the import of what she had just read.

"I remember reading this when I was a child," she said. "The events of this passage began at the dawn of the last age, though what it implies has never before occurred to me."

"What?" Elliott asked. "The passage is talking about Griogair, right?"

"Correct," she said. "And at the end of his life, according to the book, Griogair returned to his home in Gaya, never to be seen again." She grew excited. Later passages talk about his heir, 'a shamalan from Gaya'—which is you," she said, grinning.

Elliott looked at the floor. "I still have a hard time believing that," he said. "I know the bracelet is only supposed to work for Griogair's heir, but I have never understood that part."

"But that's what I'm trying to show you," she said. Think again about the passage I just read to you. It says Griogair is from the daughterland of Gaya, which is clearly our name for your home."

"Okay," he said, still trying to grasp her point.

"Griogair was a Gayan," she said. "Nowhere in the passage does it say he is shamalan. It says he united the great warring factions, the mightiest of which was the shamalans, but nowhere does it state—or even imply—that he himself was shamalan."

"I don't understand."

Sarintha smiled. "Like Griogair, you are from Gaya." She paused. "But you are a *shamalan* from Gaya," just as was prophesied. Once in Pangrelor, Griogair interbred with the shamalans, but the scrolls tell that he returned to Gaya before the end of

"From the shores of Gaya,"
Sarintha began, tracing the lines with her finger,
"the new king will arise to thwart Malgothar's plan."

his life. Perhaps he took with him a descendant. Perhaps a seed from the shamalan race returned to Gaya with him. You are the heir to that seed, Elliott. It explains how a boy from Gaya could possess the abilities of a shamalan—which is the part of your story that makes the least sense. Jingo has shared with me the story of your father. I have struggled to understand how you might be of shamalan lineage, but this must be the answer." She closed the book. "The shamalan seed has been passed down to you in Gaya. Whoever and whatever your father was, he must have carried that seed."

"I suppose it is possible," Elliott said, thinking of his wretched father. "But does the book, or anything else, indicate that Griogair took an offspring back to Gaya with him?"

"Well, no. But it *has* to be the answer. Somehow, you inherited the shamalan traits without ever having set foot on Pangrelor. Somehow, from the land of Gaya, you are the great heir to our king Griogair. You are the one we have awaited."

"I have other relatives back home that seem more likely to have passed on the shamalan traits," Elliott said. He looked at the birthmarks on his hands.

"Who, then?" she asked.

"My grandfather and my mother bear the markings of shamalans," he said. "And my grandfather seemed to know something about this whole affair. On the day before I crossed over to Pangrelor, he told me about the cultivation."

"Oh," she said. "Jingo didn't tell me that part."

"When I think back to my grandfather's words, I think he must have known about all this—about what was going to happen to me once I came over here. I think my mother also knew. She didn't want me to learn anything about it. She wanted to protect me."

Sarintha sat enthralled, urging him onward with her silence.

"My grandfather told me I must complete a task that he had been unable to complete. I believe the task was the act of crossing over into Pangrelor." He grew excited. He had not talked about his trip to his grandfather's basement with anyone, at least not in any detail, and he was hungry to share the experience with her. "On the evening of my passage, I found a journal that was written by a shamalan of Pangrelor. It told of his banishment to Gaya and how he could not find his way home. He spoke of my own home, though his description of it was many years old, as if the banishment had occurred long ago. My grandfather told me that the journal's author was my ancestor."

"So you have known all along of your connection to Pangrelor, despite your misgivings. But who could this ancestor have been?"

"My grandfather said his name was Darius Orion."

Sarintha's brow crinkled, and for a moment she was silent. "I have never heard that name before," she said at last.

"Whoever he was," Elliott said, "he must be the key to everything. But that's the only name I've heard, and I don't know much about him. And even if he is my shamalan ancestor, I still don't understand how I can be the heir to King Griogair."

"Nor do I," said Sarintha, "Griogair's lineage in Pangrelor became muddied long ago. Many have claimed to be his heir, but no one has been able to wield the bracelet of the nine clans—not until you arrived. And the bracelet itself has been missing since the time of the Great Betrayal." Sarintha was excited but was also as confused as he. "However you got here, and however the bracelet ended up in Gaya—and in your possession—is less important. I just thank the elders that you are here, Elliott. I don't know what we would have done without you!" She laughed and reached out to hug him in the near dark. He recoiled in shyness, glad that the shadows hid his blushing face.

"I'm sorry," she said softly. "I don't wish to make you uncomfortable."

"It's okay," Elliott said, changing the subject and guarding himself from the awkwardness of the gesture. "I have so many questions."

"Like what?" She settled back into her corner, *The Book of Valderon* still on her lap.

"Where to begin?" he said. "For starters, what's a wedjat?"

She laughed. "Where did you hear of the wedjat?" But before he had time to reply, she said, "There is no such thing as a wedjat, Elliott. It's a mythical creation of our world—an enchanted being that accompanies heroes, protecting them from the forces of darkness. Our mythology claims that each visit from a wedjat heralds the death of someone beloved. For anyone to gain a wedjat's protection, someone who protected them in life must have died. But this is only myth. No one has ever actually *seen* a wedjat. They are a creation of days long since passed. Even the scrolls don't lend much credence to their existence. The legend of the wedjat is the stuff of peasants' fairy tales. No such creature exists."

"Hmmph." *Each visit from a wedjat heralds the death of someone beloved.* He played the words over in his mind. He didn't tell Sarintha of his visits from the wedjat. If what she said was true, then the wedjat in the forest of Golroc would have something to do with Crosslyn. The wedjat in the well, however . . .

He shuddered, not wanting to believe what he already feared might be true. He sat straight, determined not to get emotional. Thoughts of his mother crept to the forefront of his mind, though he pushed them back. "Who . . . or what is Valderon?"

"Oh, Elliott," she said, touching the volume in her lap, "his is a long tale, and one that you will come to know well. "He is an ancient foe. An angel fallen from Antilia at the dawn of the world. During the cultivation, we learn of the complex order of beings created at the dawn of time. Among these are the arch-angels—the Vajir and Extera—the first beings made by the great creator Baruna. Valderon was conceived as a lower order of the most powerful of these beings, but soon he became a powerful foe of the creator. At the dawn of the world, before the creation of even the first daughterland, he led a revolt against the creator and was banished forever from Pangrelor. In the ages since, he has traveled throughout the stars, existing only as a shadow of his former self. It is said he was imprisoned in the great Shadow Mountain, though none of that is important right now.

The scrolls prophesy his return, as does *The Book of Valder-on*. They tell of his desire to retake the first world, which is Pangrelor. In his return, and from the events of recent seasons, we can glean that the new age is dawning. The world is chang-ing, Elliott, and you have helped usher in the change."

She smiled at him and reached out to touch his cheek. "No doubt, Valderon will gain in strength, and many will aid him in his quest to return to power. That is what all this has been about. Malus Lothar and the serpans fell under his spell. They are hap-less participants in the most ancient of battles. The scrolls tell of the final battle but do not convey who the winner shall be. We are all charged with the difficult task of following our faith and choosing the side that we believe to be righteous. That is why so many have been willing to place their faith in you. In you, they see righteousness. In you, they see the one who will for-ever defeat the ancient foe and restore order to the world. And not only to Pangrelor," she said, giving him that mischievous smile again, "but to all her daughters as well. Events in Pangre-lor have far-reaching consequences. A tremor in Pangrelor will be felt as a quake in her daughterlands. And disaster here will bring the daughterworlds to their knees. This is taught during the cultivation. No doubt, even this most recent battle for Har-welden has been felt in some manner in the daughterlands. If

Valderon were to succeed, it would change the order of things entirely. This is what he and Lothar seek. And stopping them, we now know, will depend largely on you." She beamed at him.

"Whoa!" Elliott said. "Slow down. Whatever role I've had to play, I'm pretty sure I am not meant to defeat Valderon. I may be able to control the bracelet, but even that is a limited power. Every time I use it, I go to sleep for three days."

"But your power is growing," she said. "We cannot deny the importance of your latest feat. You channeled the creator himself."

"If you say so." He was unable to remember anything from his final confrontation with Valderon. "But I don't want to stay here, Sarintha. I want to go back home." *For someone to gain a wedjat's protection, someone who protected them in life must have died.* He couldn't get the words out of his head.

She looked at the floor. "That is a difficult topic, to be sure. But I am certain your future lies here. Indirectly, you are of this world. And the mantle of its survival falls squarely on you."

"Well, I pass the mantle back to you," he said. "Because I'm not staying. Somehow, I'm going to find my way back home."

"In time, you will see that I am right," she said. "Soon, after I have been crowned, my first act as queen will be to ask you to travel into the forest, to the tombs of the elders, where you will seek further instruction." She looked at him, gauging his response. "To defeat Valderon, the Antiquitas Trident must be rediscovered. There is so much I have to teach you. The scrolls tell us that Griogair's heir will strive to reunite the Antiquitas. That is you, Elliott, and this will be harder than anything you have yet done for us."

He was getting annoyed at her refusal to understand that he just wanted to go home. "I'm tired," he said, standing up. "Let's get back to the castle."

In the darkness, he headed for the stairs. And grudgingly, Sarintha got up and followed him.

Chapter 66

Reunion

The next morning, Elliott woke to a knock at his door. Rubbing his eyes, he pulled on his shirt and got up to see who might be calling so early. When he opened the door, he was surprised to see the massive form of Hooks, grinning ear to ear. They had hardly spoken since their appearance before the chieftan in Susquatania. Smiling, Hooks reached out and bear-hugged him, lifting him off the floor.

Elliott laughed, returning the hug as his feet dangled above the floor.

"We did it!" Hooks roared.

"Yes," Elliott said, still grinning, "we did."

"It's so good to see you! Now, let's go get some breakfast. They've prepared a feast in celebration of the coronation to-night. We've got a big day ahead! Much to talk about! And I'm starving!"

Elliott laughed again as Hooks put him down. "It's good to see you, old friend. And good to see you haven't changed a bit."

Grinning, Hooks clapped him on the back so hard, he nearly fell to the floor. Together they set out for the Great Hall.

"So, Hooks," Elliott said, "is your brother still here?"

"No. He and the others stayed a few days to lend support, but now that he has made enemies of the serpans, he must go back home to fortify the valley. He left some workmen and some of the mammoths to help with the rebuilding, though."

Hooks reached out and bear-hugged Elliott,
lifting him off the floor.

"How did you ever convince them to help us? After all the stuff that happened in Susquatania? We were all sure you were going to be executed. I couldn't believe it when I heard you and the susquats had come to our defense."

"Yes," Hooks said, grinning. "I thought it was over for me, too. But never underestimate the charms of this old susquat," he said with a gleam in his eye. "On the night they imprisoned me, Keats came to my cell." Hooks's voice grew excited as he recounted the tale. "It was as if we were children again. He came to my cell to ask my advice! He was in terrible anguish. Can you believe that? He wanted my *advice!*" There was a chuckle in his voice. "My little brother," after all the seasons that have passed, came to me just as he did when we were children, looking to me for the answers he could not find within himself. And I have to say, I dazzled him."

Elliott grinned. "What did you say to him?"

"Well, I just made the case that I've prepared in my thoughts so many times over the years. I told him the war was coming to Susquatania whether he wanted it or not, and argued that the time to enter the fray was now. If the susquats want to maintain their freedom, I said, we must stand and fight for it." He lowered his voice, adopting a more serious tone. "And I was *really* convincing,"

Elliott laughed. "There is no doubt you can be convincing. But was that all there was to it? Easy as that?"

"I wouldn't say it was *easy,* but I managed to win over my little brother. When he came to my cell, he was looking for a way to redeem me. He couldn't bring himself to order my execution—not with his knowledge of the events that led to my uncle's death." A fleeting sadness darkened his face. "But that is a tale for another time. Despite all the years that have passed, the shine of Keats's big brother, whom he cherished as a child, regained some of its luster that night." His grin spread even wider. "Keats took a risk and let me speak before the council. After my session with them, Jarius and a few of the others offered their support for my position. That is one of the things about the susquats that a lot of folks don't understand. Although they present a united front behind their leader, as they did before you and the others, our discussions behind closed doors can be quite heated. When a few of the council members sided with me, indicating they would consider forgoing my punishment, I knew I was in pretty good shape. If I could win *them* over, the masses were not far behind. After my session with the council, we convened a public debate. And I have never been so eloquent in my life."

"I don't know what came over me that day, but my royal susquat blood shone through as never before. By the time I finished speaking, all Susquatania was ready to ride against the serpans. It was historic! Some even screamed for me to take over as chieftan—said I had returned from political exile to claim my rightful position as their leader. But I would never do that to my brother," he said, lowering his voice. "My interest in politics faded long ago. The thing is, I couldn't believe how quickly they turned. Once I started talking, everyone began to turn in my favor. It was as if they knew all along that we were going to have to do something, and they were just waiting for the right excuse to act on their feelings."

"Wow," Elliott said. "I never would have guessed."

Hooks laughed. "Nor would I. I guess old Crosslyn was right all along. Somehow, the old man understood something about the susquats that even I didn't know."

As they entered the Great Hall, they saw Woolf, Marvus, and Jingo seated at a table and waiting for them.

"So our leaders gathered together," Hooks continued, growing more animated as he paused in the doorway, "and formulated our plans to ride against the serpans and join with the shamalans in defense of their empire. But here's the surprising thing: we had *no communication* with the susquats of Golroc! The fact that they attacked at the same time we did was pure happenstance."

"Or perhaps fate," Elliott said.

"Perhaps, old friend," Hooks replied, clapping him on the back again.

As they proceeded to the breakfast table, Woolf extended a hand toward Hooks. Then, thinking better of it, he grabbed the shaggy beast and hugged him.

"Have a seat, brother," he said. "And allow me, on behalf of the Grayfarer Council, to express Harwelden's undying gratitude for your service in our behalf. Truly, you have done yourself proud."

Hooks grinned. "I don't care what they say about you flying wolves," he replied. You're not half bad."

As they sat down, Woolf said, "I am truly sorry for suspecting you in the deaths of the grayfarer fledglings. It has become clear to us that Alasdar was the murderer and the traitor we have sought for these past seasons." Woolf's face grew long with sadness and regret. "And to think, you were mere hours away from a horrific execution, for a crime you did not commit. We are all thankful to Marvus and Jingo for having the foresight to trust you. For without your presence on that day—and your role in this whole affair—things would have turned out quite differently."

Jingo beamed at Hooks.

"If Elliott is the deliverer, then you were the instigator. I am amazed at Crosslyn's foresight. Through it all, he stood firm in your defense, and it was ultimately your intervention that changed the course of our history." Woolf bowed his head. "Tonight we shall crown Sarintha, but we also honor you with this celebration. And we welcome you to the family of Harwelden.

I hope you will consider staying here with us, in the city. I am loath to bid farewell to such a dear and valuable friend."

Hooks had never appeared more pleased.

"And thanks be to the elders that *you* appeared when you did, Elliott," Marvus said. "I must admit, when we found you outside that cave, I would never have guessed you would become what you have become. In fact," he said, blushing, "I must confess, I found you rather strange."

Elliott nodded. "If it's any consolation, I *felt* pretty strange."

Amid the general laughter, Jingo said, "I didn't think you were strange. I knew all along who you were and what you would become."

"No doubt, that is true," Marvus said, smiling. "I sometimes find young Jingo rash in his actions, but his faith in you never wavered, Elliott. If not for him, we never would have freed Hooks and fled Harwelden to search for Crosslyn."

"Well, I guess we all had our roles to play," Elliott said. "So let's raise a toast. Here's to the Sons of Crosslyn, each as important as the next, and without each of whom this fair city and realm might have fared far worse than it did."

"Hear, hear!" they said, clacking their cups together.

"Today will be a joyous one," Jingo said. "Waldemariam has set great plans for the coronation this evening, and the ceremony will be followed by a memorial honoring Crosslyn's life."

At the mention of the memorial, the tone grew more somber.

"It will be an honor to celebrate him," Marvus said quietly. "He was a shamalan from a different age—the last of his kind."

"And he was a friend to me when I had no others," Hooks said, lowering his head.

Elliott frowned. "I'm curious about something. What's the story behind the dagger he gave to Marvus? I used it against Lothar and later against Valderon. It seemed . . . I don't know . . . *strong*."

"It is known as the Amulius," Marvus said. "The dagger of brotherhood, forged in the Age of Malgothar. It is the first of the hidden shamalan relics to surface. At the dawn of the first age, it was crafted by Valderon himself."

"I don't understand," Elliott said.

"Well," Marvus said, "then allow me to tell you its story—and the story of the Antiquitas Trident, for the two are inextricably linked. The last shamalan king before the Great Betrayal was King Dagnar. Dagnar was the ancestor of the great king Rasmussen and was rumored to be the heir to the family line of Griogair, though it is not known whether this is fact or fiction. Dagnar was the eldest of three brothers, and first in line for the throne. At his father's death, he was crowned king of the Shamalan Empire, as was his birthright."

Elliott leaned forward, becoming engrossed in the tale.

"It was during Dagnar's reign, of course, that the Great Betrayal occurred, although the winds of war with the serpans had begun to blow long before then. Many believed, even way back then, that an attack on Harwelden was inevitable. Even all those many seasons ago, there were whisperings of a traitor within the castle, much the same as during our recent history. But suspicions regarding the identity of the traitor back then were not as ill-focused as in recent days: everyone knew who the traitor was, though no one knew quite what to do about him. The suspected traitor was one of King Dagnar's brothers, a fully vested prince of the Shamalan Empire—I don't suppose I need to mention who."

Everyone at the table, except Elliott, nodded.

"The brother of King Dagnar, and the mastermind behind the Great Betrayal, was Lothar."

Everyone turned and looked at Elliott, who had surmised that Lothar was a fallen shamalan, though he appeared stunned nonetheless by the revelation.

"Indeed," Marvus said somberly. "Lothar was once the next in succession for Dagnar's crown. And the gift of magic was powerful in him. Before Dagnar's coronation, Lothar beseeched his father, then on his deathbed, to name him, not Dagnar, heir to the throne. He was fiercely jealous of his eldest brother, and in his quest for power, he began to experiment with the dark magic. It was he who first made contact with Valderon. Using the most ancient magic, he conjured a meeting with Valderon, who entered into an unholy covenant to assist Lothar in his quest for the shamalan crown. In return, Lothar vowed to help Valderon rise from his prison in the Shadow Mountain. It was this chain of events that led to the Great Betrayal itself, and to Valderon's reemergence. Indirectly, Lothar even cursed Alasdar, in whom the spirit of Valderon took up residence.

"In any event, as Lothar plotted against his brother for the reins of power, he studied the dark art of Vaundarx with great zeal. Vaundarx gives one the ability to cast disease into others, and Lothar's goal was to magically infest his brother Dagnar with the dreaded flesh-eating disease leshwart, for which there is no treatment. Lothar experimented with these abilities in great depth, using various incantations and blood runes against animals in his quest to perfect his skills. Many of his experiments were carried out on rats, which has inspired their great hatred against him—working in many ways to our own advantage."

"But what does all this have to do with the Amulius?" Elliott asked.

"Patience," Marvus said. "We are getting to that. When Lothar felt that his skills were sufficient, he cast a hex on his brother, the newly crowned Dagnar. But as we have seen recently with Slipher, one has to be exact in one's dealings with the old magic. It is a complex skill. As with Slipher, the dark magic backfired on Lothar, and he cast the leshwart upon himself. This is why he covers himself with the steel mask. Though he was once beautiful beyond description, the leshwart horribly and irreversibly marred his appearance. Undoubtedly, to look upon him without the mask would be horrifying.

"Before Lothar tried to cast his hex on Dagnar, everyone knew that Lothar wished to be king, and all were concerned about what he might do to achieve his goal. But no one had the power to act against him, save for Dagnar, who refused to believe the worst about his younger brother."

"I can certainly understand that," Hooks said.

"So it fell to the youngest of the three royal brothers," Marvus continued, "to act in secret against his brother Lothar in the empire's defense. Prince Galeren was Dagnar's youngest brother, and he feared that Lothar would succeed, for he had a clearer understanding than Dagnar of their brother's character. He took it upon himself to ensure that Lothar would not gain the ultimate prize. Without anyone's foreknowledge, Prince Galeren destroyed the shamalans' greatest asset to keep it from falling into Lothar's hands. In so doing, he irreparably weakened the empire."

Hooks was on the edge of his seat. "The Antiquitas Trident!" he exclaimed. "Prince Galeren destroyed the Antiquitas Trident! That explains everything!"

"Yes," Marvus said. "Galeren disassembled it into the seven components from which it was forged: the six daggers of Weldar, which fit together to form its shaft, and the trident head itself. Each of the daggers has a complex history dating back to the dawn of the world. One was made by Valderon, and the others, under his guidance, were made by men, shamalans, and gimlets. Each had a specific purpose, though Valderon, before his imprisonment, secretly guided their construction, for he planned to use their combined magic to build the most powerful weapon ever made: the Antiquitas Trident. He never guessed that he would be defeated and that his weapon would end up in Griogair's hands."

"Anyway, Prince Galeren sensed Lothar's desire to steal the

trident, and the shamalan throne, from Dagnar. He embarked on a journey to hide the daggers and the trident head in the darkest corners of the world, where neither Lothar nor anyone else could ever lay hands on them. The Antiquitas, you see," said Marvus, looking at Elliott, "has been the key to shamalan dominion since the time of King Griogair. It was Griogair's wise use of the Antiquitas that led to his founding the empire. And it was the shamalans' possession of the Antiquitas that resulted in the empire's uninterrupted continuity throughout the past age. It possesses the most powerful magic ever known and holds the key to ultimate power. Galeren was the only living soul who knew the location of its parts. Soon after his return from hiding the daggers and the Trident head, Lothar killed him in a fit of rage. Soon thereafter came the Great Betrayal, and the rest you largely know. It is said that for Galeren's act, despite its noble intentions, his soul has been forever banished to Hulgaar. And none of the components of the Antiquitas has been seen since . . . until now.

"You mean . . . ," Elliott said.

"Yes. The Amulius, the dagger forged by Valderon, is one of the components of the lost Antiquitas. How it came to be in Crosslyn's possession, I shall never know."

"Even I did not know the tale in its entirety," Woolf said. "But it all fits together. Waldemariam and Oskar have discussed the loss of the Antiquitas Trident on many occasions. Waldemariam says that reassembling it is the key to the empire's survival."

"Whoever holds the Antiquitas holds the key to unbridled power," Marvus said. It is the key to the control of Pangrelor and all her daughterlands. Since the time of the Betrayal, Lothar has been actively searching for the daggers. He wants more than anything to reassemble the Antiquitas Trident."

"I never even knew if the daughterlands were real or myth," Hooks said, "though Susquatanian lore speaks of them as well."

"They are real enough, as Elliott can attest, for he is from one of them." Marvus turned again to Elliott. "Since the dawn of time, Pangrelor has given rise to more daughterlands than there are droplets of water in the oceans, and they continue to form to this day. And the fate of the daughterlands falls in line with the fate of Pangrelor, with whom they are forever connected. Pangrelor is the mother to all the stars in the sky, and a ripple here is felt as a flood by her daughters. When evil is done here, it spreads in countless echoes throughout the daughterworlds."

"And that is why Waldemariam says we must seek out the components of the Antiquitas and reassemble it," Woolf said. "So we can restore order to Pangrelor and ensure the stability of her daughters as well."

"And that is where Elliott comes in—once again," Jingo said.

Elliott kept silent.

Jingo continued, "Today we rejoice because we have won the battle for Harwelden. But it is a hollow victory. Lothar and Valderon have all but destroyed our armies. Though the battle for Harwelden is won, the war for Pangrelor goes on. The scrolls tell us that the prophesied shamalan from Gaya—you, Elliott— will assemble the Antiquitas, just as your forefather Griogair did, and reunite the empire under its banner, restoring order to the mother world. This will prove even more difficult than the feat you have just accomplished. The battle for Harwelden is the beginning of the story, not the end."

"I'm sorry," Elliott said, "but all I care about is getting back home. Gaya may be a daughterland to you, but it's home to me, and it is where I intend to spend the rest of my life."

"Oh, Elliott," Jingo said, "can't you see? If Pangrelor falls to Lothar and Valderon, your home in Gaya won't be *worth* returning to. In fact, even though we won the battle for Harwelden, your fate back in Gaya—and the fate of Gaya itself—may already be irrevocably altered."

Woolf's face lit up. "You've just reminded me of something. Elliott, after Crosslyn took you to the bottom of the river, he told me what the sprites said about you. I don't think he ever told anyone else."

Elliott leaned forward, remembering. Crosslyn had never mentioned what the sprites whispered to him—the words that had spooked him so badly at the bottom of the river. "What did they say?"

"They told him you were a powerful shamalan but that great tragedy lay in your future. He believed that the tragedy would be his own death. Though you did not know it, he prepared himself for it. He forfeited his life so that you might maximize your power as quickly as possible. At first, he was unsure how to proceed with your cultivation, since most shamalans spend their entire youth discovering themselves and unlocking the individual secrets of their power. But Crosslyn knew that you had very little time to mature, and he let you tap into his energy so that you might learn to wield your power more quickly. Indirectly, by allowing you such free access to his energy, he sacrificed himself for the greater good of Pangrelor. In doing this, he hoped to fulfill the vision of the great tragedy that lay in your future, so that your only suffering would consist of his own loss and nothing more."

Elliott looked downcast. "Enough of all this," he said. "Let's have our breakfast. Tonight Sarintha will be crowned, and I don't want to talk about tragedies anymore."

"You're right," Woolf said, looking at the others. "We should all be content to thank you for what you have already done."

After finishing their breakfast, they walked to the courtyards, where a grayfarer ceremony of first flight was about to take place. It was a welcome reminder of Harwelden's return to normality, and it helped take Elliott's mind off the conversation about Crosslyn, and off everyone's hopes for his future in Pangrelor.

Chapter 67

Coronation

Late in the afternoon, Elliott split from the group and returned to his room to prepare for the coronation. By courier and word of mouth, news had spread like wildfire throughout the realm. Already, the entire city, nearly emptied during the battle mere days ago, was packed to capacity with men and gimlets from all corners of the land. The whole place was abuzz over the evening's ceremony, although Elliott had not seen Sarintha since the two of them returned from the temple last night.

He arrived at Marvus's bedchamber to find that some-one had laid out clothes for him. The garb was old-fashioned: a silken shamalan tunic, complete with shining armor breastplate and a belt with a scabbard for the Amulius. The shamalan crest, depicting the Antiquitas Trident surrounded by ravens carrying olive branches in their talons, was emblazoned on the breast-plate. With great care, he dressed himself in the garments, then stood for a moment in front of the mirror, admiring his appear-ance, when someone knocked at the door.

He opened the door to Marvus, also dressed in traditional finery.

"Magnificent," Marvus said, smoothing Elliott's silken sleeve. "It is time. Come with me."

Going up to the throne room on the top floor, they could hear music in the distance as well-dressed stewards raced to light the torches in the hallways. The mood of the grand occa-sion was everywhere.

The throne room was much larger than Elliott had imagined, and its walls were entirely of carved stone cut into busts of shamalan notables or carved in bas-relief scenes from Harwelden's long history. Not an inch of wall was left unadorned.

"It's breathtaking," he murmured to Marvus.

Row after row of ornate stone benches, fitted with fine silk cushions, faced the oversize throne, which sat atop a dais at front and center of the room. An orchestra sat on a pedestal to the left of the dais, where its many members assembled and tuned their various instruments. Still smiling, Marvus led Elliott past the musicians to the dais, where he directed him to a seat next to the throne. Marvus sat beside him. But for the orchestra, they were the first to arrive. The leader of the orchestra nodded to his musicians, and they began to play.

Elliott looked at the mural on the wall behind the throne. "Unbelievable!" he whispered to Marvus, grabbing his hand. His heart began to race, for above his head was a painting of a man he recognized instantly. In the picture, the man was sitting in the very throne beside him and held the Antiquitas Trident. He wore a flowing beard, not yet gray, and his eyes were at once wild and keenly focused—a look Elliott had seen many times. The man was wearing a silken shamalan tunic and wore a breastplate adorned with the shamalan crest. Beside him was a beautiful little girl. Wearing a flowing white dress, she stared up at her father and reached out to him.

Beneath the painting was a line of text: "King Dagnar of Ondor and his daughter, Princess Mary." The realization flooded over him. *Dagnar of Ondor . . . the initials "D. O."* These were the initials of the man in his grandfather's tale—the mysterious builder of the mansion in New Orleans, Darius Orion. Incredulous, Elliott gazed at the painting. The man was a younger version of his own grandfather, and Darius Orion was the name he had chosen after his banishment to New Orleans. The little girl, of course, was Elliott's own mother.

From a door to the right of the dais, Jingo approached. He nodded to them and sat quietly beside Marvus as the orchestra played. Hooks followed. He had bathed and brushed his shaggy fur and wore a smart purple sash. Like Jingo before him, he nodded and quietly took a seat. The pomp and pageantry was almost palpable.

From a door to the left of the dais, Waldemariam entered the room. Behind him filed Woolf and the rest of the Grayfarer Council. Woolf nodded to Elliott as he took a seat beside Waldemariam. General Grimaldi followed the grayfarers of the council. Each of them wore the shiniest armor Elliott had ever seen, with ornate matching swords hanging from scabbards at their waists, and with the golden shamalan crest emblazoned on each breastplate. When they all were seated, all the chairs on the dais, except for the throne itself, were taken. The orchestra played a new composition, and the volume of the music increased as, from the opposite end of the room, the guests began to file in. Row after row, the seats were filled, until the massive room was packed to capacity. Finally, with everyone in place, the orchestra broke into a stirring rendition of "The Majesty of Home." At the first note of the anthem, the entire room stood. The guests turned and looked to the door at the rear of the room, where Sarintha entered, wearing a flowing white gown. She was radiant.

The orchestral choir gave voice to the composition in the ancient Albian tongue.

Slowly, majestically, Sarintha marched down the aisle, the train of her gown streaming behind her and attended by two gimlet stewards. Another pair of gimlets walked ahead of her, strewing the aisle with fragrant petals.

As she neared the front of the room, she looked at Elliott, and he thought her smile the most beautiful thing he had ever seen. Reaching the throne, she stopped, then turned to face the crowd. At that exact moment, the orchestra struck the last note of its composition, and the room fell silent. With Sarintha standing in front of the throne and facing the guests, Waldemariam stood. His strong, deep voice echoed throughout the room.

"Tonight is among the most joyous affairs any of us shall ever encounter, as we are assembled to honor our new Queen, Sarintha, of the line of Gwendyl, daughter of King Gregorus, and rightful heir to the throne of Harwelden."

Lifting a golden crown from its purple cushion, he stepped in front of Sarintha and placed the crown on her head. With it in place, he knelt before her. And taking her hand, he bowed his head and gently kissed it.

"I pledge my fealty to you, Queen Sarintha, daughter of Gregorus, and pray that the elders guide your hand as you embark on your journey."

She smiled and nodded at him. "And I pledge my fealty to the Kingdom of Harwelden. Stand, Chancellor, and take your rightful place beside me. Together, with the guidance of the elders, we shall work together to bring prosperity to all the inhabitants of this land." Her voice seemed fuller and richer than Elliott remembered. Truly, he thought, she sounded the part of a queen.

One by one, the grayfarers went to her, knelt, and kissed her hand. "Long live the queen," said each in turn. When General Grimaldi, the last in the row of grayfarers, had paid his respects, all eyes turned to Elliott.

Marvus nudged him. "Honor her as the grayfarers have done," he whispered.

Nervously following Marvus's instruction, Elliott stepped before Sarintha. The affection in her gaze was apparent. Following the grayfarers' example, he knelt and reached out for her hand. But unlike before, she did not offer it.

With Sarintha standing in front of the throne and
facing the guests, Waldemariam stood. His strong,
deep voice echoed throughout the room.

"Rise and stand before me," she said.

Confused, and terrified that he had done something wrong, he stood and faced her.

"Elliott of Ondor," she said, still smiling at him, "bow not before me."

"Why not?" he whispered.

A few of the guests close enough to hear him tittered softly.

To his astonishment, she knelt before him and, bowing her head, kissed his hand.

As the crowd gasped, she looked into his eyes. "For your service to Harwelden, it is I who honor you. Thank you, Elliott of Ondor, for all that you are, for all that you have become, and for all that you have done in behalf of Harwelden. The gift you have given us is great and cannot be repaid. As long as I am queen, you shall bow before no one in this realm." Smiling at him as if no one else were present, she stood. "Without you, there would be no queen, no crown, no kingdom. For you are our deliverer, our prince, and undisputed heir to the line of Griogair. Stand beside me as my equal and as my friend."

Blood rushed to his cheeks, and he stood beside her as she had bidden.

Marvus grinned, then rose to bow before her. He kissed her hand. "Long live the Queen," he murmured. Jingo and Hooks did the same. When they were finished, Sarintha reached out for Elliott's hand and addressed the crowd.

"These are sad times," she said, "for we have lost many. But thanks to our deliverer, they are joyous times as well. Though the tasks before us are daunting, Harwelden lives on." She turned to smile at Elliott. "And the strength within her can be undone by no one."

Though she spoke to the crowd, she looked at Elliott. "Tonight, as is our custom, you offer me praise. But let it be heard throughout the land that your new queen praises you equally."

Squeezing Elliott's hand, she faced the crowd. "From the farmers in the field and the shepherds on the mountainsides to the mighty Grayfarer Council, it is the citizenry of the Kingdom of Harwelden that makes her great, not the edicts of the wellborn or the voice of one small sovereign. With the help of our deliverer, it is together that we have prevailed, and it is together, as a kingdom of many strengths and many voices, that we enter the new age."

The crowd erupted in cheers. Chants of "Long live the queen!" repeated over and over.

"But let us praise not only the few, for others, too, have had a hand in our recent victories, and each of you know who they are."

The crowd whooped.

"Hooks, of the Valley of Susquatania, come and stand before me."

Appearing shocked, Hooks grinned and went to her, towering over her.

"For the first time in our great history, we honor a citizen of the Valley of the Beasts. The susquat who stands before us has performed heroic feats in service to Harwelden, and these shall not go unrewarded. Without his brave service, I would not have the privilege of standing before you. And for your heroic endeavors, Hooks, Harwelden is forever grateful." She lowered her voice and spoke directly to him. "With all my heart, I thank you. Kneel before the throne of Harwelden."

Hooks knelt.

Waldemariam unsheathed his sword and handed it to her, nodding. She laid the sword gently on Hooks's shoulder. "From this day forth, you are hereby made a knight of Harwelden. Rise and stand with me, Sir Hooks."

Grinning sheepishly, Hooks stood and straightened his fur. "Thank you." He nodded and walked back to his seat, where he remained standing.

"Marvus, my loyal ally and friend, come and kneel before me."

Appearing uncomfortable, Marvus did as instructed.

"For your heroic and wise efforts in the service of Harwelden, from this day forth, you are hereby made a knight of Harwelden." She tapped his shoulder with the sword. "Rise and stand with me, Sir Marvus.

Unaccustomed to being the focus of such pomp, he stood and went back to his seat.

"And finally," said Sarintha, "loyal Jingo, come and kneel before me."

Jingo did as instructed. He was grinning from ear to ear.

"Dearest Jingo is the youngest gimlet ever to be advanced to the level of steward of the royal family." She smiled at him. "We have known of his talents and of his great faith since he was a child. But never did we imagine the might of the lion that lives inside him. For your faith," she said, tapping his shoulder with the sword, "and for the great strength you have mustered from within yourself to serve our cause, you are hereby made a knight of Harwelden. Stand before me, Sir Jingo."

Staggering for a moment on his new wooden leg, Jingo stood and returned to his seat.

"And so, as the new age begins, so begins the new order of Harwelden. Before you stand your new queen and your new prince, she said, grasping Elliott's hand and lifting it into the air. "And the new order of the Knights of Harwelden."

The crowd cheered so loudly, the very room shook.

Laughing, Sarintha hushed them. "And for our final order of business this night, it is my great privilege, with the blessing of the chancellor, to invite General Grimaldi to fill one of the vacancies on the Grayfarer Council. General," she said, "I beg you to accept this seat, for no one is more fit than you to fill it."

From the end of the row, Grimaldi nodded. "It would be my honor."

"Then it is done," said Sarintha. "Long live Harwelden!"

"Long live Harwelden!" shouted the crowd. "Long live the queen!" From throughout the room, roses flew into the air.

"Thank you all," said Sarintha, "from the bottom of my heart. In closing tonight's ceremony, I invite each of you to attend a memorial service in the courtyard, where we will honor the life of the great priest Crosslyn, whose wisdom transcends his death." She bowed to the crowd and turned to leave, pulling Elliott along with her.

A short time later, the crowd reassembled in the courtyard, around a raging bonfire. A piper played a solemn tune, and the new knights of Harwelden, known to themselves as the Sons of Crosslyn, took turns regaling the crowd with anecdotes about their lost friend. At the end of the service, a scribe read a biography of Crosslyn's life and told of the positions he had held in the royal court, his presumed loss during the Great Betrayal, and his reemergence in the Forest of Golroc, where he had saved Elliott's life and set him and his companions on the historic path to making allies of the susquats. It was a heartfelt tribute, and at its end, not a soul present had gone without shedding a tear.

Chapter 68

The Tombs of the Elders

The next morning, Elliott awoke early and dressed quickly. He had plans for the day. Though servants had filled his wardrobe to capacity with royal garments, he donned the leather clothes that he had worn for most of his time in Pangrelor—the very clothes Marvus had given him when they first met. He filled his grandfather's knapsack with all the personal effects he could locate, and included everything that he had carried with him upon his arrival—except for the bracelet. After much consideration, he removed it from his wrist and laid it on the dresser, next to the Amulius, the golden vibrissae shirt, and Slipher's pipe and mirror, where all might easily be found. Then, with the knapsack on his back, he looked about the room one last time and stepped out into the hall.

He had no trouble getting past the guards who stood watch over the royal chambers, and Sarintha opened the door to her new room after a single knock. With sleep in her eyes, she smiled and embraced him. "Oh, Elliott," she said. "It was wonderful, wasn't it?"

"It was." He smiled. "Congratulations to you, Queen Sarintha. You've earned it." He added with a sly grin, "Harwelden will never be the same."

She laughed. "You are too much," she said, hugging him again. "Why aren't you dressed in your royal clothes? You're a prince now," she said, pointing playfully at his leather jerkin.

"It's important that you look the part. People take notice of these things."

Elliott looked at the floor. "About that," he said. "There is something I want to talk to you about."

"We shall have much time to talk. But there's something I need you to do."

"What's that?"

"True to my word, my first edict as queen shall be directed at you." The playfulness had left her voice. "I want you to go to the Forest of Ondor, alone. Follow the trail in the valley into the center of the forest. There you will find a circle of great stones. These are the tombstones of our elders. I want you to spend a night in the center of the tombs. When darkness falls, I have no doubt, the elders will speak to you. The guidance they offer will be beneficial to you and to all of us." She looked into his eyes, beseeching him. "Will you go?"

Elliott shuffled his feet. "I will go to the Forest of Ondor."

"Excellent," she said, kissing his cheek. "Spend tonight in the presence of the tombs and return tomorrow. We will have much to talk about, I am sure."

Elliott stared at her for several seconds. "Good-bye, Sarintha."

"Good-bye, and make haste. I will see you tomorrow."

Elliott nodded and turned, stealing a final glance at her as she closed the door to her bedchamber, smiling at him all the while.

As he left the castle courtyards and entered the Boulevard of Kings, he turned and paused for a moment, staring at the castle. After a while, he turned and marched down the boulevard, past the fine statues of the many kings and queens of Harwelden.

During his walk down the boulevard, he paused only twice. The first pause was to look at a statue near the Grand

Plaza, just a few paces away from the newly completed statue of Sarintha's father, King Gregorus. The statue he looked at was one he had not noticed before, though it stood in plain sight. On the pedestal, a nameplate declared that the carving was an homage to King Dagnar, slain during Lothar's Great Betrayal, though the character immortalized in stone, Elliott knew, was not dead at all. It was his grandfather, the shamalan king Dagnar, eldest brother of Lothar and Galeren.

The second time he paused was in the Grand Plaza itself, where he took a final look at the statue of King Griogair. He paid particular attention to Griogair's hands. Gloves covered them, masking any shamalan markings that may have been present. And then, without fanfare, he walked across the drawbridge and down Mount Kalipharus, where he saw an old gray donkey grazing halfway down the mountainside. The donkey was fitted with a serpan-made saddle, but the saddle was cracked and dry-rotted, and the donkey was quite thin. Surmising that its owner must have fallen in the war, he continued down the mountain.

By midday, Elliott reached the edge of the valley, where the trailhead beckoned him onward into the Forest of Ondor. Before entering, he paused again, this time taking one last glimpse of the majestic castle atop the mountain, with the chain of Azure Mountains fading behind it as far as the eye could see. Lining the roof of the castle, Elliott saw the familiar silhouettes of the grayfarers watching over the city, and he smiled one last time before turning to enter the forest.

The trail was as he remembered, though the ravages of war, which had not touched this place when he first walked here, were everywhere evident. The purity of the forest, at least as he had known it, was gone.

With twilight approaching, he found what he was looking for. He stood at the mouth of the cave and stared at it for several

The statue Elliott looked at was one he had not noticed
before...It was his grandfather, the shamalan king Dagnar,
eldest brother of Lothar and Galeren.

seconds, recalling the first time he had stood here. Taking the knapsack off his back, he reached in and pulled out the seer stone that he had taken from the chest in his grandfather's basement. With stone in hand, he entered the blackness of the cave, summoning the yellow light of the stone.

As before, the crunching of the cydonia shells beneath his feet disrupted the silence as he walked into the cave. And as before, he heard the distant cawing of the latest magby to take up residence here. But his heartbeat did not quicken, and he walked deeper, determined to locate the wall from which he had gained passage to Pangrelor. After a time, by the dim light of the seer stone, he came across a section of wall covered by crude markings. In the center of many ancient symbols, he saw the tracing of a hand. He placed his hand perfectly within the tracing.

Epilogue

The day after he arrived back in the basement of his grand-father's house, Elliott decided to take a walk through the Garden District of New Orleans. Though his grandfather had offered to accompany him—had all but insisted, in fact—he chose to go alone. The day was overcast though not altogether unpleasant.

Much had changed in his absence. A great flood had rav-aged New Orleans, along with a wide swath of the Gulf Coast of the United States. Months before, a tsunami of historic proportions had rippled across the Indian Ocean, killing hun-dreds of thousands in Indonesia, Thailand, and Sri Lanka. In El Salvador, the country's highest volcano had erupted, displac-ing thousands, and an earthquake of historic magnitude had wreaked havoc in parts of Pakistan and India. In Niger, a plague of locusts had descended on the crops there, resulting in wide-spread famine and death. The list went on and on. Since Elliott's departure to Pangrelor, his grandfather had chronicled these and many other events in the worst year for natural disasters in anyone's memory.

And all these events had coincided with the past season in Pangrelor. Though Sarintha and others had warned Elliott that "a ripple in Pangrelor is felt as a flood by her daughters," he could never have guessed the degree of destruction brought down upon his own homeland. Walking through the Garden District, he could see that much of its beauty was gone. Many of the grand homes lining the boulevard had fallen into disrepair, and the blue tar-paulins lining many of the roofs had become the stuff of local lore. Waterlines up to three feet high marked the walls of the homes of the District, serving as a grim reminder of Hurricane Katrina, and the doors of each home he passed remained emblazoned with a big orange X to notify rescuers that the search for bodies within that dwelling had already occurred. A few of the doors had numbers spray-painted next to the orange X, indicating the number of bodies that had been found within the house and needed to be recovered. Like Harwelden, New Orleans had already begun to rebuild itself, though much remained to be done.

As he wandered through the district, he saw a pack of boys turn their bicycles in his direction. As the bullies approached, shouting their familiar taunts, he sighed. And with a hint of irritation, he turned to face them.

The heavyset kid who was their leader rode right up to him and dropped his bike on the ground. "Well, well," he said, rubbing his fist in his other palm, "look who's come back to see us. I do believe it's little Stripes. I think he wants to play."

Elliott faced the boy. "Get away from me."

"Oooohhh!" said the fat one as his pals collected in a circle around Elliott. "Little Stripes has gone and gotten tough on us. I think he needs to learn some respect."

The others laughed, closing their circle around him. Then, without warning, the fat one lunged at Elliott. His fists windmilled around him as he closed in.

Elliott sidestepped him, pushing his backside hard on the way by, so that he fell face-first into the dirty gutter.

Instantly, the others were on Elliott. But this time, instead of curling up on the ground, he dodged and ducked their blows, delivering counterpunches, bruising ribs, bloodying noses, until every one of the bullies was hurting and ready to get away from him.

As the boys gathered themselves up, he stood right where they had tried to jump him. His breath was still even, and his heart rate had hardly risen.

From the surprise in their faces, he could see that they were afraid of him. As they rode their bicycles on down the boulevard, a few of them shouted hollow threats, vowing revenge, but their tone lacked conviction, and he knew they wouldn't bother him again. When they were out of sight, he continued toward his destination.

When he reached the old Lafayette Cemetery, the skies had darkened considerably. Another storm was brewing, and by the look of things, it was going to be a real gully washer. As he walked through the cemetery gate, his thoughts turned to Pangrelor and to his encounter with the river sprites at the beginning of his cultivation. *There is death in your future,* they had said. *You will not succeed in your goal.* At the time, he had misunderstood what they meant, though he had wanted to save his mother above all else. With thunder rippling through the sky, he meandered through the many rows of crypts until he found the one he sought. It was a simple aboveground crypt, less ornate than its neighbors. Carved into the tombstone were these words: "Here lies Princess Mary, daughter of King Dagnar, heir to the line of Griogair, once heir to the throne of Harwelden. She was a cherished daughter and loving mother, whose absence from this world shall be missed. May she rest forever in Antilia, where she stands at the side of her fathers and watches over us all."

Beneath the epitaph, his grandfather had painted a picture of her. Elliott recognized it as a reproduction of the picture of Dagnar and Mary that adorned the throne room at Harwelden. The old man must have gone to great effort, for the painting was remarkably lifelike.

A tear formed in the corner of his eye as he reached out and touched the cool stone of the tomb. Beneath the epitaph and picture, one more line was carved. It was something his mother had repeated throughout his childhood: "The Journey Begins in the Heart of the Traveler."